The Professor of Eventide

MEREDITH ALLARD

The Professor of Eventide

Lemon Moon Books

Cover design by Stefan Prenich

ISBN: 979-8-218-57127-6

The Professor of Eventide/Meredith Allard – 1st paperback edition 2026

{1. Fiction. 2. Literature and Fiction—Gothic. 3. Mystery, Thriller & Suspense—Suspense. 4. Literature and Fiction—Literary Fiction. 5. Mystery, Thriller & Suspense—Mystery. 6. Psychological Thriller—Fiction. 7. Maine—Fiction.} I. Title

One

Without music or an intriguing idea, color becomes pallor, man becomes carcass, home becomes catacomb, and the dead are but for a moment motionless.

One.

Two.

Three.

That is how many of my students were murdered.

Thomas.

Amandine.

And...No. I still cannot say the name.

At the time, all I knew for certain was that it wasn't me, though some came to suspect otherwise. Somewhere in my horror, I knew that if I were going to survive with my freedom and my sanity, it would be up to me to discover who murdered my students and why. Perhaps I should have seen how the pieces of the puzzle fit sooner. Perhaps I should have seen it all along.

I have dedicated my life to words. Words are what I do.

When I cannot articulate my thoughts, I am bereft, a man grasping at ideas falling like air through my fingers, my thoughts refusing to be strung together in any coherent way. I am not entirely certain I can tell the tale in a way that helps you understand, but I will try. The story I have to share is one of memory, madness, and revenge. You will judge for yourself how well I tell it.

Langston Hughes said, “My soul has grown deep like the rivers.” I am not certain I have a soul, but my memories are deep like the rivers. They have width, depth, velocity. Often, they run amok, twirling into the distance like toy tops spinning over cliffs, drowning under the abyss, never to be seen again. In time, almost everything becomes insignificant. Tomorrow and tomorrow and tomorrow.

My routines are largely the same. Until they aren’t. I wish I could predict the times when, without warning, something happens, perhaps for no reason at all, and my predictable world is fractured beyond recognition. The questions still haunt me. Should I have seen it coming? Could I have prevented it? Perhaps. But by the time I realized what cruel terrors awaited us, the damage was done. It is not until after events happen that we realize we should have taken our first impressions more seriously. Only by then it is too late.

With me poetry has not been a purpose, but a passion.

I arrived in the coastal town of Southshore, Maine, in August 2010. On my first night, I set down my belongings in my newly rented cottage, then headed to the bay where I stood on the midnight shore under the light of a vanilla moon. The fog rolled in dense from the sea, smothering Casco Bay in a steely silence that swallowed sound itself. The dark outlines of the islands, jagged and unmoving, hovered in the distance as if waiting. The lighthouse on Great Diamond Island flashed once, vanished into the mist, then flashed again, the lonely eye blinking in the gloom. I felt, as I stood at the edge, a sorrow colder than the stones beneath my feet. At the time, I could not name the cause of my melancholy. Perhaps the anger of the oncoming storm should have been a sign, but in that moment, it was simply another nor'easter blowing in high winds and heavy rain. The gusts whipped the water against the rocky coast, the white-tipped waves creating whirlpools. The shroud-like clouds grew more menacing, so I turned away. I could not settle my mind, or my legs, so instead of going back to the cottage, I went to Eventide College, my new academic home.

Standing at the edge of campus, I admired the eclectic combination of colonial and neoclassical architecture. The roaring of the wind and the crashing of the waves dropped to a whisper, and in the near silence I felt separated from my surroundings, as though I were the only one left in the world. Past the witching hour, there was not a soul to be seen. Edgar Poe's words ran through my mind.

Merely this and nothing more.

I recited The Raven aloud as I followed the winding stone-paved walkway through the plentiful trees, still green in late summer. Dim campus lights flickered and dimmed, leaving puzzle-like shadows on the ground. Footsteps slapped the ground behind me, quick, light, but unmistakable, and I sensed a preternatural watchfulness nearby. Something stirred my senses. I stopped, listened, heard nothing more, and moved on until, again, I heard the rhythmic slapping and I turned around. No one.

Darkness there and nothing more.

Poe understood the gloom.

I shook my head in an attempt to push away the creeping sensation that someone was watching me, intruding into my private night. Then I saw the intruders—two ravens, soaring side by side, their wings dark like midnight, their eyes like molten bronze. Seeing the ravens where I was about to begin my new job made perfect sense to me. I appreciated their watchful presence as I walked home, desperate to leave the forlorn feeling behind.

If you asked me, I would say that I've grown used to the late hours. I enjoy my solitary walks in the gloaming. I'm most at peace when not a single soul in the world knows where to find me. Most people are frightened of the night because so much remains unseen. Unknowing is more fearful than knowing. Who knows what lies between shades and shadows? Nightmares spring from behind the blackness, monsters with talons for fingers who crush your very bones. Crime lurks in the darkness, anxiety in the darkness, terror in the darkness. With little light to see by, phobias are exposed, to be picked at like scabs that hurt more than help, so we peel them away until we bleed.

Yet I am alive under the somber sky. I live in the half-light. Instead of dwelling on the possibility of phantom torments, I have learned to find darkness comforting. I find solace in the unseen. Few people are awake at that hour to mind whether I come or go. Of those I encounter, they are not so very curious at night. Until they are.

Eventide College was supposed to be just another job on just another campus. No red flags waved, informing me that this particular job on this particular campus would soon turn into a circus of horrors. Perhaps it's more accurate to say that I didn't see the red flags. I have thought about it often since. Did I miss the warnings? Was there some invisible finger jabbing me in the ribs, some sign that I should beware? How often have we looked back on events and realized that the signs were there all along, yet at the time they were easily explained away? It's only in hindsight that we understand.

I had been aware of Eventide College for so long that when the phone call came, I was immediately intrigued. The message on my voicemail was clear. Her name was Deborah Bronwyn, but you could call her Debbie. She was the Department Chair of the English department at Eventide College. They had a sudden vacancy, and she wanted to speak to me. I was familiar with the process. At most colleges and universities, departments have to advertise the position, even if the person they want to hire comes by recommendation or personal acquaintance. Professor Bronwyn said that the vacancy was for someone who specialized in nineteenth-century American literature, my area of expertise. I heard the voicemail in the evening, so I gave myself the night to decide whether I wanted to pursue the position. In truth, I had been happy at Yale, but I glanced at my calendar and realized, with some sadness, that it was nearly time to move on. Besides, it might be nice to work on a smaller campus with fewer students. I wanted to focus on teaching for a change.

I asked some colleagues what they knew about the college in Southshore, Maine, and they had only good things to say. Gabriel Sweeney's twins were students at Eventide, both studying Mathematics, and he said they were quite happy. Max Stewart, a former professor at Dartmouth, said EC, as Eventide College is known, has a solid reputation for its rigorous academic programs.

"There are many brilliant minds in the English department at Eventide, Jonathan. Many of the scholars who shape our current views of literary theory are there." He laughed as he added, "Some people say EC is haunted." When I asked how it was haunted, he said he didn't know, and it was likely just a silly rumor anyway.

When I asked Gabriel Sweeney what his twins knew about the supposed hauntings, he said they knew nothing, adding, "They say it's just the English department that's haunted." As an English professor, I did not find that particularly reassuring.

I discovered that the English department at Eventide College—beyond the possibility of ghouls, imps, and I could only guess what else—was known for its exemplary American literature department. English students from EC go on to become respected scholars, authors, poets, editors, and publishers. I decided that I could handle an ogre or two for the opportunity to work there. I've dealt with worse than that in my time. The next night, I returned Debbie Bronwyn's call.

"Excuse me," she said in her vibrant voice, "but I left a message for Dr. Jonathan Ferrars, the professor of English at Yale whose scholarship on Poe I've so greatly admired. Are you calling on his behalf?"

"I'm Jonathan Ferrars."

Silence. Then, "Forgive me, Dr. Ferrars. I wasn't expecting someone who sounded so young. You are old enough to teach at a college, aren't you?"

"I am indeed Jonathan Ferrars, I assure you."

I established my identity by speaking in depth about my Poe scholarship, and she accepted that I was who I claimed to be. She spoke enough for both of us, and I was left with little to add except for an occasional "Yes" or "That's right." She praised some of my more recent scholarship on Poe and the Imp of the Perverse, and we discussed Poe's personal imp of the perverse, which wreaked havoc in his life despite his plethora of literary talent.

"We all have some inner imp whispering into our ears, prompting us to do whatever wrong thing is in front of us, don't you think, Jonathan? May I call you Jonathan?"

"Of course. And if you're asking me if I believe that we each have our own personal devil on our shoulders, then indeed I do."

"To be honest, I wasn't sure at first because you do sound so young, but you've convinced me that you're at least old enough to drink." She laughed enough for both of us. "How soon do you think you could find your way to Maine so I can show you around EC and introduce you to everyone? I'd like you to have the opportunity to get settled here before the autumn term starts."

"Is this an offer?"

"As a matter of fact, not only is it an offer, but I'd like you to fill the Eleanor C. Geddes Chair of American Literature."

I knew enough about the English department at EC to know that the Eleanor C. Geddes Chair of American Literature was fully endowed and, if I recalled correctly, funded by Eventide College's leading patron. The Geddes chair was highly respected and one of the premier positions for literary scholarship in the country. Could she be offering it to me that easily? No preliminary interview? No job talk? For a flash, I was elated. Then reality set in. It sounded too good to be true, and I said so.

"We do things differently in the English department at EC," Debbie explained. "I assure you, Jonathan, this is an offer. You've come highly recommended, and your scholarship is top-notch. I have the necessary approval to hire you on the spot if I decide that you're right for the Geddes chair, and you are."

I still thought it was too easy, but I was caught up in the thrill of receiving a well-respected position at a fine institution, and I accepted.

The next night, as Debbie and I worked through salary negotiations and arranged my move from Connecticut to Maine, she told me about Eventide College.

"Do you know about the founding of EC? The story is lore in Southshore." She took my silence for a no. Her voice took on a friendly tone, as though reciting an oft-told fairy tale.

"You see, Cornelius Everett Eventide was the youngest son of an English viscount. Like younger sons of the nobility, his eldest brother received the title, the house, and the money, leaving Cornelius to make his own way in the world. Instead of testing his luck in the army or his patience as a parson, Cornelius left for the United States in 1836.

"His brother, Anthony, was now the viscount, and his

lordship took pity on his youngest brother, who had to leave England, the center of the world, for the sticks of the colonies, which hadn't been colonies for some time by then. Cornelius invested whatever money he had and ended up making a fortune." She sounded like an actress in a play whose character laughs at the same lines every night. "Instead of New York or Rhode Island, Cornelius settled here in Maine. He married a local woman, Eleanor, which made him a local as far as his neighbors were concerned. As a matter of fact, the Eleanor C. Geddes Chair was founded in her honor. He was a great scholar, Cornelius. Nothing in the world was more important to him than learning. Upon discovering that there was no Harvard or Yale in his immediate vicinity, he created a haven of higher learning in his own backyard, literally his backyard, using the land surrounding his house for the campus. He founded Eventide College in 1850 with the intention that everyone deserved the opportunities that a good education would bring. Remember, this was a time when, according to the elites, only the privileged deserved to know things. When you arrive, you'll see the house he built, Eventide Manor. The house had been passed down for several generations until it fell into disrepair and was abandoned. About ten years ago, it was bought by our benefactor, Mr. Rhys Grimshaw. He's a nice man, even if he has his eccentricities."

"Don't we all."

"That's what I say. And no matter what, he's a generous benefactor to Eventide College. He has a soft spot for the English department, which is lucky for us. He's an amateur literature scholar, actually, and he's had several papers published. Did I tell you that he endows the Geddes chair?"

"I didn't know that."

"I think you and Rhys will get along famously. I can't wait for you to meet him."

"It all sounds rather impressive."

"I thought you should know a little about the college where you're going to make your home. Now, did you have any questions for me?"

"Is it true that Eventide is haunted?"

Again, the canned laughter. "Haunted? Whatever gave you that idea?"

"A professor at Yale mentioned it."

"Leave it to Yalies to spread rumors. Honestly, the things people say. They're jealous of us here at Eventide, of course. Our English students go on to some of the premier literary positions in the world."

Be careful what you wish for, they say, because you might get it. I have learned the hard way how true that is.

After I arrived in Maine, I spent the nights walking the roads, getting to know my new surroundings. Always the bay called to me. Casco Bay is a grandeur both beautiful and unsettling in equal measure. The sea's surface rolls under currents that gleam like broken slivers of moonlight while islands lie like ancient fortresses, their rocky silhouettes softened by a misty veil. The salt-heavy winds stir the creaking boats, the waves knocking against the hulls with an echo like organ tones. The lighthouse sits in the distance, a solemn, steady presence. Near the bay, I felt the fragility of existence, and terror and wonder washed over me the way the tide washed over the shore.

I came to like the quaint seaside village of Southshore. For those first nights, I felt the closest to peaceful I had in some time. The night before classes began, I stared into the deep horizon, seeking something, perhaps an answer to a long-held question. And then I realized what I wanted. It was a memory buried deep in the muddy river of my mind. The wind blew my hair from my eyes, and I wondered if it took my memories with it, casting them into the dark water. Sometimes my memories are close to the surface, ripe for the plucking. Other times they are so far down in the depths that I think I will never find them again. As I grappled with my memories, the good and the bad, I watched the tide lick the jagged stones while the old boathouses lurched drunkenly, their windows empty like a skeleton's eye sockets. The wooden pier jutted like the bones of an ancient ship, the ferries and fishing boats long since docked for the night.

Again, that sense of being followed tingled along my spine. This time, there were no ravens. I heard a faint, rhythmic tapping, too deliberate to be natural yet too slow to be nothing. My pulse quickened. Though I could not see the source, I knew that, whatever it was, it was out there, watching and waiting. The bay had a way of holding its secrets close, and whatever it knew, it would not share. I was certain that my imagination was getting the best of me. Crackling, a sound like someone stepping on rocks, came from behind. I turned around. No one. Then someone tugged on my jacket.

"Hello?" I called.

No one answered.

Was Max right about Eventide College being haunted? Perhaps it was Southshore, or Maine, that was visited by phantoms. Did ghosts pass in the night? I would have company then. The soft slurring of waves and the gentle press of the wind kissing the shore twisted my imagination into strange shapes. I felt exposed standing alone, and a sense of dread unnerved me. Whatever it was—real or imagined—it was gone. I sprinted away, and the movement of putting one foot in front of the other at a quick pace kept my body active while my mind searched for peace, which it doesn't often find. There are times when I might find a few moments of respite, but they are only moments. They say that no matter where you go, there you are, and no matter how fast or far I walk, I am no better than I was before. There is always something I'm trying to outrun, someone at the forefront of my thoughts. She is the one memory always close and true. I see her always —her beautiful face, her sweet smile. I am only half myself without her.

Down Frantick Road, I passed the old Victorian mansion that Debbie Bronwyn had told me about—Eventide Manor, all the windows but one dark at that late hour. The architecture was Gothic in temperament and Victorian in detail, with sharp gables that cut into the fog, narrow lancet windows glimmering with warped glass while stone gargoyles crouched at the roofline, their faces worn smooth by years and weather. Ivy, dark as old blood, clung to the façade like heavy drapes, crawling around an arched doorway and into the cornices. A wrought-iron gate fenced the property, the spikes flecked with late-night haze, and a single tower loomed above it all, its clock long dead, its hands forever fixed at some old hour, showing the correct time twice a day. Nestled into the open space of the clock was a conspiracy of ravens, their croaks rising above the whipping wind. The mansion seemed to breathe in the shifting mist. Perhaps it looked friendlier in daylight. But no, sunshine wasn't likely to help. The old mansion was too gloomy. As if the manor had projected its thoughts onto me, I suddenly felt as melancholy as the house looked.

Overtaken by an odd lethargy, perhaps a residual effect from standing in the shadows, I was unable to resist any longer, and I let the memories have their way. I remembered everything about her. Sometimes my memories are deep like the rivers. Other times they are a squall, like Hokusai's Great Wave, pressing me under until I'm certain I've drowned. I heard her voice, like a whispering wave.

"You should have seen it coming."

"Seen what coming?" I asked.

I turned into the dark cul-de-sac where my rented cottage waited. As I unlocked my door, the rain pelted me with dart-like drops, washing her away.

Three

Ah, not in knowledge is happiness, but in the acquisition of knowledge!

Eventide College burst into life with the new autumn term. Students, their youthful vivacity flashing from them like beams of sunlight, walked or rode their bikes across the pathways, crowded the coffee shop in the bookstore, and lingered on the stone steps of the amphitheater, chatting happily with friends not seen during the summer months. Freshmen walked the campus carefully, their maps tight in their hands as their eyes scanned the buildings. I took my time crossing the campus, enjoying the sights. A bubbling excitement always sparks the air at the beginning of a new school year. It never grows old for me.

Walking the campus, I passed Richfield Chapel, the four spires of the bell tower pointing forever upward, toward God, if you believe. The chapel blended into the surrounding trees, its brown bricks providing effective camouflage in the darkness. I followed the winding walkway, passing the grassy lawn of the Chisholm Library and the Beckham School of the Arts. Eventide College was an eclectic fusion of two distinct architectural styles, with half the buildings boasting a neoclassical appearance while the other half wore their colonial aspects proudly. Four Greek columns, two large and two small, lined the pathway toward the Main Quad with its Italianate gazebo and mosque-like dome. Somehow, with the abundance of summer green grass and low-hanging trees, everything worked in harmony. That night, the waning moon burnished the old-world charm of the campus. Half-faced moons symbolize letting go to prepare for new beginnings, so it seemed an auspicious start. I hoped that perhaps this college in this quiet New England town near the shore, a land of tidal marshes and coastal wetlands, would be some Gilead for me, my own private refuge.

I stopped at the center of campus near the statue of the college's founder, Cornelius Everett Eventide, his hand stretching heavenward as though posing for an immortality he was desperate for. Except for his top hat and full beard, Cornelius reminded me of Augustus of Primaporta, which shows Caesar Augustus in his breastplate alongside Cupid and a dolphin. Cornelius Everett Eventide was rather too lanky to be considered a well-muscled man. He had not been a great military leader or an instigator of the Pax Romana. He had been a brilliant scholar. Perhaps too great in the end. Posed for his statue, he appeared to be what he was: an ordinary man with an extraordinary intellect who, with his extraordinary wealth, created a college that he hoped would do some good in the world. Perhaps he adopted the pose because he believed he was leading his students toward greatness. More likely, it was, as it was for Augustus, a piece of personal propaganda. The longer I stood there admiring the marble, the more I decided that Cornelius resembled Napoleon more than Augustus. All the college's founder needed were gold epaulettes to complete the look.

From the statue, I found my way to the Eliot School of Humanities, a six-story red-brick colonial with white trim and a modern glass walkway connecting the second floor to the Kaufmann School of World Languages, part of the larger Humanities department. Everything taught under the banner of Humanities—Classics, Philosophy, History, Languages, and English—was based there. I had been to the Eliot School once since arriving, to meet Debbie Bronwyn in person. She did as she had promised, showing me my new office and introducing me to the colleagues who were there. They weren't effusively friendly, but they weren't overtly unkind, like faculty everywhere. The gossiping and backstabbing don't begin until they see the new hire's list of publications and determine where the newbie fits into the department's pecking order. My goal, as always, was to stay away from the drama. Sometimes I succeed, and sometimes I don't.

Inside the Eliot School, I took the stairs to the fourth floor, where the English department was located. The fourth floor was H-shaped, with two long hallways separated by a shorter hallway between them. Bulletin boards lined the off-white walls, proclaiming important dates such as the start of the Autumn and Spring terms and add and drop dates for courses. Some boards listed groups for students to sign up for, and one board featured recent publications by faculty. Near the elevator was a directory with the English professors' names, office numbers, and office hours. My name and office number were there, with the addendum of my holding the Geddes chair. By the time I arrived, most of the professors had left, their doors locked for the night. A few remained, shuffling around, gathering their belongings, or chatting with colleagues. Two professors welcomed each other back, asking what conferences they had attended and what papers they had submitted over the summer.

My office, number 412, was located at the far end of the hallway near the fire escape. The room was square, off-white, and just large enough to hold a metal desk with a faux-wood top in front of a small, bare window. Completing the industrial look was an old office chair, an out-of-date computer with a printer on a rolling shelf, and two empty metal bookcases. It was a standard university-issued office. If I thought that the professor holding the Geddes chair would receive special treatment, or at least a bigger office, I was mistaken.

I dropped the two boxes I had brought onto the floor while deciding how to arrange my few belongings. Other professors turned their offices into personal playgrounds, with family photographs, colorful paintings and prints, coffee makers or tea kettles, small refrigerators, and books, along with other knick-knacks such as trinkets collected on their travels or Shakespeare action figures. Nothing of my personality showed in my office, which is how I like it. The fewer personal possessions I have, the easier it is to walk away when the time comes. I grab my two boxes, and I'm gone as if I were never there.

I checked the time and saw that I had 30 minutes before my first class. I found a pair of scissors in the desk drawer and sliced open the first box. Then I removed my bomber jacket, set it across the top of my office chair, then slid the books onto the shelves: Poe's works—his fiction, poetry, and literary criticism—as well as biographies about Poe and literary criticism discussing his work from every angle from Feminism to Marxism. Then I organized the works of other nineteenth-century American authors: Emily Dickinson, Henry David Thoreau, Ralph Waldo Emerson, and Walt Whitman. Next to these, I included my own books about the same nineteenth-century American authors. It never hurts to display them.

With my belongings put away, I hung my PhD diploma from Cambridge on the wall behind my desk. I like that to be the first thing people see when they walk into my office. It doesn't hurt for them to know that I'm qualified for this job, especially since everyone likes to comment on how young I look. On the wall beside my desk, I hung reproductions of the standard portraits of Emily Dickinson, Ralph Waldo Emerson, and Henry David Thoreau. To the right, I hung up my series of daguerreotypes of Edgar A. Poe. Poe would be my object of scrutiny that term, after all.

I logged onto my computer and answered emails from students, most of whom had questions that could have been answered by reading the syllabus, which I had already sent them. Debbie Bronwyn peeked around my open door.

"I know I've already welcomed you, Jonathan, but tonight is your first class and I wanted to see how you are."

"I'm doing well, thank you. Starting a new term isn't new for me."

"Oh, I know, I know. You're old enough to drink, though you barely look like it. See, I remember what people tell me." She laughed. "You've never started a new term at Eventide before, and our students are special."

Debbie Bronwyn was a short, slender woman of indeterminate age with a youthful face and striking silver hair cut into a pixie. That night she wore a gray pantsuit and a cream blouse, her diminutive height helped by a pair of high heels that clicked loudly on the linoleum floor. She looked more professional than most of the professors I'd seen, certainly more than me in my chino pants and button-down shirt.

"I think you'll be happy here, Jonathan. We're one happy family in the English department at EC."

I smiled politely. I knew all too well that when someone says they are a happy work family, the opposite is almost always true. Everywhere I've worked, there has been nonsense, whether it was illicit affairs, academic rivalry, accusations of plagiarism, stolen research, or competition for the same grants. Professors, supposedly some of the most bookish, benign people in the world, will fight to the death to maintain their fragile authority in their fields. Rarely, but still possible, were motives of financial gain with the embezzling of university funds or other fraud. What appeared to outsiders to be a happy family soon revealed itself as a hotbed of factions and betrayals. It's always the same. My way of dealing with the nonsense is to keep my head down and stay away. I smile at everyone and make polite small talk. I don't gossip myself, though I may listen when it suits me. It's important to keep your ear to the ground and be aware of what's going on. Unfortunately, the fact that I'm silent about myself makes me an object of speculation. Since I volunteer nothing, they make up stories, fitting me into one of their handy boxes so that I make sense to them. When someone doesn't make sense, they become the object of scrutiny, which is when trouble begins. By staying silent about myself, I appear less trustworthy among the troops because no one knows where I stand on anything. That night, at the start of the new term, I hoped that Eventide College would be different and that my live-and-let-live attitude would be respected.

"Professor Stewart at Yale said you'd make an excellent administrator, Jonathan. Are you going to challenge me for the English department chair?"

"Not at all. I've had no particular aspirations to go into administration. I enjoy teaching too much."

A friendly voice rang out in the hall. "You're the first person I've heard say that in a *long* time." A middle-aged man with close-cropped salt and pepper hair, his wide tie pointing to the paunch visible under his brown jacket, appeared in the doorway. His smile was warm, the kind that invites confidence. "You must be the new Geddes Chair. I'm the post-modern guy around here."

"Jonathan Ferrars," said Debbie, "this is Leonard Harris."

"Why Eventide?" Leonard asked. "You were at Yale. Eventide is a step down, if you ask me."

"What a thing to say!" Debbie waved her finger at Leonard as though he were a naughty child. "Eventide College is highly respected. Our English department is top-notch. We're..."

"A sort of Ivy League school, yes, Debbie, I know. But Professor Ferrars had a position at an *actual* Ivy League school. Asking why he left is a legitimate question."

"Aren't you happy here?" Debbie crossed her arms over her chest. "Would you like the position Jonathan left behind?"

"I wouldn't mind it, to be honest with you, but I'm too close to retirement to leave, so I guess you're stuck with me."

Debbie turned her back on Leonard. A happy family indeed. "You'll love our students, Jonathan. They're some of the greatest young literary minds in the country. Many of our students are proud to be the first in their families to attend higher education. We have students who work two jobs to afford their courses, believing that a degree from Eventide College will make them more competitive in their chosen fields. Our students come from all over the world and speak many languages. Some professors, who do not belong here, believe that such students only serve to bring an institution down."

Debbie and Leonard watched me, waiting. The committee interview I had missed was now taking place.

"Privilege has always existed, and there have always been those who feel entitled. The terminology has changed, nothing more. My father grew up in poverty, and through his own intelligence and diligence, he created a successful business, and then he did everything in his power to give me every opportunity. When I wanted to attend university, he stopped at nothing to send me. He knew that anything that challenged your way of thinking could expand your mind. Over the years, I've come to believe that being exposed to thoughtful prose and verse is the best way to create a fully formed human being. Poe said, 'I would define, in brief, the poetry of words as the rhythmical creation of beauty.' I couldn't have said it better myself." I studied their faces, wondering if I had passed. Since they waited for me to continue, I did.

"I believe everyone deserves access to the same opportunities that I received. Even during my darkest times, I had my love for learning, and it gave me a purpose beyond my mere existence. When a student walks into my classroom, whoever that student is, they are my student for that term, and I will do everything I can to help them succeed."

"Teaching is well enough," Leonard said, "but it's not the focus of the professor, and it hasn't been for some time, if it ever was."

He was right, of course. If that had been an actual interview, they would have been more interested in my publications and grants than in my teaching.

The door across the hall opened, and the professor joined Debbie and Leonard. Debbie introduced him as Stephen Trevelyan, the modern poetry professor. Stephen was lean, angular, and finely dressed in a well-fitted iron-gray suit that matched his iron-gray hair. His black leather shoes were so well-shined that I could see my face reflected in them. "I'm glad you're here," Stephen said. "They were going to stick me with the Poe seminar. What a ghastly prospect."

"Don't care for Poe?" I asked.

"Good heavens, no. He's not what you'd call a prose stylist, and his rhymes are too perfect. Too obviously constructed."

"Poetry is constructed," Leonard said. "Who speaks in rhyme and meter?"

"Gentlemen." Debbie held her hands out, a referee separating boxers. "Let's not have this argument again. We're going to scare Jonathan away before he gets started." She smiled in my direction. "I know I've already said it, but I do hope you'll be happy at Eventide, Jonathan. Let me know if you need anything at all."

Debbie and Stephen walked away, heads leaning toward each other as they whispered about me, though I pretended not to notice. I grabbed my lecture notes and stuffed them into my backpack, then locked my door and took the stairs to the third floor where the English classes were held.

Leonard Harris followed me. "I wanted to be sure you knew the way. Your class is there at the end." He pointed four doors down. "Trevelyan is okay, you know. He's a little tight about poetry, but that's what he's paid for."

"And Debbie?"

"What have you heard?"

The suddenness of his question startled me.

"I haven't been here long enough to hear anything about anyone."

"She's, well, she's exactly what she seems to be."

"And what is that?"

"What is that?" Leonard glanced over his shoulder as though checking that no one was close enough to overhear. "She's a good enough chair. She's well-published. Early Modern is her field. She's a good face for the department. She's good at getting us funded. She knows the right people, you know? She's a special friend to everyone in admin, from the college president to our benefactor, Rhys Grimshaw. Have you met Grimshaw?"

"Not yet."

"You will. And you should know that he and Debbie are special friends. There's talk that she's gunning to be the next Mrs. Grimshaw. Just be on your guard."

"With Debbie?"

"With everyone. Some faculty members are annoyed that you're coming in with the chair when they've been struggling to leap from associate to full professor for years. Especially with you being so young."

Leonard was full of information, though it was a bit much a bit soon. I would have preferred to finish unpacking my boxes before I had to make sense of department gossip. To change the subject, I said, "I'm surprised anyone is still in their office. Even at Yale, most professors had gone home by now."

"You'd be amazed at how late some professors stay. I've had emails from colleagues time-stamped at 4:30 a.m."

"I'm afraid I'm guilty of that as well."

"You'll never get an email from me at that time. That's how I've survived this job for 25 years. I know when it's time to go home, and I know when it's time to sleep. It's too bad Larry Presspitch never learned that."

"Larry Presspitch?"

"He held the Geddes chair before you. You're in his office now. You knew you were taking over for a dead man, didn't you?"

"I knew the position had come up suddenly."

"Suddenly is one way to say it. Old Presspitch's heart gave out on him. Sitting there grading papers one minute, gone to meet his maker the next. Did you know he died in his office? I guess it's your office now."

"I didn't know that."

"He was in his 80s, so at least he made old bones. Past retirement age, you know, but he couldn't let go of the work. He thrived on it, and his students loved him. He used to have them over to his house at the end of every semester for a fancy dinner his wife cooked. A lot of his students thought of him as a father figure, and they've taken his death pretty hard. So has a lot of the faculty."

"When did he die?"

"Over the summer. One of his students, Simon Hayes, had an appointment with him. Simon banged on Larry's door, your door, but Larry never answered. Simon ran and got Leigh. Have you met our department secretary?" I nodded. "Leigh used her key to open the door, and there Larry was, calm as could be, his chin on his chest, his pen still between his fingers, smiling like the happiest man in the world. He was writing something and dropped dead as a doornail."

"What was he writing?"

"Something about at the end of exploring we'll arrive where we started." I must have looked surprised because he said, "You know it?"

"It's T. S. Eliot's poem Little Gidding." The familiar words passed behind my eyes. "And the end of all our exploring will be to arrive where we started and know the place for the first time."

"Old Presspitch has certainly arrived where he started. Let's hope the rest of us avoid the same fate any time soon."

"Let's hope we do."

Leonard nodded at some passing students as if he knew them, and then he disappeared into the crowd. I entered the classroom at the end of the hall and nodded at the waiting students. My time at Eventide College had begun.

Four

We commence, then, with this intention.

My first American Literature 1776-1865 survey class was uneventful. I took attendance, reviewed the syllabus, and prepared for the groans when I explained that our *Norton Anthology of American Literature* was in two volumes for our purposes—Volume A (Beginnings to 1820) and Volume B (1820-1865). I reviewed the important assignments and the due dates, and I let them go. I took the long way home, across campus to Southshore Road, so that I could walk along the nighttime coast. The salt spray was heavy, the rhythm of the waves rolling and slow, the fog heavy with a peculiar gloom. I continued down Frantick Road to the scenic cove where forest meets ocean, the maritime forest of pine, fir, and spruce lining the shore in majestic style. I walked as far as the edge of the dense woods, then turned toward home, stopping near Eventide Manor, its melancholy darkness calling to me as if some force bid me to it. The black brick mansion resembled the classic picture of a haunted house, mysterious and forlorn. It seemed to grow out of the shadows like an apparition, a spectral character in a Gothic tale, its mournfulness out of place in Southshore, which was a seaside village of harbors, brightly colored cottages, quaint shops, coffeehouses, and touristy bed and breakfasts. That night, the ground-floor windows of Eventide Manor glowed from within. Someone must have been awake at that late hour. A flutter of heavy curtains from the third-floor window, then the shadow of someone peering at me flickered and disappeared. I waited a while, wondering if the shadow would return, but it never did.

The following night, on my way to campus, I passed the two five-story Queen Anne mansions remodeled into student apartments—Clovis House, painted sea green, and Cavendish Hall, painted sky blue. Both houses boasted asymmetrical façades, wrap-around porches, and red brick chimneys. Students, with their backpacks over one shoulder, some walking and some riding their bicycles, came and went toward campus. Outside the student housing was a vast green lawn shaded by red oaks and sugar maples, where some young people sat chatting with friends. Beyond the trees, the open space of campus was dissected by gray stone pathways studded with benches under white pines. Near the Main Quad was the amphitheater, the Omnis Vir Odeon, as it was known, sitting on a semicircular hillside with granite slabs and stone steps. I passed the Johnson School of Mathematics and Engineering, a neoclassical-style building with a symmetrical façade and marble statues of Pythagoras, Euclid, and Hypatia in the recesses. I lingered near the sundial, curious about the students, who they were, what they studied, and where they expected to go after their time at Eventide was done. It will go by so quickly, I wanted to tell them. Enjoy this moment because it will never come again.

In my office, I dropped my backpack on my desk. I answered a few emails from students, again with questions about assignments and due dates, which, again, were in the syllabus. These were students from my survey course, and if tradition held, they would not share the attention to detail my graduate students did. I was reviewing my lecture notes when Stephen Trevelyan appeared at my open door. He smiled, a flash of a moment, which was a flash more than I had seen from him the previous night.

"Good evening, Jonathan. Are you on your way to the faculty meeting?"

"I am, but I can only stay a while. My first graduate seminar is tonight."

"The only time I wish I were teaching the late classes is when we have our nighttime faculty meetings so I'd have an excuse to skip out early. And how was your survey class last night?" He shuddered at the words *survey class*. "I'm glad I don't have to teach those anymore. The students are terrible."

"The students were fine, Stephen—perfectly normal and anxious about the new term."

"It's as if they've never read a book in their lives."

"Most of them aren't English majors, and maybe they never have read a book from beginning to end. Their interests are mathematics, music, or some other subject, but they have to take a survey course to get the humanities credits they need."

"A waste of time, if you ask me."

I was rescued by Leonard Harris, who passed Stephen's lanky form to sit in one of the two metal chairs near my desk. "Stephen doesn't believe in the general survey classes."

"So I gathered."

Stephen was unabashed. "We should concentrate on our own fields of study and take courses only in what will further our intended endeavors."

"Reading and writing are skills everyone needs," Leonard said. "Nurses, scientists, everyone needs reading comprehension and critical thinking skills. If we teach those skills more generally to students not studying literature or creative writing, I see no harm in that."

Leonard and Stephen looked at me as though I were the deciding vote.

"Since I'm the one teaching the American literature survey course, I'm inclined to agree with Leonard. But not all the students are from other departments. There are undergraduate English students in there as well, and they balance the ones who grumble about reading lists and writing assignments. And if one or two of the students from other fields decide they like poetry or fiction as a result, so much the better."

"Well said," said Leonard.

Stephen grimaced at this first opinion from the Geddes chair. "You said tonight is your first grad seminar?"

"It is."

"Well then. I wish you luck with your students. I'll see you at the meeting."

Leonard shook his head as Stephen's long shadow disappeared.

"Is he always this much fun?"

"Wait until you see him at the faculty meeting. Stephen has opinions—that I can guarantee. He likes to strut around like a peacock with his tail feathers high, but the truth is he's published little poetry lately, and his research hasn't been particularly well received. He's trying too hard to compensate. If he thinks you're standing in his way, he'll try to pull you down."

"We don't even study the same subjects. How could I be in his way?"

"If you win more grants than he does, if you publish more papers, if you speak at more prestigious conferences, he sees all that as standing in his way. And he'll spread rumors about how you accidentally plagiarized your latest paper, or how you got the job by being too friendly, if you know what I mean. What about that gossip about Debbie being too friendly with Rhys Grimshaw? Where do you think it came from? People have always said that Grimshaw has too much power in the department for a mere benefactor, but if you've got money, people will give you more power than you deserve." Leonard leaned back in the uncomfortable chair, likely chosen to keep students from lingering during office hours. "So how's it going so far?"

"As Stephen pointed out, tonight is my first graduate seminar. Ask me again tomorrow."

"Is this the Poe seminar?"

"It is." Stephen's words crossed my mind again. "What did he mean when he said he wished me luck with my students? Was he referring to the students in the survey course? He didn't seem too thrilled by the Poe seminar either."

Leonard folded his hands in his lap as he looked out the window into the night. "He meant your graduate students, actually, the ones you're going to meet tonight. What did Debbie tell you about your Poe seminar?"

"Nothing."

Leonard closed my door so that no one would overhear. He nodded as he seemed to consider his words. Finally, he said, "Our graduate students are, well, let's say they have a reputation for being tough customers. Everyone in your Poe seminar is applying to be the next Poet of Eventide, which means they're competing against each other, and that's never pretty."

"The Poet of Eventide?"

"She didn't tell you about the poet laureate thing either?" I shook my head. "She probably didn't want to scare you away. Every October, Rhys Grimshaw hosts a ball at Eventide Manor to name the new poet laureate, the Poet of Eventide. Becoming the next poet laureate is a big deal here."

"Can all students apply to be the poet laureate?"

"It's only open to grad students in the English department, and they all apply, and they all want it. Badly. Our poet laureates are virtually guaranteed to leave here with their careers made. Henry Feldstein is our reigning Poet of Eventide, and by the time he graduated last spring, he had a literary agent shopping his first novel. I haven't heard if it's been picked up yet, but I wouldn't be surprised if it were." Leonard lowered his voice as though the walls had ears. "They all want it, and some of them will play nasty to get it. Simon Hayes, he's one of your seminar students, he's always in Debbie's ear, talking down his cohort, telling her stories about how they cheat, how they lie, how they're not to be trusted."

"Sounds like Simon and Stephen should get along."

"Stephen is Simon's adviser, so you're more right than you realize. Stephen has taught Simon everything he knows." Leonard chuckled at the thought.

"Go on. What else do I need to know?"

"You need to know that your seminar students are wrapped up tight in this poet laureate thing. It's the most important thing in the world to them right now. I think they'd kill each other if it would assure them of the position."

I put my notes down for a better look at Leonard. He was a friendly looking man with bright eyes, an easy smile, and a pleasant laugh. He was gregarious, always chatting with someone in the halls—colleagues or students, he didn't seem to mind which. For a moment, I thought he was serious. When he smiled, I wasn't sure.

"You need to know that Simon Hayes and Thomas Lambert hate each other. They've been rivals since they both arrived here two years ago. The Hayes family is old money, you know, and Thomas hates everyone who has had an easier time than him. Thomas, for all his faults, is highly intelligent and more than capable. He also likes to catch professors out. Someone your age? You'll look like fresh meat to him."

"I've been doing this long enough that I can handle myself."

"Long enough is relative, young man. And you should know that Thomas likes to discover little tidbits about everyone."

"Tidbits they don't want known?"

"Exactly. Now, old Larry Presspitch knew how to handle him. Larry was good with all of them, right until the end, of course." Leonard tugged at his wide tie as he leaned further back in the chair. "Cordelia Reed, she's in Media Studies with Eric Michaels, but I don't know either of them well. Oliver Chatterjee is probably the hardest-working student we have. Seems like the kid studies 24 hours a day. He's always in the library, always reading or writing something with his ridiculous quill pen, or banging away on his laptop. He's driven, but they all are. He's on work experience, and he doesn't want to lose his place, you know? He helps in the department office. He's a bit of a pet for Debbie. I wouldn't say anything in front of him that you don't want repeated to our illustrious DC. They've all got their special pets around here."

"And who is your pet?"

Leonard's hearty laugh filled the small room. "I'm allergic to pets. And if you know what's good for you, you will be too." He paused as if he waited for me to add something, but I had nothing, so he continued. "They're not all cutthroat. Maeve Lang is a nice girl, a talented poet, maybe a little mystical, a little woo-woo."

"Woo-woo?"

"You know, dreamy, a bit of a hippie. I heard she's a wood fairy, you know, a dryad, those spirits who are tied to oak trees."

"Indeed."

"They're supposed to be beautiful women, these dryads, and Maeve is a pretty girl. Not that I've noticed or anything."

"Of course not. But why do people think she's a wood fairy of all things?"

"Simon told Stephen that he saw her in the woods doing some spell or ceremony or something. You know how poets are—all bohemian and far out and that sort of thing."

"You seem well-informed."

"As a matter of fact, I am. I was the department chair before I was bumped for Debbie. You know how it goes. Someone above my pay grade decides they want to make changes, shuffle things around. Rhys steps in with his money, and he wants Debbie to have the job because she's a good face for the department. The truth is, I don't mind the guy, but there's something about him I don't trust. But he's got the money, so he's allowed to stick his beak in, even though he's not actually a member of the department, and when he talks, everyone listens. Skinny shrimp of a guy, too, but everyone seems to be spellbound by him."

"He's taller when he's standing on his money."

"That's the truth." Leonard laughed. "I wouldn't have minded staying on as DC. I thought I was good at handling the details and the office politics, but it wasn't my call. I prefer to focus on things within my control." He checked his watch. "We ought to head to the meeting."

As I locked my door, I said, "I heard from some colleagues at Yale that Eventide College is haunted."

If I had expected Leonard to laugh, I was mistaken. He exhaled a long, slow breath. "I've seen some things happen here and there. Were they hauntings? I don't know."

"What sort of things?"

"Silly things if you look at each one on its own. Once I left my research files on my desk and they ended up in the faculty lounge."

"Could you have misplaced them?"

"I can't remember the last time I set foot in the lounge."

"What were you researching?"

"The use of the supernatural by post-modern American authors such as Octavia E. Butler and Toni Morrison. Then there was the time I found satchels of peppercorns, salt, bay leaves, and rosemary scattered here," he gestured down the hallway, "and a note that said, 'With this salt and herb, I charge these wards to protect this place.' I was like a kid on an Easter egg hunt, scavenging the whole Eliot School in search of these satchels."

"Sounds like a warding spell."

"You know it?"

"Warding spells repel negative energy or malevolent influences."

"You mean like a malevolent supernatural being?" Leonard leaned closer to me as we stopped outside the conference room. "I think, and this is just between us, but I think that there may be something supernatural out there." He nodded toward the fire escape. Whether he meant the campus, the town, or the whole of Maine, I wasn't certain.

"Did anyone else notice the satchels?"

"No one else in the department seems to care. Debbie got a good laugh out of it. She said she'd take them home and use them to scent her linen drawer. The other professors wouldn't care if something evil bit them on the ass as long as it didn't interfere with their scholarship."

He opened the door, and the meeting was already in progress. Leonard and I found two empty chairs at the far end of the long table in the center of the room. Debbie was leading the conversation, or the argument, and she clapped her hands when she saw me.

"Jonathan! I was worried you wouldn't make it tonight. I know you have to leave for your seminar soon, but I'm so glad

I can introduce you to your colleagues. Everyone, this is Jonathan Ferrars, our new Geddes chair."

There were some smiles, some nods, some blank faces, some grimaces—in other words, the usual. Stephen, his lips pulled thin, looked as pleasant as usual. A kindly, bird-like woman sitting next to him said, "Welcome, Jonathan."

"Let me introduce everyone," said Debbie. "All right now, you know Leonard, obviously, and you know Stephen. And I think you know who I am by now." She laughed as if she had said something funny. "This is Lavinia Cruz, and she's in charge of our creative writing program." Lavinia was a handsome woman with a stern smile, her hair pulled into a tight plait and left to dangle over her shoulder. She nodded in my general direction. "And next to Stephen is Elise Spencer. She studies Victorian-era British literature." Elise was the frail, bird-like woman who had welcomed me. Her white-blond hair, also plaited, was hardly discernible against her porcelain-white complexion. Her smile was gentle and sincere, and I already appreciated her. "This is Eric Michaels." Eric was young, in his mid-20s at most, and he held his head high with absolute confidence that he was on his way in the academic world. "Eric is also new to us this year. He just finished his doctoral program at Stanford, and he's leading our new Media Studies program."

"Ha!"

Stephen brought his fist to his mouth as though covering a cough. Debbie grimaced at him and moved on.

There were other faces, other names that didn't register. Leonard whispered to me that many of the professors were puffing themselves up with resentful self-righteousness because they had been called back for a late meeting. Fortunately, I was not likely to see them again. In the back, in the shadow created by the overhead fluorescent lights and the tall metal bookcases, sat a man with his legs stretched before him, his hands on his knees, watching the proceedings with interest. When Debbie saw that he had my attention, she laughed.

"Oh! How on earth could I forget? I'd leave my head behind if it weren't attached to my neck, I think."

"Sounds uncomfortable," Lavinia said.

Leonard laughed. "Doesn't it just?"

Debbie grasped the shoulder of the man in the shadows. "Rhys Grimshaw, this is Jonathan Ferrars. But of course, you know Jonathan is the new Geddes chair."

Rhys Grimshaw stood and pushed his glasses back up his nose. He was the sort of man you might pass a dozen times a day and never notice. He was of medium height, with a slight build, not young but not old, perhaps in his fifties. Everything about him screamed anonymity. He was balding, and what remained of his hair was an uncertain shade between brown and blond. His eyes had a weary tint, changing from dark to darker depending on where he stood in the shadows. His clothes were neither stylish nor shabby, and he wore a white button-down shirt and tan pleated trousers. Even his posture seemed undecided, with his shoulders neither proud nor slouched. He looked as if he existed in some permanent middle ground. If he sat beside you in a lecture hall or walked past you on the quad, you'd forget him before he turned the corner.

"I'm so pleased to see you here tonight, Professor Ferrars. I've been so eager to speak to you."

I returned his polite greeting. When Rhys Grimshaw said nothing more, everyone turned back to the meeting. With the introductions done, the argument (it was definitely an argument) continued.

"You've been outspoken about the budget, Leonard," Debbie said. "What do you think about our plan for next year?"

Leonard nodded sagely. "We're at the tail end of a global

financial crisis, and the reality is that there just isn't as much money to go around. I agree with Debbie. We're going to have to make some cuts."

"Except for the fact that we're funding a new Media Studies program," Stephen said. Lavinia snorted. Eric Michaels looked as though he was about to speak, but Debbie jumped in.

"We've been over this, Stephen. If we want to stay relevant, we need to change things up. Media Studies is booming as a focus for scholarship, and we don't want to seem out of date. As a matter of fact, that Media Studies program is already full, which brings in revenue for the school. That is always a good thing."

"If you say so."

"Thank you, yes, Stephen, I do say so. You should also know that there will be a hiring freeze next year. When Professor Jackson," she nodded at a distinguished-looking man in a corduroy jacket with elbow patches, "and Professor Ludwig retire at the end of the Spring term, we will not be replacing them."

"Then who will teach their classes?" Leonard asked.

"We'll be hiring part-time faculty to take some courses, but some of you may have an additional course or two."

The professors groaned on cue.

"Look, everyone, I know this isn't what we want to hear, and it isn't ideal, but Humanities departments all over the country are grappling with post-recession funding cuts, as we are. Our benefactor," she smiled sweetly at Rhys, "has been generous, but it's not his responsibility to keep the entire department afloat. We're going to have to cut corners to make ends meet. The Dean of the Eliot School is adamant about this."

Stephen pointed at Rhys. "You could cut the pointless chair position." He smirked at me. "No offense to the new guy, but the money you spend on one position could be spread around."

"I'm a new guy too," said Eric. No one heard him.

"You're as clueless as ever, Trevelyan." Leonard flattened his tie. "It's not just a matter of money. The board of Eventide College is pressuring departments to justify their costs. Knowledge for its own sake is being questioned because higher education has suddenly become more about preparing people for jobs than educating them to be intelligent, thoughtful members of society. Now, Jonathan here," Leonard touched my arm, "believes that teaching is the most important part of what we do."

"So do I," said Elise in her bird-like voice.

"Which brings me back to my point," said Stephen. "What is the money to endow the Geddes chair doing but funding a single position? What else could it be used for?"

Debbie smirked at Stephen. "If we eliminate Jonathan's position, then you can teach the Poe seminar. And the American literature survey class."

"I take it all back." Stephen smiled toward Rhys in the shadows. "Please continue funding the Geddes chair."

I checked the clock on the wall and saw that I had twenty minutes before my seminar began. Instead of defending myself, I said, "Speaking of teaching, if you all will excuse me, I need to get to class. If someone could let me know the fate of my position, I would appreciate it."

I grabbed my backpack and left as the professors began bickering amongst themselves, Stephen loudest of all. Debbie followed me into the hall. "I'm so sorry about that, Jonathan. Of course, your position is safe. Don't mind Stephen. He likes to run his fast mouth like he's on the New Hampshire Motor Speedway. Rhys is thrilled with you. He told me so."

"I've hardly done anything yet."

"He has a good feeling about you, Jonathan. A good feeling from Rhys is a useful thing around here."

"Indeed. Good night."

"Good night, Jonathan. And good luck with your Poe seminar."

I watched her return to the conference room, concerned that everyone felt the need to wish me luck with my graduate students.

We gave the Future to the winds, and slumbered tranquilly in the Present, weaving the dull world around us into dreams.

I needed a moment to myself before heading to the seminar room. While animosity between professors was nothing new, I had hoped for some time before the nonsense began. I left behind the red bricks of the Eliot School and wandered into the cluster of trees on the wide, stretching lawn. Although it was night, the campus was still busy with students coming and going. Stretched out on the lawn were six students, three young men and three young women, sitting together on a flannel blanket. One of the young men held up his coffee cup and said, "Here's to our final year at Eventide." The others responded in kind, their coffee cups raised in salute. They appeared to be an interesting but mismatched group, though why mismatched, I couldn't have said then. According to the clock tower, I still had fifteen minutes, so I loitered for a few moments more.

One of the students on the flannel blanket was a handsome blond young man who looked rather like a Nordic prince. He held out a book I knew well, *The Complete Works of Edgar Allan Poe*, to the young woman in sage green who smelled like jasmine. I suspected that these young people would soon belong to me, so I did what anyone would in that circumstance—I lingered behind a tree, just out of their sight, so I could eavesdrop. From what Leonard said, I half-expected them to be Minotaurs confined to the labyrinth of academia. And one poetic wood fairy. Instead, they appeared to be ordinary young college students.

"This is the book I was telling you about, Maeve," the Nordic prince said.

The sage-looking young woman took the book and turned it over to read the back cover. An auburn-haired young man looked over her shoulder with a rather stern expression.

"Harrison is not the definitive text," he said. "Mabbott's book, *Collected Works: Tales and Sketches*, is the definitive text. Harrison's books were published in 1902. Who reads anything written in 1902 in 2010?"

"What a ridiculous thing to say. Poe was published in the nineteenth century, and we still read him." A dark-haired young man pressed his tortoiseshell glasses against his nose. "Besides, Harrison is still respected, Thomas. Since you're studying Poe for your thesis, you should know that."

"Thomas knows better than the rest of us, of course," said the Nordic prince, his old-money voice blistering.

A young woman, wearing a green and olive tartan dress that resembled a school uniform, lifted her head from the open book in her hands, a volume of poetry by Elizabeth Barrett Browning. "Are you starting already, Thomas? I was hoping to at least get through the first week without having to listen to your grumbling."

"My sentiments exactly."

The young woman next to her, her red hair fiery under the

campus lights, finished her coffee and tossed the paper cup into a nearby trash can. "It's all Thomas knows how to do—complain as if his life depends on it." She turned to the Nordic prince. "Don't you think, Simon?"

Simon shrugged. "It's nothing to me. I have bigger fish to fry."

"Do you?" said the auburn-haired young man. "Did you need to ask your daddy for the money to buy the fish?"

The Nordic prince turned to the sage-looking, jasmine-scented young woman. "I thought maybe we could go to the pub tonight after class."

She shook her head. "Thank you, Simon, but I'm afraid..."

"You can't possibly have papers to write already," said the young woman with fire-like hair. "It's only the first week of class. Besides, can't you wiggle your nose and *ta da*! Your work is magically done for you."

"She's not that kind of witch, Amandine." The auburn-haired young man, the one they called Thomas, seemed to spit the words in Amandine's direction.

Amandine shrugged. "Maybe she is, and maybe she isn't." She leaned toward the Nordic prince. "I can come if you want, Simon."

"I'll see how I feel after class," the Nordic prince said. If Amandine felt the slight, she didn't show it.

Thomas lay on his back on the grass, stretching his arms above his head. He stared into the night sky as if counting stars. "What have any of you heard about the new Geddes chair?"

The dark-haired young man tugged at his black turtleneck as though he were nervous, or warm, or both. "Only that his doctorate is from Cambridge and he's here from Yale."

"Yale? Are you sure it was Yale?" The dark-haired student nodded. "What the hell is he doing here from Yale? What's wrong with him?"

"What do you mean, what's wrong with him?" said the fiery-haired Amandine.

"I mean, who goes from Yale to Eventide College?"

I stepped further into the plentiful trees. I didn't want them to hear me laughing.

"You ought to be nice to him," said the dark-haired young man. "You'll need him to be your new adviser since Larry..."

"Popped his cork?" When no one laughed, Thomas shrugged. "I'll be nice to him if he's nice to me."

Amandine threw her hands in the air. "We know what that means."

The sage-looking young woman touched his shoulder. "Thomas..."

"Don't worry, Maeve. If he checks out, he'll be fine."

Maeve's voice quivered. "I still can't believe it about Professor Presspitch. He was such a nice man."

"Believe it," said the Nordic prince. "I was the one who had an appointment with him, and I was with Leigh when she unlocked his door."

"You found him dead?" said Amandine. "You never said."

Simon shrugged as if it didn't matter. These things happen every day. "He went quietly. He looked as if he were sleeping. He had it better than most of us will." He checked his expensive-looking watch. "We'd better go."

They gathered their belongings while the young woman in the tartan dress rolled up the blanket and pushed it into her Shakespeare and Company tote bag. The six students shuffled toward the Eliot School while I followed discreetly behind. They headed toward the elevator, and I took the stairs. As I found my way to the seminar room, I considered Leonard's helpful attempt to fill me in about my students, but I've learned not to trust other people's opinions. I prefer to make my own judgments. Two people can be in the same place at the same time and explain the situation completely differently.

Truth is a universal concept, but reality is different. What Leonard knows from his perspective will differ from what I know because our realities are different.

The seminar room was a white rectangle with three small windows facing the glass walkway. The six students I had just seen were now sitting around the long conference table, three on either side, chatting amongst themselves. The Nordic prince was texting on his BlackBerry while the fiery-haired Amandine opened her MacBook. The others had notebooks and pens in their hands. When I appeared, they fell silent. I didn't look at them. I didn't acknowledge them. I took my time sitting down, opening my backpack, and pulling out my lecture notes. Yes, I was playing with them, but there was a certain satisfaction in knowing that we wouldn't begin until I said so.

I thought about the students in my survey class from the previous night. Instead of being three-headed dogs, as Stephen seemed certain they were, I found them to be friendly, polite, some more interested than others. Graduate seminars always have a different tone than survey courses, but that's to be expected. I gathered that these six students had high opinions of themselves, but people often do.

When the bubble-like tension was ready to burst, I began.

"Some people feel an inchoate longing to explain the unexplainable. Others have attempted to know the great unknowable—death—while they live. Many dwell in fear of the unknown, and they allow that fear to spiral until it becomes madness. Perhaps that's why we continue to feel a cosmic connection to that dark-haired, sad-eyed man named Edgar Poe. In this seminar, we'll study the man whose name is synonymous with American Gothic literature, with darkness, with melancholy, and with the never-ending sadness that comes from knowing that a human's time is all too finite."

I turned on the computer, pulled up my PowerPoint, and

clicked to the slide of the famous daguerreotype of Poe, his dark hair lank, his clothing untidy, his eyes a river of woe. Finally, I looked at my students. Six young faces stared at me with such intensity that I felt it in my bones.

"Perhaps it's the mystery of Poe, his writing and his life, that continues to fascinate us. Readers want to know about Poe's alcoholism, about the strange man who married his 13-year-old cousin, about the starving artist who lived with his consumptive young wife in a freezing room where she had only a cat for warmth. They want to know about the man obsessed with death. But there is more to him than the mythology that has arisen from misunderstood facts."

The atmosphere shifted, as I noted with some satisfaction. The students exhaled in unison. From my spying on them under the trees, and seeing them there in the seminar room, they didn't appear to be Minotaurs, nor were they three-headed, nor gorgons. They were six young adults sitting on the edge of their chairs. Under the harsh fluorescent lights, they appeared younger than they were—like children waiting for the next words of their bedtime story. I let them stew. Part of this job is being a showman, and I've learned to play that part well. I heard an exasperated sigh, but ignored it. I wouldn't let them ruffle me so easily.

Maeve shook her dark hair, and it flowed in waves down her back. She flattened her oversized knitted sweater over her long sage-green dress and smiled at me in an encouraging way. Leonard had called her a wood fairy. She certainly looked the part. Next to her sat Amandine. Under the fluorescent lights, Amandine's hair appeared more copper than fire. Her honey-brown eyes, fixed firmly on me, were direct and intense. The young woman in tartan across the table wore her gold-brown hair tucked neatly under a thin headband. Her wide blue eyes made her appear almost childlike as she waited for me to continue. The three young men looked like visions from some fashion magazine in their tailored jackets, turtlenecks, and vintage watches.

"Almost everyone has at least a passing familiarity with Poe's poem The Raven. What other works by Poe are we familiar with?"

"That's easy." The one called Thomas ran a hand through his unruly auburn hair. "I'm researching Poe for my thesis. I know everything he's written."

"We have a Poe scholar amongst us. What about the rest of you?"

Maeve, the sage-looking wood fairy, said, "I've read The Tell-Tale Heart."

"What do you remember about it?"

"It's about an unnamed narrator who murders an old man who has what the narrator calls a vulture eye. After the narrator murders the old man by suffocating him under his bed, he dismembers the body and hides it under the floorboards. The police come because of the screams, and it seems like the narrator is going to get away with the murder until his guilt gets the best of him and he confesses to the police."

"Very good. What other stories by Poe do we know?"

The Nordic prince was stylish in a white knit turtleneck under a finely cut tan trench coat he kept on indoors. His gold hair was parted on the side, and he brushed it away from his face with a quick sweep of his fingers. He leaned toward the wood fairy, but as she did under the trees, she leaned away. Whatever the prince liked about the wood fairy, it didn't seem to be reciprocated.

"I know The Murders in the Rue Morgue," Amandine said.

"What can you tell us about it?"

"Two women, a mother and her daughter, are murdered in their apartment in Paris. The mother is found in the courtyard with broken bones and her neck slashed so severely that her head falls off when her body is moved. The daughter is found strangled and stuffed up the chimney. The police are baffled, and C. Auguste Dupin, an amateur detective, uses his analytical skills to find the murderer."

"Who was an orangutan," Thomas said.

I pulled the class roster from my backpack, pushed my glasses back up my nose, and cleared my throat. Thomas raised his hand.

"Yes?"

"Where have you published? You look too young to be an accomplished professor, certainly too young to hold the Geddes chair."

"Don't start, Thomas," said the Nordic prince.

"I don't mind answering the question. I've been published in the same journals as other literature scholars. And I'm older than I look."

"How old are you?"

"Does it matter?"

"What if I say yes?"

The sage-looking wood fairy shook her head. "It's none of our business, Thomas."

"I'm closer to 40 than 30, if you must know."

Thomas pulled the collar of his gray jacket closer around his throat as though he were cold, and his eyes, the same gray as his jacket, gleamed. All right, I thought. I'll play along. I recited a list of my most recent publications, all concerning nineteenth-century American literature, most concerning Poe, all in well-respected journals. As if to prove me wrong, he typed into his laptop to check the online databases.

"How about I take attendance so I know who you are, since you know who I am?"

"You're Professor Jonathan Ferrars," Thomas said.

"That's correct."

I called their names from the roster.

1. Oliver Chatterjee—the serious young man in the black turtleneck and tortoiseshell glasses.

2. Simon Hayes—the Nordic prince.

3. Thomas Lambert—the auburn-haired smart-ass.

4. Maeve Lang—the sage-looking wood fairy.

5. Cordelia Reed—the earnest young woman in tartan.

6. Amandine Wesson—the fiery one.

"How much experience in this job do you have, Professor Jonathan Ferrars?"

Perhaps young Mr. Lambert would provide some comic relief that term.

Amandine Wesson rolled her eyes. "You've just checked his publications, Thomas. I saw your screen while you were checking. How could he have all that scholarship if he was a brand-new professor?"

From their conversation outside and their exasperated sighs in the seminar room, it seemed that, first, Thomas Lambert usually behaved this way, and second, the others were already annoyed with him. Simon and Oliver leaned away from Thomas as though distancing themselves.

"Thank you, Ms. Wesson. And you needn't call me Professor Jonathan Ferrars, Mr. Lambert. Professor will be fine, or Professor Ferrars. Dr. Ferrars, if you prefer."

"Very good, Professor. Where else have you taught?"

"Don't you remember what Oliver said? Professor Ferrars is from Yale." Simon typed into his laptop and turned the screen toward Thomas. "It's listed on his EC staff page."

Thomas seemed to take the information as a personal affront. "Really, Professor Ferrars, you seem to have lost your way a little."

"And how is that?"

"You left Yale for Eventide College?"

"Not this again." Amandine closed her eyes as if wishing Thomas away.

Thomas's brittle laughter snapped across the room like a slap in the face. "I think my question deserves an answer. Why would anyone leave Yale to come here?"

"You're not the first person here to ask me that question. The truth is, I enjoyed my years at Yale, but it was time to move on."

"But Yale is so much more prestigious than Eventide College."

Simon Hayes raised his hands in the air in dramatic fashion. "We've had this discussion at least 500 times, Thomas. Eventide *is* a prestigious college. The question is, what are *you* doing here if you hate it so much?"

The other heads bobbed in agreement.

"*Prestigious* is an interesting concept, isn't it? We grant prestige to certain institutions, certain cars, certain watches, certain zip codes. In the end, these things are valuable only because we choose to give them value."

"Usually because they're expensive, so only certain people can have them," Amandine said.

"Agreed. But if something is expensive, does that make it better? There are hardworking professors at schools across the nation, around the world. If their school is more affordable, does that mean the education granted by that school is less valuable?"

"No schools are affordable," said Cordelia.

"Ms. Reed has an excellent point. The cost of post-secondary education is rising exponentially. Does that make it more valuable?"

"It depends," said Oliver. He had the intense look of someone who knew what he was about. In his long brown trench coat, black turtleneck, and tortoiseshell glasses, he appeared to be someone who gave his education his undivided attention. "Eventide College continues to have one of the premier English departments in the country. Our students go on to attend some of the world's highest-ranking PhD programs. Our poet laureates are virtually guaranteed a leg up in the literary world, and our graduates become award-winning authors and editors. There's value in something beyond what it costs."

Amandine shook her head. "But if you're not getting an education for a specific reason, if you're not training for a certain occupation, then what's the purpose? Doesn't a diploma then become just a piece of paper?"

"All right, then. In other words, a college degree for the sake of a college degree is not valuable?"

"Not really," said Cordelia. "I mean, if it doesn't help you find work that will meet your basic living needs, then that education hasn't been valuable. A degree for its own sake is not valuable. It has to teach you something—how to be a lawyer, how to be a doctor, or a dentist, or how to run a business."

"Funny you should say that, Ms. Reed, since the professors were just talking about the same thing at the faculty meeting. We are now in an era that believes that the sole purpose of higher education is to prepare people for work. So then, repeating my point, knowledge for the sake of knowledge has no value?"

The students stopped to think.

"Let me put it another way. Universities are cutting their humanities departments. SUNY Albany has suspended some of its humanities programs, like World Languages, Classics, and Theater. In the UK, public funding for the humanities has been cut. We're facing budget cuts here at Eventide. Students these days want what Ms. Reed was talking about—an education that will put them forward in an emerging career. Fewer people see value in learning about literature for its own sake. We've all heard the joke about English PhDs lining up to work at McDonald's. Mr. Chatterjee has already pointed out that some of our graduates here at Eventide College go on to illustrious literary careers. Not all writers, poets, and editors will have such glowing results. The focus of our seminar, Edgar Poe, was himself a brilliantly imaginative, well-published author. Was he successful?"

"It's almost 200 years later, and we're still talking about him," said Cordelia. "He's still widely read and influential on other writers, so yes, I'd say he was successful."

"Was he financially successful?"

"No," said Simon, "he died a pauper." Simon's face tightened, as if he'd bitten into something sour, as if even saying *pauper* was too much. I wondered if he learned that look from Stephen.

"So then, is our argument that something must be financially viable in order to have value? If reading in English literature is not necessarily going to help you find a lucrative career, is it worthwhile to study the humanities, literature in particular?"

"Yes." Maeve gestured towards the other students, who sat forward in their seats. "My passion is nineteenth-century American poetry. I adore Emily Dickinson. I see so much of myself in her. And I love to read and write poetry. It's what I live for."

"So it enriches your life without offering financial gain?"

"I could be an English professor like you," said Thomas. "And if I ended up at Yale, I wouldn't leave."

"Yes, Mr. Lambert, I can see that. But only a small percentage of professors are making what we'd call a livable salary, and you have to be promoted up the tenure track before you get there. We've just experienced the Great Recession, and universities have implemented hiring freezes and budget cuts nationwide. In fact, this year, 2010, is one of the worst academic job markets in years."

"You were hired here," said Thomas.

"Yes, I was, but I'm filling an empty chair that is independently funded. I've had to search for jobs like any other academic. I was interviewed at one of the most prestigious public universities in the country, and their salary for a full-time teaching professor was half that of a high school teacher's salary. And not everyone who wants a tenure-track position will find one. Many universities are cutting back their full-time staff and filling empty positions with adjunct professors who make a pittance. You can pursue your passion to its ultimate end, in our case PhDs in our chosen fields, and still not be financially rewarded. So I ask again: is what we're doing here valuable?"

"Yes," said Oliver. "It's valuable. Knowledge for knowledge's sake is valuable. Learning more, thinking more, challenging myself more, focusing on a subject that's closest to my heart, that's valuable to me. I love learning about literature. I love writing poetry. Literature teaches me what it means to be human. It teaches empathy because we learn to relate to those who seem different from us on the surface, but underneath we want the same things."

Amandine nodded. "Literature helps us see the bigger picture. As we grapple with these narratives, we learn more about themes such as identity, obsession, revenge, and redemption. We can study the big questions about what life means, or if it has any meaning at all."

"And critical thinking," Maeve said. "By studying literature, we learn how to analyze and interpret the world. My brother is an attorney, and he got his undergraduate degree in English. When I asked why, he said studying English helped him learn how to form a cogent argument."

"I want to be a published poet," Oliver said. "I want to be respected, and I wouldn't mind winning an award or two. Studying other poets allows me to tap into my creativity."

Cordelia shrugged. "I just like to read." The others

nodded. "I love making friends with characters and sharing their journeys. It helps me understand my journey more clearly."

I leaned back in my chair, arms crossed over my chest, a smile on my lips. "Forgive me, Mr. Lambert, but I seem to have taken a roundabout route to answering your question about why I came to Eventide College, and all of you, with your thoughtful responses, have helped me. I'm here because I want to be somewhere like Eventide, where most students are not privileged. Some of you in this room may be here on grants, scholarships, or financial aid. Of course, I had students who needed financial assistance to afford a Yale diploma. I enjoy working with students who have everything to gain from an education, and there's more to an English degree than meets the eye, for the reasons we've discussed. I'm looking forward to sharing one of my favorite authors, Edgar A. Poe, with all of you. There is so much about the man and the myth, and his way of leaning into the darker side of human nature, that continues to fascinate us. Poe was a man of contradictions. He had a relentlessly analytical mind, yet at his heart he was a romantic. He was outwardly reserved, yet inwardly tempestuous. For all his severity, there was in him a profound gentleness, which surfaced unexpectedly, such as when he spoke of his beloved wife, or of the fragile nature of human happiness. In those moments, he appeared almost otherworldly, a man who walked the border between the waking world and some deeper realm most of us fear entering. Yet as gentle as he could be with his emotions, he was fearless and brutal as a literary critic."

The students were silent. Then Oliver said, "It sounds like you knew him, Professor Ferrars."

"I'm afraid that's what happens when you spend your life studying certain authors. They can feel like friends after spending so many hours together." The students nodded.

"Poe essentially invented the detective story with C. Auguste Dupin in The Murders in the Rue Morgue. He helped to make suspense and horror popular genres. As Ms. Reed said, he continues to influence authors today. All I can say is that I'm very happy to be at Eventide, and I'm looking forward to learning with all of you this term."

Thomas, however, had more on his mind.

"Why do you call us by our titles? You're the professor. You don't need to acknowledge us that way."

"Since you call me by my title, it seems only fair. I'd be perfectly fine if you called me Jonathan. I've never been one to stand on ceremony, and you've already seen that I'm qualified to teach this class." I nodded at Thomas. "You don't need to remind yourselves every time you address me."

I knew Thomas wasn't done with me, but I was fairly certain I had won over the others. All in all, it was a good night's work. I passed out copies of the syllabus, went over the reading list and a few of the assignments, answered questions about the term, and let them go.

Six

There are certain themes of which the interest is all-absorbing, but which are too entirely horrible for the purposes of legitimate fiction.

The week passed quickly, as weeks do when you've hit the ground running at the beginning of a new term. There is something that never grows old about being on a college campus when it is alive with students—the beautifully tended grounds, the plentiful trees, the rush and bustle of young lives searching for meaning—all of it makes me happy. When I grow weary of my work, as I do at times, I stand in the center of campus, wherever I happen to be, and my desire to continue is ignited. Whenever I walked to the Eliot School, I took my time along the stone-paved, tree-lined paths, enjoying the view. By then, in early September, the summer humidity had wandered away, hopefully for another year, leaving comfortable weather behind. Green foliage still brightened the landscape, the grass dotted with buttercups, coneflowers, and daisies. Eventide College appeared to be a peaceful, pleasant place, and I hoped I would be happy there.

The second Poe seminar began calmly enough. There was the occasional aside from Thomas, followed by rolling eyes or shaking heads from the others. When Maeve held up her hand, Thomas backed off. Maeve seemed to be the only one whose opinion Thomas cared about. Simon, the Nordic prince, would whisper to Maeve, and Amandine would respond. Oliver and Cordelia would sneak shy glances at each other when they thought no one was looking. I was growing to like my grad students, quite a lot, in fact. They were knowledgeable and interested. They were driven, perhaps distractedly so, but one expects that in graduate classes. I began the night with some general background on nineteenth-century American literature. The students pulled out their notebooks or laptops and took notes.

"The nineteenth century in America was a time of great change and social upheaval as the country went from an agricultural society to an industrial one as manufacturing became more readily available. There was a widening gap between the wealthy and everyone else. Sound familiar?" The students laughed. "Whenever we're tempted to say that what we're experiencing is unprecedented in history, we don't have to go too far back in time to find a similar situation. As any student of history will tell you, the more things change, the more they stay the same."

They murmured their agreement. I clicked the PowerPoint to pictures of Ralph Waldo Emerson, Henry David Thoreau, Emily Dickinson, and Walt Whitman.

"Here are some of the authors we're most likely to think of when we think of nineteenth-century American literature. When we consider literature in the U.S. during that time, we're likely to think of the American Romantic or Transcendentalist movements, which grew out of the Age of Reason.

The Age of Reason focused primarily on logic and science. It was the beginning of the recognition of individual and human rights."

"At least in theory," said Cordelia.

"Indeed, Ms. Reed. At least in theory. Previously, people thought of society as a collective, as We. With the Age of Reason and continuing through the Romantic and Transcendentalist periods, people were more likely to think of themselves as individuals, as I."

"I celebrate myself, and sing myself, And what I assume you shall assume, For every atom belonging to me as good belongs to you."

"A Whitman fan. Very good, Ms. Lang. Even before Whitman published Song of Myself, Emerson wrote about how conforming to the larger society was a great evil because it stifled a person's unique genius and prevented them from living a deep, meaningful life."

"A foolish consistency is the hobgoblin of little minds."

"You know your Emerson, Mr. Chatterjee. Can you tell us what that means?"

"It means that sticking blindly to past beliefs after new evidence or ideas emerge is small-minded. Just because something has always been a certain way doesn't mean that it's the best way. Good thinkers should challenge themselves and be open to new ideas."

"That's right. For Emerson, following society's rules just to fit in was a betrayal of one's own inner voice. He encouraged us to be courageous in our convictions, even if it means being misunderstood."

"To be great is to be misunderstood."

"You're on the mark with your Emerson quotes, Mr. Chatterjee."

"I'm studying Emerson for my thesis."

"Excellent choice. Many American writers in the nineteenth century wanted to explore the depths of human emotion. They believed in the power of human imagination. Authors such as these," I gestured at the slide, "were inspired by nature, by the imagination, by idealism. Then there was the darker side to nineteenth-century literature, which we call Dark Romanticism or Gothic literature. This is where Edgar Poe fits in, as well as Herman Melville and Nathaniel Hawthorne."

I flipped the slide, and Poe stared glumly at us once again.

"Gothic literature explores themes such as the supernatural, the grotesque, and the psychological darkness that all humans share. Jung called it the Shadow. Instead of focusing on nature's beauty, it was seen as a destructive force. Think of Melville's *Moby Dick*. Poe is widely regarded as the leading voice of American Gothic literature, and his stories are often about the gloomy, the grotesque, and the wicked."

"What did Poe think about the Transcendentalists?" Cordelia asked.

"Poe despised the Transcendentalists," Thomas said.

Cordelia grimaced. "Ralph Waldo Emerson and Henry David Thoreau are two of the most quoted authors of all time. Their messages about simplicity are as important now as they were then. I'm interested in the Transcendentalists, and I want to know what Poe thought of them."

"And I'm telling you he despised them," said Thomas.

"Poe was certainly opinionated about other authors, Ms. Reed. When Poe worked as a literary critic, he was known as the Tomahawk Man for his fearlessness in chopping other authors down to size. His criticisms of respected authors such as Longfellow and Hawthorne were brutal. He would criticize others' spelling and grammar mistakes, yet if someone made similar observations about his own writing, he became furious. Poe engaged in some fearsome public battles using newspaper editorials as his weapon. And yes, as Mr. Lambert points out, despised is not too strong a word for how Poe felt about the Transcendentalists. He considered the Transcendentalists pretentious. He believed that the purpose of art was beauty, not moral instruction. He believed that the arguments of the Transcendentalists lacked substance when he valued precise, clear language."

"Which is why Poe's language is boring." Cordelia received an irate glance from Thomas for her trouble.

"Poe had very specific views on language. He called it the single-effect theory, by which he meant that every element of a story should contribute to evoking one dominant impression in the reader. He meticulously crafted his narratives to achieve this singular impact. As we read Poe this term, you'll see that there are no unnecessary details, no wasted words, and everything serves one emotional goal."

"He saw the Transcendentalists as sharing speculations as absolute truths," Thomas said. "The Frogpondians, he called them."

"What does that even mean?" asked Cordelia.

"Poe meant it as a satire," I said. "It was a jab at the Boston intellectuals around Frog Pond on Boston Common."

"Poe thought they were pompous and self-important," Thomas said. "He thought they were shallow."

"They weren't shallow," said Amandine. "They were explaining some of the deepest truths a person can grapple with."

Thomas laughed. "Nothing pompous or self-important about that."

"In the end," I interrupted, "Poe saw the Transcendentalists as the antithesis of his own literary values. He felt that the Transcendentalists presented foggy metaphysics and unclear morality."

I backtracked to cover Poe's early life, his abandonment by his father, the death of his young mother, his unofficial adoption by John and Fanny Allan, which left him materially provided for until Fanny's death, when his relationship with John Allan became increasingly strained. Poe had a habit of running up debts, and he was constantly asking for money that John Allan wasn't happy to give. The students took notes, nodded at my extrapolations, and laughed at my silly jokes. They asked questions and offered opinions.

"I already know all this," Thomas interrupted. "We came here to learn something. This is a graduate seminar."

"I'm fully aware of that, Mr. Lambert, but I like to begin with some background to ensure an even playing field. You already know this because you're studying Poe. Mr. Chatterjee is studying Emerson. The others may not be on the same page as you. Are you studying Thoreau, Ms. Wesson?"

"I'm in the creative writing module, but I'm interested in the Transcendentalists."

"Very good. What are the rest of you studying for your graduate theses?"

"I'm studying with Professor Trevelyan," Simon said. "I'm focusing on T.S. Eliot."

"Emily Dickinson," Maeve said. This week, instead of sage, she was amethyst in her long smock dress.

"I'm focusing on Media Studies," said Cordelia. "I'm with Professor Michaels."

"Professor Trevelyan said that Media Studies isn't a real subject," Simon said. "He said that people should find an actual discipline to study."

"Since Professor Trevelyan isn't on my thesis committee, I don't actually care what he thinks," Cordelia answered.

"You see, Mr. Lambert, it's always best to provide information instead of assuming your audience knows what you're talking about."

Maeve nodded at me as if we were in this together. "As I

said, I'm studying Emily Dickinson, and she's Romantic Era, not Dark Romantic. Please continue, Professor Ferrars."

"Actually," said Amandine, "you could classify Emily Dickinson as Dark Romanticism since she speaks about the darker side of human nature in much of her verse."

"She talks about death and mortality, but..."

"And she talks about isolation and the personal self."

"But she didn't write anything we associate with Gothic literature. There's nothing grotesque about her poetry. She focuses on the struggles someone faces in their inner life."

"She also talks about the mysteries of existence, which you should know since you wrote a paper about it last year."

The Nordic prince held up his hand, which stopped Amandine from continuing. Before Maeve could reply, Thomas sat upright in his seat, his arms stretched out before him on the table.

"I'm here for you to teach me, Professor Ferrars. We're in the second week, and I'm still waiting for you to teach me."

It was the first time in a long while that I wanted to yell "Shut the hell up!" at a student. With some difficulty, I refrained myself.

"Very well, Mr. Lambert. What would you like me to teach you that you don't already know? As graduate students, you should be focused on your areas of study, and you should also be learning how to write literary criticism. I believe there's a way to explore Poe that you may find interesting and rewarding. If any of you are planning on pursuing careers in academia, this will allow you to learn what it's like to prepare a lesson."

I pulled my lesson plan for the evening toward me. With dramatic flair, I crumpled the pages, balled them up, and tossed them into the trash can. "I'm willing to tear up every lesson I have for this seminar, but if I do, then I need everyone's promise that you're going to be active participants each week."

Cordelia raised her hand.

"Yes, Ms. Reed?"

"What do you mean when you say we have to be active participants?"

"I mean, you're going to teach this class. Each of you will devise your own topic of study regarding some aspect of Edgar Poe, whether you choose to focus on his life, his works, or some combination of both. You're going to create a lesson plan for your assigned week, which we'll designate tonight, and when your week arrives, you'll teach that night's lesson based on what you learned from your studies. You'll have handouts for your classmates and discussion questions. When your lesson is over, we'll spend the duration of our time dissecting what we learned. For the next two weeks, we'll continue to cover background information on Poe and nineteenth-century American literature, and I'll teach two model lessons. After that, you're each responsible for your assigned class." I leaned back in my chair, drumming my fingers on the table. "Are you game?"

"What about the weeks after everyone has taught their lesson?" Thomas asked.

"We can decide that further down the road. I'm open to whatever you think might be most beneficial to your learning, Mr. Lambert."

"I've never had a professor who ditched his entire plan before," Maeve said.

"I'm not just any professor, Ms. Lang." The whispered conversations died down. "Does everyone agree? Everyone has to agree or this won't work and we'll go back to my original lesson for the evening. I can fish it out of the trash can." I waited a dramatic moment. "Raise your hand if you're willing to teach one class during our seminar and you're willing to learn from one another." Every hand went up, Thomas's first among them. "Very well, then. If you'll give me a moment, I'll print my class roster, and we'll decide who will present each week. One brave soul will need to teach the first student lesson. I vote for Mr. Lambert."

The students laughed.

"That's right, Thomas," Oliver said. "You started this. You should go first."

"I agree," said Amandine.

Thomas brushed a lock of auburn hair from his eyes and stood, towering over the others. "On behalf of the class, Professor Jonathan Ferrars, I accept your challenge, and I will faithfully execute my duties to the best of my ability."

"Excellent. Those of you not studying Poe for your thesis may need help to discover what you want to focus on. I can help with that and offer some ideas for research sources. I'm your first line of defense. If you need help, any help at all, then ask. That's what I'm paid for, after all. Isn't that right, Mr. Lambert?"

"Indeed it is, Professor Ferrars."

After class, with the six of them watching, I left for home, taking a roundabout route in case someone followed. They were curious about me, I knew, though they were going to have to stay curious. They didn't want to know me, as much as they thought they did.

Seven

In forever knowing, we are forever blessed; but to know all, were the curse of a fiend.

My rented cottage sat quietly, minding its own business under a broken street lamp in a tree-lined cul-de-sac. The house was a two-story structure of red-brown slats, asymmetrical casement windows, a red brick chimney, and a pitched roof. It was an easy walk to campus and came furnished, which suited me. Mrs. Griggs, the elderly landlady, handed me the keys the night I arrived in Maine. She was exactly the kind of person I was used to renting houses from—small but spry, the kind of older woman you'd want to help cross the road until she beat you with her cane because she moved more quickly than you did. When I first arrived at the red-brown house, she opened the door warily, as though expecting a masked bandit with a popgun and a pillowcase for the cash. She carried a basket with a spray bottle and rags for cleaning.

"Mrs. Griggs? We arranged to meet tonight so I could get the key."

She searched me up and down, her round glasses perched on the tip of her nose. She wiped her hands on her frilly apron as she nodded. "Ayuh. Ferrari, was it?"

"No, ma'am. Ferrars."

"Hmph. You mean like them terrors?"

"Well, yes, I suppose the words do rhyme."

"That's hard tellin' I'd say. Not knowin' your own name, that is." She shivered though the late summer humidity left everything warm and hazy. "Come on in, then, since the wind off the shore's blowin' colder. The wind is changin' and it's wicked sharp early this year, I'm tellin' you."

She stepped aside to let me enter a whitewashed hallway. I glanced at my new home and thought it seemed a rather pleasant place to be.

"You come from far, Mr. Fairfax?"

"No, not far. I was at Yale, and now I've taken a job at Eventide College."

"A Yalie, huh? You see that shingle-style over there?" She pointed through the window at the blue house across the road. "Ayuh, he went to Yale. Thinks he understands the ocean because he read about it in a book. He tried to tell me my boat was aesthetic, but I says what the hell color is aesthetic? Any nut can see it's orange so I can find it in the fog."

"Indeed," seemed the proper response.

"You and those college kids around here with all your book learnin' you'd think you'd know how to tie a proper knot or fix a clogged pump, but I'll bet you don't know none of that. All them ten-dollar words you like to flash around without one practical thing in your heads. There's nothing wrong with reading, and I like a good book myself, but you need to learn how to do things in this world, or else what good are you?"

"I'm afraid you're probably right about that. And it's

Ferrars, Mrs. Griggs. As you pointed out, it rhymes with terrors."

Her eyes grew wide and she smiled. At least I took it for a smile. "Oh, you mean *Ferrars* like that Edward fellow in that book."

"*Sense and Sensibility*, yes."

"Well, why didn't you say so? Now I love a good Austen. That gal knew how to spin a yarn. When you check out the bookcase, you'll see every one of them Austens, including that one with Edward Terrors. I have quite a collection of mysteries too. Nothing like a good whodunnit to keep you awake all scared-like in the night."

I seemed to have passed her test, whatever exactly the test was, and she gave me the grand tour of the quaint cottage. The sitting room was comfortable with its hunter green walls boasting a gallery of oil paintings of lush scenic views. A sea-green Turkish rug covered the dark wood floor, while two Chesterfield chairs sat before the wood-burning fireplace. There was a partially filled Hepplewhite bookcase, which left room for my own library, meager though my traveling collection was. A cabriolet sat in the center of the room, and there was a rolltop desk pressed against a window that looked onto the tree-lined road. Privacy was provided outside the front windows by the tall-growing lilacs, the serviceberries, the switchgrass, and the two Norway spruces on either side of the front door. Upstairs were two bedrooms, a third room used as a study, and a bathroom. Above that was the attic, an open, triangular space with a few odds and ends and a circular window that opened onto the road. The bedroom I chose for myself, facing the front of the house toward the sea, had a four-poster bed with an old-fashioned burgundy velvet canopy. Beside the bed was a nightstand with a banker-style lamp, and on the opposite wall sat a wardrobe of dark teakwood. The curtains, the same burgundy velvet as the canopy, gave the room a heavy feel. It was old-fashioned, and I liked it.

After the tour, we returned to the sitting room, where she pointed to the Hepplewhite bookcase. "You're welcome to read any of these. I keep the books here to keep their dust out of the house where I live. Like I said, there's some Austen, some mysteries, you choose what you like, sonny. You're a Yalie, so at least you know about books. Now, as for maintenance, I'm low-key, you see. I don't do windows, I don't do floors, and I don't do ovens."

"I'm house-trained, Mrs. Griggs, and I don't cook."

"Ayuh. Typical man. No wife to look after you?"

"Not now, no."

"Then I'll drop by a couple of days a week for some light cleanin'. You need your shoppin' done?"

"No, thank you. I can tend to the shopping, and I'll look after my bedroom myself."

"Now you're talkin'. There may be some hope for you college folk after all."

She dropped the key into my hand and left me with pointed instructions for caring for the potted plants sitting patiently along the windowsills and in the corners of the rooms. I paid close attention since I did not want to answer to her for accidentally killing them.

My favorite room in the cottage, where I spent most of my home hours, was the second-story study. It resembled a gentleman's smoking room with ecru walls, gilt-framed portraits of unknown people, most likely purchased from a charity shop, and a red brick fireplace with a dark teakwood mantel. A leather sofa and matching recliner sat comfortably before the fire. I spent many pleasant hours going through Mrs. Griggs's books. Indeed, she had a complete collection of Jane Austen, as well as some Georgette Heyer, Agatha Christie, Dorothy L. Sayers, Margery Allingham, Ngaio Marsh, and P.D. James, among others. I would make myself comfortable with whatever book I happened to pull off the shelf and sit in the recliner before the fire with a warm cup beside me. Sometimes, wishing for a different view, I'd sit in the back garden, which provided more privacy than the front garden with its tall wood fence, sweet pepper bush, and red twig dogwoods. The yellow asters, white chrysanthemums, and lavender lupines left pastel dots in the shrubbery, fading a little more each night as it inched closer to autumn.

After the second Poe seminar, I returned to the cottage and took my book outside to sit at the picnic-style bench, enjoying the clear night, the half-moon bright and dominant against the twinkling stars. There are times when I feel like the moon, with important parts of myself hidden away. Carl Sandburg said, "The moon is a friend for the lonesome to talk to." Indeed, the moon has been my constant companion. After contemplating my rocky friend in the distance, I closed my book, Christie's *And Then There Were None*. I heard wings flutter, branches creaking, and then there were two ravens perched on the topmost branch of a dogwood tree. With their beaks touching, they looked like a heart-shaped shadow, living fragments of midnight. I watched them until late into the night, fascinated, then went inside.

At the sight of my research books scattered across the desk, I remembered that the due date for my revise and resubmit for "Poe: Grief, Loss, and the Death of the Beautiful Woman" was drawing near. It was not the best choice of topic for a widower. I laughed at my own foolishness, as if I enjoy poking myself with a pointed stick, and perhaps I do. I saw her face so clearly in that moment, and then she faded away. My revisions were nearly done, only line editing left, so I sat down with my books, my notebooks, and my pens and worked contentedly for about an hour, until my mind wandered away of its own accord, as it tends to when faced with tedious tasks.

There.

I saw her face flash in the gilded mirror on the wall. Such beauty is ephemeral and impossible to keep, and it always carries an ache with it. I covered my eyes with my hand. When I looked again, she was gone.

"Where are you?" I called.

I searched the house, up the stairs, into the attic, down the stairs, into the basement, searching high and looking low. But no. My overactive imagination, needing desperately to see her, must have conjured her in my mind's eye. Grief, Loss, and the Death of the Beautiful Woman, indeed. Poe's words visited me once again, as they often did in such moments.

"Wretch," I cried, "thy God hath lent thee—by these angels he hath sent thee

Respite—respite and nepenthe from thy memories of Lenore;

Quaff, oh quaff this kind nepenthe and forget this lost Lenore!"

Quoth the Raven "Nevermore."

She was here, she was gone, and I shall see her. Nevermore.

I shuddered with a pensive melancholy, my inexorable guilt overwhelming me. There are so many things I have done, so many things I shoulder the burden of remorse for, and she is one of them. Some amends can never be made. I shook my sorrow aside, once again certain that I felt her presence. She was there. She had something to tell me. My rational mind told me to get a grip, but the phantasm of memory was too strong. That permanent hole inside me, that place of never-ending emptiness, widened perceptibly. A strange agitation seized my nerves, and I needed to distract myself from my gloomy thoughts. Searching for something to occupy my time, I noticed the bottom drawer of the desk. It was bulging and lopsided, as though it had been tugged off the track. Odd that I hadn't noticed it before. I opened the drawer above it and found paper, old-fashioned dip pens, envelopes, a wax-seal stamp with an ocean-wave design, blue wax, and two tapered candles. When I tried to open the offending drawer, it was locked, so I searched for the key, which was conveniently located on the top corner of the desk, as if it were waiting to be discovered. Mrs. Griggs, who did not strike me as a forgetful person, must have left it there.

And then I wondered. What could Mrs. Griggs possibly be hiding that needs to be tucked under lock and key? If I felt guilty for looking through a locked drawer, I reminded myself that I paid monthly to rent that house and so I had a perfect right to see what was inside. What if I needed to use the space for something?

The lock looked old, but the key turned easily. At first glance, the drawer appeared empty, and I was disappointed. I wasn't expecting a pirate's map pointing to a treasure, though perhaps Mrs. Griggs was hiding love letters from a forlorn beau from ages past. I laughed at the thought and couldn't quite picture it. I wondered what kind of man Mr. Griggs was. A patient man, certainly.

When I tried to close the drawer, it fell off the track again, and something jammed. I reached in and pulled the offending object from its hiding place. Instead of a pirate's map, I found an old-looking journal with a russet-colored calfskin cover stamped *The Journal of...* in a simple gilt line with a name that had been scraped away. When I opened the cover, the ivory-colored pages, citrine at the edges with age, complained. I turned to the first entry, saw the date, and thought that perhaps I had found that love letter after all.

Wednesday, 10 October 1843
Southshore, Maine

. . .

The room smelled of lavender and candle wax, the faint sweetness mingling with the sharp scent of her cod liver oil and creosote, all prescribed by the doctor, all known to do nothing in cases of consumption. The Ayer's Cherry Pectoral, with its morphine, at least helps her to sleep. Helen lay against the pillows, her skin translucent, her breath thin and irregular, like the fluttering of a butterfly in a draft. I sat beside my beloved wife, holding her hand in both of mine, my eyes fixed on the shallow rise and fall of her chest.

"You do not study today, my love," she said.

"How can I study when you are ill?" I pressed her fingers to my lips. "I will return to my library when you are better. Whatever new things there are to learn, they will still be there tomorrow."

"But your studies are so important to you. Learning is so important to you."

"Nothing is more important to me than you."

She attempted to lift her head. "I've seen them," she whispered. Her voice was so faint I had to lean close to hear. "They come at night, when the wind is quiet. They say they are not bound by time as we are. They come seeking the voices of those they've lost."

I frowned, brushing a strand of her dark, damp hair from her forehead. "You were dreaming, my love."

"No," she said. Her fingers tightened around mine. "Not dreams. They were real. I speak to them. You know I do. You've seen me communicate with them many times."

"And they speak to you now, my love?" I asked.

Her eyes, luminous and far away, widened as though she saw them then. "They said there are ways to cross the border between here and there, between life and eternity. You must find that border and cross it. Promise me."

I tried to soothe her, but her words lodged deep within me, unsettling and bright as a spark in the darkness.

"Helen..." My voice faltered, and I could not go on.

"This is what you need to know." She exhaled a painful breath and everything seemed to stop. I was afraid she had left me until she inhaled heavily. She spoke of Ravens and spells and invocations and charms. She spoke of beings from the Other World, some closer than we might think. She spoke of witchcraft and necromancy and Abracadabra. It all sounded like gibberish to me, but she was quite serious, so I listened.

She drew another trembling breath. "Do not search for eternity for my sake. It is too late for me to cross any border but one." When I sobbed, she gripped my hand. "Do not fear for me, my love. Death is not an abyss but a veil. It is fragile, yes, but it can be lifted. I will come back to you. Search for your own sake. If such a thing can be done, then do it. If anyone has the skill to discover the path to the Other Side, it is you, my love. There is no better scholar than you. For my sake. Live forever. So that death never parts you from what you love again."

"When we are parted, I will be forever separated from what I love."

"There is so much...so much more you can do. There is so much more for you to learn. There is so much more for you to teach. Live forever."

Her hand went still, her warmth fading as she was carried away by angels.

"Helen?" I called.

Her gaze had already fixed on the Great Beyond. I sat motionless beside my beloved, her last words echoing in the hollow of my chest.

Live forever.

And in that moment, grief-struck and half-mad with loss, I vowed to her that I would.

Saturday, 14 October 1843

Southshore, Maine

These first days after Helen's death have passed like a fever dream. I scarcely sleep. I wander the house, searching for her in every corner. I yearn for an echo of her voice, her scent, the faint warmth left behind by her body in the bed. The silence only deepens, and the world somehow manages to turn without her. Life will continue without her despite my aching pain.

Even now, as I sit in the library, her words haunt me. Are there ways to cross the border between Life and Eternity? I know that Helen helped people. They relied on her to connect them with their loved ones who had already passed into the Great Beyond. Perhaps she knew something about straddling the line between Here and There that others do not.

After her burial, her tomb was obscured by the Stygian darkness of a fast-moving nor'easter. The melancholy grew to be too much, and I returned home in silence. When I could not stir myself to action, I sat near the window, staring into the cadaverous sky. In a state of severe disquietude, I attempted to settle my mind by transcribing everything she said in her final moments, writing until the red ink seeped like blood through the paper. Soon I filled pages with fragments—names, symbols, the half-remembered lore she whispered in that last delirious hour. I scoured her journals, her letters, the books she had loved. Were there patterns in her whispers of ancient knowledge? Perhaps Helen was right. Perhaps there is a small portion of Eternity for me.

Helen has ignited this fire in my breast. I will live forever.

Eight

Either the memory of past bliss is the anguish of today, or the agonies which are have their origin in the ecstasies which might have been.

I flipped through the remaining pages, skimming, not reading too closely. There was something melodramatic about the passages, and I wondered if the entries were scraps from an unfinished novel. They certainly read like a Gothic tale about ghosts, witches, and things that go bump in the night. The handwriting was calligraphy, the words bold and sloping, which is what I would expect from nineteenth-century cursive. I flipped through the pages again, searching for the author's identity, but found nothing. The name on the cover had been scraped off and there were no other clues. The author appeared to be a husband seeking closure with his dead wife, a sentiment I understood since I was myself a husband seeking closure with my dead wife. I had my own work to finish, so the delights of those sentiments would have to wait for another time. I returned the book to the drawer and resumed editing.

Or I tried to resume editing. I could not get the man from the journal out of my mind. I thought of him, seeking the ghost of his wife. I no longer seek ghosts, though for years she lingered as fresh as the day we married. Her scent, sweet like strawberries, followed me everywhere, even in my sleep. Often, I awoke to a faint murmur, as though someone had spoken my name and leaned close to hear my reply. Sometimes a woman's laugh would pierce the air, a laugh so like hers that I searched everywhere for her. Other times, I'd swear I saw her silhouette reflecting in the glass of a house window. And then the pernicious realization that she wasn't there, along with the overwhelming guilt that it was all my fault. Memory, I reminded myself. It is only memory.

Unlike other memories, she is not deep like the rivers. She is there on the surface. I cannot say that such memories are unwelcome. There are times when thoughts of her steady me, reminding me in a good way of our life together. Sometimes I allow her memory to walk beside me, not as a torment, but as a blessing. Sometimes I feel her hand on my shoulder, a gentle reminder that love does not vanish, yet grief seeps into every corner of my being, like the Maine fog. Some part of her always lingers beside me, ethereal and luminous.

I wished I could speak to the man who wrote that journal. I wanted to tell him that the pain is too hard at first. You are so certain you will never survive the heartbreak, and your only wish will be to join her. In time, though, you will get better at going on. You may never love again, but you might create a different kind of life for yourself. It might only be a second-best sort of life, but it is still a life. Whether or not you want to, you will go on, so you might as well make the best of it you can.

. . . .

The first monthly graduate colloquium was held on the Friday of the third week of term. It was twilight as I walked toward campus and the Carlson Auditorium. I made my way down Whitley Way to Southshore Road, taking the long way as I often did, and I basked in the weak rays of sunlight. The softened sky, pastel and warm, illuminated the calm sea washing the rocks along the bay. Each night, I grew to love the rugged Maine scenery more. I loved the jagged shoreline and the contrasting forest. I loved the lighthouse and the shadowy islands in the distance. I never agreed with Poe's dismissal of the Transcendentalists. I too believe that nature is our most powerful connection with the divine. I too believe that by observing the profound beauty of nature, we can learn to live meaningful lives. When I need to settle myself, I walk in nature, and I find connection and healing, even if only for that moment. If that makes me pretentious, so be it.

By the time I arrived on campus, the air had sharpened and the sky was bruised with oncoming rain. A brisk wind stirred the leaves clinging to the stone-paved path. I arrived at the auditorium, its windows glowing like watchful eyes, in good spirits. I've attended many colloquiums, and they are normally pleasant, if perhaps boring, gatherings where students share their research interests and faculty share tips and tricks. The department colloquium was one of those traditions that seemed to exist only to remind the faculty of their own importance and the students of their low place in the pecking order. The scene was often the same—the coffee-stained name tags, the nervous grad students clutching their annotated copies of *Critical Inquiry*, the senior professors sprawled across the front row like a jury waiting to declare the defendant guilty without trial. There were presentations and then Q&As. Packaged sandwiches were served with bottles of water, soda, or tea. Everyone would linger and chat for a while, then leave for home.

I arrived fashionably late and found an unobtrusive place at the back near a shelf of abandoned anthologies. The air smelled faintly of coffee and old carpet. I scanned the list of presentations and was pleased to see that Cordelia Reed was one of the presenters, along with her adviser, Eric Michaels, the new young hotshot straight out of his doctoral program at Stanford. Attendees were seated in folding chairs set out in neat rows with an aisle in between. True to the pecking order, professors sat in the first row and the students behind them. Stephen, Leonard, Debbie, and Lavinia Cruz, the creative writing professor, were clustered in the corner while Maeve, Amandine, Simon, and Oliver sat together in the back. Thomas stood not far from me near the bookcases. There were other professors and students I wasn't familiar with, and most of the seats were taken.

I was so engaged in watching my students interact that I hadn't noticed Rhys Grimshaw, wearing the easy smile of a patient mystic, standing before the microphone waiting for everyone to quiet down. At the colloquium, Grimshaw was much the same as he had been at the faculty meeting. When he was silent, he was easily overlooked, yet when he spoke, he commanded your attention.

"Welcome, everyone. I am very happy to host the first of our monthly English department colloquiums for the 2010-2011 academic year." A polite smattering of applause. "If you're new at EC this year, my name is Rhys Grimshaw. Though I am not an official member of the department, Professor Bronwyn is kind enough to indulge me by allowing me to participate in this wonderful gathering of colleagues." Debbie stood and waved as though none of us knew who she was.

"You can do anything you want if you're willing to pay for it," Thomas whispered to no one in particular.

"Tonight we'll hear from some of our student scholars,

and we'll have a chance to learn about some of their recent research. As I said, I'm not officially a member of this department," ("Who needs to be official when you can buy your way in?" Thomas whispered) "but most of you know that literature has always been my intellectual home. Though I am not myself a professor, I have a great interest in Edgar Poe. Some of his works are quite visceral. For example, he wrote The Cask of Amontillado, his tale of the perfect revenge, in 1846. I have recently submitted a paper affirming the prevalent theory that Poe wrote Amontillado as a form of literary revenge against Thomas Dunn English, with whom Poe had a bitter public feud."

Thomas raised his hand.

Grimshaw turned his benevolent smile onto Thomas. "I expected to hear from you tonight, Thomas." Everyone laughed. "How may I help you?"

"Didn't Poe have a public feud with nearly every literary figure then?"

"Indeed, you're quite right. He was always battling something out in the newspapers with someone, as though he were trying to settle his inner demons by clashing swords with external ones. In this case, Poe was quite correct in his desire to retaliate. English had published a novel entitled *1844* with a character named Marmaduke Hammerhead, which was widely believed to be a mockery of Poe. Hammerhead was a journalist and author, and he was portrayed as a drunk and a liar who had published a poem called The Black Crow, which was a mockery of The Raven. Hammerhead also used phrases like Nevermore and referred to a lost Lenore. You can see why Poe would be furious. With its theme of the perfect revenge against a thousand insults, we believe that The Cask of Amontillado was Poe's response to English. The fact that Poe was living in extreme poverty while his young wife was dying, well, you can see why Poe would write this story with such a cynical tone. The reason we still love Poe's work today is that he makes something horrible beautiful, and I mean beautiful in the sense of its being mournful and poetic. Poe treats the macabre with reverence, creating a mood that lingers long after the story ends, and we, the readers, are left in awe. Such sentiments are perfectly portrayed in his story The Tell-Tale Heart as well. And let's not forget about The Murders in the Rue Morgue. Our very own Professor Ferrars recently published an eloquent study of Poe's influence on Arthur Conan Doyle, who created Sherlock Holmes."

Maeve smiled at me, and I appreciated her kindness. Thomas shrugged as though he couldn't help but acknowledge my accomplishment. He moved beside me, his arms crossed over his chest, his face pulled tight, which was not so different from how he looked in class. I nodded at him, and he at me.

"Thank you all for indulging me. I wished to share some of my insights into Edgar Poe, as I do at every colloquium." Everyone laughed. "Now we're in for a treat as some of our students will share their latest research with us."

Yes, I decided, there was something magnetic about Rhys Grimshaw after all. Rhys nodded benevolently as he seemed to take in everyone at once. "Now, friends, I proudly call to order the first Eventide College English Department Colloquium for the 2010 Autumn Term." Everyone applauded. "To begin tonight, we have one of our brightest students, Miss Cordelia Reed, and her adviser, Professor Eric Michaels, to discuss her research in Media Studies."

Cordelia, her bright blue eyes wide as she took in her audience, and Eric Michaels, grinning with overconfidence in his too-tight suit, stood near the microphone. The projector flickered to life, and the title of her talk flashed on the screen in bold type.

Consuming the Other: The Vampire in Post-Millennial Media Through a Derridean Lens

Amusement rippled through the room. Stephen leaned toward Leonard and whispered something that made Leonard smirk into his shirt collar. Lavinia folded her arms, her expression exasperated. Poor Cordelia didn't stand a chance. Her performance had been judged and found wanting before she spoke her first word. Despite the negative energy in the room, she carried herself well. Her voice trembled at first, but she steadied herself.

"The vampire functions as a signifier of both attraction and repulsion," she said, "embodying the post-modern collapse of boundaries between self and other."

Young Eric Michaels clicked through slides of screen stills —*Twilight*, *True Blood*, *The Vampire Diaries*—as Cordelia continued.

"If we deconstruct the late-capitalist appetite for vampirism, we find Derrida's notion of différance embodied in the undead, who are ever present and always deferred to."

A stage sigh escaped Stephen. "*Dracula* and Derrida," he muttered loud enough to be heard. "Now I've seen it all. I can die happy."

Lavinia replied dryly. "I wouldn't recommend it. Some bloodthirsty bitey thing might eat you for dinner and use your bones as a toothpick." She earned a snort from Leonard for her trouble. The audience's laughter snapped through the room like a blast of cold air. I had to fight back my own laughter, not at Cordelia's expense, but at the sheer theatricality of the scene. There were the scholars scoffing at the pop culture they publicly sneered at but secretly consumed. There was the young professor so caught up in his belief in his own brilliance that he didn't realize he was being mocked. And there, at the heart of it, was Cordelia, who appeared both proud and earnest, her blue eyes nearly circles while she tucked a lock of hair behind her ear. She continued her presentation while defending her right to find meaning in popular stories.

Simon slouched forward in his chair, his chin on his chest, sleeping, it seemed. Amandine looked remarkably similar to Lavinia, with her arms crossed over her chest, clearly unimpressed. She whispered something to Simon, who shrugged in response. I wondered if it was intentional, the students mimicking the professors they admired. For a moment, I worried about what my students might have taken from me. Oliver whispered something to Amandine that drew a chuckle.

Maeve appeared to be the peacekeeper among them. She ignored the asides and leaned forward, nodding at everything Cordelia said, intent on the presentation. When Simon whispered something sarcastic to her, Maeve shook her head. "Cordelia is making a good point about how culture feeds on itself," she whispered. "It's clever. Besides, everyone *is* consuming vampires these days. You can't escape them."

Thomas coughed into his hand. "Bullshit!"

Cordelia finished her presentation with poise. If she registered the negative energy, she didn't let on.

"The vampire's immortality is not only a fantasy of escape from death but a mirror for our obsession with repetition as we devour the same stories over and over again."

The applause was tepid. Then it was time for questions. Stephen raised his hand.

"So, Ms. Reed." His voice took on the collegial tone of someone who meant to slice her neatly in half. "Are you suggesting that Derrida would have considered *Buffy the Vampire Slayer* a philosophical text?"

Cordelia blinked once, then smiled. "He might have. He was interested in hauntings."

A ripple of laughter from the students. Even Stephen cracked a grin as he straightened his jacket. Rhys Grimshaw appeared on stage.

"Thank you, Miss Reed, Professor Michaels. I find studies of the supernatural fascinating. As a matter of fact, I think we should hear from our newest professor, Dr. Ferrars," ("I'm a new professor too," said Eric Michaels. No one heard him) "about Poe's use of the supernatural in his fiction."

If I thought I would be able to hide, I was mistaken.

"I'm afraid that the supernatural isn't my area of expertise, but I'll do my best." Rhys bowed in a gentlemanly manner. "Ligeia and Morella are two of Poe's stories where the supernatural plays a role. In both stories, a woman of superior intellect has died, though their deaths do not remain final. In Ligeia, the narrator's second wife appears to resurrect as Ligeia, and in Morella, Morella dies in childbirth, but her identity has consumed her child."

"This Poe guy sounds like a hoot," said Leonard.

"He had his moments. But the two stories are about deaths that did not remain final. Ligeia and Morella are about the power of will. The narrators in these stories cannot tell the difference between presence and memory. Poe is asking us to consider two metaphysical questions: what if the mind, whether plagued by love, grief, or obsession, can force reality to obey it? And what if the deaths of our loved ones are not final? Perhaps we can will them back to life."

"Ah." Rhys closed his eyes and nodded sagely. When he opened his eyes, he stared at me. "So then, Professor Ferrars, what is real in these stories and what is not? Are the women truly resurrected, or was it wishful thinking?"

"It's difficult to say. Poe is showing us how the human mind may be capable of rewriting reality. Perhaps sometimes we want something so much that we make it our reality."

Rhys smiled. "Isn't it fascinating to think that death may not be the end? That death may be negotiable?"

"I'm not sure that obsessive fixation to the point where all reason collapses is ever a good thing."

"Ah," said Rhys.

"Poe shows us the psychological hallucinations that can overtake us if we cannot let go, especially if we truly loved the person who is gone."

"I was never really insane except upon occasions when my heart was touched."

"That was from a letter Poe wrote to Maria Clemm, his aunt." Thomas shouted as though we were too far to hear him.

"She was also his mother-in-law, the mother of his 13-year-old wife." Lavinia seemed to spit venom as she spoke.

"Yuck," a student said.

Whenever Rhys smiled at me, something rankled. Had I seen him before? My memory, sometimes clear, sometimes cloudy, returned nothing. In his ordinariness, perhaps I had seen him somewhere, or perhaps I had seen him everywhere.

"That was excellent, Professor Ferrars," Rhys said. "Perhaps you'll present something at next month's colloquium?"

"I'd be delighted."

Debbie teetered onto the stage, her high heels slippery on the waxed floor. She laughed at some joke only she seemed to know as she tugged the microphone down. "Yes, thank you, Cordelia, and thank you, Professor Ferrars."

"I was there too," said Eric Michaels. No one paid attention.

"Now we'll take a fifteen minute break before we continue with Anthony Lorne's research with Professor Harris concerning Langston Hughes's use of blues and jazz rhythms in his poetry." She gestured to the student-led jazz quintet setting up behind her. "Thank you to our fantastic music department for helping us out tonight."

The room broke into the usual scraping of chairs and polite chatter. Cordelia gathered her notes from the lectern, her cheeks flushed, while Professor Michaels clasped her shoulder, murmuring something encouraging. I lingered until the crowd moved away.

"A bold choice of topic, Ms. Reed. I suspect Professor Trevelyan will be having nightmares for a week."

"About vampires?"

"About Derrida."

She laughed, the tension leaving her shoulders. "Maybe I should consider that a success."

"I believe you should."

I tilted my head towards those gathered around the refreshment table. "You handled that well. It's not easy defending something you believe in before a room full of skeptics. You should know, for future reference, that all scholars are skeptical of any research that isn't their own. You'll face worse if you present at professional conferences."

She hesitated, studying my expression. "You don't think my research is ridiculous, then?"

"You've obviously given your subject a lot of thought. You are your own best judge about whether or not it's ridiculous. You get to decide what is meaningful to you. You get to decide what topics you want to research."

Cordelia clutched her papers closer, her hands still trembling from the adrenaline rush, and we joined the others near the refreshments. I liked Cordelia. In fact, I rather admired her. The earnestness of the young. They are so fierce yet so fragile. As I stepped back to let Cordelia and Maeve commiserate, Debbie offered me a styrofoam cup of coffee.

"I'll take that." Leonard grabbed the cup from Debbie's hand and wandered toward the music students running scales on their instruments.

"There's always something here to keep you on your toes, that's for sure." Debbie was speaking to me, though her eyes were on Rhys, whose eyes were on Thomas, who stood alone in the shadows of the tall bookcases. As I was about to respond, Simon crossed to Maeve. He whispered into her ear and set a hand on her shoulder. Thomas watched while Simon and Maeve fell into a quiet conversation. Rhys, making the rounds with something pleasant to say to everyone, said something into Thomas's ear before crossing over to some creative writing students.

"Don't you think, Jonathan?"

I had forgotten that Debbie was there.

"I'm sorry, Debbie. I was miles away. What did you say?"

"I said that sometimes professors can get carried away with their own pride, don't you think?"

"Of course, though it's no different here than anywhere else. There are always interesting frictions between professors or cohorts."

"Fun with personalities, right?"

I was about to respond when Thomas charged to where Simon stood huddled with Maeve.

"Leave her alone!" Thomas yelled, pushing himself between them.

"What the hell are you doing?" Simon looked ready to manhandle Thomas out the door.

"Can't you see that Maeve wants you to go away? Leave her alone. Even the great Simon Hayes can't win every prize."

Maeve held her hands out. "Thomas, please. Everything is fine. And I'm not a prize. Simon and I are just talking."

The colloquium fell into silence, and everyone's eyes were glued to the scene playing out before them. Stephen and Lavinia stepped closer to the fray, their wide grins betraying their amusement.

A student in the back said, "Finally, something interesting is happening."

Amandine joined in. "What the hell are you doing, Thomas?" She pushed his shoulder. "Leave Simon alone. He's not bothering you."

"He's pressing in on Maeve and anyone can see that she's..."

"Thomas." Maeve stepped closer to him. "Simon and I were just talking about our portfolios for the Poet of Eventide competition because the submission is due tomorrow by midnight. He wasn't..."

"You don't really want to talk to him, do you?"

Maeve turned away. "Maybe you should go home, Thomas."

"Go home, Thomas," said Cordelia. "I was standing right here, and Simon didn't do anything but ask Maeve a question."

Oliver stood defensively behind Cordelia. "She's right, Thomas, go home."

Simon, in his Nordic prince glory, pressed his hair away from his intense eyes as he challenged Thomas to go right ahead and continue his rant. Stephen leaned close to Leonard and said, in a stage whisper, "This ought to be good."

Debbie stepped between Maeve and Simon. "Maeve, is Simon bothering you?"

"No, Professor Bronwyn. As I said, we were only discussing our Poet of Eventide portfolios. Tomorrow night is the submission deadline, and he asked me if I was getting mine in on time. That's all."

"All right then, everyone." Debbie waved her hands above her head. "This has all been a misunderstanding. Thomas, I'm sure you meant well, but next time you might find out what's happening before jumping to conclusions."

"You mean the way you mean well when you flirt with our wealthy benefactor?" Thomas smirked at Rhys, who, with his radiant eyes and twinkling smile, appeared highly entertained, much like Stephen and Lavinia. "Isn't that how you got the department chair, Professor Bronwyn? Getting down with Mr. Grimshaw, also known as Mr. Moneybags?"

A collective "Oh..." filled the room.

Debbie stood as tall as her short stature and high heels would allow. "I beg your pardon, Thomas. I graduated from Eventide College, and I was the Poet of Eventide for my year. I received my PhD from UCLA. I am well-published in my field. I have every right to be the department chair here."

Thomas threw his hands into the air. "You all know that the poet laureate position is a farce, right?" He nodded at Maeve. "It's a joke. I was putting my portfolio together, and then I realized, what was I doing? He," he pointed at Simon, "is going to be the next Poet of Eventide because he," he pointed at Stephen, "is going to sway the professors into voting for his candidate, or money will change hands, or something will happen so that the person who deserves to win will walk away empty-handed." He laughed maniacally, sounding rather like one of Poe's madmen. "And you," he pointed at Stephen, "haven't published anything at all in over a year. These days, you're conning your graduate students into writing your papers for you. Isn't that right, Simon? How much work have you done for your favorite professor?"

"That's enough, Thomas!" Simon stood proud, his head thrown back. "You've made enough of an ass of yourself for one night. It's time for you to leave."

"Why don't you leave Maeve alone? Do you think your rich daddy will buy her for you like he buys you everything else? Stick with Amandine. She wants you. Even after the way you dumped her over the summer, she still has the hots for you. She wants you no matter how badly you treat her. Are you so bored with her that now you're going to try it on with Maeve?"

Maeve didn't appear hurt, only concerned. She grabbed both of Thomas's hands in hers. "Thomas, everything is fine, I'm fine, but you should leave now. Come on. I'll take you back to Clovis House."

Thomas shot a withering glare at Simon, and then he deflated like a popped balloon before our eyes. Maeve grabbed her bag and led him away. As the door closed behind them, Stephen said, "Someone ought to get rid of that kid."

"What a thing to say, Stephen."

"You seem awfully calm, Debbie. He just accused you of getting off with Rhys in front of the whole department. He accused me of submitting false scholarship."

"I know, I was here, but nothing that he said was true, so what does it matter?" She peered into Stephen's face. "It isn't true, is it?"

"Of course it isn't true!"

"All right then. Obviously, the young man is troubled, and we need to help him if he needs it."

"If?"

"I'll speak to him and try to figure out what on earth is happening."

The next presentation was less eventful. The young scholar, stuttering and unsure after the heightened emotions from Thomas's outburst, shared his research in a spoken poetry style accompanied by blues and jazz. It was creative, and despite the young man's solid work, something of Thomas's fury still trembled in the air. I snuck away before the student finished speaking. As I turned toward the door, Simon whispered to Amandine, "If Thomas tries that again, I'll kill him."

Instead of heading for home, I walked the campus, searching for some peace in the silent company of the Harvest Moon, round, mellow, and filling the sky. The wind skittered, mimicking my thoughts. I didn't know the student with the Hughes presentation, but I hoped the others were kinder to him than they had been to Cordelia. I didn't know what to think about Thomas's outburst. There was a violence to his words I hadn't seen in class. Was it a result of the stress of attending Eventide College? The students in these programs were always Type A personalities. They did everything as if the sand in the hourglass had all but fallen away. They walked, ate, studied, and talked quickly. They became easily frustrated and impatient. They set ambitious goals for themselves and stopped at nothing to achieve them. They might also be easily provoked and quick to anger. Simon, Amandine, and Thomas seemed to have those traits. Thomas, most of all, seemed to harbor deep distrust of others, except for Maeve, whom he seemed protective of. Maeve, Cordelia, and Oliver appeared to have better control over their competitive natures. My initial instinct was right. Those six students would not have gravitated toward each other if they had not been in the same cohort.

Academia is a competitive field. If those students wanted to succeed at the highest levels of the ivory tower, they were going to have to learn how to cope. Academics everywhere believe fervently in their own cleverness. Each paper, each colloquium, each question and counter-question was meant to prove one's extraordinary knowledge. I know more than you, and I will let you know so in no uncertain terms. I belong to the sacred hall of Academia. What would Academia make of Thomas Lambert? Whatever demons were haunting him, I wished him strength. Internal demons, those imps of the perverse, could be nearly impossible to overcome. Poe knew it. And so did I.

Once, a long time ago, I had been convinced that language could reveal the hidden knowledge we all seek. As time passed, I learned that words can circle the truth without quite touching it. I remember standing before my first classes, speaking about Cicero as if understanding his work was a matter of rhetoric. *De Officiis*, *On Duties*, the manual for a gentleman, spoke of the cardinal virtues—temperance, justice, fortitude, and wisdom—which were used to bridge the gap between philosophy and ethics, from which we were to learn how to lead a life of service and integrity. But time dulls all optimism. The longer I live, the more I watch meaning slip through even the most rigorous language. There is the danger that, with time, everything could become meaningless. Words, words, words.

And yet words still have value. At the colloquium, Thomas had given in to his anxieties by lashing out at others, using his words as weapons. Cordelia had been brave, using her words to instruct. She stood before a room of skeptics and spoke of our endless hunger for stories. And she was right. Stories *are* metaphors for repetition. We return to the same stories because we find value and comfort in them. And we tell stories with words.

I crossed the quad and passed a cluster of students huddled under umbrellas as protection from the thunderstorm that had split the sky in half. Their laughter was carried by the wind, and they looked bright and lively against the dark, such a contrast to the scene I had just left. My thoughts were shattered into a million little pieces, and I needed to keep moving. I walked to the shore, stopping at the scenic cove, taking comfort in the ancient trees that have seen it all before. Once again, I felt the pull of Eventide Manor, and I wandered toward the dark old house. Rhys was likely still on campus, still at the colloquium, so I paused near the wrought-iron gate, studying the perched gargoyles itching to break free. On second glance, I realized that it wasn't the gargoyles taking flight, but ravens, six of them, their gurgling croaks rising, their long wings and wedge-shaped tails flapping against the feisty storm as they settled into the home they had made for themselves in the hollow recess of the clock tower. With nothing left to hold my attention, I walked into the gathering gale. The nor'easter drenched the coastal town, and the world slipped into a dreary shadow.

. . .

By the following Monday, the colloquium had passed into department legend. In the hallway near my office, I overheard snippets about Stephen's latest barb, Leonard's feigned bewilderment, and Lavinia's insistence that "Media Studies" was a polite euphemism for cultural decay. Most of the talk was about Thomas's meltdown. Some of what they said was right. Most of what they said was wrong. All of it was typical post-colloquium gossip. I sat down to mark the critical responses from my survey class when a hesitant knock sounded on my door. Cordelia stepped inside, holding a paper cup of coffee as if it were a shield. Her cheeks were pink from the cooler early autumn air, her expression uncertain.

"I hope I'm not interrupting, Professor Ferrars."

"Not at all. Still recovering from Friday's battle?"

She smiled, a bit sheepishly, perhaps. "That's one way to put it. I mean, the thing with Thomas...I've never seen anything like that. Do you think what he said was true, about Professor Brownwyn and Professor Trevelyan?"

I had my suspicions, largely planted by Leonard, but I shook my head. "Sometimes when someone is anxious or upset they'll say whatever they think will hurt the other person."

"And you think that's what Thomas was doing?"

"I do. Have you spoken to him since Friday night?"

"I haven't, no. Maeve went to see him, and she said he seems to be calmer. Will he be kicked out of school? He already had to leave the program once. They're not likely to let him back in a second time."

"I haven't heard anything about him being kicked out. Hopefully, this was just an unfortunate incident and we can put it behind us."

Cordelia nodded. She looked as though she were going to leave, but then she sat down. "I just wanted to thank you for what you said after my presentation. It meant a lot. Most of the faculty think I'm half-mad."

"Only half?" Her eyes widened until she caught my smile. She brushed a lock of hair behind her ear and glanced at the titles of the books in the bookcases.

"I suppose I was asking for it, but I think it's fascinating to consider what might be possible, and I think that's why these myths and legends are so popular. And what's wrong with Media Studies as a subject?"

"Absolutely nothing." I leaned back in my chair, admiring her pluck. "What are you planning on doing when you leave here, Ms. Reed?"

"I want to do what you do. I want to get my doctorate, and I want to be a professor." She held up her hand as a stop sign. "I know the job market is bad, but I'm a hard worker, and I believe I have as much chance as anyone else when it comes to getting an academic position."

"I do not doubt that you have what it takes to be successful. And if you're going to do this for a living, you'll need to get used to people trying to make you look small. It's their way of trying to make themselves feel bigger."

"You mean the way Professor Trevelyan was speaking to me? Or the way Thomas was speaking to Professor Trevelyan?"

"They were both trying to make those around them seem weak, but all they were really doing was revealing their own flaws."

She made her way to the door. When she looked back, she seemed amused. "*Dracula* and Derrida. I'll never live that down."

"I suspect Professor Trevelyan will never forget it, either, which is a kind of immortality, if you think about it."

"Immortality through infamy?"

"The most reliable kind."

Her laughter faded into thoughtful silence. "You know, I started that paper as a joke. But I like vampire stories, and so do other people. I love the idea of using an imaginary world to examine our real lives. You can make observations about the world in speculative fiction that can be hard to make in other genres because people will accept the observations however they want if the world is imaginary. They can simply enjoy the story, or they can dig deeper and find meaning that applies to their own lives. These stories haunt us, in a way. Isn't that what the best stories do? Haunt us? The way Poe's stories haunt us?"

She stared at me and, for a moment, I wondered what she saw. The overhead fluorescent lights striped my desk in cold white lines. What did I look like under such a spotlight? Her gaze lingered on my face a heartbeat too long, curiosity sparking behind her eyes. Then she shook her head as though she had changed her mind.

"Well, thank you again for taking my work seriously, Professor Ferrars." She stepped into the hallway.

"Ms. Reed? Don't allow their laughter to discourage you. Every generation finds new ways to interpret old tales. It's how the stories stay alive, and we need people like you to study them."

"Maybe there's hope for me yet."

Perhaps there's hope for us all.

I feel that I must inevitably abandon life and reason together, in some struggle with the grim phantasm, FEAR.

Wednesday night, five of the students were seated when I arrived, whispering amongst themselves. A certain anxious energy filled the room, as though the very walls were waiting. Thomas stood at the front of the room typing into the computer. He didn't appear to be any worse for wear after the events of the colloquium; in fact, he didn't appear to recall that Maeve had to lead him away before he, or someone else, threw the first punch.

Perhaps he was determined to finish his degree. I hadn't heard anything about disciplinary action against him, so all he could do was hope that Debbie and Stephen, as well as the administration, were as unbothered by his outburst as he appeared to be. Thomas flipped through his PowerPoint, nodding to himself as though rehearsing in his head.

"Tonight Mr. Lambert is going to share some of his vast

knowledge of Poe with us. What topic are you addressing, Mr. Lambert?"

"Poe's use of the paranormal in The Fall of the House of Usher."

"There appears to be a fascination with the paranormal this autumn. Do you have handouts for the class?"

He passed a stack of papers around the table and handed one to me. I gave what I hoped was an encouraging nod and waited. He appeared to be in his element. He had the floor and everyone had to listen to whatever he wanted to say.

"Whenever you're ready, Mr. Lambert."

Thomas flipped his presentation to an illustration of a decaying black mansion with a crack down the wall and eyes glaring through the windows. It looked rather like Eventide Manor.

"Tonight we're going to discuss the supernatural elements of Poe's The Fall of the House of Usher." Thomas clicked his slideshow to a photograph of Bela Lugosi in the 1931 film *Dracula* to laughter from the class.

"I think you've got the wrong story," said Simon.

Thomas smirked. "As a matter of fact, Madeline Usher is a vampire."

Cordelia's staccato laugh sounded like a hiccup. When everyone turned to her, she slapped her hands on the table. "You all laughed at me when I gave a presentation about vampires." She pointed at Thomas. "You laughed loudest of all. I saw you standing in the back, laughing so hard I thought your head was going to pop off. Now *you're* talking about vampires? How is it okay when you do it?"

"Your discussion of vampires and Derrida was nonsensical. My discussion of vampires and Poe matches the requirements of our seminar."

"That was exactly my point! We see vampire legends all around us, and we still connect with them today."

Well, I thought. This ought to be delightful.

Simon's foot tapped an impatient rhythm on the carpet. "Forget that stupid colloquium talk and let's get to your lesson, Thomas, which is also nonsense. I read House of Usher twice, and nowhere does Poe say Madeline Usher was a vampire."

"Poe never explicitly labels Madeline Usher as a vampire, but she presents vampiric traits. You can read my bibliography to see my sources."

I flipped to the end of the handout and skimmed the Works Cited page.

"Madeline's illness is not made clear in the story," Thomas continued. "She has a wasting illness and a ghastly pallor. Roderick himself seems to suffer from a similar decline."

"But doesn't that point to consumption?" Maeve asked. "Now we call it tuberculosis."

"Yes, Maeve," Amandine spat, "we know it's tuberculosis. We're not morons."

"The wasting disease," Thomas interrupted, "can also point to vampirism. In 1914, in his book *Vampires and Vampirism*, Dudley Wright explains that not all vampires are bloodsuckers. Some vampires dispatched their victims by giving them a deadly disease. Like tuberculosis." He shot an angry glance at Amandine. "The wasting sickness of Madeleine Usher can be related to that moment when vampires drain their victims' blood and turn them into new vampires. Poe wrote about premature burial brought about by a cataleptic state in several works, such as The Premature Burial. Fear of premature burial was common in the nineteenth century with their more limited medical knowledge. Poe himself was terrified of being buried alive."

"What does that have to do with the story?" Oliver asked.

"Vampires appear dead when they sleep, but they wake up and return to life, which is what happens to Madeline

Usher." Thomas grinned at me. "Isn't that right, Professor Ferrars?"

"I'm afraid I'm not an expert."

Thomas clicked to the next slide—an illustration of Madeline Usher breaking free of her coffin.

"The most compelling evidence of Madeline's vampire nature is when she breaks out of her coffin. How can a sickly, frail woman with a wasting disease find the strength to break through a coffin and an iron door? She must be possessed by some supernatural power to be able to achieve such extraordinary physical feats."

"The issue isn't with Madeline," said Simon. "The issue is with Roderick. Why is he so eager to entomb his twin sister when he knows she's cataleptic? He seems to know perfectly well that she might not be dead. He gives some feeble excuse about why he buries her, but it doesn't ring true. I don't think she's a vampire. I think he buries her alive and he knows it."

"And she breaks through a coffin and an iron door?" asked Maeve.

"When people are under duress they can perform superhuman acts," said Oliver.

Thomas continued as if he hadn't heard. "Other, more minor evidence of Madeline's vampirism is the fact that her white robe is covered in blood, a common signifier of vampires."

"Or a common result of using your bare hands to break yourself out of a premature burial," said Simon. "Besides, she doesn't bite Roderick's neck, or the narrator's."

"There is such a thing as a psychic vampire," Cordelia said.

"You mean Madeline could read Roderick's mind?" asked Oliver.

Amandine smirked in Maeve's direction. "People do that, don't they, Maeve?"

I wondered why Amandine thought Maeve could read

minds until I remembered. The wood fairy. Can wood fairies read minds? I wasn't certain. Amandine had that yes, I know, and now you know that I know gleam in her eyes. Maeve stared at her notebook, ignoring the question.

"I don't mean psychic as in reading minds," Cordelia said. "I mean that Madeline is draining Roderick's life force. She's an energy vampire. She lives off other people's energy." Cordelia waved her hands in front of her face to emphasize her point. "Perhaps when Roderick buried Madeline, he was trying to rid himself of her vampiric influence. What do you think, Professor Ferrars?"

I couldn't say what I thought, so I said instead, "I'm wondering, Mr. Lambert, what you make of the hereditary evil that Roderick insists has infected his family. Some scholars believe that the phrase 'in the direct line' of Ushers means that there's a history of incest in the family."

"You mean the way Ancient Egyptian royal dynasties would marry brother and sister to keep the family line what they considered pure?" Oliver asked.

"Precisely. How do you think that connects to the idea of vampirism in the story, Mr. Lambert?"

"The Ushers are feeding on themselves. They're consuming their own family from within."

"What would Poe have known about vampires?" Simon asked.

Thomas's nose crinkled as though he smelled something unpleasant. "Vampire stories have existed for as long as there have been people to tell them. Supernatural stories regained popularity in the early nineteenth century when John Polidori wrote *The Vampyre*."

"Didn't that come out of the same ghost story challenge that caused Mary Shelley to write *Frankenstein*?" Maeve asked.

"That's right," I said. "*The Vampyre* was published in

1819, and Poe was first published in 1827. Poe could have been familiar with Polidori's story."

Thomas tapped his pen against the table and his foot against the carpet until we stopped talking.

"In The Fall of the House of Usher, there's a lot that Poe leaves ambiguous. We don't know for certain what is happening with the Ushers, but we can infer that the supernatural is somehow involved. Remember, the House of Usher refers both to the family and to the house. The setting—the house itself—becomes a character as well as a reflection of the mental states of Roderick and Madeline. The decay of the Usher mansion mirrors the moral and psychological decay of the family."

"I think it fits," Maeve said. "After all, there's that poem in the story that suggests that something evil overtook the Usher family. That evil could have been some kind of curse, and that curse might have been vampirism."

Despite a few glitches, there was nothing particularly hostile about their words or their manner toward each other. They were asking and answering questions in an appropriate way. Thomas's discussion questions prompted an interesting conversation about the evidence of Madeline Usher's vampirism in the story, and it was a good discussion—heated but not unkind. All in all, it had been a success.

Thomas lingered after the others had left.

"I do apologize for tonight, Professor. I think I understand your job better now. If I was rude when I challenged your plans for the term, I'm sorry. That wasn't my intention."

I believed that was exactly his intention, but his apology appeared sincere. I wondered if there was something in that apology that included the colloquium, but it didn't seem right to press him. He said good night and left.

I sat in the silent room for a while. It was only the fourth week of classes, and already Eventide College was proving an eventful place to be. I took the stairs to the fourth floor, and when I passed Leonard's office the door was open, so I stopped. Leonard was grabbing his keys from his desk and his briefcase.

"Aren't you the one who said you don't work long hours?"

"I had a meeting with the new Master's cohort and it ran long." He smiled as if we were co-conspirators. "So how's old Poe going?"

"He's going, same as he ever has. Are the department colloquiums always so exciting?"

His chest heaved with laughter. "Not quite as lively as that, no. When I first started here 20 years ago, some students threw some punches, but I haven't seen it go to first-round knockouts since."

"That's something, I suppose. And these students are all vying to be the next Poet of Eventide."

Leonard put a friendly hand on my shoulder. "That's what I've been trying to tell you. That whole cohort is trouble."

"Not Maeve, surely."

Leonard grinned. "The wood fairy? No, not Maeve. Though Amandine might disagree. Amandine is jealous of Maeve."

"I gathered that. But why?"

"Oh, you know how it goes with the young. They're all in love with the wrong people. Simon likes Maeve, while Amandine has it bad for Simon. It's like Thomas said at the colloquium. Amandine and Simon had a fling over the summer, but it fizzled out. Amandine still has the hots for Simon, but Simon's not interested anymore. Now Amandine is jealous of Maeve."

"Because of Simon."

"And also because Maeve is more talented than Amandine. Amandine's a smart girl, but Maeve has something special."

"Besides being a wood fairy."

"Right. Maeve is a talented literary scholar. Last year, Maeve came with Professor Jewell and me to Harvard to visit their Emily Dickinson collection. I realized then that Maeve has some interesting ideas about Dickinson's poetry, some good enough to publish. She's a gifted poet as well, and she's already published a bit."

"And Amandine?"

"She's a good thinker, and she knows how to argue a point. I'd say her literary prospects are average at best. I suspect Maeve will be the next Poet of Eventide, which will make Amandine's sniping even worse. You'll get your copies of the Poet of Eventide portfolios tomorrow, and you can read them for yourself. Don't forget to vote for the one you think should win."

"What about Cordelia?"

"Cordelia and Maeve are friends, which is good. Only Cordelia, well, as I told you before, I don't know her well. She seems like a nice girl, and I guess you can't blame a kid for their parents."

"What's wrong with Cordelia's parents?"

"Stephen told me that when Cordelia was in his class, Cordelia was doing all right, you know, just okay. She handed in a so-so essay and received a C. It wasn't a big deal, and her grade would have improved as she learned more. Her mother called Stephen to say that she had read the paper and her daughter deserved an A because she spent so long working on it."

"What did Stephen do?"

"He thanked the mother for her opinion and said that this is Eventide College and we don't speak to students' mommies here."

"I'm sure that went over well."

"Debbie had a few things to say. What those things were, he couldn't tell me since he wasn't paying attention."

I followed Leonard to the elevator. "I wonder if students realize how much professors know about them."

"As far as they're concerned, we're experts in our fields and nothing more. They think we materialize onto campus in the morning and dissolve away at night. Probably think we're even a little addle-brained."

"The absent-minded professor lives."

"Don't you know it. Do you know what you're going to wear to the Eventide ball? It's next month, you know."

"I hadn't thought about it, but a tuxedo, I imagine."

"A tux? Didn't anyone tell you it was fancy dress?"

"Fancy dress as in costumes?"

"Fancy dress as in we wear nineteenth-century finery—top hats and cravats for the men and crinolines and gowns for the women."

"Why the Victorian cosplay?"

"Rhys Grimshaw likes it, and it's nice seeing everyone dress up. The ball is usually good fun. You'll enjoy it." He nodded goodnight as he stepped into the elevator. As I turned toward my office, tremulous whispers echoed off the walls. I stopped, out of sight of an open door. Debbie and Rhys were in her office, huddled close and whispering. A third person was there, sighing impatiently, but I couldn't see who it was. Whatever they were discussing, I didn't want to know. I grabbed my papers and went home.

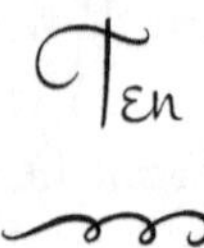

Believe nothing you hear, and only one half that you see.

Friday night, I didn't have class, but I went to my office as early as I could. Maeve Lang had made an appointment concerning her Poe presentation. I meant to review her notes before she arrived, but I couldn't concentrate. The colloquium was still on my mind. I logged onto my computer, checked the time, then stared at the coffee stains on my desk, wondering if Larry Presspitch had been a coffee drinker. A knock, and Debbie peeked around the open door, her silver pixie gleaming under the fluorescent lights. She laughed, high-pitched and forced, as though she had already said something funny.

"What about that scene at the colloquium? I don't know what's getting into kids these days."

"Will there be any sort of action against Thomas?"

"No one wants to take it that far. I've had him in my office, and Rhys and I are convinced that it was a simple misunderstanding."

"It was loud for a simple misunderstanding."

"It was rather loud, wasn't it? Thomas apologized. He said he wants to stay and finish his degree and go on to a PhD, though he isn't sure where yet. Professor Levinson, have you met her? She's the Dean of the Eliot School."

"I haven't met her yet."

"Well, she and I met to discuss the matter, and she said that if we're happy that Thomas is staying on then she's fine with it, though she made us understand that if there's another incident, even the slightest outburst, he'll have to go. Thomas has assured Rhys and me that there will be no further incidents."

"You weren't angered by what he said about you and Rhys?"

"Trust me, Jonathan, I've heard worse. People think that Rhys wanted me to be the next department chair because we were, you know. But we weren't. We're friends, that's all. We have many of the same tastes. We both love opera, so we'll head to New York to the Met together. We both love art, so we'll go to exhibitions. He may not be an official member of our department, but he's a highly intelligent man and a thoughtful scholar, and I find his ideas helpful, that's all. If people want to make it out to be more than it is, that's more about them than about me."

"You have a good attitude about it all."

"I think we're rather lucky to have a benefactor who does so much to help keep the department running smoothly. As I told you before, we're one big happy family here at EC. We go out of our way to help each other." She surveyed my office as if to be certain she hadn't missed anything during her previous inspection. Her eyes stopped on my Cambridge diploma and she nodded. "How are you finding it here so far?"

"So far, so good, I think, for the first few weeks."

"I heard you changed your seminar curriculum. You'll

revise your syllabus and share a new copy with your students and file it with the office, of course."

"Already done. Is there a problem with the changes? I didn't realize I had to ask permission."

"Not at all. Let's call it an experiment. They're not Education majors, after all."

"It won't do them any harm to put together a lesson where they teach their fellow students about something they learned, which should prompt some interesting discussions. It's a seminar, after all, which should be more collaborative than something lecture-based like a survey class."

"Don't worry. I didn't come to tell you that you did something wrong. Stephen Trevelyan may grumble, but you don't need to pay attention to him. The rest of us know to ignore him."

"His students pay attention to him."

"Hmm." Debbie squinted at the thought. "Yes, Stephen's students are rather awe-struck by him. They see him as a renegade, the one who dares to buck the system, the one who says what he thinks no matter who is listening. But his bark is worse than his bite."

"His bark is bad enough, I should think. Do you think it's true, what Thomas said, that Stephen gets his graduate students to write his research papers?"

"I know it's true. We all do. But professors have been badgering their graduate students into writing their research papers since the beginning of time. Haven't you done it?"

"No, I'm afraid I haven't. When I'm an adviser, I help my students with whatever they need, but I prefer to write the papers under my own name."

Debbie smiled. "As you should. As a matter of fact, Rhys and I like that you're willing to think on your feet. We like that you put the students first. We have some of the best literary minds in the country here, but even at Eventide, some of our older professors aren't as forward-thinking as they should be. They don't know how to relate to this generation of students. They think the students' love of Dell Inspirions and Lenovo ThinkPads is the beginning of the destruction of mankind, let alone their messengers and MySpace and all the rest of it. We have professors in our department who still can't work their email properly, let alone understand that students nowadays need something different from when they were in school. Whatever gave you the idea to have the students teach each other, anyway?"

"Thomas Lambert seemed to think he wouldn't be challenged the way I structured the seminar, and I'm all for challenging my students. I'm not trying to shape them into people who spit back my own ideas. I want them to think for themselves."

"It always seems to come back to Thomas, doesn't it? Poor kid. He seems to make an enemy of everyone. But I do like your style, Jonathan. It's important to keep the students happy."

"I thought our job was to keep them learning."

"Of course. But if we can stop their grumbling, that's always helpful."

"I'm not sure there's a way to stop Thomas Lambert from grumbling. After his exhibition the other night, I think he rather enjoys stirring the pot."

"Mr. Lambert is an interesting student in more ways than one. He had some difficulties during his first term, so we dropped him from the program. When he returned the following year, he had to take twice the coursework in order to graduate with his cohort. He seems to have pulled himself together, so hopefully he can hang on until he finishes his degree."

"Why did he fail his first year?"

"No one knows. He had a position as a student worker in

the library. Suddenly, one day, he withdrew from his courses and vanished for the rest of the academic year. He reappeared the following fall asking to be reinstated, and at the time I didn't see any reason not to give him a second chance. He has always been a good student with a lot of potential—all of his professors say so—and he hasn't broken any laws that I could see. He hadn't been in trouble with the police. He simply vanished and then reappeared."

"A magic trick?"

"It's as good an answer as any."

"I was told that Thomas takes offense at anyone who has had an easier time getting through life than he did."

"Who told you that?"

"Leonard."

Debbie rolled her eyes as she sighed. "I'd take anything Leonard says with a grain of salt. He loves to talk, but half of what he says is gossip, and the other half is just plain wrong. But he means well. He likes to shoot the breeze, so he'll say whatever comes to mind just to keep the conversation going. Did Thomas seem pleased with your changes?"

"He taught the first student lesson, and he seemed rather pleased with himself afterwards. Hopefully, that will hold him for a while."

Debbie grabbed the doorknob, then turned back, which is usually when people say what they meant to say in the first place. "I just remembered why I came by." She reached into the pocket of her lavender jacket and pulled out an envelope with *Professor Jonathan Ferrars* embossed in gold. "Rhys asked me to deliver this to you personally. It's your invitation to the Eventide ball. Everyone in the English department, students and faculty, is invited to see the new poet laureate crowned."

"Being named poet laureate is a big deal, isn't it?"

"Oh, yes, as I know from personal experience. It's quite a privilege. Our poet laureates go on to have fine literary careers.

I believe that my having been a Poet of Eventide is one of the reasons I'm the department chair today, not because Rhys and I, you know." She smiled at me as she reached for the doorknob again. "You know that the ball is nineteenth-century dress, don't you?"

"Leonard told me about the costumes."

"Rhys loves the nineteenth century above all else, and it does add an element of fun to the festivities. The fancy dress makes everything a bit grander, you know? We wear fine clothing, waltz across the ballroom floor, drink tea and champagne, and eat finger sandwiches while the top three finalists for poet laureate read their poems. It's fun, I promise." She let go of the knob and stepped closer. "Of course, you're entitled to a plus one. Who will you bring to the ball, Professor Ferrars?" Her eyes brightened. "A tall, good-looking young man like you should be out and about meeting people. Don't follow your colleagues in believing that because you're a professor you have no time for anything but work for the rest of your life. It's all about work-life balance."

"Finding a balance between work and life can be a challenge."

"Of course it is, but you're a handsome young man. You should have some fun every once in a while. Who in your family was blond?"

"Pardon me?"

"Who did you inherit that gold hair from?"

"My mother had lighter-colored hair when she was younger."

"And was your father tall?" I tried to think of a way to extricate myself from the conversation before she said, "I'm not sure there's anyone in our department for you, but I know someone in philosophy, Professor Sebelle. She's very pretty and on the younger side. I think you'd like her."

"That really isn't necessary."

She glanced again at my Cambridge diploma, then studied the Poe daguerreotypes and the portraits of Dickinson, Emerson, and Thoreau. She scanned the bookshelves. "No family photos?"

"It's just me. My parents passed away long ago."

"No wife? No significant other?"

"Not at the moment."

"At the moment?"

Was it ever acceptable etiquette to shove your supervisor into the hallway and slam the door in her face? I couldn't see how to do so politely, so I didn't, though I would have liked it very much. When I couldn't think of a way around, I went through.

"My wife died."

Debbie shook her head. She didn't appear surprised, and for a moment I thought she already knew, though I certainly hadn't told her. Something about the stillness of her expression disturbed me. I must be paranoid, I thought. That suspicious feeling of being followed was growing into an inexplicable dread of other people's curiosity. This was not how I wanted to go, because of the never-ending questions from a busybody. Finally, she seemed to understand.

"I shouldn't have pried, Jonathan. I'm sorry for your loss. I was only trying to help, and I wanted you to know how happy we are to have you here."

I thanked her as she was leaving. Before I had a chance to consider what had happened, Maeve stood in the doorway, and I waved her in. She looked feathery green in her floral print dress and chunky wool sweater, her long hair in waves down her back.

"I'm so sorry to bother you, Professor Ferrars."

"You're no bother, Ms. Lang. I'm here to help."

Maeve gave my office the once-over, as Debbie had

moments before. Maeve smiled at the portrait of Emily Dickinson.

"She's my favorite, Emily Dickinson."

"Why?"

"There's a vulnerability about her verse that makes her seem, I don't know, normal, like she's just like me except she happened to write her thoughts down."

"I understand you're a talented poet as well."

"Yes, I write poetry, and I've been lucky enough to have a few poems published in some smaller journals. I feel like I have an innate knowledge of Dickinson, as if I understand her in some profound way. I get why she wanted to hide away in her room the last years of her life."

"Why do you think she stayed so secluded?"

"Because she bared so much of her soul in her poetry. I mean, she lived as a complete recluse, yet in many ways her life was fuller than someone who traveled the world. That's what I want to do. I want to live fully in slow, quiet ways."

"Dickinson lived a life of the imagination, yet she was grounded in reality."

"That's it exactly."

Yes, I thought, I could see something of the wood fairy about Maeve. She wasn't wispy or insubstantial; in fact, she was rather the opposite. She evinced a strong sense of self, as though she knew who she was and accepted it. But there was something ethereal about her, dare I say, enchanted.

"Now, how can I help with Poe? In your email, you indicated that you're looking at a psychological examination of the darkness in The Tell-Tale Heart."

"I was wondering what I should focus on. I mean, I know what a psychoanalytic theme is in literary theory, but I can't see what I should look for in this particular story."

"Well, Poe focused on the dark side of human nature. His

characters often have issues with instability and delusions." Maeve wrote her notes in a spiral notebook. "The Tell-Tale Heart is a good example of the psychological torment someone might experience as they descend into madness under the burden of their guilt. Does the narrator feel remorse after he kills the old man?"

Maeve flipped through her notes as she considered.

"He feels guilty, but I wouldn't say he feels remorse."

"And what is the difference between the two?"

She pulled out a paperback collection of Poe's stories and flipped to the page she wanted. "He feels guilty because he knows that he committed a crime by killing the old man. Remorse is more about regret, and I'm not sure he regrets his actions." I nodded in encouragement, so she continued. "The narrator's guilt shows itself through hallucinating that he hears the heart of the man he murdered still beating. The narrator is right at the point of getting away with the murder, but he's certain the police can hear the old man's heartbeat too, so he confesses."

"Poe wants to examine how these feelings of guilt and paranoia can prompt people into acts of self-destruction. He delves into those hidden impulses that lurk beneath the surface. Even people who seem rational can slide into horrific acts when driven by such unconscious forces. The narrator doesn't have a good reason for killing the old man, and the reason he does give is feeble."

"Like in *Crime and Punishment*."

"Precisely. Like Dostoevsky, Poe doesn't present evil as an external force. Instead, he suggests that it resides within the human heart and that a potential for darkness exists in everyone."

Maeve read over her notes and nodded.

"Thank you, Professor Ferrars. I have a better understanding now of where to start. I should look into the madness, so to speak, of the narrator in The Tell-Tale Heart."

"See what you can uncover about the elements we've just discussed. Then decide how best to present what you've learned. If you need help with locating sources, I can point you in the right direction. Is there anything else you'd like to discuss while you're here?"

Maeve slid her notebook and her paperback into her brown leather satchel and sat a moment, her eyes drawn back to my Cambridge diploma. She walked close to it, leaning her face forward as if studying every detail. Then she turned to me. Perhaps I should put that away, I thought. People at Eventide seemed intent upon it, and it was making me nervous. Sounds of life in the department died away as professors and students left for the night.

"Professor Ferrars, I wanted to ask you something. I was hoping that you'd be my new adviser since I'm studying Emily Dickinson and Professor Presspitch is no longer here. He was my adviser, but you know..."

"Yes, I know, and I'd be very happy to be your adviser. It's getting late tonight, but we can make an appointment to go over what you've already completed with Professor Presspitch and see what else needs to be done. You're graduating in the spring, correct?"

"That's right. Or at least that was the plan."

"Then we'll make sure that everything is in order for a spring graduation."

Maeve exhaled loudly. "Thank you."

She shifted her satchel onto her shoulder, and I realized that I had to ask my questions now or never. I had become rather interested in young Mr. Lambert, and Maeve seemed to know him better than anyone.

"Ms. Lang, I was wondering if you knew what caused Mr. Lambert to act out the way he did at the colloquium."

Maeve nodded as if she had been expecting the question. "Thomas is, well, he can be high-strung."

"So I noticed."

"I can't say for certain because he doesn't confide in me about everything. Really, there's a lot he doesn't say. He just keeps it all bottled up inside. I know he wants to be the next Poet of Eventide. Thomas thinks that being the next Poet of Eventide is his best chance of making his way in the literary world, but he doesn't think he has a chance. He's sure it will be Simon because Simon's dad is rich and can buy the award if he wants to. He thinks Mr. Grimshaw has wormed his way into the department, planting whoever he wants wherever he wants because he paid for it. I think, and this is just my opinion, but I think that Thomas feels like it's him against the world. He tries to pick fights with everyone. You saw it yourself the first night of class when he tried to start with you. Mainly, he picks on Simon."

"However misguided Mr. Lambert's actions were, it looked to me like he was trying to protect you."

"Thomas thinks that Simon is trying to move in on me, but he's not. Simon and I are friends. I try to be patient with Thomas because I think I'm the closest thing he has to a friend. But it's hard sometimes because I've seen Thomas being pretty spiteful. Once, he tried to get Larry, that's what Professor Presspitch wanted us to call him, fired for bullying. Only Larry was the nicest man, and there wasn't anything he wouldn't do to help his students. Thomas was the bully, constantly challenging Professor Presspitch in front of everyone, and then he tried to turn it around and make it seem like Larry was the bully. It was..." Her fingers stretched as though grasping for words. "It was a hard time to be a student here. When Thomas came back, he seemed to have calmed down, or at least he did until the colloquium."

"Do you know why Mr. Lambert left his studies?"

"No, no one does. We started the program together—

Thomas, Simon, Amandine, Oliver, Cordelia, and I—and then Thomas suddenly dropped out during our first term. He came back just as suddenly at the beginning of our second year. Before Thomas dropped out, Simon said he saw him arguing with Professor Bronwyn and Mr. Grimshaw, though Simon couldn't hear what the argument was about. Then Thomas disappeared. And then he came back. It was odd."

"It certainly sounds like it."

Maeve turned toward me as she considered. Something shuffled in the hall, like footsteps.

"This," she gestured toward the hall, "the English department, Eventide, all of it, is a challenging place to be, and sometimes that brings out the worst in people. Like the big deal over the Poet of Eventide. We have to submit our portfolios to be considered, but the truth is, I don't think the portfolio ends up counting for much. I read Henry Feldstein's portfolio. Henry is our current poet laureate, and his poems were, I don't know, just okay. But Henry was Professor Trevelyan's favorite, and I think Professor Trevelyan helped boost his student in the standings."

"When I received the portfolios, I noticed that they're not judged blind."

"You're right, they're not. Our names are on them. You see, it's not just the students who win acclaim when they become the poet laureate, but it's also the professors who guide them."

She stood there, as if waiting for me to add something, but I wasn't sure what to say. I did have more questions. I wanted to know what that argument was about between Thomas, Debbie, and Rhys. I wanted to know what was eating at Thomas. I also wanted to know more about how Leonard came to find warding spells in the Eliot School. I wanted someone to verify or deny that things went bump in the night at Eventide College. I decided yes, I should ask her, then no, then yes again. When my curiosity was too much, I said, “I’m not sure if this has anything to do with what is bothering Thomas, but I was told that Eventide is haunted, of all things. Someone discovered packets of warding spells in our hallways. I must admit, the prospect of working at a haunted college is fascinating and frightening in equal measure.”

“Who told you that?”

“A student, I think. I can’t remember. However, it was the same person who told me that you’re a wood fairy.”

Maeve laughed. “I’m not a wood fairy, Professor Ferrars. I’m a hedge witch.”

“So you are a witch after all. Amandine said you were.”

“Amandine says a lot of things about me. Most of them aren’t true, but some of them are.”

“What exactly does a hedge witch do?”

“Don’t worry, it’s not as scary as it sounds. Hedge witches are known for working with herbs. We also do spirit work.”

“What does that mean?”

“It means we can cross the hedge, the line between worlds.”

“You’re a clairvoyant?”

“That’s right. I can speak to those on the other side. I practice divination, but that’s only a small part of what I do. I prefer to focus on healing, on natural remedies. Hedge witches are solitary, meaning that we don’t belong to a formal coven or anything like that, though I have friends who are also hedge witches. Everything, even a walk through the forest, can have a magical intent. And yes, there are magical forces here at Eventide, but then there are magical forces everywhere. I’m not sure our college is more or less haunted than anywhere else.”

“That’s good to know. I think. Do you know anything about the smudging?”

"Yes, I did the smudging. I placed the satchels of sage around the Eliot School, and then I did the cleansing spell."

"Why?"

"Because there's an evil spirit here, and it frightens me."

"Do you think your spells worked?"

"Not yet. I..." Her cheeks went pink, and she turned away, perhaps in confusion. "I think the magic is stronger than any spell I can cast. I'm sorry, Professor Ferrars. That was too much information. I didn't mean to embarrass you by telling you all that. Cordelia told me what you said to her after her presentation, and I thought you'd understand."

"You'll find no judgment from me, Ms. Lang. We could all use a little magic in our lives, though perhaps some of us have more magic than we know what to do with. Is there a spell for that?"

"Having too much magic? I don't think so."

I stood up to see her out. As I walked around my desk, Maeve grabbed my hand, squeezed my fingers, and closed her eyes. She was still as a statue, waiting. Then her eyes flashed open, and we stood there, my hand still in hers.

"Ms. Lang? What are you doing?"

"It's all right, Professor. I sensed there was..."

Footsteps slapped the floor outside my office. I tried to pull my hand away, but her grip was tight. I looked over her head into the hallway. No one.

"You're still learning about Eventide College," she said. "There is a whole invisible world here, with many things unseen." She seemed to see through me as though I were invisible. Her voice sounded far away, as if she spoke through a dream. "There are phantoms here, benign and evil. The evil means harm to the one in the realm beyond time."

"What does that mean?"

"It means someone needs to beware."

"Who?"

"I don't know. I can't make out a name or a face."

Maeve's grip loosened, and I tugged my hand away. She shook her head as though she were waking from a nightmare. In a moment, she seemed herself again.

"I'm sorry, Professor. There was something about you, some aura surrounding you, and I had to know."

I forced a laugh, a feeble attempt to make light of the situation. "Are you a good witch or a bad witch?"

"I'm just myself."

"Who else knows?"

"I think they all know, the students I mean, and some professors. I don't hide it, and I'm not embarrassed by it. I am what I am. I think people have a deeper connection to the spiritual realm than they realize, but it seems too outlandish, so they don't believe it. There are a few people here who ask me to contact their loved ones on the other side, and I'm happy to help if I can. It's hard to explain, but it's like having an extra sense, one that can see the invisible world. I can feel when there's a presence, and I know when there's magic." She seemed far away in that moment, as though her body were there, but her soul had left for another plane. "With you, I sense sorrow, the kind that lingers in your soul. Like the ache of remembering something beautiful that is now gone, or the sense of loneliness after saying goodbye. I sense the act of gradually fading away from others, not out of melancholy or madness, but from a desperate need for the peace that comes with solitude. Here." She dropped something round and hard into my hand. "This will bring you some serenity."

I spoke before I considered my words. "I've stopped talking about it because no one else can understand."

Maeve smiled, a bit sadly. "There is beauty in surviving the wounds you thought would destroy you."

"Sometimes I think they have destroyed me."

"No, Professor. You're still here."

I was tempted to say more, to bare my soul. It had been so long since I had someone to confide in about the things closest to me, but I stopped myself in time. I was still her professor, and the professional boundary had to remain, no matter how good a hedge witch she was. Before I could speak again, she was gone, and Amandine stood in the doorway.

"Ms. Wesson, good evening. Have a seat."

I sat behind my desk and dropped the object Maeve had given me into the top drawer. It was an amethyst, meant to ward off negativity.

Amandine made herself comfortable in the student chair. She flipped her long copper hair behind her neck and adjusted the shoulder of her red and black plaid dress. "Is everything all right with Maeve? She seemed upset just now."

"Ms. Lang is fine. Do you need help with your Poe presentation?"

"No, I can handle that. I was just talking to Professor Cruz, and I saw that your door was open, so I thought I'd say hello."

"And how are things going so far this term?"

"Pretty good, I'd have to say. I spent the beginning of the term finishing my portfolio for the Poet of Eventide. Now that it's done, I'm working on my portfolio for my creative writing thesis. I'm also the assistant editor of the school's literary journal, and I'm preparing for my brown belt in Taekwondo."

"It sounds like you have a lot on your plate."

"I do, but I'm enjoying it."

We sat in silence until she said, "Did you know that Professor Presspitch passed away in this very office? Creepy, isn't it? He was probably in that chair you're sitting in now when he died. It was kind of sad that he died, but he was old, so what can you do? Professor Trevelyan said that when you get to be that age, your heart just gives out."

I looked at the ceiling, half-expecting to see Presspitch's ghost. I would have recognized him since I had recently seen his photograph on the EC English department website. No one had taken his picture down, and he was still listed as a faculty member. Instead of anything spectral, all I saw was institutional off-white paint.

Amandine glanced over her shoulder into the hallway.

"Are you sure Maeve is okay? Like I said, she seemed kind of off, but then, she's always a little scatterbrained. She's never entirely here, you know? Simon said her head is always in the clouds. Her head is always in the forest, from what I hear. I don't think Simon really understands how disconnected she is from even the most basic reality. She thinks she's a witch, you know, boiling cauldrons, eye of newt, that sort of thing."

"Sounds more like Shakespeare."

"I feel sorry for her, that's all. So does Simon. That's why he's always talking to her. But I understand Simon in a way no one else can. Simon and I take Taekwondo together. We get each other, but because Maeve seems so sweet, everyone lets her get away with nonsense. Thomas went with her into the forest so she could cast a spell, and he told me all about it. One of these days, people will see how cracked Maeve really is. It's not like she can hide forever." Amandine smiled sweetly. "I just wanted to say hi, Professor Ferrars. Have a great night."

Thomas peered around my door.

"Can I have a moment, Professor Ferrars?"

Before I could answer, Amandine was gone, and Thomas was sitting near my desk. I wondered if I might find a more uncomfortable chair for office hours.

Thomas checked that we were alone. "You should beware of anything Amandine says to you, Professor Ferrars. She's in love with Simon and jealous of Maeve. But Maeve is in love with me."

Silence appeared to be my safest course. As I pondered

why my students were coming to me with their personal problems, Thomas stared at my Cambridge diploma, not with approval as Debbie or Maeve had, but with curiosity. He pointed his chin at the framed paper.

"That's impressive, Professor. So young, with such an extraordinary academic pedigree. You really are rather a prodigy. I concede your point about why you would come to Eventide, but I still think you should have stayed at Yale."

"You're still not happy with our seminar?"

"The seminar is fine. I like the changes you made. I feel like I've been challenged, which happens rarely enough. I've been helping Cordelia and Oliver with their presentations so I can put my knowledge to good use."

"That's generous of you to help your classmates."

He seemed to wait for me to say something more. When I didn't, he leaned forward so that his head and shoulders were halfway across the desk.

"How do you do it, Professor? How do you keep up the momentum night after night for so long? It must be tiring."

"It's only the fourth week of the semester, Mr. Lambert. I can assure you that I don't normally start flagging until the term is nearly over."

He leaned over even more, and our noses nearly touched. His sneer appeared deformed, as if he were ogling me.

"You know what I mean, Professor Ferrars."

I stayed where I was, a hair's breadth from him, and stared back. "I have no idea what you're talking about, Mr. Lambert. Can you please explain what you're referring to?"

"Very well, if you want to take the slow road. I wasn't entirely convinced about your credentials the first night of school. I know what it says on your EC faculty page, but I wanted more information. I've become rather curious about you."

"Your point, Mr. Lambert?"

"My point is that I saw you. In the forest. I went with Maeve so that she could cast a banishment spell. It was midnight, so I went with her to make sure she was safe. She told me she was going to try to trap a malevolent spirit beneath the root of a beech tree."

"You seem too practical to believe in malevolent spirits."

"I've come to know differently. You'd be amazed at what you'll find at Eventide College. And then we saw you. You didn't realize we were there. You blew right by us, but we both saw you. You were...strange. And then you were gone." He grinned as though rather pleased with himself.

"You're looking at me now, Mr. Lambert. Do you see anything strange?"

"No. But I've seen you other times too. I've seen you walking alone at night."

"I'm not aware that walking alone at night is a criminal offense. I suffer from insomnia. When I can't sleep, I walk. The movement helps to settle my mind." I stood to leave; rather, I stood hoping he'd get the hint that he should leave. "Mr. Lambert, is there something about the Poe seminar that I can help you with?"

The arrogance he had entered my office with had fled. He looked dubious, his fingers twisting knots in his lap, his knees bouncing in quick time. It was similar to the way he behaved at the colloquium, where he ranted and raved with self-righteousness until he deflated.

"No, Professor Ferrars. Thank you."

He remained where he was as though he wanted to say more. I moved to the student chair beside him.

"Mr. Lambert, is something wrong? Is there anything I can do to help? I know I've only been here for a few weeks, but if you'd like to speak to someone, I'm here. If you'd prefer to speak to a professional, I can help you find someone at the health center."

He laughed. "I had been and am; but why *will* you say that I am mad?"

"I'm not at all saying that you're mad, Mr. Lambert, certainly not in the way Poe meant it. I do know that sometimes life can feel lonely, like there's not one single person in the whole world we can rely on. Sometimes we feel as if we're being actively pursued by some invisible something that we can't name. I'd like to help if I can. That's all I'm trying to say."

He closed his eyes as he exhaled, perhaps properly for the first time since sitting down. His voice took on a quieter, defeated tone. "It's nothing. I've just been, I don't know. I've discovered some strange things since I've been at Eventide."

"Forgive me, I'm not trying to pry, but I know that you left the program your first year and returned. Someone said they heard you arguing with Professor Bronwyn and Mr. Grimshaw. It's just that I was wondering if your argument had anything to do with your leaving. Was there a problem with Professor Bronwyn or Mr. Grimshaw? Something that needs to be addressed?"

"There are so many problems with Professor Bronwyn and Mr. Grimshaw that I don't know where to start." He smirked at my startled expression. "It's nothing illegal, nothing like that, and I don't think it can be formally addressed. It's only that I'm not sure what's true anymore. You don't have to call the helpline, Professor. I'm not going to do any damage to myself. I came back to Eventide to finish my degree and move on."

"Will you at least think about seeing someone? It never hurts to talk about things, especially if they're causing you anxiety or pain."

He stood, stretching his back after the confines of the hard chair. "I'm sorry about what I said. I was...and then I saw you...I don't know. Maybe it was being out in the forest at midnight and watching Maeve cast a spell. I'll think about talking to someone. I promise."

"Then I'll see you at our next class."

When he was gone, I looked at the ceiling again, this time with a prayer.

Eleven

That which you mistake for madness is but an overacuteness of the senses.

This is when my madness began.

"You should have seen it coming."

Perhaps I should have.

In the fifth week, Simon gave his presentation on symbolism in Poe's detective fiction.

"In Rue Morgue, a mother and daughter are murdered viciously. Madame L'Espanaye is found in the courtyard of her apartment building, her bones crushed and her throat sliced so severely that her head is severed. Her daughter, Camille, is discovered strangled to death and stuffed into the chimney of their apartment. With the clues available, C. Auguste Dupin, Poe's detective, deduces that the murderer was not human, but an escaped orangutan. The orangutan itself is a symbol of the force of primitive, brute irrationality."

Simon presented well. He knew his material and his arguments were sound. He lingered in the seminar room with Amandine, and after everyone else had gone, he handed me a cream envelope with the faint scent of vanilla, my name written in swirling calligraphy.

"I hope you don't find this too out of the ordinary, Professor, but I'd like to formally invite you to join us at our little gathering tomorrow night."

"I didn't realize you had a study group."

"I wouldn't call it a study group as much as a poetry appreciation society. We discuss poetry and read some of our original work. This is where we first read aloud the poems we submitted for our Poet of Eventide portfolios."

"Oh, yes, Professor Ferrars," said Amandine. "Do come."

"It sounds charming, but I'm afraid I have a class to teach."

"No matter. Our gatherings begin at 10 p.m., and we go until the early hours of the morning. You could come after you've completed your work. We'll just be getting started."

Well, I thought, why couldn't I go? What was so wrong about seeing them outside of class to discuss poetry and hear some of their original work? Many professors invite students to their homes for discussions. Professor Presspitch had students over at the end of every term. Professor Cruz often took her students to Portland, Boston, or New York City. Perhaps such a gathering could help me understand my students better.

"Are you sure you want your professor there? I'm afraid I might cramp your style."

"We would love to have you, Professor Ferrars. Besides, we need you there for a reason." Amandine glanced at Simon, who nodded for her to continue. "We've read your paper on the meaning of death and loss in Poe's poetry, and we think you're the perfect person to judge our original poems based on that exact topic. The theme for this particular meeting is also death and loss."

"But the submission date for the poet laureate portfolios has passed."

"You're right, it has," said Simon. "These are poems we're hoping to submit to literary journals for publication. We'd like your honest opinion."

"Which brings me to another concern. If I have some notes about a particular poem and the poet thinks I'm being harsh, that could make the rest of the term awkward for us all, don't you think?"

"Not at all," said Simon. "We've agreed that your well-formed opinion will stand. The poet whose work you're critiquing will listen silently, as at any writers' workshop."

"Nothing I say means that the poet has to change anything. It's up to each poet to decide what criticism is valid for their vision for their poem."

"That's right," Amandine said. "But we'd still love your opinion. The meeting is at Simon's house, and he lives off campus on Frantick Road down the street from Eventide Manor. Do you know it?"

"I do."

Simon grinned. He had won the battle. "Shall we say tomorrow at 11 p.m.?"

The next night, I was floundering through a first draft of a new Poe-inspired article when the clock chimed the hour. Not wanting to show up empty-handed, I grabbed a gift tin of tea, thinking it was appropriate based on what Simon said. I dropped the tin into a green Harrods of London bag, grabbed my backpack, and crossed Main Street to Frantick Road to Simon's house, located two miles from the melancholy oppressiveness of Eventide Manor.

In October, the plentiful birches, maples, oaks, even the pines along the bay, whirl into a kaleidoscope of reds, purples, oranges, and yellows of such exquisite beauty that I am forced to believe in a higher power. Every year, when the fall foliage bursts into bloom, I challenge myself to name the variety of colors: tortoiseshell, sepia, lemon, goldenrod, amber, tangerine, scarlet, and russet were among those I saw that night. I admired the scene as I passed, knowing full well that such brilliance is fleeting. Cold-weather clothing had been taken out of storage, and the few people I passed looked like fishermen in knitted sweaters, hats, and scarves. Harvest festivals, apple picking, hiking, and leaf peeping on the scenic routes were thriving, though all was quiet at that late hour.

As if to make a point, an angry storm dropped suddenly while I walked, whipping the trees. Colorful leaves flapped as if waving goodbye, while others bent toward the rain-soaked grass. As I pulled up my hood, I found one perfect purple maple leaf, picked it up, and held it close to my face, which prompted a razor-edged pain when I recalled how she would stand under the autumn trees, reaching toward the branches with both arms as though she wanted to hug the beauty close. I held the leaf toward the sky, offering it to her, then let it fly away.

Simon's house was easy to spot, a blue and white three-story Queen Anne. The houses on Frantick Road had an eclectic feel, as if the neighborhood couldn't decide what it was. Eventide Manor presided at the end, closest to the shore, grand and gloomy, while modest, one-story colonial-looking homes in reds, blues, and greens dotted the road inland. Simon's home was somewhere between since it was stately in a royal way but not bleak like Eventide Manor. Heavy-looking apple trees in Simon's front yard stood guard, the grass covered with overripe apples. The scent of a wood-burning fire and apple cider wafted from inside, while lace-like ivy added thoughtful bits of draped greenery. From the flurry of dropped curtains, I guessed I had been spotted. It was too late to turn around, which I had been considering. It will be fine, I thought. I'll listen to their poems, do my best to be useful in a way that isn't overly critical, and then I'll go home. It will all be over soon.

I took one stone step at a time, admiring the stained-glass circle in the center of the door as it cast a patchwork of green, yellow, and blue at my feet. Before I raised my hand to the knocker, an elderly maid in a black dress, white apron, and cap opened the door and asked if I was Professor Ferrars. When I admitted I was, she let me in, taking my wet raincoat and the bag of tea from my hands.

"Professor Jonathan Ferrars," she announced. She stepped aside and curtsied to no one in particular.

Simon Hayes, the Nordic prince himself, looked the part in his black cable-knit sweater, black and white houndstooth trousers, and Oxford-style shoes. He stood when he saw me.

"Welcome, Professor Ferrars. We're all so pleased you could come."

I thanked him, then turned my attention to the wall of portraits of various generations of his family, many with the same gold hair and pale blue eyes. For a moment, that sense of being spied on returned, only in this particular case I wasn't being paranoid. I was, in fact, being watched. Five pairs of eyes stared at me.

"Will I be meeting your family tonight, Mr. Lambert?"

"Oh, no, Professor. My parents always spend the autumn in France and the winter in Switzerland. The house is all mine for the next four months."

"I'm so happy you could join us tonight, Professor Ferrars." Amandine stood from the chaise lounge and extended her hand in an old-fashioned gesture. I grasped the tips of her fingers as I bowed my head. She appeared to take on the role of hostess as she gestured toward the silver tea set on the sideboard. I watched as she poured tea into a delicate bone china cup, which she handed to me. I sat on the settee near the bay window and set the cup and saucer on the side table. Amandine sat near Simon and smoothed down her white wool dress, pressing her fiery curls from her face.

"Where is Ms. Lang?" I asked.

"She had a paper to finish for Professor Harris's class," Simon said. "She'll join us as soon as she can."

I had interrupted a conversation about the Poet of Eventide ball.

"I understand it's quite an honor to be asked to read at the event."

Oliver nodded as he set his cup and saucer aside. "That's right, Professor. Only the top three applicants are asked to read."

"If you're asked to read, you know you made the short list," said Simon. "The main poem in my portfolio is entitled An Ode to a Raven, whereby I pay tribute to two of poetry's most important birds, Keats's Nightingale and Poe's Raven."

They were watching me, so I maintained a straight face. It was a struggle, but I won. I lifted my teacup as if to take a sip, looking into the amber liquid and wishing I could read the tea leaves. Unable to stall any longer, I said, "What an interesting way you have of combining two of the world's most beloved poems."

Thomas slapped his hands on his knees, then pointed at Simon. Even Thomas's finger mocked the Nordic prince.

"He submitted the same portfolio this year that he did last year, and he expects to become poet laureate with those banal excuses for poetry. His daddy plays golf with the dean's husband, and he has a finger in with our illustrious benefactor, Mr. Grimshaw. Did you know that Daddy Hayes pays the administration to fuss over his son? Old Hayes pays almost as much to the department as old Rhys does." Thomas pointed at me. "There is some real literary talent at EC, Professor. John Noone, who graduated last year, had a poem published in the New England Review, and he didn't even get a look-in as the Poet of Eventide. He didn't know the right people, I suppose, hadn't brown-nosed enough professors or shagged Trevelyan or kissed Grimshaw's freakish ass or whatever it is you have to do to get a chance around here."

Simon, his face revealing nothing, tugged at his sweater. "I beg your pardon, Thomas, but I've had three poems published in the Southside Standard."

"The Southside Standard is Eventide College's literary journal, of which you are the editor-in-chief, and your little pet here," he gestured at Amandine, "is your well-trained assistant. Are we expected to be amazed that you chose to publish your own poems? Where have you been published that you're not the editor or your daddy doesn't pay your way in?"

As if on cue, the elderly maid entered, refreshing the teapot and the silver tray of crumpets. Simon waved her away. The room was dim, lit only by the flickering flames of the fireplace and the taper candles. Everyone's faces were in shadow. The atmosphere thickened around me, charged with something unspoken, until Amandine moved to the wing chair beside me.

"You must have the ear of Professor Bronwyn, Professor Ferrars. Can't you persuade her that one of us should be the next poet laureate? I know all the English professors vote for their favorite portfolio."

Thomas scoffed. "Or their favorite student."

"Enough, Thomas!" Cordelia yelled. "Can't we have even one night without listening to you complain about every single thing on earth?"

"We all know what you think, Thomas." Amandine puckered her lips, giving her a grotesque look in the candlelight.

"Have you put in your vote for the next Poet of Eventide, Professor Ferrars?" Oliver asked.

And there it was. The reason I had been invited. In fact, I had voted. When I received the portfolios, I suggested to Debbie that perhaps the voting should be blind so that professors couldn't play favorites. I was told every which way why that wouldn't work, so I dropped it. I knew who I voted for, even if I wasn't about to say so.

"I know each of you would like to be the next poet laureate, but I'm only one vote, and I'm afraid there isn't much I can do about the choices of the other professors."

I sensed that they wanted to ask who I voted for. Thankfully, no one did.

"I have every confidence that the right poet will be chosen."

Thomas scoffed. "That only goes to show that you're new, Professor Ferrars, and you're still learning how things work around here."

Oliver paced to the window, peering at the wool-like clouds bringing more brisk rain. The apple trees in the front yard swayed, and overripe apples fell with a thud. It was warm in the parlor with the fire, though Oliver shivered as though he had been caught without a coat in the wet weather. Everyone gathered near the window, huddled together as they watched the flapping wind, the snapping rain, the jolting thunder, and the flashing lightning. The storm grew fiercer, as did the energy in the room.

Amandine spoke as if the conversation hadn't stalled.

"You sound as if you think things are fair, Professor Ferrars. Nothing is ever fair." She looked around, her eyes narrow. "Where is Maeve? Getting away with murder, as usual, I see?"

"Ms. Lang is what...?"

"Amandine thinks Maeve murders people with her witchy powers," said Cordelia.

Amandine stamped her foot like a pouting child. "She's always late to these meetings. Or she doesn't bother showing up at all. Not that you care." She flicked a careless finger at Simon. "She could plagiarize her whole thesis and Simon wouldn't care at all. In fact, he'd probably help her. Maeve Lang can do no wrong in Simon Hayes's eyes."

Simon shrugged but said nothing.

Watching with a cool eye, Thomas was all nonchalance, as though it was no concern of his. He sighed as he spoke. "I chose Eventide College because I wanted to find a community of like-minded people who thrive on literature and poetry. I see now that I made a mistake."

Cordelia gestured toward me. "That's a lie. You asked Professor Ferrars why he would leave Yale to come to EC. You said EC was a step down. To me, that means you don't really want to be here."

Thomas shrugged. "Apparently, the joke is on me. What are we doing here anyway? Or a better question—what am *I* doing here?"

"What *are* you doing here?" Amandine laughed in Thomas's face. "You can leave any time, you know. You've already left once. What's wrong? Is nothing going your way? You already tried to get Larry Presspitch in trouble, though it didn't work. You were horrible to Professor Bronwyn and Rhys."

"Oh?" Thomas said. "It's Rhys, is it? Is he your bosom buddy? Or your sugar daddy?"

Amandine's face grew as fiery as her hair. "You're the one who's always causing problems! You're the one who makes it seem like you think you're so much smarter than we are and we're not good enough to meet your exacting standards!

Maybe instead of always putting everyone else down, you should get off that high horse of yours!"

And then I remembered why I never went to social functions. What would Professor Cruz do if her students broke out in a fistfight in New York? Should I interfere? Should I try to settle everyone down? I should have left, but I was worried that things would escalate even more without me.

Simon stood with his back to the crackling flames in the hearth. "I'm not certain what our esteemed colleague means when he asks what we're doing here. We've already established our purpose. We're at Eventide for the outstanding reputation of its English department. We're here to be educated by respected faculty like Professor Ferrars."

"And your poetry is always the finest," Thomas said. "Your own father says so."

Simon stood as straight as he could. Though he wasn't gifted with height, he had width enough for two men. He wasn't heavy, but he was broad, and even without the height to back it up, he would have been intimidating. He looked particularly so in the flickering reddish shadows cast in the dark room. Thomas, taller and lankier, pulled himself upright, towering more than a head over Simon.

"Honestly, Thomas," said Oliver, standing a safe distance away, "I don't know what your problem has been lately."

"Lately?" Amandine laughed. "He's been nothing but an ass for as long as we've been here, and I'm sick of it." She stood less than a foot from Thomas. "You're a goddam bastard!"

Cordelia took a step forward, to help or hinder Amandine, I couldn't tell. Thomas leaned casually against the bookcase, his eyes level with Cordelia's, his hands clasped behind his back. Cordelia was shouting now.

"What have any of us done except try to be your friend? If you hate it here so much, then leave. Eventide College existed before you arrived, and it will exist after you're gone."

"For the better," added Oliver.

Amandine and Cordelia stood shoulder to shoulder in a show of solidarity.

"Cordelia is right, Thomas," Amandine said. "You're obviously unhappy here. Like you said, Eventide isn't Yale. So go to Yale."

I inserted myself between Thomas and everyone else. "Everyone, please sit down. Becoming the next poet laureate shouldn't be this acrimonious. I know it can lead to future opportunities, but ninety-nine percent of people in the literary world made their way without being the Poet of Eventide. There's no reason to be so upset about it."

They took a step back, away from each other. Cordelia dropped her head as though she were sorry for her outburst.

"I agree with Professor Ferrars," Oliver said. "We're here to read our poems, and the professor has been kind enough to come tonight to listen. Let's begin before he has to leave. What do you think, Simon?"

Everyone waited as if Simon were the presiding judge. It was his house, after all.

"I do agree, yes, thank you, Oliver." He tapped his spoon against a teacup, and everyone turned to the tinkling sound. "Our poetry reading will now come to order."

The students, including Thomas, pulled out their notebooks with their pages of verse. I found it disconcerting how quickly they switched from contemptuous to contented, though no one else seemed to find the sudden shift of mood odd.

Oliver informed me that each week they assigned themselves the task of writing one original poem, which meant that each of them would have completed sixteen new poems by the end of the term. Each week was given a theme, something lofty like love or resilience. The theme that week was death.

"I wonder if you might start us off by sharing some ideas

about Poe and the theme of death, Professor Ferrars," Simon said.

I considered each word carefully. One misspoken observation and all hell would break loose.

"Poe lost his mother when he was a child. Other women he loved, some of whom he looked upon as mother figures, also died young. As we mentioned in class, Poe's wife died of tuberculosis. Poe himself died at only 40 under mysterious circumstances. To those of us who study his work today, it seems as if he used his writing to work through his fears about death and dying."

"My mother died when I was eight," Oliver said. "Maybe that's why I've always been drawn to Poe. He expresses an inner melancholy I didn't have the words for at such a young age."

"My grandparents died within two months of each other," Cordelia said. "Since starting this seminar, I learned that Poe shares a depth of sadness that only the best writers can convey."

Point for Ms. Reed. Someone was paying attention.

The students read their poems in turn, and I offered some gentle suggestions. As anyone might expect, some poems were better than others. Cordelia spoke about the deaths of her grandparents and how they affected her. Simon and Amandine chose to deal with death metaphysically by focusing on what one human death means on a cosmic scale. When it was his turn, Oliver stood with his poem in his shaking hands, his voice soft but intent. He had taken care with this poem, his work written in calligraphy on parchment paper, and he read something strong and fine.

Then it was Thomas's turn. When he read, the rest of us waited on edge for his every word. I thought his poem was brilliant, and I was surprised at how touched I was. Yes, he relied a little too heavily on sound effects and allusions, like

Poe, and perhaps there was more style over substance, also like Poe, but style has its place in literature. With maturity and more life experience, I thought, this young man might make a fine poet after all. And I meant to tell him so.

Thomas finished reading, and he dropped onto the chaise lounge. A gloominess settled over the room that matched the melancholy eye of the storm raging outside. Except for the sound of the sputtering flames, it was silent, with everyone lingering in their own thoughts. Until Thomas turned to me.

"What about you, Professor Ferrars?"

"What about me?"

"We've been sharing our verse on the topic of death. What is your experience with the great equalizer?"

"I'm afraid I'm going to have to bow out respectfully."

"But this is what we do at our meetings. We bare our souls through our poetry. That's what it means to be a poet."

"I don't write my own poetry, Mr. Lambert. I study the poetry of others. My knowledge lies in research, not practice."

Thomas leaned forward, his hands on his knees, his whole body tipped in my direction. "Do you really believe you're so much more knowledgeable than we are because you have some pieces of paper with your name and a university stamp?"

"My job is to question, Mr. Lambert, to push the boundaries of what we think we know. Once we think we know everything about a subject, it's time to put that subject away and find something new. I see no reason why, in a few years, with some hard work, you can't have the same diplomas on your wall if that's the direction you wish to go. All of you. You're all capable of achieving anything you want if you're willing to work for it." Simon looked as if he meant to say something but changed his mind. "While I'm happy to discuss any point of literature with you, I have to draw a line at discussing my personal life."

"Are you married, Professor?" Thomas asked.

I leaned my head against the back of the chair. I should have listened to my first thoughts. I shouldn't have been there.

"Oh, come now," Thomas continued. "Surely, there's no harm in telling us whether you're married."

"He doesn't want to talk about it." Cordelia stood, her long skirt billowing around her ankles. "Besides, it's none of our business." She turned to me. "I'm so sorry, Professor Ferrars." She gestured at her fellow students. "We're literature students who hope to become poets and scholars..."

"Unless your name is Simon Bernard Hayes. Then your daddy pays for you to become whatever you want."

Amandine rolled her eyes. "Here we go again."

"He'll have a house, awards, and all the money in the world to fund the publication of his watery writing. I want to get back to the point. What do you have to share with us, Professor? You've listened as we've shared our grief. It's your turn."

What could I share with them? So much of my knowledge is formless, weightless, beyond basic understanding. How do I put that into language they could understand? I let the silence linger until I found some words to share that would release me from any obligation.

"I lost my wife under difficult circumstances."

Oliver sat beside me, his eyes soft with concern behind his tortoiseshell glasses. "Professor Ferrars, I'm so sorry." He glared at Thomas. "I think that's enough, don't you?"

Meeting her cue once more, the maid returned with another fresh pot of tea. Seeing that the dainty plates with crumpets, clotted cream, and raspberry jam were untouched, she rolled the cart to each guest so we could help ourselves to the tasty-looking treats. When the cart appeared beside me, I shook my head.

Thomas scoffed. "Even our tea and crumpets aren't good

enough for the illustrious Professor of Eventide? Perhaps you'd prefer something else?"

"*Our* tea and crumpets?" Simon laughed. "I believe the refreshments have been provided by me. Professor Ferrars is my guest, and if he chooses not to partake, that's his right."

Simon exhaled with frustration, an expression of fatigue pulling his lips into thin lines. Without warning, Thomas charged toward Simon and punched him in the face. The impact was so hard that Simon's head snapped back. His nose was bleeding, and Amandine rushed to him, bringing him napkins. Meanwhile, the maid stood near the door, the handle of the cart in her hand, staring into the distance as though this was nothing out of the ordinary.

Oliver grabbed more napkins from the cart and held them out to Simon. "Pinch your nose and hold your head back. If it doesn't stop bleeding, you'll have to go to the hospital." Oliver turned to Thomas. "What is wrong with you?"

Simon removed the napkins from his nose, staring at the blood as though he hardly knew what it was. Amandine stepped closer to him as she examined his face.

"The bleeding has stopped," she said. "He should be okay."

Simon stepped around Amandine and confronted Thomas as though ready for another round.

"What is your problem, Thomas? Did we not applaud politely enough for your poem?"

Thomas raised his fist as if to punch Simon again. "Maeve is in love with me, you know. I know you're trying to steal her away, but you can't fool her. She's too smart for you."

"You're both delusional," said Cordelia. "Maeve is not in love with either of you, so get over yourselves."

Simon dabbed the rest of the blood away with the napkins. "Maeve and I are friends, that's all. Not that it's any of your business." He waved a bored hand before his bloody face.

Now Amandine was flaring. "How many times do they have to tell you that they're not dating, Thomas?"

Thomas stormed away, clutching his coat and his backpack, his fist covered in blood, looking rather like a Victorian body snatcher making away with a victim. He slammed the front door behind him, the maid still staring into space. The rest of us sat in silence.

Amandine stood. "Simon, you'd better get yourself cleaned up."

Simon followed Amandine into the hall. As he walked away, he said, loud enough for everyone to hear, "If he tries that again, I'll kill him."

"You said that at the colloquium," Amandine said. She closed the door behind them.

It was my turn to head for the door. "Forgive me, but I think it's rather time I left you all to...well, whatever it is you're going to do now."

"I'm so sorry, Professor Ferrars," Cordelia said. "This is usually just an informal gathering where we share our love of poetry. This was..." she glanced at Oliver, who was glaring through the window in the direction Thomas had left. "This was unusual, to say the least."

"Is Thomas worse this year than he was before?"

"I'd say he's worse. He's always been uptight, but this year, I don't know. I don't know what's going on with him."

I thanked Cordelia, said good night to Oliver, grabbed my raincoat, and walked outside. The storm had cleared, for that moment at least, so I went toward the bay. It was a new moon, and with the rain clouds gone, the stars were brighter and more beautiful without the moonlight washing them away. Then, as if the fog parted and a figure emerged, someone trembled at the edge of my recollection. A man from long ago. His face was blank, lost somewhere at the bottom of my memory. The more I tried to tug his features into place, the more the image disintegrated, leaving my thoughts half-formed in the darkness.

To take my mind off the phantom image, I stopped at the edge of the shore where the rough tide kissed land, rocking on my heels to the rhythm of the waves. I missed the moonlight. How many fears, nightmares, and wishes have I told only to the moon? Why be afraid of the dark when the veils people wear under bright lights are so much more terrifying? I had been upset by the scene at Simon's, the impatience, the bickering, the violence barely restrained from exploding into something even more dangerous. There was rage in that room. Standing at the edge of the shore, the lack of moonlight did not help to quell my concerns. A lone raven braved the night to perch in a pine, my only company. I wondered where its partner was.

A deep fatigue tormented me, a mournful, soul-crushing exhaustion I hadn't felt in some time. You can only carry the burden of sorrow for so long before it overwhelms you. Like the moon, I have weaved in and out of phases in my life. Sometimes I was in control. More often, I was not. That night, I was certain that I was not in control of anything. I know full well what terrors arise when you are not in control. With the water brushing my shoes, I stood with my arms out, my eyes closed, allowing the gales to blow through me as I sought comfort in the knowledge that the moon doesn't fight the darkness, and it doesn't always need to be whole. The moon can be but a fraction of itself, and it is still beautiful. Sometimes, as on that night, it disappears. Yet in time it will shine again. Light and shadow always dance together, and one cannot exist without the other. I thought of her and smiled, hoping that somehow we would always be connected under that same moon. Victor Hugo said, "Whatever causes night in our souls may leave stars." I wondered how many of the stars in the sky were mine.

Did I know, as I stood on the shore with my arms outstretched, that there was a horrific act of violence occurring at that very moment? Of course, I've asked myself since. What I know for certain is that an extreme melancholy overwhelmed me. I felt as if I were slowly separating from myself, as if there were some detached part of me, just out of reach, and no matter how hard I tried, I could not rein it in. Eventide College had already become uncomfortable. There was too much strangeness there, and somewhere, in the back of my mind, I was already making plans to leave.

Her screams pierced the night. I ran toward her, cutting across the side road between Whitley Way and Main Street. There she was, Maeve, in Simon's front yard, her delicate face frozen in a mask of horror. I followed her terrified gaze to the too-still body lying at odd angles on the wet ground. I pushed past the fence and joined the others as they peered at Thomas Lambert.

"Is he dead?" Amandine asked.

I didn't need to look too closely to know.

"Has someone called 9-1-1?"

"I did," said Oliver. "The police are on their way."

"Come on, everyone. Come away. The police will need space when they get here, and there's nothing more we can do for him."

Amandine stood, transfixed, staring wide-eyed at the blood oozing on the wet grass, trailing from Thomas's throat, slashed so deeply that muscles and veins popped out at grotesque angles. I realized with horror that he appeared to be decapitated. Then the sweet scent, earthy and metallic, overwhelmed me. I closed my eyes, steadied myself, and stepped as far away as I could without making myself obvious. Maeve gagged, and Simon set a hand on her shoulder.

"Please, Maeve," he said gently. "Come away."

The others stared at the body as though they couldn't believe it—boisterous, argumentative Thomas Lambert with his throat slashed and his limbs sprawled at awkward angles as though he had fallen from a great height. The upstairs rooms were dark, the windows closed. A balcony extended from the second floor. A thought occurred to me, something so bizarre I nearly laughed aloud. It was a flight of fancy, certainly, and I kept my thoughts to myself. I didn't want to upset the others.

Oliver followed my gaze to the balcony. "But Thomas left, didn't he? The whole house shook when he slammed the door as he stormed away."

Simon shrugged. "I think he did."

"Did Thomas come back in?" Cordelia asked.

"I didn't see him." Simon followed Oliver's gaze to the balcony. "Do you think he jumped?"

"I don't know what to think," said Oliver.

"Who did this to you?" Maeve asked the corpse. I half-expected the poor boy to answer.

I listened for sirens, and I shuddered. I was taking a chance by being there. When I heard Maeve's scream, I had to make sure she was all right. Now, knowing the reason for her scream, I was afraid. I knew there was no reason I should be implicated. I didn't kill Thomas. I was at Simon's house, but I left. I was at the shore, and then I returned. But I was on the shore alone, and you can't take anything for granted—even the truth.

There were no sirens. The ambulance arrived first, then the police. Flashing red lights reflected off the windows, leaving everyone a devilish shade. When the police walked toward us, I was tempted to run, but it was pointless. My students knew I had been there, so the police would know soon enough. I stayed where I was, sitting on the steps with the others. There were two uniformed officers. One walked toward the body, and the other came toward us.

"Who found the body?" he asked.

"I did," Maeve said.

"And you are?"

"Maeve Lang."

He wrote it down. "And what were you young folks doin' out here this time of night?"

"I was coming to Simon's house for our poetry group. We're students at Eventide." She began crying as the area around Thomas's body was sectioned off with yellow tape.

He took the students' names and wrote them down. When he saw me, he asked, "You know him?" He gestured toward Thomas.

"He's my student, Thomas Lambert."

"And you are?"

"Professor Jonathan Ferrars."

"Also from EC?"

"Yes."

"What do you teach, Professor Ferrars?"

"American literature."

"You just happened to be here, and now one of your students is dead?"

"I was invited to attend the poetry group, but I left to go home. I heard Maeve screaming, so I came back."

"What time did you arrive?"

"About 11 p.m."

"What time did you leave?"

"Maybe midnight. I wasn't looking at the time."

"You see this young man," he gestured toward Thomas, "alive when you left?"

"I didn't see him at all when I left. He had already gone."

"You see anyone loiterin' about, anyone nearby besides yourself and your students?"

"No one."

"What was the meetin' about?"

"The students wanted me to evaluate their poems."

"Seems late for class."

"It was an informal meeting."

"Did he," the officer nodded toward Thomas, "have a mobile phone? Or a car, maybe with a GPS?"

"He had a BlackBerry," Maeve said. "But he didn't have a car."

The officer nodded as he wrote everything down.

"All right, Professor. Where can we find you?" I gave him my office number at the Eliot School and my home details. "We'll have more questions for all of you. You're free to go."

Maeve sat on the top step and cried into Simon's arms.

"Are you all right, Ms. Lang?" I asked.

She nodded through her tears. "I'll be all right, Professor."

"I'll make sure she's all right," Simon said.

I stopped outside the fence where neighbors gathered to watch. I moved quickly toward my cottage with my head down, my hands in my pockets. I glanced at the sky, but there was no comfort to be found. The buzzing in my ears, that paranoia that had been creeping up on me, was overwhelming. Eyes tracked me, I was certain of it, while voices whispered behind my back. I was being followed, and I spun around to see. No one. A quick movement behind a beech tree, and a human-shaped shadow crept near. I drew closer to a wide space between branches. No one. I checked the sky and saw my friends, two ravens, flying overhead. They turned their heads in sync, a deliberate, precise movement, and their eyes glimmered with a bronze luminosity. I recognized that gaze. I had seen it before—the cool appraisal, the confident knowledge. The ravens were not merely observant, but aware. As I turned the corner, they flew away.

The next thing I knew, I was inside my cottage, my hand on the mantle, the fireplace black with soot. I had no idea how I got there. A thin, reedy sound pierced the fog inside my skull and escaped my throat. I blinked, finding the familiar outline of the study, the desk where I worked, my books, the bookcase, the window glazed with night. Yet I did not recall opening the front door. I did not recall crossing the threshold. Or walking up the stairs. I shivered as if I had brought the October chill indoors. The room felt wrong, not in any particular way, but in the sum of small dissonances. The chair was drawn out from the desk, as though someone had been sitting there, waiting. The old leather-bound journal was in front of me, open to a page I did not recall reading. In fact, I did not recall leaving it on the desk. I was certain I had returned it to the drawer. There was a faint scent of ash, as though someone had lit the fire and it burned away.

I retraced my steps in my mind. The last thing I recalled was the path home from Simon's, the old oaks whispering overhead, their branches tracing silhouettes on the ground. I heard Maeve's scream as though it were happening again, then the dreadful sight of Thomas mangled and dead. I hoped it was some terrible nightmare, some B-grade television movie. And then I woke up! But no. The night had been all too real. Poor Thomas was dead. Suddenly, the world tipped sideways, and I grasped the desk to keep myself upright. Again, I was overwhelmed with the sense that I was not connected to myself, or anything else, that my thoughts were drowning me, my memories perishing one by one.

"What is happening to me?" I said aloud.

The cottage, silent and waiting, did not answer. Only the gilded mirror, reflecting the surrounding room, seemed to know.

When I felt steady enough, I let go of the desk and sat in the office chair, staring into the smoldering fireplace. The reality that Thomas was dead hit me hard, and I grieved him. He was too tempestuous for his own good, but he had promise, as all young people do. He had the potential to grow into a solid researcher and a respected poet. Yes, he tried to challenge me, but when his volatile mood passed, I saw something else in him, something vulnerable. If he had believed more in himself instead of always looking for someone else to tell him that he was okay, if he could have stopped pointing his finger at others and turned that energy onto his own promise, perhaps he could have had a happier ending. Not that he deserved to be murdered. Never that.

The vision of his body splayed like a doll discarded in a child's fit of anger burned behind my eyes. I considered my other students and was overwhelmed by dread, for them, and for me. I have my secrets, as most people do. And I know all too well how easily things get twisted out of proportion. How easily things fall apart.

Twelve

Who has not, a hundred times, found himself committing a vile or silly action for no other reason than because he knows he should not?

Everyone at Eventide, in the state of Maine, all of New England, it seemed, knew about Thomas Lambert's death. The police were less than forthcoming. They were a small force, and the local chief said that they were not equipped for this kind of case. People aren't murdered in Southshore, he said, and help from the Maine State Police and their major crimes unit was imminent. By the following week, the only update we received said that two detectives from the state police had arrived and all options were being considered. They had Thomas's BlackBerry, they said, and had downloaded the track log in an attempt to use the satellite signals and cellular data. The problem, the state police said, was that the young man didn't have Google Maps or Foursquare open, so the GPS in his phone wasn't actively pinging. In coastal Maine, cell towers were few and far between, meaning they might not be able to triangulate his location so easily. The time between Thomas leaving and Maeve screaming wasn't long—perhaps half an hour. To me, that meant that he was likely killed near Simon's house, possibly even inside Simon's house. Whatever the police knew, they were keeping it to themselves, and they said as little as they could get away with at the press conference.

Had Thomas Lambert been anywhere besides campus, his room at Clovis House, and Simon Hayes's house the night he was murdered, a reporter asked?

At this time, the police officer said, they had no further information.

Everyone who had been at Simon's that night had gone to the local police station to give our official statements. If I had Facebook, MySpace, or even a television, I'm sure I would have seen more about the murder, but I pulled even further into my bubble. Even there, I couldn't escape the horror of Thomas's death. I had seen the horrible reality of it myself.

When I arrived at my office the following Monday, Leonard stood outside my door, waiting for me.

"Good heavens, Jonathan. You're here for two months and you're already having your students murdered out from under you. That's got to be a record."

I knew he meant it in jest, but the sentiment struck too close to home. I unlocked my door and let us both in. I dropped my backpack on my desk and pushed my glasses back up my nose. I was too agitated to sit, so I pulled the latch on the window, pressing it open, feeling the sea gusts blowing my hair from my eyes.

"So what happened that night? You were there. Do you think it was one of the students? Do you think Thomas killed himself?"

"I honestly don't know what to think."

"What did the police tell you?"

"Nothing. They asked where I was after I left Simon's and how I came to be there when Thomas's body was found. Then they let me go."

"No suspects?"

"If there are, I haven't heard about it."

Leonard whistled, a long, slow sound. "And here I thought I'd seen everything." His hearty laugh sounded awkward in the quiet room. "There are all sorts of stories going around the school, you know. Some people say Thomas ran into some random burglars who wanted to ransack Simon's house. Some say Thomas was on drugs and ran with the wrong crowd. Others say he was depressed and committed suicide by slitting his own throat while leaping from the balcony."

"Sounds a bit theatrical."

"Too theatrical for Thomas? I doubt it."

"I suppose we'll have to wait for the police to figure it out."

"It's a shame that you were there when it happened."

"I wasn't there when he was murdered. I had already left. When I heard Maeve scream, I went back."

Leonard considered me with a curious expression. "Well, whatever happened, Thomas Lambert has already passed into legendary status. I wouldn't be surprised if they put a statue of him next to old Cornelius in the center of campus."

I leaned back in my chair and closed my eyes. Thomas's demise suddenly felt distant, blurred, as though the events of that night were visible through a foggy window. I thought of the young man who had sat in the same chair as Leonard. He had come to challenge me. And now he was gone.

"How well did you know Thomas?" I asked.

"I knew him a bit. I had him in my class that first year when he left halfway through the term. Then I had him again when he returned, and he wasn't the same."

"How do you mean?"

"He was angrier, lashing out at everyone. You saw how he was at the colloquium. He tried to get Larry Presspitch fired for bullying, you know, but everyone saw through that."

"What did Debbie tell you about him?"

"About Thomas? That he hailed from Baltimore. His father was a lawyer, his mother was a teacher, you know, an ordinary family. He attended the University of Maryland, College Park. He showed some promise there and published a few poems in some of the better university literary journals. He chose Eventide College for his Master's degree based on the prestige, but he became bitter when he was no longer the top dog and had to contend with some of the brightest young minds academia has to offer."

"It sounds like something inside him, some sense of inadequacy perhaps, reared itself in ugly ways, and he lashed out." Through the window, I watched the storm moving in across the bay. "They really should have cancelled classes this week. Whether people knew Thomas or not, whether they liked him or not, he was still a student here. As far as any of us know, his murderer may still be out there, perhaps even waiting for their next victim."

Leonard grunted as he stood from the uncomfortable chair. "You know how it goes. The board decided that classes should proceed as usual. The Poet of Eventide Ball will go on as planned."

"No one will feel like going to a ball."

"Maybe. But we'll all be there just the same. By the way, did you hear who the finalists for the Poet of Eventide will be?"

"No, I haven't heard."

"It's Maeve, Simon, and Cordelia. Debbie said that Thomas actually made the top three, but, well, you know."

That night, my American literature survey class was only half full, but I didn't take attendance and didn't press the matter. The next night, everyone, with one obvious exception, was at the Poe seminar. When I arrived, there was an eerie silence as the five students looked everywhere but at each other. Cordelia tapped her pen on the table while Amandine and Simon stared at their laptops. Maeve ran her finger over a water stain on the table, her foot tapping a rhythm muffled by the carpet. Only Oliver sat expectantly, his tortoiseshell glasses on the tip of his nose, his spiral notebook open, his ballpoint pen in hand.

They looked so young, so innocent, yet I couldn't help but wonder. Did one of them murder their classmate? What reason did they have? Yes, they disliked Thomas. Yes, they were all vying for the title of Poet of Eventide. That was not enough of a reason to kill someone, surely. I recalled reading in one of those detective novels from the bookcase in the cottage that motive was the last thing the police concerned themselves with. First, they had to find clues, some proof that someone, whomever it may be, had committed the crime. The *how* was more important than the *why*, at least in the beginning. Studying the open faces of my students, I was glad that the job of uncovering Thomas's murderer didn't fall on me. Did the students suspect that one of the others sitting around that table was the killer? It was hard to tell from their distracted faces. I asked Amandine if she would mind presenting the following week. When she said no, I let them go. They took a moment to start gathering their things.

"Thank you, Professor." Maeve packed up her satchel. "I wasn't really in any condition for class tonight, but I didn't want to miss anything. I don't like that the Poet of Eventide Ball is still scheduled for next weekend. I don't feel up to it."

"I know Thomas could be an idiot," said Oliver, "but he didn't deserve to die for it."

"Calling him an idiot is being too polite." Simon checked the time on his pocket watch. "He was an ass."

"He's dead now, Simon. Let him rest in peace." Cordelia looked at each of us, her round eyes welling with tears, as she left.

"His being dead doesn't change anything," Simon called after her, yelling into empty space. "It doesn't change how rude he was, or how he was always challenging everyone. It doesn't change the punch he threw at me. He broke my nose." As the others drifted away, he shrugged, grabbed his satchel, and left.

I stayed where I was, giving them time to leave. I had nothing to add, no words of wisdom, nothing to profess. I was as blindsided as they were. Alone in the seminar room, I tried to recall the events of that sad night. There were six of us in Simon's library. Maeve had not arrived. There was an argument, a punch thrown, and Thomas left. Simon and Amandine left the room after Thomas stormed away. Did Simon kill Thomas? Did Amandine? Did they work together? It was Simon's house, after all. He would know the secret passageways, the shortcuts. He would know the best way to drag someone upstairs unseen. Perhaps he didn't have to drag Thomas. Perhaps Thomas returned, and then Simon, or Amandine, or both, lured him upstairs, and they sliced his throat and threw him from the balcony. Did either of them have that kind of violence within them? I certainly didn't know. The similarity to Poe crossed my mind again. The Murders in the Rue Morgue. That was how the mother died —her throat was sliced and she was thrown through a window. The realization hit too close to home. It had to be a coincidence. At least, that's what I allowed myself to believe.

"There are few persons who have not, at some period of their lives, amused themselves in retracing the steps by which particular conclusions of their own minds have been attained," said C. Auguste Dupin, Poe's detective. "The occupation is often full of interest and he who attempts it for the first time is astonished by the apparently illimitable distance and incoherence between the starting-point and the goal." Dupin, or Poe, was right. No matter how many times I retraced the events of that night in my mind, all I found was incoherence.

Back at my cottage, I dropped my keys into the porcelain bowl on the side table and wandered into the sitting room, looking out at the Norway spruces that surrounded the house like bodyguards, their branches heavy with red, gold, and russet. Then I opened the sliding glass door and sat at the picnic bench in the back garden under the red twig dogwoods, breathing in the scent of the salty sea, soothed by the whispers of the waves rustling against the shore.

I went back inside, intending to be productive. I had already sent in my revise and resubmit, so that was done. I made a valiant second attempt to start my next paper, but despite my best intentions, I couldn't concentrate. I went to the sitting room and scanned the titles of Mrs. Griggs's books and chose another Agatha Christie. I turned a copy of *Death on the Nile* over in my hands and wondered how long it would take Hercule Poirot to find Thomas's murderer, that is, if Thomas was murdered. He may have committed suicide, though, to my limited knowledge of such things, it seemed unlikely. Perhaps C. Auguste Dupin could make a go of it. When I replaced the Christie with Ngaio Marsh, I found the bound leather journal jutting from the shelf. Life had become busy, and then Thomas's death, and I had forgotten about the old book. But I had seen it on the desk in the study. Hadn't I?

I held the journal close to the light, wondering if it was really from the nineteenth century. The ivory pages, yellowing at the margins, appeared authentic. The paper itself had a woven pattern, one of the better quality papers from that era. I flipped through the entries until once again my curiosity got the better of me. I lit the fire, warmed myself a cup, settled on the sofa, and turned to where I had left off, hoping that the rest of the journal would be as entertaining as the pages I had already read.

Saturday, 11 November 1843
Southshore, Maine

I am not a man prone to superstition. My beloved Helen died one long month ago. My true love lies buried in the gloomy churchyard, her coffin and the ground it is buried in chilled in the autumn storm. Life is too hard. I cannot live without her. I cannot find peace here in the home we shared. I cannot find it in the Scriptures that the parson reads in a rigid monotone. My soul is shattered anew every night when our dear children weep for their departed mother.

I am restless and cannot sleep. Some specter haunts our home. Is it Helen? She would not have meant to frighten us. I reach out for her, and though I grasp at nothing, I feel her presence everywhere. I am certain that she is searching for a connection between us so we can communicate, just as she communicated with the others, only then she was here and they were there. Now she is there and I am here. For years, I watched, first in skepticism, then in awe, as she helped the grieving by contacting their loved ones in the Great Beyond. If she could make contact with strangers, why can't she make contact with me, the husband who loves her dearly?

I must speak to her, but I haven't her gifts, and so I require an intermediary, as she was an intermediary. Last night I visited a woman whom others proclaim to be an expert spiritualist. The results were not promising.

I was recommended to this woman by a dear friend. "Madame Desiree can help you," Mrs. Lewis said. "I've been using her to contact my Alexander since our dear Helen passed.

Madame Desiree has done wonders for setting my mind at ease. She'll do the same for you."

I made an appointment with Madame Desiree. I traveled to Boston to see her. I found myself seated in a parlor in Beacon Hill, every flat surface covered with luminous candles while a hearth raged, crackling and red, against the biting air. Besides myself, there were four women: two widows, one woman whose son died of consumption, and one woman hoping to contact her deceased father. We sat at the round mahogany table, its surface worn smooth by previous hopefuls. The walls were lined with black velvet, leaving us shrouded in sepulchral gloom. A single beeswax candle stood in a silver holder in the center of the table, its flame flickering to the rhythm of a heartbeat.

Madame Desiree appeared, nodded once, and sat at the table. She was a small woman, her gray-black hair pulled severely from her face in a tight knot. When she raised her veil, I saw that her features were childlike, a contrast to her wizened complexion. Her mourning crape was wrinkled and well-worn. She closed her eyes and rocked in her chair. Then she sat preternaturally still. When her eyes flashed open, she seemed to stare through the table. Perhaps she was receiving a message from the Other Side.

"We begin," she said. "Everyone must close their eyes and join their hands. Come forth, spirits of the departed. Tonight we open the Veil between the Worlds."

The two women on either side of me, whose hands I held, shivered. I, however, felt nothing. When I watched Helen call forth the spirits, static flashed invisible through all participants, even me, and I wasn't taking part in the proceedings. With Madame Desiree, it was all a blank. Perhaps it's me, I thought. Perhaps I only believe in Helen.

"Hello?" Madame Desiree called. "Is anybody there?"

Her accent sounded more Eastern European than French to

my ear, but I let that go as unimportant. Curiosity got the better of me, so I opened my eyes, only a little.

Madame's head fell back, her breathing shallowed, and her eyes rolled until only the whites showed. Then the tapping began. First a single rap from beneath the table. Then two more. Then three.

"A man. Recently passed. He is near."

The woman to my right shuddered, her palm sweaty. "My husband recently passed," she said. "Is it my Matthew?"

"Matthew, yes." Madame Desiree nodded. "Matthew Harrow."

"Oh!" The woman jumped in her seat. "Yes, Matthew dearest. I'm here!"

"He regrets that he could not say goodbye. He has lingered in this realm to speak to you one last time."

The woman let go of my hand. She opened her reticule, removed a handkerchief, and honked as she blew her nose.

"What is it, Matthew? Oh!" Another honk. "He died so suddenly, the poor dear, and I never...and I never..."

"He says there was nothing more you or anyone else could have done. He is no longer suffering, and he says for you to be at peace. He says that he knows that you love him and that you miss him every day, as he misses you."

"I feel him here!" she said. "I feel his breath on the back of my neck."

I felt something as well, only it wasn't like someone's breath but rather a lady's fan. I was afraid I would be too obvious if I turned to see. The soft patter of slippered feet skipped away. The woman beside me grabbed my arm while her hand shook uncontrollably.

"Oh, Matthew! Oh my dear, dear Matthew!"

Everyone jumped, including me, when the table trembled and the single candle slipped. Madame Desiree cried out and slumped forward. A low moan that didn't sound human filled the room. Then stillness. Then silence.

Madame Desiree sat as upright as her small frame allowed. "He is gone. I listen now for the next visitor." A hush settled while Madame Desiree trembled. "There is a woman here seeking her husband."

Since I was the only man present, I assumed she referred to Helen.

"Is that my wife?" I asked.

"Oh yes. Your wife wants to speak to you. To tell you..."

She waited. And so did I.

I know what a true conduit looks like. It looks like Helen. She had a true connection to the Great Beyond. Her gift was real. There was no tapping, no yelping, no ghoulish whispers. There was no false trembling, no lady's fan waved by an unseen hand. I was the most skeptical man alive when I met Helen, but in time, I saw the truth of her gifts. Often I'd arrive home to see her in the drawing room, her embroidery in her hands as her fingers worked the needle through the linen, all the while having a conversation with an invisible somebody the same as she would speak to anyone. Madame Desiree was a trickster. I did not doubt that. She was enacting a well-rehearsed scene she had played many times.

In my desperation to communicate with Helen, I had hoped I could find a conduit. But Madame Desiree was a sharper, nothing more. I guessed that she was waiting for me to give her some clue as to what I wanted to hear, but I would not play her game. If my Helen were there, if she had a message for me, she would make sure that I received it.

I watched as Madame Desiree opened her eyes to look for some clue from me. I nodded at her without hiding my gaze. She shrugged.

"She is gone," Madame Desiree said. "Your wife has left.

She has no message for you." She smirked as she said it, as if it were hurtful to me to be cut in this way. She continued the charade with the other women there, the women gifting Madame with clues about their lost loved ones. Madame gratified them with positive messages all around. Your loved ones see you. They love you. They want you to be happy. Does no spirit ever wish anyone ill, I wondered? Not everyone showers their family with love. What about stories of vindictive spirits? Sometimes vengeance is all we have.

My quest to contact Helen has become even more urgent. I must find her. I must speak to her.

Live forever, she said. My dearest, I'm trying.

I pressed the book between my hands, wondering. Again, I held the book under the light, checking the paper, the binding, the stitching, the penmanship, and the type of pen it appeared to be written with. The journal seemed authentic from the 1840s. I wasn't sure what to make of it. I believed in the author, or at least, I believed he felt that his words were true when he wrote them. I flipped through the pages one more time, still searching for clues about the identity of the author, still finding nothing. I was curious about what Mrs. Griggs would be doing with such a book. Perhaps it was something passed down in her family, though I had a hard time associating the dark romantic sentiments in the journal with Mrs. Griggs or anyone in her family, then or now. I would have to ask her about it the next time she came to clean.

A fragile recollection began to gnaw at my consciousness. Some vision pecked at me, determined to be known yet not breaking through, as though my past were written on a palimpsest—blurring, dissolving, and nearly coming into focus until vanishing altogether. Here and gone. Again, I tried to make sense of the shadowy face, and again it evaded me. Whoever he was, I could only hope that he would make himself known in time.

Thirteen

There is no exquisite beauty without some strangeness in the proportion.

The night of the Eventide Ball arrived. I was not looking forward to it, especially since everything was curiously quiet. The people were quiet. The campus was quiet. Most disturbing of all, the police were quiet. They were pursuing several leads. That was all they said. I wanted to beg off the ball, but I didn't want to make myself even more conspicuous by my absence. I was already the subject of some speculation since I had been at Simon's the night Thomas died. I had visions of the police appearing at Eventide Manor, handcuffs at the ready, as they loaded all the finely dressed guests, myself included, into old-fashioned paddy wagons.

After a fair amount of grumbling, I pulled out the clothes I had set aside. Black seemed easiest, its funereal color matching my mood. I pulled on black trousers, a freshly pressed white shirt, an embroidered black waistcoat, and a black frock coat. For good measure, I added a gold watch and chain across my waistcoat and tied a silk gray cravat around my neck, groaning all the while. I never did like that style of clothing, but I consoled myself with the knowledge that it was only for a few hours. I checked that my black leather boots were shined, slid on white gloves, and added a top hat to complete the look. If I could have seen myself, I would have laughed.

When I arrived at the black brick mansion, it looked the same—sepulchral in the night, heavy and somber. A blanket of flannel-like clouds blew in from the bay. Everywhere was gray and foreboding. While the house could not be called decayed, its shadows suggested decrepitude, as though the building had stood in one place for too long. The House of Usher came to mind since I was certain I saw eyes in the windows and a crack in the wall. An unkindness of ravens dived and rolled toward the old house, a black cloud searing the sky, their loud knocks echoing toward the sea as they communicated to each other about where to find food. The ruckus stopped as some coasted into the clock tower and others settled into the thickest branches at the tops of the tallest oaks. The iridescent, sharp-eyed birds fluffed out their feathers, tucked their heads, and pulled one leg up under their bellies, resembling puffy black balls. One of the birds, with one eye closed, turned its other eye on me. I shivered and went inside.

As ominous as the exterior of the house was, the open door beckoned guests inside, where the warm glow of gaslight reflected off marble floors scrubbed to a brilliant shine, leaving the room mellow and gold. The space was wide and inviting despite the dark wood trim. Past the threshold, I heard conversations, laughter, and clinking glasses.

"I'm glad you made it, Jonathan."

Leonard doffed his top hat to me. He appeared every bit the gentleman in his gray woolen trousers, quilted silk waistcoat, and maroon frock coat.

"Hello, Leonard. I'm impressed by how elegant everyone looks tonight."

"It's hard to believe these are the same students who show up to class in hoodies and jeans."

The fine-looking ladies and gentlemen appeared relaxed, relieved, even. We had all been under such strain since Thomas's death. Perhaps for that one night, we could leave our worries behind for a few hours. Perhaps holding the ball was the right decision after all, not from lack of concern or callousness, but because everyone needed permission to move on.

Leonard gestured to the grand display of dishes spread buffet-style. Two long tables held the choicest bites—salmon finger sandwiches, asparagus tarts, stuffed mushrooms, savory pies, cakes, biscuits, shortbread, and trifles—while a third table held glasses of negus, orgeat, wine, water, and champagne. A round table offered coffee and tea. Guests hovered close, sampling a few dishes while enjoying repeated glasses of champagne.

"Where is Rhys?" I asked.

"He'll be down in a bit. He likes to make an entrance."

Leonard turned to speak to a colleague I had only met once, so I began exploring the house. The interior looked like a museum of nineteenth-century artifacts. This is how people lived then, the house said, as if boasting of its heavy wood furniture, antiques, Turkish rugs, ornaments, and portraits of perfectly proper ladies in ringlets and gentlemen in top hats.

I made my way through the Great Hall, admiring everything, until I found the library at the end of the east wing. The room was dimly lit, with a high ceiling of dark wood beams and towering bookshelves carved from the same dark wood. The stone hearth, carved with serpentine flourishes, crackled with a high fire, its embers illuminating the nearby guests in flickers of amber and bronze. In the center of the room sat an ornately carved writing desk cluttered with open books, an oil lamp, and candles, while the scent of old paper and leather-bound tomes lingered in the air. The velvet curtains were open, revealing tall, arched windows where slivers of moonlight filtered in, casting elongated shadows on the floor. An ancient globe, fraying at the edges, stood near a wall adorned with framed maps and oil paintings of bucolic scenes. As I stood near the desk, I noticed that a quill pen, its ink still fresh, rested beside a half-written manuscript. I was curious and stepped closer, but Stephen Trevelyan, his wife, and Lavinia Cruz appeared. I nodded at Lavinia's sapphire-blue satin gown.

"You look wonderful, Lavinia."

"Thank you, Jonathan. You clean up very well."

After the polite small talk one must make at such moments, I excused myself to continue exploring. The drawing room had the cluttered look favored in the nineteenth century, with ornate dark mahogany furniture upholstered in burgundy damask. Every surface was covered with doilies and filled with decorative porcelain figurines, vases with flowers, and other curiosities. Silver-framed portraits and landscape paintings filled the walls. A piano sat expectantly in the corner as though waiting to be played. The round window facing the street was stained glass, a garden scene resembling the view outside the house—a charming effect. For a moment, standing in the flash of color, I was disoriented, as if the scene weren't real. Perhaps I passed into some dreamy shadowland. It was happening more often, this sense of disconnection from my own thoughts, as though I wasn't sure where I was. I sat on the settee, taking a moment to pull myself together.

When I felt well enough to rejoin the festivities, I found my students huddled near the ballroom, whispering amongst themselves. Simon Hayes approached me first. He was particularly handsome in his finely tailored black coat and trousers, a crisp white shirt, a gray brocade waistcoat, a matching cravat, and a gold pocket watch hanging from a gold chain. His fair hair was neatly parted on the side and brushed away from his face. He looked less like a Nordic prince and more like an actor preparing to perform in a costume drama. Instead of seeming overly formal in the tight-fitting clothing, he looked more relaxed than I had ever seen him, as if this era, the nineteenth century, was where he truly belonged.

"Welcome, Professor Ferrars. We're glad you're here." He bowed in a gentlemanly manner, then extended his hand, which I shook politely. "Eventide Manor is rather fine, isn't it? Mr. Grimshaw is always so generous about hosting the Poet of Eventide Ball."

I admired the marble statues, the antique vases, and the winding staircase. I gestured at Simon's fine attire. "Heavens, Mr. Hayes. What a difference a day makes."

Simon's voice, already old-money, took on an affected quality, as if striving for an aristocratic English accent but not quite finding it, like film actors in the 1930s. "Thank you, Professor. I do look forward to the ball every year, and I shall miss it when I'm no longer a student here." He led me toward the south-facing windows with a fine view of the bay.

I caught her jasmine scent before I saw her. Maeve stood from a wing chair and extended her hand in an old-fashioned gesture, which I took gravely as I bowed. Her dark hair was curled and pinned with violets, while her lavender silk ball gown fell in graceful lines, though the crinoline hampered her movements and she had to step carefully in her short-heeled shoes.

"You look lovely, Ms. Lang."

She waved her fan before her face and laughed. "Thank you, Professor. You look rather handsome yourself."

Simon excused himself to escort Amandine, lovely in

ivory, to the refreshment table. I watched them with some curiosity.

An upbeat swell of a quadrille soared from the ballroom. Then the musicians, also in nineteenth-century garb, played something by Haydn I couldn't place. Professors and students waltzed across the ballroom like a scene from a historical film. Candlelight from crystal candelabras flickered, the room shimmering as though it breathed. Ladies, students and professors alike, brushed past, their skirts rustling like whispers. Debbie danced with Leonard, old animosities forgotten, for that night, at least. Her peacock-blue taffeta gown suited her, and her face lit up as she laughed. Amandine, her ivory dress swinging behind her, looked rather like a Rossetti painting as Simon swung her to the rhythm of the music. She beamed at him with an expression of adoration. Elise Spencer, the bird-like professor of nineteenth-century British literature, danced with her bird-like husband. Stephen Trevelyan danced with his wife, who was younger than I had expected.

Maeve stood beside me as she scanned the room with quiet alertness. I bowed in courtly fashion and extended my hand. "May I claim the next waltz, Ms. Lang? If you don't mind that I'm a rather inept dancer, that is."

Her expression, though proper for a nineteenth-century lady, held a glint of mischief. "I'd be delighted, Professor." She dipped into a graceful curtsy.

The next waltz was the *Valse des Roses*. I offered Maeve my arm and led her to the dance floor. The music rose, and we turned. Around us swirled lace, satin, champagne-heightened laughter, and floral perfumes mingled with wax and old wood. Simon, standing with his back against the wall, didn't take his eyes off us. Rather, he didn't take his eyes from Maeve.

"You're rather graceful, Ms. Lang. I'm afraid I can't say the same for myself."

"Don't worry, Professor. You're holding your own."

She smiled, and for a fleeting moment, I forgot the other dancers and the weight of Thomas's horrific death. For that moment, there was only music, and turning, and laughter, and the way the light caught the amber in her eyes.

After I had embarrassed myself enough on the dance floor, we went to the library and sat in leather wing chairs near the roaring fire. Maeve drank tea from a dainty porcelain cup while we watched the others enjoying the night. Though it was the middle of October and cold outside, the many guests and the fires lit in every room meant that Eventide Manor was beginning to feel like the tropics. We wandered through the long hall lined with what looked like family portraits, perhaps from the original owner of the house, Cornelius Eventide. I was fascinated by the aristocratic faces, some male, some female, some older, some younger, but all with a similarity of feature that was hard to miss. I stood before one particular portrait of a woman, her dark hair parted down the middle and curling at her ears, her heart-shaped face serious but not unkind, until I felt a hand on my shoulder turning me away. It was Rhys Grimshaw, dressed in a black tailcoat with a resplendent emerald green waistcoat. He extended his gloved hand to Maeve.

"Maeve, I'm so pleased to see you. How are you finding the ball this year?"

"I think it may be the best ball I've seen since I've been at EC, Mr. Grimshaw."

"Mr. Grimshaw. What nonsense, my dear. We're friends now, so I expect you to call me Rhys. I'm so pleased that you're enjoying the ball." He turned his warm smile on me. "I'm so happy to finally speak to you, Professor Ferrars. I know we've seen each other, and we had that fun chat at the colloquium, but we haven't had a chance to sit down and talk."

"I'm glad to speak to you as well, Mr. Grimshaw. I owe the funding of my position to you, I believe."

"We should have the greatest literary minds at Eventide College, and funding the Geddes chair is my way of ensuring that happens. EC has always had a very special place in my heart, a very special place indeed. And I insist that you call me Rhys if I may call you Jonathan."

"Certainly." I gestured at our surroundings. "This is a fine place you have here. Did you buy it from the Eventide family?"

"I bought it from an investor who decided not to pursue the renovations. The house had been neglected and had gone into some disrepair after the last member of the Eventide family left. I've loved Southshore for as long as I can remember, and I was planning on making my home here again, so I took Eventide Manor as my residence."

"This is certainly the perfect place for a nineteenth-century ball. It rather reminds me of a museum."

"I was compelled to return the old house to its former glory. It was quite something in the days of Cornelius. To many, the house was out in the sticks of Maine, nowhere near the society of Boston or New York. Cornelius loved entertaining his friends, though, and he always managed to draw quite a crowd to stay during the summer and the Christmas holidays. He knew many of the great literary and scientific minds of the nineteenth century—Mitchell, Gray, Maury, Emerson, Fuller, even Poe himself was an acquaintance. Many of them visited him here at Eventide Manor."

I looked toward the back of the long hallway and saw a closed door. Noting my curiosity, Rhys smiled.

"Just some construction in the room behind the library. Nothing can ever be quite perfect in an old house like this."

"You're very generous in opening your home to us."

"It's my pleasure. The ball is always so highly anticipated, and it's the highlight of our English department calendar. If dressing up in nineteenth-century clothing and dancing in a nineteenth-century setting brings some joy, especially in these dark times, then I'm highly gratified to be able to do it." For a moment, he reminded me of a mute, a paid actor of grief. All he needed was a black sash around his waist. He shook his head, and his face crumpled. "Poor, dear Thomas. He should be here with us tonight, but I know he would have wanted us to press on." As quickly as his face darkened, it brightened again. He nodded at Stephen and Lavinia as they wandered toward us. "Ah, Professor Trevelyan, Professor Cruz. How magnificent you both look." He smiled at Stephen's charcoal frock coat and perfectly knotted cravat. "Stephen, I'm half expecting you to pull out a pocket watch and quote Tennyson."

Stephen's smile seemed sincere, perhaps for the second time that term. He did, in fact, pull out a pocket watch, and we laughed. He slipped the watch back into place and adjusted his coat. "I considered bringing my annotated *In Memoriam* but decided it might be a bit excessive."

"Nothing is too excessive when it comes to Tennyson, my friend. He's one of my favorites."

And then I heard it.

The Gentleman of Shadows.

Like an ancient echo reverberating across centuries.

The Gentleman of Shadows.

The voice, vaguely recognizable, shattered something deep within me, something long forgotten, and a hollow terror shook me. I searched the nearby faces for the speaker. Stephen and Rhys were still speaking about Tennyson. Others paid no attention to me. I shook my head, fearful that my sanity, already fragile since arriving in Maine, was detaching from itself once and for all. Debbie's laughter helped bring me back to myself. She grabbed Rhys's gloved hands in hers.

"Yet another magnificent ball, Rhys." He brought her white-gloved hand to his lips. "You never cease to amaze me. Every year you seem to outdo yourself." She gestured at the flickering sconces on the walls and the garlands of ivy and white roses draping the handrail of the winding staircase. "I always feel as though I've stepped into a Brontë novel when I'm here for the ball."

Lavinia accepted a cup of tea from a server in livery. "Hopefully without the madwoman in the attic."

Rhys laughed as though that were the funniest thing he had heard all night. "Ha ha, my dear, no, there are no madwomen here. At least not in the attic." He winked at Maeve, who dropped her eyes.

Elise Spencer chirped in. "Oh no, Debbie, not a Brontë novel. You mean Jane Austen when you're referring to balls."

"You're right, Elise. I do mean Austen. Perhaps I'll meet my very own Mr. Darcy tonight." Debbie smiled sweetly at Rhys, who smiled sweetly back.

Cordelia, dramatic in black velvet and a cameo at her throat, wandered in with Oliver, who chose a more bohemian interpretation of the theme with his loose white shirt, paisley waistcoat, and a velvet artist's cravat. He looked as if he'd wandered out of the Pre-Raphaelite Brotherhood. He and Amandine would have made quite a pair that night.

"I can barely breathe in this corset," Cordelia muttered as she munched on a cucumber sandwich.

"That's the authentic experience," Oliver said.

"Thank God I live now." Cordelia put her sandwich on a side table and tugged at her middle. "How did those women live like this?"

"By fainting every five minutes and being called insubstantial and weak. Don't worry, Deelie. I have smelling salts in case you keel over."

"Thanks, Oliver."

Simon navigated toward us, balancing two cups of tea. He handed one cup to Maeve, which she accepted.

The musicians shifted into another waltz, and Rhys moved to the center of the room, raising his voice enough to carry. "Who will join me for the dance?"

Lavinia stepped forward with an outstretched hand and an amused grin. "I would be more than happy to accompany you, Rhys."

He extended his arm in a gallant gesture, and as they left for the ballroom, other couples formed. Leonard and Debbie appeared to be having quite a night in each other's company, fueled by repeated glasses of champagne, and they too left for the ballroom. Stephen gallantly approached Amandine, who smiled coquettishly as she accepted. Oliver bowed theatrically to Cordelia, who rolled her eyes, though she beamed as she took his arm. Simon presented his arm to Maeve, and they walked onto the floor together.

After the waltz ended, Maeve was back by my side. I nodded toward three newcomers, business-looking women in fashionable modern pantsuits standing apart from the rest of us, drinking champagne with their heads pressed together in conversation, bearing a striking similarity to a chimera.

"Who are they?" I asked.

"Literary agents from New York," Maeve said. "They come every year to meet the new Poet of Eventide. They almost always sign the new poet laureate to a contract." She pushed a curl from her face.

"Are you nervous about reading your poem tonight?"

"I think I'm ready. But it's so strange, isn't it? All of us are here, in fancy dress, enjoying ourselves, while poor Thomas lies dead in a morgue. He should be here to read his poem. It doesn't seem right without him."

"If I've learned anything, it's that we have to grasp whatever joy we can when it's there. Life is too unpredictable.

There's too much that we can't control. Sometimes we're going along fine, taking our joy for granted, and then the next day it's gone forever." I turned away. "I shouldn't have said that. I'm sorry." I looked for the door. "It's getting a little warm in here. If you'll excuse me, I'd like to go outside to get some air."

Maeve curtsied, and I dodged around other guests to the open door and the autumn-crisp night. The storm had passed, the sky layered with gradients of gray, the full moon there to commune with. What would I tell her, the moon? How could I express my sorrow over recent events? A few other guests found their way outside, the ladies pulling their shawls closer around their shoulders, the men shivering in the breeze.

"You look as if you belong in this era."

Rhys stood near the front door. As the other guests returned inside, he greeted each of them with a slight bow that would have done any nineteenth-century gentleman proud.

"I've certainly studied the nineteenth century long enough to feel comfortable in similar environs."

"As you know, Professor Ferrars, I've read your work on Poe, and I was rather impressed."

"I know that you're a Poe scholar yourself. Debbie showed me your research into the different variations of The Raven. I found it fascinating."

"These days, I find myself curious about biographical criticism, the intersection of an author's biography and the interpretation of their literary works. I'm fully aware of the argument that an author's biography is irrelevant because it's only the words on the page that matter. Where do you stand, Professor?"

"I don't agree with treating literature as if it were created in a vacuum. Writers are people, and they can't help but put their own experiences into their writing. By leaving the human being outside of the literature they create, you're also leaving out the context in which the stories were written, which leaves for a weaker understanding of the text."

He waited for me to continue, so I did.

"There are times when an author's biography can provide clues about their writing. Knowing that many of the women in Poe's life died young goes a long way in explaining his preoccupation with the death of young women. Poe said, 'The death of a beautiful woman is, unquestionably, the most poetical topic in the world.' He examined the subject of death in his writing since he couldn't do it any other way." I smiled. "Forgive me. I appear to be waxing poetic on the subject of Edgar Poe, though I suppose that's what you're paying me for."

"Don't apologize. I'm pleased to know that after all this time, Poe is still a topic of fascination for you. While I agree with everything you say, I think that our friend has become more of a myth than a man. Poe was reserved, brilliant, fragile, and formidable. He was a gentleman whose conversation was a privilege, even if we had to tread carefully since he was so easily bruised. The man's intellect was as sharp as any I have known. Too many scholars love to cite alcoholism, drug abuse, necrophilia, or insanity when the reality is much more complicated."

"That is the most accurate assessment of Poe I've heard in some time."

"I'm pleased you think so. The fact that he quenched his need for revenge through fiction is probably a good thing."

"Are you a fan of Jacobean revenge tragedies?"

He laughed heartily. In the shadows, his ordinary features became menacing.

"Who doesn't love a good revenge tragedy? Madness, murder, death, moral ambiguity. They're brilliant."

"And an occasional ghost or two."

"Ah, indeed. *Hamlet* is an excellent example. Though Poe's

The Cask of Amontillado wasn't written in the time of King James I, it is still a quintessential revenge tale."

"If you like stories about pride, deception, and punishment."

"I do indeed. The Cask of Amontillado is the description of a perfect crime."

Leaning into the light from the streetlamp, he seemed an ordinary man again. He led us back inside, where he disappeared into the crowd, and I found my way to the refreshment table. Professors and students noticed me and bowed and curtsied with good humor. I couldn't help but bow back. I joined a polite discussion about nineteenth-century authors from both sides of the Atlantic. Servers in livery offered guests trays with an assortment of cakes. Guests ate their cakes and drank bergamot-scented tea between glasses of champagne. Soon the topic turned to the main event, which was the poetry reading and the crowning of the new Poet of Eventide.

Maeve and Rhys appeared, coming out of the drawing room together. They were chatting pleasantly. In a chivalrous move, Rhys brought Maeve's gloved hand to his lips.

"You are enchanting, as always, my dear Maeve," Rhys said.

"I'm happy to help," Maeve answered.

Debbie arrived, putting her arm through Rhys's, leading him toward the ballroom, while Maeve joined me near the staircase. I wasn't going to ask, it was none of my business, but she said, "Rhys asked me to do a reading for him. He knows I'm a conduit. I shouldn't have told you that. I can't tell you anything about the reading. Whatever I learn about someone is private."

"Of course."

She sighed. "The police questioned me about you, Professor. I wasn't going to say anything because I didn't want to worry you, but they asked because the only time you were at Simon's was the night Thomas was killed."

"What did they want to know?"

"Where you were before you came to Eventide and who your family and friends are." She watched as Simon and Amandine slid across the ballroom floor. "I told them that you were at Yale and your wife had died. They asked me if I knew how she died, and I said I didn't." She turned her back to the rest of the room and whispered. "The police told me that they're treating Thomas's death as murder. Something about the way his throat was sliced," she shuddered, "the angle or something, it couldn't have been self-inflicted. Someone must have cut his throat and thrown him through the window." We must have looked like two spies in a TV show, meeting in a park, pretending not to know each other. "I told you there's dark magic at work at Eventide. I think that dark magic is responsible."

"For Thomas?"

Her voice dropped so low that it sank beneath the thrumming of the music. "I haven't been able to read anything from anyone that points me in the direction of Thomas's killer." She paused, her amber eyes searching mine. "I haven't found any clues."

"Let the police do their job, Ms. Lang. You shouldn't get involved in this."

"I was the closest thing to a friend Thomas had. Everyone thought he was in love with me, but I think it was just that he felt comfortable with me when he didn't with anyone else, so he gravitated toward me."

I thought of what Thomas had said on that score, but I kept quiet. It was none of my business anyway.

Debbie appeared at the top of the spiral staircase, her silver hair glowing under the gaslight. She tapped a spoon against a crystal goblet, the dulcet tones echoing, and everyone quieted.

"Welcome to our annual Poet of Eventide Ball, hosted by our generous benefactor, Mr. Rhys Grimshaw."

Rhys stood at the top of the staircase, and the polite applause became thunderous appreciation. With exaggerated humility, he waved the cheers away. He scanned the crowd, a king acknowledging his loyal subjects, bestowing benevolence and goodwill. Our eyes locked, and he bowed. The professors closest to me nodded, as though that acknowledgment from Rhys made me an official member of the department. When the applause died down, he spoke.

"Welcome to this year's Poet of Eventide Ball. Tonight we meet in mournful circumstances. I know many of you thought that we should have postponed or even cancelled this year's ball due to the loss of our dear student, Thomas Lambert, but I believe going forward is the right thing. As students of literature, we understand the battle of life. Under such struggles, we can be cowed, or we can be courageous. Thomas would have wanted the Poet of Eventide Ball to go on as planned." He paused for polite applause.

"And now, we proceed to our main event. The three finalists for this year's Poet of Eventide are Simon Hayes, Maeve Lang, and Cordelia Reed." More polite applause. "Our three talented finalists will read one of the poems they submitted as part of their portfolios. Our reigning Poet of Eventide, Henry Feldstein, will be our Master of Ceremonies tonight. In addition, Henry will read one of the poems Thomas Lambert submitted. Young Thomas was one of the finalists, and he should have been here tonight. Although Thomas is no longer with us, he will always remain in our hearts. Then we'll conclude our evening with the naming of our new poet laureate."

"Who got bumped up because Thomas is gone?" Stephen whispered.

"Cordelia," Lavinia answered. "Cordelia was in fourth

place. With Thomas in the morgue, she was promoted to third, so she gets to read tonight."

Henry Feldstein appeared, handsome in his early nineteenth-century costume of pantaloons, coat, white linen shirt, and white linen neckcloth.

"Ladies and gentlemen," Henry said. "Can we please take a moment of silence in remembrance of my friend, Thomas Lambert?"

I wasn't aware that Thomas had any friends other than Maeve, but grief makes for strange bedfellows. After we bowed our heads, Henry introduced the three finalists—Simon, Cordelia, and Maeve. Simon and Cordelia's poems were fine, precisely what I would have expected, similar to what I heard that fateful night. Their poems were full of other voices since they hadn't yet found their own. Maeve read an emotional sonnet about the challenges of being different from those around you, and it was lovely. Then Henry Feldstein read Thomas's poem. Sobs filled the Great Hall as he read.

"And now, ladies and gentlemen, administration, faculty, and students, it is my honor to announce..." Henry paused, and not a sound was heard, "that Simon Hayes is our new poet laureate of Eventide College. Congratulations to our newest Poet of Eventide."

Simon. Not Maeve. So much for my vote.

I found Maeve near the refreshments, sipping a cup of tea.

"I'm sorry you're not the new Poet of Eventide. I voted for you."

"Thank you, Professor. It's okay. I had a feeling Simon would win. Thomas was argumentative, but he wasn't always wrong."

"Money and connections might open doors, but in time those doors will slam shut if there's no talent. Some writers begin with an edge because they have wealthy parents, like Simon, or a wealthy spouse. Poe was adopted into a wealthy family, but John Allan cut him off, so Poe was forced to make his own way in the world."

"He didn't do a very good job of it."

"No, he didn't. He died in poverty. Yet we still appreciate him for being one of the most influential authors in American literature."

"It's all right, Professor, really. I wasn't expecting to win. I wasn't even going to apply, but I thought I'd regret it later if I didn't at least try. I tried, and it didn't happen, and that's okay. It's better than not trying at all."

"That is the attitude that will get you far in life, Ms. Lang."

Cordelia and Oliver stayed behind, whispering, while they threw stone-like glares at Simon, who was engrossed in a conversation with the chimera who were likely going to take him on. Debbie stood beside Simon, nodding at whatever they said, beaming like a proud mother.

Maeve tugged my sleeve. "Where's Amandine?"

"Perhaps she left."

"I've been standing by the door, and I didn't see her leave."

"She must be around here somewhere."

After the announcement of the new Poet of Eventide, the festivities slowed. The hours had taken their toll. Those who had been bright-eyed and glowing from the excitement drooped. Satin slippers dragged, smiles shrank, hair feathers sagged. As guests took their leave, they seemed to throw the anxieties they had left at the threshold back over their shoulders like suffocating shrouds. Eventide Manor was nearly empty by then. But there was no sign of Amandine. I walked into the library in search of her. Instead of Amandine, I saw Debbie and Rhys embracing. I turned away as quickly as I could, but I had been spotted.

"Oh, Jonathan!" Debbie patted her lips as if checking her

lipstick. "I was just thanking Rhys for yet another fabulous ball."

"Of course."

As I walked back to the door, I felt a presence by my side. Rhys looked as if nothing out of the ordinary had happened.

"I'm so glad we finally had a chance to speak tonight, Jonathan. In fact, I'd like to continue our conversation. Did you know that I lived in Baltimore near Westminster Hall and Burying Ground for a while? I visited Poe's grave often."

"It's good that he was reburied." I scanned the few remaining guests for Amandine but did not see her. "He deserved better than an unmarked grave."

"He would have preferred the pauper's grave himself."

"Do you think? He always seemed rather sure of himself, as if he understood his place in literature even if no one else did at the time."

"That's why you and I need to meet again. I do enjoy speaking of Poe with those who also found him fascinating."

"I would like that."

Maeve stood outside, shivering with only a thin cloak to cover her.

"Have you found Amandine?"

She shook her head. "Should we be worried, Professor? I mean, after Thomas?"

The chimera left, so we—Maeve, Simon, Oliver, Cordelia, Stephen, his wife, and I—were the last guests. Rhys joined us near the door.

"Is everything all right?" Rhys asked. "Maeve? You look as if you've seen a ghost."

Oliver scanned the hallway, empty now except for the hired help there to clean. "I don't see her."

"Just because we didn't see her leave doesn't mean she didn't slip out when no one was looking."

"I'm sure Professor Ferrars is right," said Rhys. "I'm sure Amandine is fine."

"No," said Cordelia. "Amandine was supposed to come back to Cavendish Hall with Oliver and me. We arrived together, and we were supposed to leave together."

"Maybe that's why she left so suddenly," said Stephen. "She wanted to get away from you." His wife scowled at him.

"I'm going to find Amandine," said Cordelia. "You can do what you want."

We split up, with Maeve and me searching the rooms downstairs while Rhys, Cordelia, and Oliver went upstairs. Simon followed Stephen and his wife out the door.

Maeve and I searched the drawing room, the ballroom, the library, and the basement kitchen. I paused outside the door where Rhys said there was construction and turned away, guessing there was nothing to see there. A sliding glass door led to the garden, so we stepped outside. Even at that late autumn hour, the flowers put on a show. Blue anemones and red hydrangeas lined the borders, while chrysanthemums echoed the yellows, oranges, and reds of the overhanging trees. The backyard was vast, stretching into the forested area.

"Amandine?" I called.

"Amandine?" Maeve echoed. She squinted into the darkness. "Do you think we ought to call the police?"

"More than likely, she's gone home. I'm sure we're worrying for nothing."

Maeve pulled her shawl closer around her shoulders and shivered.

"You're not really dressed for this weather, Ms. Lang."

"I don't own a Victorian-style coat, and my hoodies didn't quite go with the gown."

Eventide Manor was gloomy in the silence.

"Where do you live, Ms. Lang? With everything that's going on, I'd like to see that you get home in one piece."

"I'm in Cavendish Hall."

No one else was around when we walked away.

Fourteen

Truth is not always in a well. In fact, as regards the more important knowledge, I do believe that she is invariably superficial.

We passed professors and students on Southshore Road who were cutting a fine show in their nineteenth-century finery. They chatted away, reliving the festivities, recounting the food, the champagne, the music, the dancing, and the new Poet of Eventide. For me, the joy of the ball already felt far away.

"I hope Amandine is all right," Maeve said.

"I know we're all expecting the worst because of what happened to Thomas, but I'm sure she's fine."

"Actually, we still don't know what happened to Thomas. Why are the police being so quiet about their investigation?"

"I wish I knew."

The Queen Anne mansion of Cavendish Hall beckoned with bright electric lights, a stark contrast to the glowing gaslight of Eventide Manor. English students blundered into the building with laughter buoyed by champagne and good spirits. Maeve and I stood on the lawn, watching the others pass, while the trees shuddered under the heavy weight of the whipping winds, the rust and lemon-colored leaves dropping skittishly to the ground.

"There's something you need to see, Professor. It's, well, it's a secret, I think. I don't think I'm supposed to know about it. Will you come?" Without waiting for my reply, she walked toward campus. She must have seen the indecision on my face. "Do you know about the underground library?"

She had my attention. "It sounds like something from an Agatha Christie story."

"One night, about a week before Thomas was killed, I couldn't sleep, so I went for a walk and ended up on campus. I saw Thomas going into the library."

"The underground library?"

"No, just the Chisolm. It was long past closing, though, and everything was dark. He pulled a key from his coat pocket and used it to unlock the door. He was in there for some time, and then he came out, went around the back, and disappeared."

"Disappeared as in *poof*?"

"Disappeared as in I couldn't see him anywhere. Then I saw him hiding behind a tree, hunched over, his hands on his knees, and he was panting as if he couldn't breathe. I wanted to call out to him, ask him if he needed help, but there was something about the way he was holding himself, like he was trying to hide, so I stayed quiet. I went back the next night, but I couldn't get into the Chisolm because it was closed and I didn't have a key."

The beam of the full moon was muffled under a blanket of wool-like clouds. The campus was deserted, the neighborhood silent. Instead of walking up the steps to the Chisholm

Library, we went around the back to the grassy knoll where students liked to drink coffee and read between classes. When we arrived at the back door, Maeve pulled a key from her reticule. She smirked when she showed it to me.

"I told Thomas the next day that I had seen him. That's when he told me about the underground library, and he gave me the key."

"Where did he get it?"

"He didn't exactly say. He also gave me the passcode for the alarm. He told me he thought I should keep the key, just in case."

"Just in case? Did he think someone was after him?"

"I don't know. He didn't say. But then Thomas kept a lot to himself."

She used the key to open the door, then punched the numbers into the alarm system on the wall. I may have peeked at the code. She led me to the back of the library, behind the circulation desk, and we went through a door and then down a staircase to the basement. She opened another door, and we walked into an open space that looked like an abandoned office. A few scattered chairs and a desk were all that remained. Another door stood closed at the far end of the room. "There's a tunnel through there. After Thomas died, I came to take a look at it. I was wondering if there was something here he wanted me to see."

"That was dangerous, Ms. Lang."

"Maybe. But I was curious. When I came the first time, I got to the end of the tunnel, but I heard voices. I was too far to hear what they were saying, but I could tell they were arguing. I didn't want them to see me, so I left. I went back the next night, and no one was there, so I had a chance to look around. It's really rather fascinating."

"Did you tell the police what you just told me?" Maeve

shook her head. "Someone killed Thomas. Perhaps more than one someone. If he was sneaking around the library and someone saw him, that could have something to do with why he was killed."

"I can't imagine anyone from EC being that brutal."

"Sometimes people don't realize how much violence they have within them until they're pushed to their limit."

Maeve opened the door. I stiffened, expecting an alarm to sound, but nothing. The space was just wide enough for one person to pass. There was nothing immediately to fear except a thin metal ladder, which didn't seem too dangerous. I gripped the ladder and stepped down, one slow foot at a time, as my eyes adjusted to the dimness. What the hell am I doing? I wondered as I descended deeper into the black hole. Maeve followed, stepping carefully in her ball gown and low-heeled shoes. When we were both at the bottom, she put a finger to her lips. Anyone could have been there—the police, Thomas's murderer, anyone.

"The light is here." Maeve flipped a switch, and electric lights, white against the darkness of the tunnel, illuminated the way. Was there whispering? I was certain that I heard half-remembered tales calling to us, begging us to know them. Then I heard it. *The Gentleman of Shadows*. I brushed it aside with the thought that my mind was playing tricks on me. As we neared the end of the tunnel, a stone door creaked and swung open. Maeve jumped back. Above the archway, it said *Rex Quisque Habet Regnum*. Every king has his reign.

"Are you sure you want to do this, Ms. Lang?"

Maeve looked more certain than I felt. We stepped through the doorway into a cavernous room, windowless, close, as though the place had never known fresh air. The room was lit by candles and gaslight. Dust scattered and cobwebs covered the walls. The scent was unmistakable—aged paper, rotting leather, and something sweet and metallic, like iron, a scent I recognized but Maeve didn't seem to notice. I chose not to draw her attention to it. Towering black bookshelves groaned beneath the weight of ancient tomes—scrolls, codices, grimoires, tablets, and books from the earliest days of the printing press. Some cloth-bound volumes showed gilded spines etched in Ancient Greek or Latin, while others revealed sigils and forgotten alphabets. In the center of the room was a long obsidian table, its glass top scratched with cryptic shapes and diagrams, graffiti-like scratches, as if someone had etched their notes into the furniture. Some of the books were filled with marginalia in a language that looked like German, perhaps, or Old Norse. In the center of the table stood a candelabrum, its white candles burned nearly to their nubs. I thought I had stepped into another dimension.

"May I help you, sir?"

The man's voice was as wizened as his face. He was of medium height, slim and well-built, as though he had cut quite a fine figure in his younger days. He would have fit in quite nicely at our nineteenth-century ball with his black coat, blue waistcoat, pressed white shirt, and black trousers. His thin white hair appeared in tufts across his head. There was something about his pallor, ghostly and waxen, that appeared ghoulish in the gaslight. He stepped closer, inspecting my features. "I have been expecting you."

I struggled to place his face, but couldn't. "I don't believe we've met."

"Your name, sir?"

"Jonathan Ferrars."

He closed his eyes, and his eyelids fluttered as though racing through a list of names in the Rolodex inside his head.

"I do not know a Jonathan Ferrars."

"You must be thinking of someone else."

He didn't press the point, so I let it drop. It took me a

moment to place his accent. It was German, or at least I guessed it was German. "Since you know my name, perhaps I could know yours?"

"Elias Venn, sir. The librarian."

"Of course."

He didn't appear to notice Maeve, who was standing near the tallest bookcase, examining the titles.

"Would you like a tour, sir?" Elias Venn asked.

Curiosity killed the cat, my father used to say. One of these days, perhaps I'll listen. I turned to Maeve, and she nodded.

"Certainly."

"Very good, sir. Please to follow me."

He led us into the next chamber, which looked more like a museum with its artifacts lining the shelves.

"Is this the special collection of the Chisholm Library?"

"You might call this a special collection, sir. Only the most sought-after knowledge can be found here."

"I see."

I didn't see, but it seemed the best answer. Venn showed us a beautiful gold scroll-shaped hand mirror, like a treasure from the Palace of Versailles, stored in a velvet-lined box. He held up the mirror, and when I stepped back, he smiled. "Looking into this mirror reveals not one's reflection, but a scene from the past."

"What kind of scene from the past?" Maeve asked.

Venn looked at Maeve as though noticing her for the first time.

"A scene that would break your heart to remember." He held it out to me, but I didn't reach for it. He smiled again. "Quite right, sir. As tempting as this beautiful object may be, repeated use leads to insomnia, hallucinations, and paranoia."

He brought our attention to a heavy book bound in time-worn leather. He flipped through it so we could see that the pages had been overwritten dozens of times. I tried to make sense of the scribbles, but it was gibberish to me. Venn opened another book, and there, in a fine calligraphy hand, Maeve and I read, *Do not trust the one who reads this next.* Since we would not see who read the book next, we would not know whom we shouldn't trust. Rather clever, actually.

Elias Venn gestured to a jagged iron key hanging from the wall on a strip of leather. "Touching this key induces a trance-like state, sir. Some who have worn it claimed to hear whispers giving commands."

There were other artifacts as well, including a smooth, egg-sized stone. When I stood over it, an iron-smelling red liquid seeped onto the shelf. Maeve watched it pulse and backed away.

"According to eighteenth-century sources, sir, that stone feeds on memories."

Maeve leaned over a leather diary bound with silver clasps. "What is this?"

"The writer claimed he opened the book and saw the end."

"The end of what?"

Elias Venn waved his white hand as though the answer should be obvious.

"Some books are not meant to be opened. Once readers begin down the path of seeking forbidden knowledge, they become obsessed, unable to stop until they know it all. But one can never know everything. Knowledge, human or otherwise, is not quantifiable and therefore cannot be contained. Even in a library." He bared his long eyeteeth, and his grin seemed more like a growl. "Many have tried to capture the most elusive knowledge. All have failed or gone mad trying. Such quests don't lead to more knowledge. They reveal what becomes of knowledge when you take it too far. I tried to tell him. I tried to explain, but he insisted. He could not, or would not, understand. But I am his friend, you see. In truth, I am his only friend. He has been good to me in his way, so if he asks for my assistance, I must do all that I can for him."

"Who?" Maeve asked.

Venn looked a little too eagerly at Maeve. I didn't care for the way he was leaning toward her, biting his lower lip. She clutched her shawl close to her chin as I moved closer to her, ready to protect her if need be. The whey-faced librarian stepped away, watching us.

"That was fascinating, Mr. Venn. This is, well, this is certainly a library. You have some fine artifacts here."

"Certainly, sir."

"Do scholars use this library for research?"

"Oh no, sir. The knowledge here is strictly forbidden."

"Forbidden?"

"There are no visitors allowed here."

"But we're visitors."

"As you say, sir."

After another leer at Maeve, Venn slammed the door in our faces. We climbed up the ladder, made our way back through the main part of the Chisholm Library, and out the back door, which Maeve locked before returning the key to her reticule. We stood under a street lamp, both of us staring at Eventide College as though we no longer recognized it.

"What on earth just happened?" Maeve asked. "Who was that strange man?"

"He was Elias Venn, the librarian."

We must have looked a sight, our nineteenth-century finery dusty and disheveled. We walked in silence. Maeve seemed distracted, her eyes staring everywhere except in front of her, as though she were afraid that Elias Venn, librarian, might jump out from the shadows. The thought had crossed my mind as I too scanned the darkness. We stopped outside Cavendish Hall.

"Perhaps you should stay above ground from now on, Ms. Lang."

She nodded, still distracted, as she went inside.

I was awakened by a persistent banging on my front door, which I opened to find a uniformed police officer and a man in a brown suit with no tie, his white button-down shirt open at the collar. Officer Yellin was a young man in a uniform perhaps one size too big for him. The man in a suit introduced himself as Detective William Strongwater. Strongwater was a tall, well-built man with long salt and pepper hair pulled into a neat ponytail.

"Professor Ferrars." Yellin's voice was frustrated, as were his tight eyes. "We've been trying to get in touch with you since this morning."

"Is something wrong?"

"Where were you last night?"

"I was at the ball at Eventide Manor."

"And afterwards?"

"I beg your pardon?"

"Where were you after the ball?"

Great, I thought. How could I explain that my student and I were alone together in a creepy underground library? I could tell them, of course. It wasn't as if they couldn't search the library for themselves. Perhaps they could make sense of Venn. Instead, I lied.

"I was tired after the ball, so I came home and went to sleep."

"It's after 6 p.m., Professor. Are you just waking up now?"

"Yes."

"Can anyone verify when you arrived home last night?"

"I live alone."

"Rhys Grimshaw said he saw you leave the ball with one of your students, Maeve Lang."

"That's right."

"Where did you go with Miss Lang?"

"I walked her back to her lodgings at Cavendish Hall."

"And?"

"And?"

"What did you do afterwards?"

"I came here and went to sleep."

"And didn't wake up until nearly 6 p.m.?"

"Yes."

One thing I learned from reading Mrs. Griggs's mystery novels is that the best lies are those that stick mainly to the truth. What I said was mostly true. I'm not sure why I didn't tell them about the library, or Venn. Perhaps because I didn't have time to consider the curiosities I saw. Perhaps I didn't tell them because I sensed that there were secrets in that library meant only for me. Perhaps I simply felt like being petty.

"Is this about Thomas Lambert's death? I've already given my statement at the police station."

Detective Strongwater stepped forward. He looked grim.

"I'm sorry to have to inform you, Professor Ferrars, that your student Amandine Wesson was found murdered last night."

Amandine. I had forgotten all about her.

"What happened?"

"One of your students, Oliver Chatterjee, was searching for her. He was concerned about her whereabouts after the death of Thomas Lambert. Mr. Chatterjee noticed a large amount of soot on the sitting room carpet. Upon further investigation, he discovered Ms. Wesson's body shoved up the chimney. When our team dislodged her, they discovered that she had been strangled."

"Up the chimney? That can't be."

"Why not?" Strongwater's voice wasn't unkind, but I could tell by his expression that he had already seen the same connection I made after Thomas's peculiar death. "Does her death remind you of something, Professor Ferrars? When you gave your statement after the death of Mr. Lambert, you said that you're teaching the Poe seminar at Eventide College this term. Surely it rings a bell."

"In the story The Murders in the Rue Morgue, Mademoiselle Camille is found choked and thrust up the chimney."

"And the odd circumstances of Mr. Lambert's death?"

"Madame L'Espanaye was found outside the house with her bones shattered and her throat cut so deeply that her head fell off when her body was moved."

"Which is what happened to Mr. Lambert. We'd like to speak to you down at the station, Professor Ferrars. Will you come?"

The October trees bowed under the weight of their colorful autumnal beauty, and kaleidoscope-colored leaves fluttered and swirled in a drifting dance. It was cold—a chill wind, or an ill wind, I wasn't certain. The sky was clear. Endless stars sparkled in the distance as though winking. If two of my students hadn't died, I might have said it was a beautiful night.

The police station on Randall Lane was three miles from campus. Detective Strongwater hadn't dropped his calm demeanor, and I wondered if that would change once we were at the station. We walked through the small offices, since the police force in Southshore consisted of one chief and three officers. The other officer on duty that night stood near his desk, where his small, box-like television showed the Giants versus the Phillies game. When Yellin passed, the officer grumbled about another Red Sox season of missed playoffs.

"They just won three years ago," Yellin said. "What else do you want?"

Detective Strongwater grimaced at Yellin as if baseball were not the most important thing at the moment.

"In here, please, Professor Ferrars."

Strongwater was joined by a young woman in a blue pantsuit, also from the Maine State Police, whom he introduced as Detective Anna Ji-Yeong. Strongwater gestured to the table, which looked similar to those I had seen on television, where the bad guys sit on one side and the good guys on the other, the good guys trying every trick they knew to get the bad guys to confess. Detective Strongwater took the lead.

"We needed to speak to you more formally, Professor Ferrars, because two of your students have been murdered in very particular ways. Can you tell us where you were last night?"

"At the ball at Eventide Manor with the rest of the English department."

"We understand that Ms. Wesson seemed to have disappeared toward the end of the night and some of the remaining guests searched for her. Did you help to look for Ms. Wesson?"

"I did."

"And you didn't see her?"

"No. Maeve and I looked downstairs and in the back garden, but she wasn't there."

"And you didn't find that strange?"

"I thought perhaps she left rather suddenly, but I didn't notice anything to make me suspicious. I guessed she had gone home when no one happened to see her."

"So you searched with Maeve Lang?"

"That's right."

Detective Strongwater consulted the file in front of him. "How would you say your students get along?"

"I'd say it's complicated. There have been various issues between them, but there are always clashes of personalities in cohorts. The students at Eventide College are highly competitive."

"How well do you know Ms. Lang?"

"I know her as well as any professor knows his students." Strongwater didn't blink as he waited for me to elaborate. When I said nothing more, he nodded.

"What did you do after you left the ball?"

"I walked Maeve to Cavendish Hall, and then I returned home."

"Why did you walk her home?"

"Because it was late, and I wanted to be sure she was safe."

"Did you know that Amandine Wesson was dead at the time?"

"I didn't know until you told me tonight."

"Were you afraid that whoever murdered Thomas Lambert might be on the lookout for another victim, and that's why you walked Ms. Lang home?"

"Not necessarily. I walked her home because it was late and dark, and some of the guests at the ball had been drinking rather heavily."

"Had you or Ms. Lang been drinking heavily?"

"I don't drink, and I only noticed Maeve drinking tea."

"What time did you leave?"

"I wasn't looking at my watch, but it was perhaps after midnight."

"How long after midnight?" Detective Ji-Yeong leaned back in her chair, her arms crossed over her chest, a disapproving look on her face. She would have done well in a televised police drama.

"I'm not sure. As I said, I didn't look at the time."

"And then you went to sleep?"

I did some quick numbers in my head.

"I was up for a while."

"Doing what?"

"Reading, I suppose. I went to sleep around dawn."

"And you slept all day until we arrived, which was after 6 p.m.?"

"Yes."

"Do you often keep such late hours, Professor?"

"Yes."

"A night owl?"

"Yes."

"And did anyone see you?"

"No. As I said, I live alone."

My alibi was flimsy at best, and if they were any good at their jobs, which I sensed they were, they had probably already guessed that I was lying about something. Again, I thought that I should come clean about the underground library. If I were going to tell them, that was the time. Perhaps they could make something of the dungeon-like rooms with the ancient-looking tomes flickering in the gaslight. But I stayed silent.

Strongwater looked through the file he held in his hands. "As I stated earlier, Professor Ferrars, we recognized the unusual way Thomas Lambert and Amandine Wesson were murdered. Can you tell us more about that?"

"From what you've told me, they both appear to have been murdered in the manner of the deaths in Edgar Poe's The Murders in the Rue Morgue."

"Isn't it a bit coincidental that two of your students were killed in the same way as Poe's characters?"

"Coincidental?"

"That students taking a Poe seminar should be murdered in the style of a Poe story?"

"I don't know if it's coincidental."

"Did you kill your students, Professor Ferrars?"

"No. Perhaps it was an orangutan."

Ji-Yeong looked ready to lay into me until Strongwater held up his hand.

"I've been doing this job long enough to never say never, even to orangutans. But then there's this other death we're concerned about." He opened an accordion file on the table beside him. "Did you know Professor Lawrence Presspitch?"

"No, but I've heard of him. He held the Geddes chair before me."

"Did you know he died?"

"Yes."

"Did you know he was murdered?"

"Murdered? I was told he died of a heart attack."

"Who told you that?"

"Leonard Harris. And Amandine said something about his heart giving out on him."

Strongwater nodded at Ji-Yeong, who wrote the information down.

"Upon the deaths of the two students, we thought it might be prudent to reexamine the post-mortem results for Dr. Presspitch. The official cause of death was a heart attack. Are you familiar with nitre?"

"Nitre? I don't think so."

"I think my question is, are you familiar with a Poe story that uses nitre?"

Nothing immediately sprang to mind. Then I remembered.

"The Cask of Amontillado. Montresor points out the nitre on the walls as he leads Fortunato to his death. Montresor feels that Fortunato belittled him, so Montresor decides to get his revenge. The nitre is not just a physical substance in the story. It represents deceit and danger, and it looks like a spider's web on the walls. Fortunato is caught in Montresor's web, which leads Fortunato to his demise. Fortunato begins to cough from the nitre, and in his weakened state and his drunkenness, Montresor buries Fortunato alive by building a wall around him in the catacombs where no one will hear his screams."

Strongwater nodded. "All this because of some slight Montresor felt."

"Poe was particular about revenge, in his stories as well as in his life. Why do you ask?"

"We have reason to believe that Lawrence Presspitch was murdered using potassium nitrate. Nitre, also known as..."

"Saltpeter. I remember now. It's a soft, white, highly soluble mineral found primarily in arid climates or cave deposits, like in Montresor's underground vault."

Ji-Yeong sent a meaningful glance Strongwater's way.

"That's right, Professor Ferrars. Nitre is the mineral form of potassium nitrate. Low doses aren't harmful, but high doses can cause methemoglobinemia, which is reduced oxygen in the blood, which could have caused the heart attack. There was a high dose of potassium nitrate in Dr. Presspitch's blood at the time of his death. You see, Professor, that makes three people at Eventide College who were murdered in the style of Poe's characters in two months."

"I'm afraid I didn't know Lawrence Presspitch. I'm familiar with his scholarship, but I didn't know him personally."

"Never met him at conferences?"

"Never."

"Do you know of any reason why anyone might want to hurt him? Or your students?"

"No."

"What was Thomas Lambert like as a student?" Ji-Yeong asked.

I told them the truth as far as I was able, that he could be difficult but he was also talented, though I had only been his professor since the beginning of the term and I didn't really know him that well. I chose not to tell them about the night he confronted me, thinking that information wasn't necessary under the circumstances. Ji-Yeong asked why I was at the study group the night Thomas was murdered. Once again, I explained that I had been invited to critique their poems. Had I noticed any tension between Mr. Lambert and the other students in the study group? I told them what happened that night: the arguments and the punch thrown. There seemed to be a certain animosity between all the students in one way or another, and I had been told about a particular rivalry between Thomas and Simon, which I had witnessed myself that night.

"Who told you that?" Ji-Yeong asked.

"Leonard Harris."

Again, Ji-Yeong wrote it down.

They had a few more questions for me, questions I had already answered when I gave my official statement after Thomas died, and they let me go. They seemed satisfied with my responses, for that moment anyway.

Walking home, the October night was calm, the wind fluttering like butterfly wings, the night-tide waves meandering to and from the shore like stolen kisses, the scent of autumn freshening the air. It was just as well that the night was calm since a squall raged within me. What began as a quiet term at a peaceful New England college was now a nightmare. It can be so easy for the innocent to appear guilty. One wrongly worded sentence, one importune action, and fingers point guilt at the guiltless. The weight of my secret hung like a noose around my neck, and I was overwhelmed by my lack of an alibi. I regretted not mentioning the underground library to Strongwater. I almost went back to tell him. Almost. What if Maeve tells the police about our visit to Mr. Venn? Well, I thought, then I'd have to come clean.

Back at the cottage, I paced the small study from window to door so many times that I felt the friction of the carpet as I wore a groove into the Turkish rug. Certainly, I would hear from Mrs. Griggs about it. I considered the questions the detectives had asked—and my answers. Strongwater had been kind in his way, and I hadn't felt pressured, as though they were trying to force a guilty secret out of me. They had their suspicions, but the direction of their inquiries didn't appear to include me—not yet, at least.

After Amandine's death, classes were cancelled for a week. Notices about the availability of mental health professionals were distributed. There was some discussion about cancelling the term, but students pushed back, arguing that such a move, especially for those close to completing their degrees, could prove disastrous. A week was chosen as appropriate, not that any time away could help us make sense of the brutality that descended like a beast upon this quiet corner of Maine.

During the week of mourning, I went to my office at my usual time. There was a police presence on campus, but I wanted to keep to some kind of routine in an attempt to stay focused. Lights were on in various windows in the red brick building of the Eliot School, showing life inside. I took the stairs to the fourth floor and let myself into my office. There were no open doors in my hallway, and I felt more alone than I had in some time. I turned on my computer but realized that I had no heart to work. I sat there, staring at the myriad of coffee stains like a Kandinsky painting on my desk. I remembered what Strongwater had said: that Presspitch had large amounts of potassium nitrate in his blood when he died. If someone had poisoned him, it was likely put into his coffee. He seemed to drink enough of it.

Leonard peeked around my open door. "Care for some company?" I gestured to the student chair, and he sighed as he sat. "I can't believe this. Now Amandine Wesson. On the night we were dancing and drinking champagne, that poor girl was being killed."

"How well did you know her?"

"She was in a couple of my classes. She could be jealous, like I said, but overall, I thought she was a good kid. Her literary talent might have been just okay, but she would have made a great lawyer."

"Do you think there are two murderers?"

"One for Thomas and another for Amandine? I was just wondering the same thing myself. Although they may have a suspect. I heard from Debbie that the police kept Simon Hayes overnight. His wealthy parents are on their way back from Europe, and they got him a top-notch attorney. Do you think he did it?"

"I honestly don't know. My instinct tells me no, but then none of us can really know another person. I know there was antagonism between the students, but this seems excessive for academic rivalry."

"Not at Eventide, it isn't."

"Students have murdered each other to be the next poet laureate?"

"Well." He watched me shut down my computer. "Maybe they haven't gone that far, but they've bribed assistants to lose things like applications and the portfolios of their competitors, you know, that sort of nonsense."

"But Simon is the new Poet of Eventide. He got what he wanted."

"Maybe the murder was over something else. As you said, you never really know another person. What are you doing here?"

"To be honest, I don't know. I came in to get some work done, but now that I'm here, I realize I'm not in the mood to concentrate."

"Same here."

I grabbed my backpack, followed Leonard to his office, watched him lock up, and we left the building together. We said goodbye near the Chisholm Library. I was tempted to go for another peek underground, but I resisted and went home. As I turned down Whitley Way, footsteps slapped the grass behind me. I turned, expecting to see Leonard. No one. I pressed the palms of my hands into my eyes, trying to will away the paranoia. Perhaps it wasn't paranoia after all. Thomas was dead. Amandine was dead. Larry Presspitch was dead. And all in the style of a Poe story. Detective Strongwater was right. It was too convenient to be a coincidence.

I leaned against an overhanging beech, pressing my head into the scratchy bark, enjoying the sharp October air, inhaling the burnt smoke scent of the leaves, imprinting the color into my brain before it faded. Fog and rain clouds settled in, and iridescent pockets flashed across the sky where the mist intermingled with streetlamps, the moonlight invisible under the cloaked sky. Where were my friends, the ravens? Likely, they had met, conversed, and were now resting for the night.

Back at the cottage, I went to the study, lit the fire, and pulled aside the curtains so I could watch the rain leave mirror-like puddles on the road. The dim room was shadowy from the dancing flames, so I lit the two sconces on either side of the hearth, the sweet scent of honey from the beeswax candles filling the air. The oil paintings, the landscapes and the portraits, flashed in the firelight, winking with hidden knowledge. I couldn't settle myself, so I wandered around, examining the room as if seeing it for the first time. I ran my hand over the black Corona typewriter and clicked the stiff keys. I had been messy, leaving my research books and notes scattered in unorganized piles, so I attempted to restore some order to my work as well as my thoughts. With nothing more to distract me, I settled onto the sofa. I stretched my legs on the ottoman and picked up one of my research books, Silverman's biography of Poe—*Mournful and Never-Ending Remembrance*. I wondered what Poe would make of recent events. This is all rather like one of my stories, he would have said in his cultivated, logical way. I flipped through the pages, then glanced over the bric-à-brac on the bookshelves, the faded globe, the busts of Shakespeare, Darwin, and Aristotle, the half-burned candles. One of the portraits kept catching my eye—a young dark-haired woman. I studied her a moment, then forgot her as I noticed that the Limoges vases were filled with fresh autumn mums left by Mrs. Griggs.

The last time I had seen Mrs. Griggs was before I left for the ball. Usually, we missed each other since she cleaned during the day, though sometimes she might come later, and I would see her as she was finishing up. After I dressed myself in black, I found her in the kitchen wearing long yellow gloves as she gave the table a good scrub (heaven knows how dirty it could have been since I never used it). When she saw me in my nineteenth-century finery, she dropped the sponge into a soapy bucket and shrugged.

"It's like none of you have any idea what's happenin' in the real world."

"I'm fully aware of the real world, Mrs. Griggs."

"A student from your college is dead now."

"Yes, and the police are investigating."

She placed the soapy bucket on the kitchen counter and began scrubbing the sink with a slight oath. She turned to me suddenly, wiping her hands on her apron as she squinted at me through one eye of her round glasses.

"Did you know the student who was murdered?"

"He was my student. Yes."

"Did you murder him?"

"No, Mrs. Griggs. I can assure you, I'm not in the habit of murdering my students. The police are still checking his BlackBerry to see if they can find his location at the time he was murdered."

"Ayuh. Technicolor police work. They can check their

little screens all they want, but you're lookin' for a ghost in a machine."

"A ghost in a machine?"

"It's a strange event, that's all I'm sayin'. I knew somethin' was up. I saw those ravens circlin' before the murder. They do that when there's a rot, you know."

"I don't understand, Mrs. Griggs. A rot?"

"Ravens are secret keepers. When they gather together and spy like that, somethin' is up. I was feeling unsettled when I saw them, like the end was nigh, and not three days later, that young boy was dead. Ravens are a bridge between the livin' and the gone. Maybe they were actin' as a connection between here and there. A group of ravens is called a conspiracy, you know."

"Yes, or an unkindness."

"An unkindness of ravens. Think on it."

She left while I was checking my shined shoes. I had meant to ask her about that journal I kept finding, but she had taken me off-guard with her comments about the murder, and the ravens, and I forgot.

Still lost in thought about that conversation with Mrs. Griggs, I warmed something to drink and sank heavily into the sofa, staring into the hearth, allowing the flames and the woody scent to mesmerize me. All was silent but for the crackling and the rain slipping down the windows. I realized suddenly how sad I was about Thomas and Amandine. It was too fantastical to be true and nearly impossible to believe. There were times when I woke up expecting to find myself in Connecticut, in my apartment near Yale, the way Dorothy awakens in Kansas after that bizarre technicolor dream. Thomas and Amandine should have had many years ahead of them.

Still restless, I considered going for a walk until I decided that it was probably better for me to lie low just then. I wasn't certain why, but I felt better staying hidden. I was good at that after all, staying in the shadows. I went to work, I taught, I kept my office hours, I came home and finished whatever needed finishing—grading papers, submitting papers for publication, revising when necessary, completing my lesson plans, writing books when a good idea struck me. Occasionally, I came up with an idea for an original work—perhaps a memoir, perhaps a novel. I had been eager to break away from the structure of academic writing for some time. The only people who read scholarship are other scholars seeking citations for their own works. Many times I have sat, sometimes at my computer, other times with quill and ink, writing down ideas that seem suitable. Then I declare the whole thing a bust and stick to scholarship. Better the devil you know.

I threw another log into the fire, then lit the candles on the mantel. It was a comfortable cottage where I enjoyed spending time, and I hadn't felt at home anywhere in a while. That night, though, something was not quite right. An odd static lingered near my head, buzzing all around. The fire flickered low again, so I grabbed the poker and jabbed it back to life. When the light flared, the portrait faces smiled, and the dark-haired young woman appeared to leap out of her frame. I gasped aloud when I realized. She was the spitting image of my wife.

How could that be?

I stepped closer, my face nearly touching the oil as I examined her dark hair and dark eyes. Her peach-like complexion and berry-stained lips. Her sweet smile.

"That's nonsense. You are nonsense!" I yelled, hoping the sound of my voice might snap me back into reality. "Memory. She is only memory."

The portrait artist could not have seen inside my mind and discovered her, could not have caught hold of my most sacred memory and painted her perfect likeness. I wasn't seeing the portrait correctly, or I was seeing what I wanted to see. I had been beaten down by the deaths of my students, and this was some trick my mind was playing on me. I leaned forward, my eyes squeezed tight, as I struggled to convince myself that it was wish fulfillment. When I opened my eyes, I was certain I'd see some other dark-haired young woman. But no. She looked just as I remembered. Whoever she was, she looked like my wife. Had the resemblance been there all that time, since I moved in, and I hadn't noticed?

I began ruminating on madness and how easily any one of us could fall down the never-ending spiral into insanity. For Poe, madness was not a disease but a terrifying state we all had within us. In his stories, in his poetry, he explored the idea that even the most unhinged among us could be logical, even rational, that madness itself was a consequence of extreme obsession. He thought madness might even be a heightened form of perception. "Men have called me mad; but, the question is not settled, whether madness is or is not a loftier form of intelligence," he said.

In The Tell-Tale Heart, Poe's nameless narrator says, "The disease had sharpened my senses—not destroyed—not dulled them." The narrator does not believe he is insane. He believes his meticulous planning of the murder of the old man and his ability to hear the sound of the old man's heart are a result of his superior senses. Poe used madness as a means to examine our deepest anxieties. He wanted to show how logic and reason can be twisted into prisons of our own devising.

There are times when I have felt myself on the verge of madness. I have too many faces blurring, one into the other, and there are times when I cannot say if the memory is my own or borrowed from some distant shadow. Right and wrong, light and dark, good and bad, all of it can become dulled in time if I do not remain diligent. Doing good, doing right, staying in the light even in the darkness—that was how I chose to be. But there are times when the line between guilt and innocence wavers like flames in a draft.

Even worse, there were times during those gruesome weeks when I was terrified that I had done the deeds myself. I was overwhelmed by waking nightmares of my dead students, their bones crushed, their necks slashed, and the knife in my own hand. Other times, I saw myself standing on the balcony, grinning at the lifeless bodies below. Or standing near the fireplace, shoving the corpses up, up, up. I began to distrust my own mind, which is a fearful way to live.

Fifteen

I am among strangers, and my wretchedness is more than I can bear.

I did not see Mrs. Griggs again until Halloween. She had her dusting rag in one hand and an Agatha Christie novel, the appropriate *Hallowe'en Party*, open in the other. She was so intent on her reading that she didn't hear me come into the room. When she noticed me, she slid the book onto the shelf.

"Goin' to the festival near the harbor?"

"I'm not much for Halloween, I'm afraid."

"Me neither. Some folks say people put on masks so they can act like fools. I say people put on masks so they can act like themselves, which is even scarier if you ask me. Around here, we don't need to remove a mask to see who a body really is. Besides, it's gonna be a cold night. That's a bone-setter wind, you know—a wind so cold it makes your skeleton ache." As she dusted the windowsill, she peered at the shadows, stretching like fingers tracing circles in the sky. "Sun's gone, young man. Now the woods belong to the ravens, though I don't see them out tonight." She turned toward me. "Are you lookin' for ghosts?"

"Not tonight, no."

"You won't need to search for ghosts around here. Ghosts in Maine don't need an invitation."

I did go out, in fact, but not in search of ghosts. I had already been followed by several since arriving in Maine. That night, the streets of Southshore, the houses, the shops, the pubs, and the bed and breakfasts were decorated for Halloween. Skeletons dressed as pirates were posed at steering wheels in the boats as though ready to launch into the next tide. Jack-o'-lanterns carved with nautical themes like anchors and sea monsters decorated porches, while friendly scarecrows kept guard. Houses showed red, orange, and yellow potted mums in their yards, and front doors proudly wore black and orange wreaths. Lobster buoys painted autumnal colors bobbed in the bay, their fishing nets hung like cobwebs inhabited by plastic spiders, all of it set off by skulls and glowing fairy lights. The night was biting cold but clear. It was a dry Halloween, so the children went about in their Buzz Lightyear or Woody costumes as they took their plastic pumpkins from house to house for their goodies. As soon as the sun went down, a few trick-or-treaters arrived at the cottage, so I handed out bite-sized Snickers bars, wondering, with a smile, what they would think if they knew. When I was ready to leave, I put the rest of the candy into a bowl outside my door and hoped that the children wouldn't be too greedy as they helped themselves.

Down Southshore Road, near the bay, the festivities were in full swing. Apple bobbing, pumpkin carving, pumpkin weighing, face painting, cider pressing, and scary storytelling kept the visitors happy. I stood aside and watched, somewhat wistfully, as the families laughed and made memories together. I turned down the cobblestones of Main Street, bustling with college students dressed in their Lady Gaga meat dresses and zombie costumes as they enjoyed the restaurants, pubs, and coffee shops. Cordelia and Oliver were outside the tavern, Cordelia dressed as Alice in Wonderland and Oliver as the Mad Hatter. When the beat of a Taylor Swift song bellowed, Oliver grabbed Cordelia around the waist, and they danced to the upbeat music. Oliver, normally so uptight, his tie knotted so closely to his throat he looked as if he might accidentally hang himself, his shoulders perpetually hunched from long hours of study, appeared lighthearted, carefree, and so did Cordelia, her earnestness left behind, for that night at least. They danced, and they kissed, and they glanced shyly away from each other and giggled, and they danced again. I was happy for them. For one ridiculous moment, I wondered if they were responsible for Thomas or Amandine, but no, there was nothing about them that resembled guilt, only release and joy.

"They're dating."

Maeve stood at my shoulder, following my gaze to her classmates, their arms entwined, their lips close as they swayed to a slower song.

"I gathered."

Maeve looked lovely in a plum velvet dress under a charcoal knit shawl. Wrapped around her waist was a silver belt dangling with sun, moon, and star charms. She wore a floppy, low-brimmed felt hat with a slightly pointed crown, with eucalyptus and other dried herbs wrapped around the base. Her laced Victorian-style boots added an inch to her height. She wore fingerless gloves, her fingers stacked with amethyst rings. She clutched a broom close to her chest, and the scent of cinnamon mingled pleasantly with jasmine.

"Dressed as a hedge witch, Ms. Lang?"

"As a matter of fact, I am. I was supposed to meet Oliver and Cordelia, but they seem preoccupied and I don't want to intrude." She looked into the night sky. "It's a perfect, clear night. The moon won't rise for a few more hours. A Dark Halloween night like this is perfect for stargazing since the lack of light from the moon makes the Milky Way more visible over the ocean."

"My thoughts exactly. I was just on my way to the scenic cove near the bay."

"Would you mind some company?"

"In fact, I would prefer it."

We walked down Southshore Road, past the festivities, through the rugged forest to the water. I paused to help Maeve over the stones, difficult to navigate in her high-heeled boots. Two ravens, perhaps the same two who had been keeping me company, crisscrossed in the sky. I thought about what Mrs. Griggs had said and hoped that all would remain calm that night.

"The ravens in Maine seem to be out later than the ravens in other places I've been."

"Ravens symbolize the keepers of secrets and knowledge. They connect the veil between worlds. Some people believe they carry messages from beyond."

"You're the second person to say that to me lately."

"They also symbolize the importance of transformation. If a raven has flown into your life, then magic will be plentiful."

"I've been followed by ravens since I came here. My landlady seems to think that ravens predicted Thomas's death."

Maeve's eyebrows pulled together as she considered. "I'm not familiar with ravens predicting death, only carrying messages once someone has died."

"Perhaps Thomas had a message for us."

"Maybe he did." Maeve stopped, balancing her high-heeled boots on the stones as she watched the two birds barely visible in the moonless sky.

"You know a lot about ravens, Ms. Lang."

"The raven is my spirit guide."

"You're not going to tell me that my spirit guide is something else, like a wolf, a serpent, or a bat, for example."

She laughed. "Poor bats get such a bad rap. They're good spirit guides. They represent seeing in the dark and following your instincts in times of crisis, so you could do worse. But no, Professor. Ravens are your spirit guides. Our spirit guides are the same."

We stopped at the edge, stunned into silence by the luminous river of spilled celestial milk circling in the black velvet sky. Dark bands of stardust split the galaxy into sparkling silvers and ghostly grays. The stars reflected off the water, engulfing us in a labyrinth of glittering diamonds. We leaned toward the rhythmic waves as they washed the stones, the brisk wind sharp against our exposed skin and whipping Maeve's loose braid behind her.

She hugged the nearest tree. "Thank you for being strong and brave." To the sea, she said, "Thank you for stretching far and wide." The world needs more people who thank the trees and the sea, I thought as I watched her. We remained silent, watching the stars, for a long time. What is there to say in the midst of such ethereal beauty? Poe said, "Beauty of whatever kind, in its supreme development, invariably excites the sensitive soul to tears." I was as close to tears in that moment as I had been in some time, even closer than after the deaths of my students. Perhaps it took the beauty of Nature to crack me open.

Maeve shivered, pulling her knit shawl closer to her chin. As we turned away, she plucked one smooth, polished silver stone from the water and dropped it into her pocket. She shivered again, and I offered her my coat, which she accepted, gladly. Next, I offered my arm, and we made our way deeper into the forested area. She stopped near a pine tree.

"Ms. Lang? We should go. You're cold."

"I'm fine, Professor. But I came here to do something. Tonight is a special night when the veil between worlds is the thinnest it will be all year. I still think there's an evil force at Eventide, and I think that force is responsible for Thomas and Amandine. So far, my magic hasn't been strong enough to do anything, but I have another idea."

"Do you think the underground library has something to do with it?"

"Most of the books we saw were grimoires. I think there's probably some connection, but I couldn't tell you what it is yet."

"I don't see why an evil spirit would want to murder in the style of Poe's stories."

"There's a reason, Professor. There always is."

She ran her hand across her felt hat, removing the eucalyptus and other dried herbs. She moved deeper into the pine woods and began whispering. Her plum velvet dress brushed against fallen leaves, each tiny rustle echoing in the rhythm of the waves. She clutched my coat closer around her shoulders. Though it was heavier than her shawl, it offered little defense against the cold. She stopped in a clearing dominated by tall pines, their massive branches reaching like arms toward the mesmerizing sky. From the wide pockets in her dress, she pulled out her tools—three small, gnarled pieces of driftwood, a pinch of coarse sea salt, and the river stone she had collected a moment before. She knelt on the cool earth. Her voice was a low hum against the Atlantic, a distant shush like an ancient lullaby.

"The turning of the wheel, the thinning of the veil, the turning of the wheel, the thinning of the veil." She removed her fingerless gloves, and with her bare hands, she carefully arranged the driftwood into a triangle. She sprinkled the sea salt within, and then, with deliberate slowness, she placed the stone in the center. She closed her eyes and tilted her head, listening. I listened too, but all I heard was the scurry of the rising wind in the underbrush, the gentle sigh of the waves, and the distant, mournful cry of a loon across the bay. She opened her eyes and stared at the river stone, allowing the starlight to gather on its smooth surface. She spoke as if to herself and no one else.

"Salt for the earth, and smoke for the air, keep out the shadow, the grief, and the snare. By iron and silver, by hearth and by stone, leave only the light in this sacred zone. No spirit of malice may enter this door, by the sky overhead and the sea-beaten shore."

A shiver of energy flashed through me, and the air thickened. For a fleeting moment, I saw tiny lights, like fireflies, flickering around the stone, an almost imperceptible glow—a promise of warmth, protection, and the deep, enduring magic of the Maine woods on a moonless night. Maeve smiled. She had shared her secret with the whispering trees and the ancient stars. And me.

We walked toward Southshore in silence until Maeve said, "Samhain is a sacred pause when the veil between the living and the dead thins. It's a time when we can honor those who came before us and let go of what no longer serves us. Now is when we begin the cycle of rebirth." She grabbed my arm gently and turned me toward her. "What do you need to let go of, Professor?"

"I think you know."

"Who does not remember that, at such a time as this, the eye, like a shattered mirror, multiplies the images of its sorrow, and sees in innumerable far-off places, the woe which is close at hand?"

"You've been reading your Poe, Ms. Lang."

"My seminar professor is pretty strict."

I laughed. "The boundaries which divide Life from Death

are at best shadowy and vague. Who shall say where the one ends, and where the other begins?"

"The Premature Burial?"

"We'll make a Poe scholar of you yet."

"I think I'll stick to Emily Dickinson. But the answer to your question is you do. You say where the one ends and the other begins. When you're stuck in the past, it's hard to live in the moment, and the moment before you is the only one you really have. I think you suffer from a tender form of sorrow, the kind that lingers in the background, over your shoulder. No matter where you turn, it's always there. It's the sorrow of remembering what you've lost, you know, like the silence after goodbye. It's the bittersweetness of missing something deeply meaningful to you."

"Or someone."

"Yes, or someone. It's just that I've never seen anyone who looks as sad as you do, Professor. Even when you're smiling, there's this melancholy longing behind your eyes."

"I suppose that makes me the perfect person to teach the Poe seminar." She didn't laugh, and neither did I. She looked through me with those glowing amber-tinted eyes that contained wisdom far beyond her years.

We stopped at the edge of the forest near Southshore Road. Something prompted me to speak to Maeve. Perhaps it was loneliness. Perhaps it was horror prompted by two murdered students. Perhaps I sensed that she would understand.

"There are times, especially now, since Thomas and Amandine, when I feel soul-tired, this," I reached out with my hands, my fingers grasping for the right words, "this never-ending fatigue of heartache and sorrow. I feel myself longing for a home I lost long ago. I've been overwhelmed by an odd nostalgia for a place I can never return to."

"You wish to return to where you were happiest."

"Only that place doesn't exist anymore."

"But you've built a new life for yourself. I know that you think of yourself as a shadow." When I tried to protest, she raised her hand. "Your melancholy eyes can't lie, Professor. They can misdirect, but they can't lie. You should know that the world is full of shadows."

"And monsters."

"And monsters. We see them every day. They smile, and they laugh, and their friendly expressions coax us into tolerance while the angels hide away their scars. In the shadows."

"The jury may still be out on whether I'm a shadow, or a monster, for that matter, but I am most definitely not an angel."

The wind picked up, whipping the pine trees until the sharp needles fell like darts around us. Maeve brushed the needles from my coat, then stepped closer to me. She closed her eyes and raised her hands to the heavens. She stood there, statue-like, for a long time. When she opened her eyes, she stared at me.

"She wants you to be happy."

I remembered the leather-bound journal, the man desperate to contact his dead wife, who found instead a charlatan ready to profit from his grief. It was the generic response —that the spirits of those you loved want you to be happy. He had been right about that, at least.

Maeve's eyes narrowed, as if she could read my mind. "That's what everyone says, I know, but it's true. I felt her presence when we were in your office, and I feel it again now. She has only love for you. I feel her struggling to be near you again. She's closer than you might think."

"Since I've been in Maine, I've been feeling this presence, as though someone is always behind me, following me, but whenever I turn around, it's gone. I keep hoping it's her, that I'm not imagining it, that she's here with me." I threw my hands into the air in exasperation. "I don't know what I'm trying to say."

"On nights like tonight, when the veil between worlds is thin, if you feel a presence, it's not your imagination."

"What about the other nights?"

"If a spirit wants to contact you, they can do so at any time. They don't have to wait for Samhain."

"Perhaps. But I'm not the same man I was. I'd be amazed if she even recognized me."

"We're all different from what we used to be." A sliver of the moon appeared, faint and ghost-like behind the clouds. "There's a saying that if you love someone, you love them twice. The first time, you love them for their outside—for the way they look, their voice, their presence. But then the curtain drops, and you see them for who they really are, with their wounds, their scars, their traumas. We no longer see our beloved as perfect. We understand them as complete beings. This is the kind of love she has for you. The kind of love that stays through everything. I've helped other people on campus contact their departed loved ones. I've helped Mr. Grimshaw communicate with his deceased wife several times now. Professor Bronwyn has a twin brother who died, and I've helped her contact him. Would you like me to do the same for you?"

"I don't think it would work for me."

"Of course it would."

We neared Main Street, where the pubs and coffee shops stayed open late. Eventide students were still out drinking, laughing, and enjoying the night. Oliver and Cordelia were nowhere to be seen.

"Think about it," Maeve said. I nodded, though I had no need. I knew what my answer would be.

. . .

In November, the last of the autumn foliage dropped away, and everywhere was stark and bare, the skeletal branches bleak under a gray sky.

The official week of mourning ended. Campus flags were raised from half-staff. Some students and faculty wore black. A makeshift memorial appeared near the main entrance to the Eliot School. After the revelries of Halloween night, everything fell silent once more, as if we had that one Sunday night to forget until reality came roaring back on Monday. Everyone, from those running the ferries, to local fishermen, to shop owners, to students, to faculty, shuffled about their tasks with stunned expressions. A state of shock was our new normal.

We went about our usual routines as best we could. Students attended classes, researched at the library, and got coffee at the coffee shop in the bookstore. The weather turned frigid, and instead of studying under the trees, students gathered in study rooms across campus. Most professors, myself included, were not so strict about assignments and due dates. We were all doing the best we could.

The most daunting part was the police presence. Armed, uniformed officers, most from the state police, stood sentry at various points around campus, mainly the Eliot School. Leonard told me that there had never been much security at Eventide College. Southshore was a quaint little town near the coast. The locals were quiet people, self-contained and not particularly curious. The students who invaded the town ten months a year were also largely quiet except for an occasional Friday or Saturday night at the pubs and coffee shops on Main Street. Eventide College was not a party school, and the police presence set everyone on edge.

The main problem, as far as many were concerned, was the lack of official updates about the investigation. The only new information we received was that the police believed the two deaths were related. They did not publicly mention Larry

Presspitch as a third possible murder victim. Notices went around saying that, while classes would continue, everyone should walk with a buddy and lock their doors at night.

Our Poe seminar struggled along. When I arrived at the seminar room, the door was closed, which was unusual. Then I saw why. Two armed police officers stood guard outside.

"Is this necessary?" I asked the officer I recognized, the young man named Yellin.

"Orders from Detective Strongwater."

"Does he think we're in danger?"

Yellin shrugged as he opened the door. I saw my students, facing away from each other, as though they were afraid of what they might find if they looked too closely. I placed my backpack on the table and waited for the words to straighten out in my head—to no avail. This time, my silence was not bravado. It stemmed from a broken heart. From the looks on my students' faces, they felt the same. I wanted to let them go home; more to the point, I wanted to go home, but I decided it was better to stay. Even a failed attempt at normalcy was better than running away.

When the silence strained to breaking, I said, "I'm sure you're all waiting for some wise words from me regarding the deaths of Thomas and Amandine, but I'm afraid I have nothing. I'm as shocked and saddened as the rest of you. While Mr. Lambert could be..." I nodded at my thoughts, which the others shared. "While Mr. Lambert could be challenging, I think we can all agree that he was a dedicated student devoted to literature, Edgar Poe in particular. Ms. Wesson was intelligent and forthright, and her voice will be missed at this table. All we can do now is move forward. As I'm sure you know, Professor Bronwyn and the Dean of the Eliot School have brought in mental health professionals for those of you who wish to speak to someone."

Cordelia raised her hand. When I nodded, she said, "I've

heard that the police are considering the two deaths connected, that someone had it out for Thomas and Amandine. Do the rest of us have to worry about some homicidal maniac running around campus murdering us? Why are there police guarding our door? Are we in danger?"

"The police are urging caution for everyone. Don't go out at night alone. Lock your doors. Campus security is working with local and state police, and they will be out in full force at all times until the case is solved. Beyond that, I'm afraid I don't know any more than you do, Ms. Reed."

I couldn't find my lecture notes, and I couldn't remember who was supposed to present that night, or if that person was even still alive. I recalled the Agatha Christie story about the Ten Little Soldiers. And then I realized. Four little soldier boys going out to sea; A red herring swallowed one *and then there were three*. Oliver Chatterjee wasn't there. Oh God, I thought. Please, not again.

"Has anyone seen Mr. Chatterjee?"

Simon, Maeve, and Cordelia shook their heads. They typed into their laptops or pulled notebooks from their bags, avoiding my gaze.

"Ms. Reed? Have you seen Mr. Chatterjee?"

"Not today, no." Her round blue eyes darkened, reflecting the concern I couldn't hide from my voice.

"Mr. Hayes? Ms. Lang?" Nothing. I looked at my watch. It was a quarter past seven. I rummaged through my papers again and found my class list. It was Oliver's turn to present that night, and he had always been on time. In fact, he was usually early. "Mr. Chatterjee is supposed to present an analysis of the uncanny in Poe's fiction. Does anyone know if he's coming?"

Simon shrugged. "I saw him this morning at the library."

"At the library?"

I didn't look at Maeve for fear of what our glances might reveal.

"We were supposed to go over our notes for a paper for our modern American poetry class. He left about noon, and I haven't seen him since."

"I'm sure something has held him up and he'll be here shortly." I hoped I sounded more certain than I felt. "While we're waiting, does anyone have any questions about Poe or the seminar in general?"

I felt as if they were barely present in class. I was barely present. What are we doing here, I wondered?

"Look," I said. "This term has been, let's use the euphemism *unusual*. If any of you want to drop the class even though it's past the drop date, or if you want to postpone completing the class, I'm sure we can come to some agreement. You've had to endure some extraordinary circumstances this semester, and if you need time before you're ready to move on, I certainly understand."

"You mean because someone is out to kill us?" Simon pointed at the closed door, where two armed police officers stood guard. "I need to keep going, Professor Ferrars. I don't want to lose the credits from my courses this term. I'm graduating in May, and I don't want to drag this out. I want to be done already."

"Ms. Lang? Ms. Reed?"

They nodded but said nothing. Maeve seemed distracted, but I couldn't ask her what she was thinking in front of the others.

"If we're going to proceed, then my suggestion is to continue as normally as we can. We have Mr. Chatterjee presenting tonight, and then Ms. Reed and Ms. Lang will present over the next two weeks. Afterwards, we can work something out for the rest of the term. What do you say?"

More nodding.

"Very well."

The door flew open, and Oliver burst breathless into the room, his trench coat flapping behind him. The police officers watched warily as they closed the door. Oliver stood there, his eyes widening under his tortoiseshell glasses when he saw Simon. He pressed his glasses onto his nose and threw his head back, his grin defiant. Words, harsh words most likely, were left unspoken between the two young men. The rest of us waited, expecting an outburst. The moment passed, and Oliver took the empty chair next to Maeve.

"I beg your pardon, Professor Ferrars." Oliver glared at Simon. "There was a mix-up that caused me to be delayed."

I was so relieved to see him that I didn't care where he had been. Simon watched Oliver with steady eyes while his poker face remained expressionless.

"Are you ready to present tonight, Mr. Chatterjee?"

"I am."

I gave him a moment to pull up his presentation. He kept his eye on Simon, who remained impassive, typing into his laptop, then scanning the handout Oliver had sent around.

"You're presenting an analysis of the uncanny in Poe's fiction, Mr. Chatterjee. Is that correct?"

"That's right."

He began with a quivering voice.

"The uncanny is a psychological phenomenon that describes a feeling of profound unease that arises when something familiar suddenly becomes unsettling. Freud called the uncanny nothing new or foreign, but something familiar and old that was established in the mind and then later made strange through the process of repression." He pointed to his handout. "Edgar Allan Poe is considered a master of the uncanny. He takes ordinary settings, characters, or situations and twists them, turns them, and flips them around until they're no longer ordinary but strange. A seemingly normal house, like the House of Usher, becomes a symbol of decay and psychological instability. A home, a symbol of safety and comfort, becomes a terrifying presence, making the familiar uncanny."

Oliver looked confused, as though he had forgotten what he was going to say. He stared at Simon, who stared back. Oliver brushed his hair away from his forehead, pushed his glasses back, and glanced at the stormy black sky through the window.

"Do you need to take a break, Mr. Chatterjee?"

"No, Professor Ferrars. I'm sorry. I can keep going."

"Take your time."

He exhaled, looked at his notes, and continued.

"Poe's horror often comes from a character's repressed guilt. In The Tell-Tale Heart, the narrator's obsession with the old man's eye and his subsequent guilt over the murder manifest as the sound of the beating heart. A beating heart is something normal, but under the circumstances, where the narrator hallucinates about hearing the dead man's heartbeat, the beating heart becomes terrifying. By making the horror occur inside the narrator's mind, Poe creates an unsettling sense of dread. Poe finds terror in the dark spaces of the human psyche that we can all relate to, since we've all imagined hearing things in one way or another."

The others listened politely to Oliver's presentation. They agreed with him where they liked his argument and made their various points respectfully known. They made connections between Poe and the authors they were reading for other classes. I leaned back in my chair, following the conversation, contributing a clarifying question where needed, but otherwise they did as I hoped they would—they had an intelligent discussion even while feeling the weight of the world on their young shoulders.

Cordelia raised her hand.

"Yes, Ms. Reed?"

"I have a question about the uncanny. I know Oliver went over it, but I'm still not exactly sure what it means."

"Would anyone like to answer that?"

"The uncanny refers to something that feels uneasy when you experience it," Maeve said. "In other words, something that would normally seem familiar becomes unfamiliar and strange, even frightening."

"That's right, Ms. Lang. The easiest way to explain the uncanny would be to say that when something normal and expected becomes abnormal and unexpected, perhaps even repulsive, then we can say that it is uncanny. As Mr. Chatterjee pointed out, Poe was a master at creating such dissonance. Unfortunately, we've been dealing with the uncanny ourselves recently. We're experiencing dissonance right now."

Simon scoffed. "You mean the dissonance of having two of your classmates murdered?"

There was nothing more to say.

Maeve, Cordelia, and Oliver left under the scrutiny of the armed guards. I wondered again—could it have been one of them? Were the police onto something, and it was Simon Hayes after all? Was it Oliver, Cordelia, or even Maeve? Did they have help? And if so, who?

Only Simon remained. He was always well put together, always Nordic prince handsome with his wide cheekbones and pale blue eyes. That night, he looked haggard, his compact frame hunched at the shoulders, as though he had aged twenty years in two weeks. Perhaps Simon murdered Thomas after all. Perhaps he murdered Amandine too. Hell, perhaps he murdered Larry Presspitch while he was at it. Why, I couldn't have guessed until I reminded myself that motive was the last thing fictional detectives looked for. I tried to read something into the young man, some inner truth that only the most discerning eye would see. Unlike C. Auguste Dupin, who would have uncovered clues everywhere, all I saw was exhaustion.

"How can I help you, Mr. Hayes?"

"I didn't do it, Professor Ferrars. I didn't kill Thomas or Amandine. I had nothing against Amandine. She was opinionated, but so am I. We hung out together, and we studied Taekwondo together. We had fun, you know? I didn't want Thomas dead either. He may have been an ass, and I may have wanted to punch him, especially after he hit me first, but I didn't do it."

"Shouldn't you be saying this to the police?"

Simon's eyes closed and his head slumped. He looked as if he could sleep right there.

"I've been talking to the police since this happened. They seem to think I'm the key suspect."

"Have they said as much to you?"

"They haven't said much of anything to me except ask the same questions a hundred times."

"They need to be certain they have the facts straight."

"That's the problem. I don't have any facts to tell them. They seemed most concerned about our study meeting. First Thomas left. Then you left. Then Maeve arrived and found Thomas's murdered body in my front yard. I heard Maeve scream and then..." Simon slumped further, as if he wanted to sink into the chair and vanish forever. He opened his eyes with a quickness that startled me. "How did you get back to my house so fast? You left some time before."

"I wasn't that far away. I walked to the shore."

"To the shore and back is still a walk."

"I was already on my way back."

"It was a cold night to be out looking at the bay."

"I don't mind the cold."

"Dark, wasn't it? I don't think there was a moon that night.

I'm not accusing you, Professor Ferrars. I was just wondering how you got to us so quickly." With what looked like a great deal of effort, he pulled himself onto his feet, grabbed his satchel, and headed for the door. "I hope they get to the bottom of this soon. I don't know how much more I can take."

"You know you're innocent. In the end, they'll discover the truth." Only I knew it wasn't true. The innocent aren't always exonerated, and too often the truth doesn't matter.

With Simon gone, I sat alone in the room. It was after 9 p.m., and the entire hallway, the entire building, the entire campus, it seemed, was silent, eerie. I grabbed my backpack, turned off the lights, and locked the door, nodding to the police as I made my way to the elevator. I remembered that I had left some research notes on my desk, so I went up instead of down. When I stepped onto the fourth floor, I saw Oliver sitting on the linoleum floor outside my office. What is the magic spell for disappearing, I wondered? Perhaps Maeve would know.

Oliver stood up when he saw me.

"I'm glad I caught you, Professor Ferrars." He glanced up and down the empty corridor, all the doors locked for the night. There were no armed guards on the fourth floor, but a knot-like tension lingered. "There's something I need to tell you."

I stood silently, waiting.

"I know Simon was just telling you that he didn't kill Thomas. I was outside the door listening."

"The police didn't stop you?"

"I was just standing there."

So much for police security.

"I didn't mean to eavesdrop, but I was waiting for you, and I heard him. I also heard him ask how you got back to his house so soon after you left the night Thomas died. But I know it wasn't you. It was Simon. He's the one who had the vendetta against Thomas."

"I'm not sure I'd call a disagreement a vendetta. And what about Amandine?"

"She wanted Simon for herself, but Simon wants Maeve. Maybe she was jealous. Maybe she knew something she shouldn't."

"But what does that have to do with Thomas?"

Oliver shrugged. "Thomas was always arguing with someone over something. Maybe something happened between them that we don't know about."

"I would wait before jumping to any conclusions, Mr. Chatterjee. Let the police do their jobs. As far as I know, both deaths are still under investigation."

"I heard some rumors that Thomas killed himself, but I don't think so. He was too fond of himself for that."

"Was he?" I thought of my conversation with Thomas in my office. Then I remembered what Maeve said, something about the angle of the knife wound couldn't have been self-inflicted. I kept my thoughts to myself.

"I know it was Simon, Professor Ferrars."

"You've spoken to the police about this?"

"They've taken my statement. That's why Simon was held for questioning, and you can tell he's still worried. That's why he's trying to drag you into this."

Oliver waited as if he expected me to share something, anything, but I kept my own counsel. At times like this, when people are worried about their own necks, they are more likely to lash out at others in an attempt to turn the attention away from themselves. At times like this, trust no one. I had already learned that lesson the hard way.

"If you've told the police your concerns, then there's nothing more you can do, Mr. Chatterjee. Let Detective Strongwater do his job. Hopefully, this will all be over soon."

Oliver looked disappointed, perhaps because I had not been more forthcoming. He thanked me for my time, bid me good night, and went down the stairs. I listened to his footsteps recede, then slipped the key into my office door. I sat in dreary silence, alone in the dark, pondering what else Eventide College had in store.

I wandered home in an ethereal fog pushing inland from the bay. That night, Southshore had an enchanting, almost magical atmosphere, and for a moment, I could forget the terror that seemed to follow my every move. My thoughts swirled into delirious confusion. As I opened the cottage door, overwhelmed by disjointed thoughts, I wondered once more how I had arrived home since I had no memory of it. Then I recalled my two flying friends, their ink-black wings fluttering silently overhead, leading the way. I sat at the dining room table, staring at the wall, for hours. When I came to myself, I saw the old bound journal, the one I kept meaning to ask Mrs. Griggs about, on the table in front of me. Did I leave it there? The journal had an uncanny knack for appearing wherever I happened to be. Perhaps Mrs. Griggs, with her understanding of the unseen world, could explain that too. Wishing to keep my mind from my other troubles, I opened to where I had left off and read.

Saturday, 25 November 1843
Southshore, Maine

In my dreams, no time has passed, and we are just as we were—together, safe and warm. In my dreams, she has weight and substance, her voice soothing and melodious, as it was in life. Then, shortly after that excuse for a séance, she appeared to me.

Was she a dream? A ghost? I do not know. When she was

alive, Helen was the go-between for so many of the bereaved. So many sorrow-stricken visitors would come to visit her, seeking comfort. Helen did not try to fool anyone. She needed no knocking or rapping, no ghostly apparitions. She helped one guest at a time, and when that person spoke about their deceased loved one, Helen took their hand, and if she had a message, she passed it on. She spoke truthfully, and people believed her. In time, I believed her. She would never take money as compensation. She told me, when we were newlyweds, that it made her happy to share her gifts with those in need. There was no trickery. No sleight of hand. No showmanship. It was simply Helen, sitting with the bereaved and sharing what she gleaned. Spirits are real, Helen taught me. They are behind a veil, yes, and difficult for mortals to view, but they are here, and we can connect with them. This is what I was desperate for—to connect with her.

It was a frigid night when a powerful storm brought heavy winds and high snow. I sat before the hearth, my feet on the bumper, drinking mulled cider. I was tired; it had been a long day, and I drifted off to sleep. Then Helen visited me. She knelt beside me and kissed my fingers.

"My dearest," I said. "Won't you come back to me? How can you leave me alone like this?"

She shook her head sadly. "I cannot come back. I am too far on the other side. But you can find immortality for yourself. The knowledge is there if you know where to seek it."

"You told me to live forever before you passed on, and I mean to do what you say. But I'm still struggling, my dearest. Why would I want to live forever without you?"

She touched the tip of my nose with her finger, as she had so many times. "Silly boy. I will always be here, like this. If you find your immortality, you will always be here too. And we will always be together in our own way."

She made it sound so simple.

My monomania is now complete. I am obsessed with that

one idea to the exclusion of all else. My life, so meaningless without Helen, now has purpose. I will spend every waking hour searching for forever. I have sent our children to live with Helen's sister because, though I love them, I cannot care for them, not now when the specter of immortality haunts me. The children are better off in a loving home than with a father deranged by some fantastical need. Compulsive delirium has become my constant friend.

She appeared to me again last night. I begged to know where I might find the magic for Eternity.

"Where the Raven cries," she said.

I am devoting my heart and my soul, my sweat and my blood, to seeking this Raven with the knowledge I need. I shall not stop until immortality is mine.

Sixteen

I became insane, with long intervals of horrible sanity.

Where the Raven cries.

That alone should have answered my questions. That alone should have tipped me in the right direction. But I dismissed it. I had heard so much about ravens in those days that one more mention seemed nothing more than another coincidence.

I had a more pressing concern on my mind—madness. It crept toward me slowly, night after night. One moment passes, then another, then still others, until, with our need to make sense of things, the disconnected beads are strung together to create a fascinating narrative. Whether that story is true or not doesn't matter. If I tell you that I saw Person A do something to Person B, you will believe me even if what I say is a lie. When Person A says, no, this is what really happened, you will still believe me because I told you my version first. We believe the first story we hear, even when it is not true, even when it is blatantly false. So much harm has been caused by this one simple truth.

I arrived late for the faculty meeting. I slipped around the open door, avoiding eye contact with anyone, slinking to the first empty chair. Their faces were dour, skin pulled tight around their skulls, skeleton-like grimaces on their lips. After a moment of silence, Lavinia Cruz closed her laptop with a thud, exasperation loud in her voice.

"We can't just ignore the fact that two of our students have been murdered! We can't go on pretending that nothing has happened!"

Rhys Grimshaw slipped in and took the empty seat beside me.

Debbie ran a hand through her silver hair. With her red eyes and swollen face, she looked as if she had spent the afternoon crying. She leaned across the table toward Lavinia.

"No one is ignoring what happened. No one is pretending it away. There are no words to express how horrible this is for all of us. But I happen to agree with the students. I don't think they should be academically penalized because they were here this term with these unfortunate events."

"Unfortunate events?" Stephen laughed. "Is that what we're calling murder these days?"

"Come on, Stephen," said Leonard. "Let her talk. We're all trying to get through this the best we can."

"Thank you, Leonard." Debbie nodded, first at Rhys, then at me, as though first noticing us. "I'm glad you could join us, Rhys, Jonathan."

"That's right, Rhys and Jonathan. So glad you could join us." Stephen made an exaggerated show of checking his watch. Others did the same.

"My point, Stephen, is that we have students who are

scheduled to graduate this spring. Why should they be held back because of this? And yes, Stephen, I'm using the term *unfortunate events* because if I have to say the word *murder* one more time, I'll scream, or I'll cry, or both."

Debbie dropped heavily into her chair as if she had been deflated, her head drooping onto her chest.

Elise Spencer, the bird-like woman, raised her hand as if she were a student.

"Yes, Elise?" Debbie said.

"I'd like to take a moment to talk about the Poet of Eventide." A general groan. "I'd like to know how Simon Hayes won when Maeve Lang is so much more talented. Even Thomas Lambert, rest his soul, had better poetic sense than Simon Hayes."

"Thomas Lambert had a tendency to fall into blank verse," said Stephen.

"Blank verse is poetry," said Leonard. "It's unrhymed iambic pentameter. It's music in language. It's Shakespeare. Since you're a poetry professor, you ought to know that."

"Is any of this really important?" Eric Michaels asked. No one heard him.

Stephen flapped his hand as if it were a speaking puppet. "Yada yada yada. Here we go again. You're talking nonsense, Elise."

"This isn't nonsense," Elise said. "I want to know why your students always win, Stephen. I want to know why it's never the most talented student who wins. I want to know who I need to know around here so that my students have a fighting chance to win this prestigious prize."

"I'm more worried about my students not getting murdered," said Eric. No one paid attention.

Everyone turned to Rhys, who smiled benevolently, once again a king bestowing grace upon his subjects.

"I don't choose the Poet of Eventide, as you all know. I

merely host the ball. Each of you is responsible for voting for the portfolio that you believe best represents the English department. The votes are tallied, and the student with the most votes is crowned the poet laureate for that year."

"I've always thought it was a popularity contest myself," said Leonard.

"Like *American Idol*?" said a professor I wasn't familiar with.

"Right. There's some vote for talent, but most people vote for personality. You can't tell me Simon Hayes has the talent, but he has the personality that agents and publishing houses love. He's young, good-looking, and comes from a good family. He comes from money, so he can live on the paltry advance they're going to pay him for his first book."

"I heard the New York agents have already signed him," said Eric, to no one. I considered giving the young man a flag to wave so that the others would notice him.

Stephen turned to me. "What do you think, Jonathan?"

"I think the portfolios should be judged blind."

"But who did you vote for?" asked Lavinia.

"I voted for Maeve."

"Maeve." Stephen slapped his knees with his hands. "That makes sense."

"Excuse me?"

"I'm sure I'm not the only one who has noticed that Professor Ferrars and Maeve Lang have become rather friendly lately."

"Here he goes." Leonard leaned back in his chair and closed his eyes. He looked ready for his evening nap.

Debbie held her hands out, and I understood why she often looked like a boxing referee.

"Enough, Stephen. We don't make unfounded accusations against our colleagues here."

"I'm not making accusations. It was just an observation.

I'm sorry if you thought I was attacking you just now, Jonathan. It must be very hard for you, what with your being at the scene of both murders."

"What?" Elise peered through her small, round glasses as though seeing me for the first time. "That's not true, is it, Jonathan?"

"Yes, it's true. I was at Simon's the night Thomas was murdered." A smattering of voices broke out in whispers.

"Why were you at Simon's that night?" Elise asked.

"The students had written some original poems, and they asked me to critique them. Though I think it's disingenuous to say I was at Amandine's murder, Stephen, as though I were the only one. We were all at Eventide Manor the night she was killed."

"That's right," said Leonard. "We were all at the ball. What are you picking on Jonathan for?"

"I'm not picking on him," Stephen said. "I just want to know what happened."

"We all want to know what happened," said Debbie. "I spoke to Detective Strongwater this morning. The police are working some new angle, and they expect to make an arrest soon. I don't really know what to say." She looked sadly at those of us sitting around the table. "The murderer has to be one of us, doesn't he?"

"Why would you say that?" Stephen yelled.

"Is it likely that a stranger happened to break into Eventide Manor the night we're all there for the ball? Who else would have had the opportunity?"

"They could have easily slipped in unnoticed if they were wearing nineteenth-century garb," Lavinia said. "Most of us were so busy dancing and drinking champagne, we might not have noticed."

"Maybe it was the New York literary agents," Eric said. No one laughed.

"What about you, Rhys?" Lavinia asked. "Amandine was murdered in your home. What did the police say to you?"

"The police have gone over Eventide Manor with a fine-tooth comb. They questioned me several times, in fact. If you ask me, they seem rather incompetent. Southshore is hardly a metropolis. Why are they having so much trouble narrowing down their list of suspects?"

"I think it must have been two people who killed Amandine," Lavinia said. "She was a strong young woman, and she could defend herself."

"That's right," Elise said. "It would have taken two people to strangle her and shove her up the chimney."

"Or one very strong person," said Leonard.

"She took Taekwondo with Simon Hayes," said Lavinia. "I think Simon should be questioned again. I bet he's strong enough to shove her up the chimney, and poor Thomas was killed in his house. I bet he has the strength to nearly decapitate Thomas and shove him off the balcony, or through the window, or whatever happened. It was Simon's house, after all. He knows the easiest way to get around."

"In fact, it's poor Simon I worry about," Rhys said. Everyone turned to him. "From what I understand, the police think he's their chief suspect. The fact that he was also there at the time of both murders, and yes, that he might be strong enough to pull off the feats requiring strength, doesn't help him."

"Do we even know the time of both murders?" Leonard asked. "The police haven't been very forthcoming."

"The police believe that Amandine died between half past eleven and midnight," said Rhys. "She was near me by the staircase watching the top three finalists read, and I saw her when Simon was named the new Poet of Eventide. She seemed extremely pleased for Simon."

"She would," muttered Leonard.

"I saw her too," Debbie said. "I was next to her when Simon's name was called."

Rhys nodded. "I'm sure others saw her as well."

"Did anyone actually see her leave?" Debbie asked.

"Obviously, she didn't leave," said Stephen. "She was strangled inside the house."

Leonard smirked at Stephen. "And how do you know that, Professor Trevelyan? Maybe she was strangled somewhere else and brought back to the house and then shoved up the chimney."

"That's hardly likely. She came for the ball and left feet first."

Debbie shook her finger at Stephen. "What a dreadful thing to say. You can all think what you want, but I'm not convinced that Simon had a reason to kill Amandine. Thomas, maybe, since they were at each other from their first day here, but not Amandine."

"Simon and Amandine were friends with benefits," said Leonard.

"I'm not going to ask how you know that," said Lavinia.

"Well, I'm not worried about poor Simon, as Rhys called him," Leonard said. "His father has already bought him the most expensive lawyer money can buy." He looked each of us in the eye. "But if Simon is the murderer, I hope they nail him, and soon. How can they let him wander the streets? Can't they arrest him so the rest of us are out of danger?"

"Obviously, they don't have enough evidence for that," said Debbie. "Now I want to make sure we're all on the same page. If students want to drop their courses instead of finishing the term, we'll allow them to do so, but otherwise, classes will continue. We need to allow the students the chance to graduate on time."

Debbie adjourned the meeting, and we dragged ourselves onto our feet. There was none of the ambient chatter one usually hears as everyone leaves. We slunk away, heads down, lost in our own thoughts. When I reached my office, Leonard put a friendly hand on my shoulder.

"Fun, right?"

"Nothing about this term has been much fun."

"I'd say welcome to Eventide, but this is something else."

I reached for the doorknob and dropped my hand. All I wanted was to return to my quaint little cottage, warm a cup to drink, open a book, and read something comforting that would whisk me somewhere far away. I turned toward the elevator to see Rhys Grimshaw standing beside me.

"For all evils there are two remedies—time and silence."

"Alexandre Dumas."

"Very good, Professor Ferrars." He gestured toward the conference room we had just left. "An exciting meeting tonight."

"That's one word for it."

"I wouldn't worry about Stephen Trevelyan. He speaks before he thinks. No one here takes him seriously when he talks nonsense like that. Are you going into your office?"

"To be honest, I think I'm going home."

"May I walk with you?"

He followed me down the stairs. Usually, I would take Marginal Road to the cottage, but something pulled me toward the opposite end of campus. I didn't want Rhys Grimshaw following me home. I didn't want him to know where I lived, though he could have found out easily enough. We walked across campus in silence. He paused near the statue of the self-satisfied-looking Cornelius Everett Eventide, his full Victorian beard glowing under the campus lights.

"I quite like the full-bearded look myself." Rhys patted his clean-shaven face as though he missed having such a beard. "It's a rugged look. Quite manly."

I wondered what Cornelius Eventide would think of

recent events. He had wanted the college so much. Nearly everything he did was toward the aim of creating a place of learning. Eventide College was one of the first colleges in the United States to accept women as students, Blacks as students, everyone as students. He created Eventide College with the conviction that knowledge was the great equalizer. It was why, when Debbie called from Eventide College, I accepted without asking too many questions. I wanted to be a small part of that vision.

As if he read my mind, Rhys said, "Cornelius Eventide was insatiable about knowledge." He gestured toward the statue. "He was, in a word, monomaniacal. His whole determination, his whole being, was bent on learning the most he could about every subject that caught his fancy. He spent every waking hour studying. His great passion was discovering little-known books. He traveled the world to track down the rarest tomes."

Rhys smiled, and his ordinary features became cadaverous in the shadows. Something about his appearance made me pause. Something trembled at the edge of my recollection, but no matter how hard I prodded, the fragment flickered away, the brief light of recognition dwindling into darkness.

We continued past the Student Union, the Chisholm Library, the Beckham School of the Arts, and the Richfield Chapel. We passed Clovis House, then Cavendish Hall, and I wondered which of the lit windows belonged to Maeve. I hadn't seen her since our seminar, and something felt off, as if the stars were misaligned somehow. I was frightened for Maeve for reasons I could not explain. I feared I was tipping into another one of those moments where my mind detached from itself. Darkness encircled my thoughts. Rhys stepped closer, watching me, so I struggled to keep my expression neutral. He opened his mouth as if to say something, but didn't. We continued down Southshore Road to the scenic cove where I had spent so many hours, and we stood under the Taurid

Meteor shower, the bright meteors streaking across the inky sky, the Milky Way as prominent as when I was there with Maeve. The temperature dropped as Rhys and I stood there, the high winds creating whitecaps on the choppy water. The spiky air presaged the first hard frost of winter. Without moonlight, the water in the bay became a black mirror, reflecting the constellations. Silvery neon sparks swirled, then vanished into liquid obsidian. The waves rose, spectre-like, then disappeared as the ghostly foam struck the rocky shore. Why had Rhys brought me there? Had he seen me loitering at the shore from his window at Eventide Manor? There was beauty in the shifting waves, and danger too. A hollow terror forced its way through every fiber of my being. I felt unmoored, like a boat in the harbor that had broken free of its restraints. Something, somewhere, was trying to capture my attention. Someone, somewhere, was trying to communicate, to tell me. But I didn't understand what it wanted, so I turned away.

The gusts grew more violent, ruffling our hair and our coats. Rhys pointed toward Eventide Manor, and I nodded, though I felt no eagerness to return to the place where Amandine had been murdered. The thought of returning to the old house made me anxious, but I didn't see how to refuse politely. I followed him to the black brick mansion with eye-like windows. At the front door, he pulled his key from his pocket, an antique-looking brass key appropriate to the nineteenth century. Rhys opened the door and stepped aside so I could enter. The mansion appeared different without the gaslight and the laughing guests in fancy dress. Now the interior matched the exterior—dark, sullen, and oppressive. The marble floors appeared icy, as though if you stepped on them you would become a frozen block. The dark wood trim was sepulchral, as shadowy inside as the black bricks outside. Rhys watched me take it all in.

"It's all right," he said. "The house is no longer a crime scene. The police have found everything they are going to find."

"It must be strange living here, knowing what happened."

"We all must do the best we can, Professor. We can do no more than that."

We made our way through the Great Hall, equally gloomy in the darkness. Rhys led me quickly past the portraits on the walls to the east wing, and we entered the library. He flipped the valve on a gas lamp, lit a taper, ignited the gas, and the room burst into an amber glow. In the shadows cast by the light, his ordinary face shifted entirely, his features exaggerated and menacing, as though he were a different person altogether. I kept going back to Stevenson's tale whenever I considered Rhys Grimshaw—*Dr. Jekyll and Mr. Hyde.*

"I hope you don't mind gaslight, or candlelight, for that matter. Electric lights can be so jarring, wouldn't you say?"

"Some people prefer the shadows."

"Indeed, Professor. Some people do."

The library looked as I remembered: towering dark bookcases, the faint scent of old books, the sweetness of aging cellulose. I glanced at the bucolic paintings and the antique maps, which I now saw were of Virginia, Maryland, and New York. The heavy curtains were drawn, and the ornately carved writing desk remained cluttered with open books. I was fascinated by the accoutrements—the quill pens, the ink fresh in its well, the pale paper, slightly yellowed at the edges and smelling of dry cloth, like an old linen chest. I noticed a door between the bookcases, and when I moved toward it, Rhys steered me away.

"I'm afraid there's not much to see through there except some construction."

"Is that the same construction you told me about at the ball?"

"As a matter of fact, it is. It should be finished soon, thank goodness, but everything worth doing should be done properly. Tea?"

"No, thank you. You've been very kind, but it's getting late, and I really should head home."

"Surely you don't need to leave yet. Won't you sit?" He gestured at two wing chairs before the unlit fire. "I would love the opportunity to talk some more about our beloved Poe."

When I agreed, he built a log fire, lit a taper, and set the logs aflame. Amber became cadmium orange became red hot, the shadows like apparitions on the walls. Again, he seemed monstrous. His features hadn't changed; he was as homely as ever, but his manner became larger than life. A sense of wariness overcame me. There was danger there, I was certain of it, only I couldn't explain why. Rhys Grimshaw was a generous benefactor at Eventide College. He funded my position. We shared an interest in Edgar Poe. He offered me tea. We sat before a comforting fire in a pleasant, old-fashioned library. What ominous foreboding was I imagining in this mansion by the sea?

I smiled to make myself more congenial. "I like Poe, but I can't say that I love him."

"No? Then why do you study him?"

"I can find someone fascinating without loving them."

"Do explain."

"Well, for example, Poe wasn't the easiest person in the world to know. Something always haunted him."

"Our dear Poe's sensibilities were delicate. One perceived insult or one unkindly raised eyebrow would wound him far more than the offender intended. Whenever he felt himself ill-used, he would lapse into silence, his expression tightening as though he were gathering his thoughts into some private chamber of his mind. Other times, he would discourse vehemently on matters of literature, his eyes alight with fervor, his entire person animated by the power of his imagination."

"But he wasn't the kind of person to inspire love."

"No, perhaps not. Yet for all his severity, there was a gentleness to him which would surface when he spoke of his wife, or of the fragility of human happiness. In those moments, he appeared otherworldly, as if he understood the great beyond."

"Where angels fear to tread."

"Ah, yes, Pope. For fools rush in where angels fear to tread. But there are no angels here, are there, Professor?"

He stoked the flames higher, and the room flushed with an oppressive heat. His face, still monster-like in the shadows, flashed fathomless for one moment. Then he smiled. Something tugged at me once again, something I was certain I could remember if only I could grab it and hold on. My reverie crackled with the flames.

He stared thoughtfully into the fire. "Perhaps I feel a connection with Poe because he fixated on the death of young women."

"Most of the women in his life died young."

"His wife was such a sweet young thing. Life scarcely touched the maidens he wrote about before the grave claimed them. They seem less like characters and more like embodiments of his private sorrows. He writes of Lenore and Annabel Lee and the others with a reverence bordering on the sacred. We have all experienced such profound loss in our lives." He stared at me, unblinking. "Do you not think so, Professor?"

I didn't care for the turn the conversation had taken. I recalled Poe, his penetrating gaze, as though he studied not only what you said but what you left unsaid, as though with one look he understood you completely. With Poe, one felt their very being was weighed and measured, he was so exacting.

Then faintly, so very faintly, in the thinnest hint of a whisper: *The Gentleman of Shadows.*

I misheard. I must have. I thought I heard it during the ball, and now, in the grainy darkness of this odd conversation with the man whose face turned light and dark, I misheard again. My mind was playing tricks on me, and I feared for my sanity. First the footsteps belonging to no one, then my lapses of time, then thinking I had seen my wife in a painting. Thomas and Amandine. In my mind's eye, I attempted to hold on to myself, fingertips clasping at the edge of my sanity, until the weight was too much and I let go. I felt myself crashing into cold, cadaverous moonlit stone, but I remained alive.

I closed my eyes for a moment, soaking up the heat of the still-dancing flames, settling myself. I did not want a quivering voice to betray me.

"If you'll excuse me, Rhys. It's getting late, and I really should go."

He escorted me to the door. "I've quite enjoyed our conversation, Professor. Do come again."

Walking home in the silence of midnight, I couldn't shake the sight of Poe's sad eyes from my mind. The never-ending melancholy. The death of a beautiful young woman. I know well how loss eats you inside out, a consumption of the soul. As I turned onto Whitley Way, there they were, my two ravens, shadows of shadows huddled on a fencepost as they watched me pass. If two ravens watch you in silence, it means that someone is thinking of you. Perhaps I would take Maeve up on her offer after all. For that moment, at least, I had my two feathered friends. In my mind, I conjured my message, and with a hopeful hand, I tossed my thoughts in the birds' direction.

"Carry it far and carry it wide," I said. My raven friends flew away.

Poe's words kept me company as I meandered home.

For the moon never beams, without bringing me dreams
Of the beautiful Annabel Lee;
And the stars never rise, but I feel the bright eyes
Of the beautiful Annabel Lee;
And so, all the night-tide, I lie down by the side
Of my darling—my darling—my life and my bride,
In her sepulchre there by the sea—
In her tomb by the sounding sea.

Seventeen

The eye, like a shattered mirror, multiplies the images of sorrow.

I discovered my new ranking in the hierarchy of the department through fits and starts. Because of my late classes, I rarely saw the other professors, so issues were not immediately apparent. I might nod to Stephen as he locked his door on his way out. Sometimes Leonard stopped by to shoot the breeze. Occasionally, I saw Debbie, Lavinia, or Elise. When the truth dawned on me, I dismissed it. My life has taught me to be cynical, and though it can be a defensive skill, sometimes my worries are only hot air. I am not always adept at knowing the difference.

The truth is, paranoia can be a precursor to madness. You think everyone is watching you, everyone is out to get you, and everyone has a cunning plan. From there, it is a short leap to believing that everyone is actively trying to sabotage you or even kill you. Step by step, the logic makes sense. But sometimes the suspicion isn't simply your mind talking riddles to itself. Sometimes suspicion is intuition. It's correct. Someone *is* watching you. Someone *is* out to get you. Someone *is* trying to kill you.

Somehow, through idle chatter, gossip, hearsay, rumors, it doesn't really matter, others in the department learned what happened after Oliver's presentation, about how Simon was on the verge of accusing me and how Oliver tried to point the accusations back at Simon. Simon's suspicion, along with my having been conveniently at both murders, prompted more whispering. When I arrived at my office the following week, Lavinia and Eric were speaking near his office door. Eric must have been pleased that someone from the department finally noticed him. He must have liked that he was finally taking part in whatever discussions arose. When she saw me, Lavinia held a file folder in front of her mouth in an attempt to muffle her words. When I passed Debbie, her eyes darted away as she looked everywhere but at me. I ignored them the best I could. But I saw enough. One night, I walked into Debbie's office to speak to her about my concerns about the growing animosity between Oliver and Simon, and she placed her arm around my shoulders, turned me around, and escorted me out the door as quickly as she could. She made it seem so casual, talking about silly nonsense between two stubborn-headed boys, but I knew what she was doing. She was acting as if she didn't want to be seen with me. Others in the department must have thought I was somehow responsible, if not for the murders, then for something.

I stayed away from campus as much as I could, holing up in my little cottage at the desk near the window, staring blankly into the cul-de-sac. I didn't read. I didn't write. Perhaps I hoped that if I sat there long enough, the puzzle of the murders would straighten itself out in my mind, the picture of the chain of events complete. I would be the Sherlock Holmes of Eventide College, calmly piecing together the clues the police failed to see. Only I didn't see any clues, and I didn't know where to search for them.

I didn't keep my office hours for a week. When I arrived at the Eliot School the following Monday, I overheard Debbie and Leonard whispering about how I was "too close" to the victims, whatever "too close" meant. Yes, I was close in proximity—I was their professor. I was at Simon's house and the ball. Suddenly, I was desperate to run somewhere far away. The campus had become a prison of whispers and suspicion. My office felt claustrophobic. Eventide College had become intolerable. Anywhere but here.

I opened my office door and dropped like a dead weight into my chair. I didn't bother turning on the light. My door swung open suddenly, and Debbie squinted until she saw me, illuminated by the moonlight streaming in an iridescent arc onto my desk. She flipped on the lights and shielded her eyes with her hands until they adjusted to the fluorescent brightness.

"Oh, Jonathan!" She sounded like some B-rate actor. "It's all too terrible, isn't it? Two students have been murdered, and everyone is so upset that no one knows what to do. It's all so ghastly."

"It has been a lot to take in."

"It's too awful for words."

If I were going to say what I was thinking, that was the time.

"I hate to bring this up again, Debbie, and I know you already addressed this at the faculty meeting, but I wonder if we should cancel the Poe seminar once and for all. It's our class that has been most affected, and if there's even the slightest danger of these murders being deliberate, then we have to take a proactive stance and protect the remaining students."

"Have the students said they want to cancel?"

"Well, no. As you said, they don't want to lose credits so

close to graduation, which I understand, but it can't be good for them to see our class of six down to four. You were a student here. Was it that cutthroat that you felt that you were in danger when you applied to be the Poet of Eventide?"

"Danger? What danger is there in studying literature and writing poetry? There was no danger. But these students today are so determined in the way they approach their studies. Things are so different from when I was a student."

"You were the Poet of Eventide when you were here. Was the rivalry that intense?"

"Of course it was intense, but it wasn't murderous. And rivalry isn't always a bad thing. It pushed me to do my best, and now I'm back at EC as the English department chair."

"Did it push you far enough to want to kill someone? Leonard mentioned some stories about how brutal the students could be."

"Remember what I said, Jonathan. Don't listen to everything Leonard tells you. He's wonderfully friendly, but he lies."

"So you don't think the students are capable of murdering each other?"

"I think anyone can kill if they feel angry enough in any given moment. It sounds to me like you don't like rivalries."

"As a matter of fact, I don't."

"Then you're in the wrong career because academia is built on rivalries. Unlike you, I think rivalries can be good. They give you the edge you need to survive in a tough world. They give you the ambition and the drive to do your best. Doing your best is the key to success. You must know that. You're successful for such a young man. You must have bested others who were older and more accomplished to get where you are."

"No one died because I may have published a few more papers than someone else."

"That you're aware of." Debbie smiled, but something closed behind her eyes, something she did not want me to see. She stared through the window as the wispy mist hovered mid-air, the waxing crescent moon peering through the endless fog. The leaves, so beautiful and jewel-toned in autumn, were now crumpled and dry, the bent-looking trees languishing in deep ochre and muddy brown. "I don't know what to make of it. To think there's some madman out there after our students and the police don't know who it is. It's terrifying."

"I think the police know more than they're saying."

"I agree. But I worry about what these deaths mean for Eventide College. I'm concerned about the media attention we've been getting. They're saying all sorts of awful things about us, mainly about how we can't keep our students safe. It doesn't look good for us right now, and we've always enjoyed such a fine reputation. We don't want that reputation spoiled because of these senseless deaths."

Well, I thought as she left, at least she has her priorities straight. Then Leonard poked his head around my door. His friendly smile was replaced with deep worry lines.

"What is it, Leonard?"

"I saw Debbie in here and I didn't want to butt in. She's been saying some things, you know."

I dropped my head into my hands and closed my eyes. "What things?" I asked.

"She's been making it seem like maybe, just maybe, and she isn't sure, but maybe you're more involved in everything than you've been making out. Did she ask you if you did it?"

"If I killed my students? No, she didn't. She was saying she didn't want the college's reputation to be spoiled because of the deaths."

"You teach the Poe seminar, and those students were murdered in ways written about by Poe. No one on campus knows more about Poe than you do. That's what she said to me. You watch out, Jonathan. Debbie is worried about her own skin, which means she's likely to lash out."

I opened my eyes, though I didn't look at Leonard, afraid of what I might see. "She didn't say any of that when she was in here just now."

"That's the way she is, right? She plays all chummy to your face and then gossips behind your back. She's two-faced, and she'll say whatever her listener wants to hear. The police have been here asking about you."

"I thought they were interested in Simon."

"Do you think he murdered them?"

"I wish I knew. What questions were they asking?"

"The same questions they've been asking all along. How well I know you, how well you seem to get along with your students, that sort of thing. This one, Strongwater, he seems to have made some kind of connection with it being a Poe seminar and the way the deaths occurred. I think Debbie might have led him onto that."

"He already knew. I spoke to him about it when he questioned me after Amandine died."

Leonard looked at me expectantly, but I added nothing more, afraid I had already said too much. "You're right, though. They still seem most interested in Simon." He waited again, and still I said nothing. "If you ask me, I think they're trying to prove that Simon did it. But wasn't he talking to the New York literary agents after he was awarded Poet of Eventide?"

I shrugged. I had no answers.

"I lost track of him after, though. Who knows where he went? I wouldn't be surprised if they found him guilty. Maeve hasn't been around much, so no one knows what she's thinking."

"You're not suggesting that Maeve had anything to do with it?"

"Not directly, I shouldn't think. But everyone knows that Thomas Lambert was in love with Maeve."

I pictured my students as chess pieces, and I moved them around on the chessboard in my mind. What did I know about them? Cordelia and Oliver were an item. Cordelia I crossed off my mental list. She seemed to have the least to do with any of it. Oliver seemed intent on proving that Simon was the murderer. Was Oliver trying to take attention off himself? It was possible. Was Thomas in love with Maeve? Maeve said no, they were only friends. But would Thomas have confessed that to her? He seemed to think that Maeve was in love with him. Perhaps Thomas confused Maeve's friendship with something else. Thomas seemed to be obsessed with the fact that Simon gets whatever he wants because he wants it. Simon seems to want Maeve, but Maeve doesn't seem to want him. Was Maeve at the heart of this somchow? No matter how I moved the chess pieces across the black and white board, nothing made sense.

"You know what, Leonard? I don't think any of this has to do with romantic entanglements."

"No?"

"No. There's something more sinister about this. Some, I don't know, inexplicable dread. There's hatred here. I don't know what the hatred is about, and I don't know why it's rearing its ugly head now, but someone out there wants something, and they're taking it from my students. This is too specific to be random."

"So you think it's an inside job?"

"It may well be an inside job. I just don't think one of my students is the murderer."

Leonard stared as though trying to see through me. "It sure seems like someone is trying to pick them off one by one."

"But why?"

"As you said, it's too specific to be random. For the past

week, Debbie, Stephen, and I have been in meetings with the dean, the provost, and the president of the college. Maybe we do need to end your seminar after all."

"I just said as much to Debbie."

"We need to be more worried about keeping them alive than making sure they get the units for their classes. I am sorry, Jonathan."

"Sorry about what?"

"I'm sorry that your students are being picked off in the style of Poe's characters. Debbie may be a blabbermouth, but she's not wrong when she says that you know more about Poe than anyone else on campus. I don't know much about Poe beyond the general facts most people know. Nineteenth-century literature isn't my area. Oh, and the police were asking about your whereabouts when you're not on campus. I told them the truth, which is I don't know much about you except that you're well published in your field and a good professor from everything I've heard."

Leonard's eyes were focused on my Cambridge diploma, though he didn't seem to see it, his thoughts far away. I wished desperately for someone to confide in. I was tempted to tell Leonard about Strongwater's suspicions about Larry Presspitch's death, which would make three people killed Poe-style—one I could not be held accountable for. Then there was that underground library I had seen with Maeve, the one with the ancient-looking tomes. And what about that oddity, Venn? I wanted to question Leonard about what else he knew, but I couldn't confide in him, no matter how friendly he seemed. I've made that mistake one too many times. Someone comes across as amiable, and you want desperately to unburden yourself, to share confidences and confusions and questions, only to discover too late that the person wasn't trustworthy after all. What you thought was a private conversation became public property. So I stayed silent, as much as it pained me to do so.

What would Hercule Poirot say? Is it ever the most obvious person who commits the crime? It could be, but it rarely was, at least according to Mrs. Griggs's mystery novels. Some professors, perhaps even some students, thought I was the most obvious suspect. But what reason did I have to murder my own students? Wasn't it too obvious for the Poe professor to commit the Poe-like crimes? I've been a professor for a long time, and now suddenly I'm a homicidal maniac? I laughed at the thought.

Walking across campus, I felt rather than saw a creeping shadow, but this time I wasn't hallucinating. I was being followed. When I arrived near the Chisholm Library, I turned so suddenly that Simon couldn't hide. I smiled to let him know that I saw him and that I wasn't afraid. I continued toward Southshore Road, and he followed me, openly now.

Had it been Simon following me all along? Was he monitoring my movements? Trying to shift police interest onto me? I could have turned and yelled, "What the hell are you doing?" Perhaps I should have.

I had to lose him. I had no choice. If he knew where I was going and why, that would be the end of me. I moved faster, not so fast that I would become a blur, but fast enough that he couldn't keep up. Near the forest, I stopped, listening to his haphazard footsteps, first to the right, then to the left, unsure where to turn. Then he retreated. I was relieved, but I had to stay on my guard. The eyes of Maine were watching me, I was certain of it. The spindly winter trees pointed at me as I flashed away.

I dreaded returning to college. The red brick colonials and the neoclassical columns were no longer friendly. The students were solitary and largely silent. The ground shimmered with silver hoarfrost while the sky, smoky, flat, and gray, remained bleak. The wide expanse of fragile, dormant trees was bleak. Everywhere was bleak. When I arrived on campus, there was a commotion near the Eliot School. Students and faculty crowded together, straining to see as two uniformed police officers led Simon Hayes away in handcuffs. So it was Simon after all. What a shame.

Leonard Harris grabbed me when I stepped out of the elevator. "Have you heard that Simon Hayes has been arrested?"

"I just saw them taking him away. What happened?"

"Apparently, Oliver Chatterjee went to the police a second time and told them all sorts of things he said he overheard Simon say, like when he was planning on killing Thomas, how he was planning on making Amandine disappear."

"That hardly seems likely. Simon and Amandine were friends. Simon seemed fond enough of her."

"Simon Hayes isn't fond of anyone but himself. Though it does seem strange that Oliver is the one who spoke out against Simon."

"Are you sure it was Oliver?"

"That's what Debbie thinks. I bet Simon's guilty." Leonard's eyes were small and sharp. "He always seemed slimy to me, you know, the kind of person who gets away with whatever just because he can."

"Even being a serial murderer?"

"When you're from a wealthy family like that, they have ways of getting around things like laws."

I cancelled the Poe seminar that week until I had a chance to sit with Debbie and figure out what to do. I started with six students. Two were murdered. One was arrested. I thought that an independent study might work, where they could still read and research Poe, but instead of meeting weekly, they could work independently. The coursework was not that important under the circumstances—except that it was. The crimes were based on Poe's stories, after all. I began to hope that this experience at Eventide College was a nightmare. Perhaps there was still a chance that I'd wake up to find myself in my apartment in New Haven.

I searched for Debbie, but she wasn't in her office. Leonard and Stephen didn't know where she was, and Lavinia had gone home. I wasn't interested in speculation about what Simon had done, how he had done it, or why he had done it. As far as the English department was concerned, Simon Hayes was the murderer. The police had their man, and everyone seemed to breathe easier because our campus was safe again.

At home, I lit some candles, lit the fire, and sat on the sofa, watching the trees through the window as they shook in rhythm with the wind. Something moved upstairs, and I sat up. A snap, a jump, and the candles on the mantelpiece sputtered. The flames went out, and the room was black.

It must be the oncoming storm, I thought. A gust must have come down the chimney. I must have imagined the sounds upstairs. And here it begins, like the mad narrator of The Tell-Tale Heart who hears the very heartbeat he stilled with his own hands. I imagined sounds that weren't there. I had been lingering just this side of madness for so long that perhaps it was time I slipped over the edge.

Another bang. I flipped on the electric lights and checked the shadows behind the doors and in the dark corners. No one. I peeked into the cupboards. No one. I checked the second-floor bedrooms. No one. I climbed to the attic and found the circular window open, but it was a 40-foot drop to the ground. I squinted into the darkness. No one. Did I leave the window open? I couldn't remember the last time I had been up to the attic. I went there once when Mrs. Griggs showed me around the house, and I went up a second time after I moved in to look around. Did I open the window? I didn't think so. Did Mrs. Griggs open the window? I didn't know.

Suddenly, the house felt as though it were being whisked away by a tornado. Kansas sounded better than Maine at that time, so I didn't mind. As I leaned against the sloping wall, the floorboards gave way beneath my feet. The entire cottage collapsed, taking me with it. Poe's words flashed through my mind, the same words Thomas had spoken before he died.

True!—Nervous—very, very dreadfully nervous I had been and am; but why will you say that I am mad?

As suddenly as it began, the house stopped spinning. Everything was fine. Nothing had happened. It was all in my mind.

Terror struck me with brutal force. Have the years finally caught up with me? My scattered thoughts felt like boiled alphabet soup, the letters melded together, unable to make distinct words. I covered my eyes with my hands as I struggled to calm myself, as my father had taught me. I had always been a worrier since I was a very small boy, and when my childish fears would run away with me, my father asked simple questions to ground me.

"Who are you? Where are you? What are you doing? What do you see, taste, touch, hear, and feel?"

These questions have acted as talismans for me ever since. Only at that moment, the answers didn't come easily. Who was I? I couldn't quite say. There are times when, if I want to survive, I have to let my very name go. I have had so many.

I answered the other questions easily enough.

I was in Southshore, a quiet village in coastal Maine.

I was standing in my attic, leaning against the wall, trying to gather my bearings.

What was I doing? I had gone to Southshore to take a prestigious position at a respected college. Two of my students were dead, and my predecessor as well. Was there an unseen presence after all, hidden and unknown, monitoring my classes, waiting to catch us unawares? What did Maeve mean when she said that she sensed something evil at Eventide? And then it occurred to me. What if that evil presence wanted me? Was that the answer? The presence didn't want my students. It wanted me. But who would try to get at me by killing innocent young people? The more I thought about it, the more confused I became.

I went down to the study, sat at the desk, pulled out ink, quill, and paper, and wrote down everything I knew about what had happened since I arrived in Maine. Instead of feeling better, my dread increased. I saw phantom threats everywhere. Everyone was a menace. Leonard. Debbie. Stephen. Lavinia. Simon. Oliver? Cordelia? Maeve?

I know what I have suffered. I know that I need peace, solitude, certainty, and safety. Sometimes, I allow myself the illusion of thinking I have found them. Other times, I admit that such safety is only a mirage reflecting what I want to see. That night, I pulled even further into myself because I knew that there was no one I could turn to. Trust no one. My fears became paranoia, which became dread, which became a self-fulfilling loop where doubt breeds upon itself. Nothing would break the cycle except death.

Perhaps I should have been surprised when I saw the old bound journal close at hand. But I wasn't.

Eighteen

There are some secrets which do not permit themselves to be told.

Tuesday, 22 October 1844
Southshore, Maine

My descent began when the Ravens whispered to me, their voices following me to places I cannot name.

Where the Raven cries.

I have become obsessed with the riddle: what is the connection between Ravens and immortality? The solution is proving elusive. I read, and I study, and I ponder until the very shadows tilt toward me. I have been fearing for my sanity. Ha! I have read the works of Edgar A. Poe, and I feel certain that he would understand. I am unwilling to fall all the way down into madness quite yet, so I pull myself up with sheer determination, and I continue my quest.

Before Helen's death, my life made sense. Sitting with my books, my tea, my comforting fire. Communing with my thoughts in my commonplace books and essays. Spending quiet dinners with my wife and our children. Reading together with Helen after the children had gone to bed. My life was simple, meaningful. I spent many happy hours studying literature, history, and politics—the subjects that most fascinated me. I was happy simply to be alive with the opportunity to sit with the great questions. Whatever wisdom I gleaned came through methodical study and determined perseverance. Now I study more than ever, but nothing makes sense. I peruse the darkest subjects, and my knowledge of thaumaturgy is hard won. The grimoires, the enchanted objects, the bewitching sense of dread—they leave me with a persistent paranoia I cannot shake. I have been watched by invisible eyes, disoriented by sneaking shadows, and bewildered by the rustling wings of Ravens. The knowledge I am now seeking is not merely collected and studied. It is secretive and as hungry for me as I am for it.

I am still making sense of the information I have gained. I have read about ritual magic. I have read instructions for incantations. I have studied methods to read omens and interpret the future, including the use of crystal balls, mirrors, tarot cards, and pendulum divination. I have recipes for transmutation that turn lead into gold. I have the secret words for invoking spirits, good, bad, or indifferent. I could summon a familiar. The Raven must be my familiar; that must be why the birds remain near. I have warding spells to shield me from misfortune or harm. If someone aggravates me, I can hex them into silence. I know salves, charms, and dream interpretation. Yet I cannot live forever, which is the only magick I seek.

Saturday, 26 October 1844
Southshore, Maine

. . .

Not long ago, I uncovered a collection of necromancy books in Boston. The books appear most promising, so I have bought them, and they are on their way. As I sit near the open window, I can see my neighbors finishing their tasks from their market day as they prepare for the Sabbath. On Sundays, the world comes to a halt in observance of the Lord's day. If those self-same neighbors knew that I studied Satan's own knowledge, I'd be arrested, or worse. Outside, I hear the men as they pile seaweed or evergreen boughs against the foundations of their houses to insulate against the coming winter winds. I should hire a man to do that for me, but I cannot pull my head away from my books. The nights grow dark early now, and it is already time to light my candles.

Since magick alone has not led me down the path to immortality, I have decided to learn more about Ravens. Perhaps it is the Raven itself that I need to understand. I hear the Ravens outside my house, perching in the trees, and I wonder at them. Are they here for me? Perhaps they hold the secret I seek. Ravens are more than beautiful black-plumaged birds. They are intelligent and powerful. They are complex and significant across cultures. They can mimic human speech, they play like human children, and often they mate for life. In most cultures, the Raven holds a special place of symbolic importance. They are no ordinary birds, and it is a sorrow that nowadays they are seen as pests and have been largely exterminated. The small-minded see these majestic birds as ill omens. They see the iridescent feathers shimmering like sapphires and believe the birds must be bad. Ravens have been persecuted, and we rarely see their wedge-shaped tails soaring above. Yet those outside my window remain. Occasionally, I see others circling the sky in pairs. When I spot them, I stop, hoping they will speak to me, not in a croak, but in words, telling me their secrets. Where the Raven cries. What does that mean? Instead of answering, they croak and fly away. The pair perched outside my window stares at me with some hidden knowledge they will not share.

I am struggling to make connections between Ravens and dark magick. Ravens are considered mystical guides between worlds, symbolizing prophecy and transformation. Many believe that Ravens carry messages from the spiritual world to ours and back again. Ravens teach us to trust the unknown and embrace the mysteries of life. Ravens guide us to trust the coincidences around us, revealing hidden possibilities. They are the guides of souls and lead fresh-born spirits to the Other Side.

I have learned all this, yet I need more. I can find no specific spells or chants that connect the Raven to immortality. How does one lead to the other? I see no answers here.

As I read, I noticed that a handful of pages had been torn from the binding. The next entry was dated nearly two years later.

Tuesday, 10 February 1846
London, England

I remain with Anthony, resting, though I leave for home tomorrow. I traveled to Ireland, where in Celtic traditions the Raven is closely connected with the goddess of war and fate, the Morrígan, who appears on the battlefield in the form of a Raven. In Ireland, Ravens are carriers of prophecy and omens, appearing at moments of death. While many wise men could tell me about the Morrígan and her Ravens, no one had any knowledge of Ravens and immortality.

I traveled to Rome, where Ravens are messengers of the gods and instruments of divination. In ancient days, Ravens were seen as omens, sometimes omens of ill will, but always they represented a message from a higher power. While many wise men could tell me all about Apollo and his Ravens, no one had any knowledge of Ravens and immortality.

I traveled to the United Kingdoms of Sweden and Norway, where Ravens are the eyes and ears of the god Odin, symbolizing Odin's vast wisdom and knowledge. Ravens accompany warriors to battle, and they are associated with war and the fallen. While many wise men could tell me all about Odin and his Ravens, no one had any knowledge of Ravens and immortality.

Finally, I braved the frigid journey to Siberia, where the Raven is a primal trickster, credited with creating the land, shaping the first human beings, and stealing the Sun, Moon, and Stars to bring light to the world. He is a cultural hero who is clever but more often foolish. There was no help for me there.

For my long, weary journey, I persevered through rough terrain, choppy seas, and physical agonies. I brought home quantities of books about the occult, the supernatural, and Ravens. In none of my sojourns had I found any examples where the Raven could bring someone back to life or grant immortality. I am frustrated with myself. I have failed. I know no more about how Ravens might bring me eternal life than I did when I began this arduous path. Helen's wish for me remains unfulfilled. My library has grown large, though I daren't show my latest acquisitions to anyone. This knowledge is for my eyes only.

Monday, 20 April 1846
Indian Territory

Before I left England, Anthony told me about the British Relief Association, which some noblemen, including himself, and some wealthy businessmen have founded. They are raising thousands of pounds while purchasing Indian corn to ship to the most distressed parts of the Emerald Isle as a result of their potato crops failing. They hope to feed schoolchildren, since the young are the most vulnerable to famine. Our ships prepare to depart with holds of lumber, along with Indian corn, and we expect Irish immigrants to come to America to seek a better life. I feel for them, truly, and I have made my donation to the British Relief Association, but my mind is occupied elsewhere.

I have discovered that Ravens are of utmost importance in several native cultures. The Haida and Tlingit peoples in the Northwest, near Russian America, have many of the same beliefs about the bird as the Russians. The Raven steals the Sun, Moon, and Stars from a greedy chief who was hoarding them in cedar boxes. Through cunning and shapeshifting, turning into a hemlock needle and being swallowed by the chief's daughter to be born as her baby, the Raven succeeds in releasing light to the dark world. Again, my hopes were dashed when I learned that there is no connection with immortal life.

Then I discovered the tale of the Raven Mocker. The Cherokee people now live in Indian Territory after being forced on death marches a mere nine years ago. As soon as I heard of the legend of the Raven Mocker, I knew I must visit them. I undertook the treacherous five-week journey over several stages. First, from Maine to Boston by railroad and stagecoach. Then on a riverboat from the Ohio River to the Mississippi to St. Louis. Then, a four-week journey overland by horseback and a hired stagecoach over rough terrain. The 1500-mile journey was a test of endurance. Whether it was fruitful, I am still not certain.

When I arrived, it was easy to see that the people still suffered from their forced marches. Even so, there is a sense of determination among them. They did not trust me at first, but I found an elder, a silver-haired, stoop-backed man, who told me tales of the Raven Mocker. We sat under a clear, cold night around a fire. Others sat and listened. One young man, tall and strong-looking, kept away, though he appeared intent on our conversation.

"The people cannot see the Raven Mocker, the Kalona Ayeliski," the elder said. "It is an evil spirit and cannot be seen by good eyes."

"What exactly is the Raven Mocker?" I asked.

"All the Raven Mocker cares for is prolonging its own life force. It feeds on others for its own purposes, not caring about those it kills. It tortures the dying and hastens their deaths so it can consume their hearts. It receives one year of life for every year the victim would have lived. The Raven Mocker preys upon the sick and dying because they are the easiest to catch. He flies through the night with outstretched arms like wings that sound like a strong wind. His flight is accompanied by a Raven's cry, the omen of death."

My heart pounded with a vengeance. "Excuse me. What did you say?"

"The Raven's cry is the omen of death."

"Of death? Not life?"

"The Raven Mocker's presence means death for those he attacks." The old man glanced over his shoulder, as though expecting to see a Raven-sized man with winged arms behind him. My thoughts were racing. Where the Raven cries. It meant death, not life. But could there be eternal life after death? Was the Raven Mocker itself immortal? Ah! My whole being swelled with the hope that my journey might finally be at an end.

"Not all Raven Mockers are evil," the young man called from the distance.

"There is no such thing as a good Raven Mocker," another elder said.

"You know there is." The young man's voice was challenging. He stood to his full height, which was rather tall. For a moment, he looked as if he might join us, but he didn't. "I was helped by the Kalona Ayeliski." He gestured toward the man who had

been talking. "My father will tell you. My father begged him to save me."

"He must have saved you," I said. "You're speaking to me now."

"He is not saved," the first man said. He nodded at the fire as though he were seeing a vision. "For he is one of them." He gestured toward the young man. "There you are, stranger. Behold for yourself. The Kalona Ayeliski."

"I'm not," the young man said. "I've never eaten anyone's heart."

"The Raven Mocker takes the heart without harming the victim's body. You could have had many hearts, and none of us would know. You should go far away. There has been too much death already."

I studied the young man. He was pale beneath the moonlight, but he didn't appear dangerous. I stepped toward him. I had so many questions, but he seemed to vanish, he was gone so quickly.

"He is...?" I asked.

"The Raven Mocker is a trickster, so you cannot believe him. I'm certain he has eaten many hearts."

"You're telling me that the young man I just saw is not human?" It took great effort on my part not to scream, to jump up and down, or to wave my arms like a madman. Finally, after so much reading, studying, and traveling, I was on the verge of my answer. How do Ravens and immortality intersect? That young man was my missing link.

A white-haired man stood, surveying the others. He nodded toward the pale young man, who was once again watching us from the shadows.

"He," the white-haired man said, indicating the young man, "is my son. He is not the Kalona Ayeliski. He is something different. Something more. He does not age. He will not die. But he is not an evil spirit." The man looked through me as if he saw

into my mind. "You," he pointed at me, "you want immortal life for your own selfish purposes, so you can speak forever to one already gone. You will do bad things with eternity. Your intentions began with good, but you will easily be led astray. Your sense of self-importance will bring you down. You should stop your quest now before someone gets hurt because you will hurt many people before you are done."

"But my wife is gone," I said. "And I want to hear her voice again."

"The essence of life is change. Everything changes. And so do we."

"Not him," the first man said, nodding toward the young man hiding in the darkness.

"You." The white-haired man addressed me again. "You want forever because it has become an obsession for you. Your desperate need has taken over. It burns you up from the inside, a raging fire in your belly. Whether your wife speaks to you or not, you wish to live on. This is not a good thing. Our lives have meaning because one day we will no longer have them. It is the impermanence that gives our time value."

"But what about your son?"

"He is forced to find meaning in other ways. And it is not easy."

"It may not be easy, but it is possible." I looked toward the shadows, but the young man was gone. "Your son was given immortality. I want some for myself. Where do I find it?"

"You are greedy. The greedy never come to a good end. You will die in a pit of fire of your own making."

"If I'm immortal, I can create any end for myself I wish. And if I do not like the first one, I can create another, and another." I raised my voice in fury. "Where do I find forever?"

The white-haired man raised his hands in defeat. "Where the Raven cries."

After that, he said no more.

Nineteen

Words have no power to impress the mind without the exquisite horror of their reality.

The Raven Mocker. Another sign. Another key that should have unlocked the mystery buried in my frozen mind. But my memory remained stubborn. My head felt heavy, as if there was one important word balanced on the tip of my tongue that I couldn't quite pronounce. My thoughts had weight but no substance. I wish I could say that reading those particular journal entries triggered something, anything. I wish I could say that this was the moment when events began to straighten themselves out in my mind. When I look back now, I see how perfectly everything was aligning. The answer was there, but I didn't see it. Perhaps my mind knew what it was doing, and it was protecting me.

I held the old journal between my hands, pressing the leather covers together so tightly the ivory-tinted rag paper nearly disintegrated into dust. Perhaps the journal writer just happened to mention the Raven Mocker, just as I happened to hear whispers of the Gentleman of Shadows. Perhaps I really was mad after all. I felt both heavy and light at the same time, as though I were a feather tied down by bricks. Everything felt like a burden, including the weight of my own body. The fire crackled while the sweet resin of the pine logs scented the air, but the warmth felt distant, as I felt distant, as if I didn't fully inhabit the space I stood in.

There.

A sense of a memory. A conversation? A face? A warning murmured in a low voice? The edges of it, shadowy and faceless, glimmered like frost catching a stray beam of light. Whenever I turned toward it, it skittered away as though frightened. I pressed my fingers to my temples and squeezed my eyes shut. Everything, all of my life, blurred into one long, dense fog, while I shifted through the shadows of things that had been. Most memories, though once deeply important, faded into the background, not with the pain of loss, but with quiet acceptance. Some memories slipped away so peacefully that I did not notice they were gone.

There.

I could have grasped the image if only it had stayed a moment longer. There was cold air, the echo of a door slamming shut, the sense of someone standing near, someone who shouldn't have been there, someone furious with me for a reason I could not recall.

I paced the study, hoping the movement would shake my memories loose. I spoke aloud to myself and answered too. "What is it?" I shouted at the flames. "What is it that I can't recall?" My voice sounded strained to my own ears, and I felt my limbs fraying at the edges. The flames did not reply.

There.

I could feel it, the memory right beneath the surface, pressing upward, like a submerged stone desperate to break the water. Yet every time I nearly reached it, it slipped back under the crashing waves. Something had happened in the past, something important, and the fact that I could not remember—that was the real danger. I walked to the window and pushed it up, allowing the November rain to drench me. Perhaps if I drowned, the memory would rise to the surface.

Like the seasons, memory has its own weather. Some days it is as sharp as winter sunlight on fresh snow. Of course, there are those memories that are with me always, crystalline details etched and illuminated as though they are not touched by time. Her scent, her voice, the particular tilt of her smile. I see her clearly, as if she were standing before me now. These memories are whole, intact, offering themselves without hesitation. Other memories become fog—too dense to see through. Such lost moments drift out of reach, moving behind a gauze that refuses to fade.

There.

An image, but then it slipped away, like water through cupped hands. Perhaps some of my memories remain vivid because they changed me. Perhaps others fade because I survived them and need not consider them again. Others wait in the mist, patient, until I am ready.

On Monday, I skipped my office hours. Tuesday, I had a total of four students in my survey class. I reviewed the reading, went over our next essay, and let them go. Wednesday, I spoke to Debbie once more about the seminar, finally convincing her that an independent study for the remaining students would be best. Instead of meeting each week, they would use their studies of Poe to produce a formal paper that, with some tweaks and nudges, might become publishable. When I mentioned the change to the students, they agreed. They would get their credits for completing the course, they would graduate on time despite the mess that term had been, and we wouldn't have a weekly reminder of how our class had been violently whittled down. Since we were no longer formally meeting, I had to check for their emails in case they had questions. I would keep my office hours in case they needed me.

The Eliot School was dreadful in its silence that late November night. It was Thanksgiving week, and though the campus closed beginning on Wednesday for the holiday, it seemed as if everyone had taken the entire week off. I went to my office, however, in case any of my seminar students turned up. I hadn't seen any police on campus recently, which made me think they were confident that Simon Hayes was their man.

That is, until I saw him in the hallway, waiting near my office door.

"I'm glad to see that they've let you go, Mr. Hayes."

"Are you?" He took an aggressive step toward me. "I would have thought that you'd be happy to let me take the blame."

"Why would you think that?"

"Because you're the murderer, aren't you, Professor Ferrars?"

No one else was there. The office doors were closed. A fluttering, like quick steps running away, then nothing. I opened my door and gestured Simon inside, though I left the door ajar. Just in case.

"Of course, I'm not the murderer. Why would you think that?"

"You had an opportunity. You were at my house the night Thomas was killed."

"So were you. So was everyone else in our seminar."

"But Thomas left, and then you left, and then Thomas was murdered. You just happened to reappear in my front yard when Thomas's body was lying there."

"If I recall correctly, you and Amandine left the room

before I did. Ms. Lang had only just arrived. Surely you don't think Ms. Lang had anything to do with it?"

"Of course not. But what about Amandine? You made a whole big show of how you were looking for her at the ball. You even cornered Maeve into helping you. And now Amandine is dead too." His eyes flashed from here to there while his right foot tapped a Morse code on the linoleum floor, his fingers dancing down his legs as though typing a message. If I didn't know better, I would have thought he was stoned. From his fidgety movements, he might have been.

"The entire English department was at Eventide Manor for the ball, Mr. Hayes. Do you think everyone who was at the ball is a suspect?"

"So you're saying it's random? When two students from the same seminar are killed only two weeks apart? You're a murderer, Professor Ferrars. And I'm going to prove it."

Murderer. His accusation landed like a blow, as he intended. The world reeled away from me, and in my mind's eye I saw myself bent over Thomas's broken body, my hands slick with his blood. My mind shattered into glass, my two halves separating, never again to be whole. Perhaps it wasn't Rhys Grimshaw who was Jekyll and Hyde. Perhaps it was me.

A horrible thought occurred to me. Did I murder Thomas? Or Amandine? Could I possibly?

I have known darkness. I have known righteous anger and seething violence. And blood. So much blood. But that was in the past. Again, my thoughts jumbled one into the next. I couldn't tell if I was here or there or some place else entirely. I was everywhere at once. A vision of me as a murderer pressed close, too vivid to dismiss, and I was bound, hands behind my back, unable to break free. The edges of my sanity disintegrated, inch by inch, leaving me hollow inside.

As suddenly as the delusions appeared, they vanished. I was fully myself again.

"I'm sorry, Mr. Hayes, but it wasn't me, and I sincerely hope for your sake that it wasn't you. For all I know, you might be turning the blame onto me to take the attention away from yourself."

Footsteps on linoleum. A shadow on the floor. I recognized her jasmine scent before I saw her.

"Professor?" Maeve poked her head around the open door. She looked confused, first at me, then at Simon. "I didn't realize the police let you go."

"Oh, they've let me go." Simon pointed at me. "They're onto you, Professor. They'll have you before long."

Maeve watched Simon leave. She turned her amber eyes, normally radiant and curious, onto me with a haunted expression. Debbie followed her into my office.

"Jonathan." As soon as Debbie spoke, I knew that something was wrong. She opened the door wider. "Will you excuse us, Maeve? I need to discuss something with Professor Ferrars."

Maeve looked at me, waiting, and I nodded. Whatever this was, I sensed it was not going to be pretty, and Maeve didn't need to witness it. Debbie shut the door behind her.

"I'm surprised you're here. It seems like everyone else has taken the week off."

"I have some work to do, and I thought my seminar students might need me."

Debbie cleared her throat. She straightened her jacket, stood as tall as her diminutive height would allow, and affected a sad demeanor. "I'm so sorry about everything that has happened since you started at Eventide, Jonathan. Normally, we teach our students in a peaceful corner of the world. Since you've been here," her eyebrows pulled together as she considered her words, "well, you know what's happened since you've been here. Forgive me for eavesdropping. I wasn't really, but

Simon was speaking loudly, and the police were here earlier looking for you. Did they find you?"

"I haven't spoken to the police since Amandine died."

"They came to our faculty meeting this morning. We were finalizing the details of our department budget for next year, resource allocations, that sort of thing, and Detective Strongwater wanted to know why you weren't there."

"We agreed that I wouldn't have to attend the morning meetings."

"I know, and that's what I told him. But then, well, it is odd, isn't it? Even professors who teach night classes come to the daytime meetings when they need to. I thought, well, I'm not sure what I thought, but it sounded like an excuse when I said it."

"It's the truth."

"The truth can sound odd more often than a lie, as I'm sure you know. The thing is, I saw Leonard whisper something to the detective this morning. Then later, Detective Strongwater asked me to verify what Leonard had told him. That you only work at night."

"I teach night classes."

"I know. I hired you to teach them. But, well, I don't know, when you say it like that, it sounds fishy, doesn't it? I can't even begin to guess what Detective Strongwater was thinking. After all, it seems a little too obvious to me. Why would you go around killing your own students in the style of Poe's characters when you're the obvious suspect for such a crime? But I wouldn't worry too much. Detective Strongwater seems to know what he's doing, and he must realize how unlikely it is. When I asked Leonard why he talked to the police, he said that sometimes the most obvious answer is the right answer after all. You didn't kill your students, did you, Jonathan?"

"No, Debbie, I didn't kill them."

"I didn't think so. And Stephen has continued talking about you and Maeve as if there's really something going on between you. We all know not to listen to Stephen when he gets like that, but I'm sorry, Jonathan, I have to ask. Is there anything going on with Maeve?"

"What does Maeve have to do with anything?"

Debbie looked at the door as though Maeve were still there. "Oh, it's nothing, I'm sure, except it's not only Stephen who noticed that you seemed to spend the entire ball together. And then..." She gestured toward the door. "Maeve's a lovely young woman, and she looks up to you. She's always quoting something you said. 'The professor said this' or 'The professor said that.' Sometimes when a young student and a younger professor hit it off, there are problems." She fiddled with the button at the bottom of her jacket.

"Is there something else you want to say to me?"

She dropped her jacket and sighed. "I'm so sorry to have to do this, I mean, we were so excited to have you as the Geddes chair, Rhys and I, but your presence here right now, with what happened to your students, and the police presence, and Simon accusing you of the murders. The truth is, it's too much. I have every confidence that it's just a coincidence that everything started happening when you arrived, and the fact that you teach the Poe seminar, and the way the students were killed, but as long as the investigation is ongoing..."

"I'm not even certain that I am under investigation. As I said, I haven't spoken to the police since..."

"The police want you down at the station. Detective Strongwater told me. I'm surprised they haven't come to find you. I am so sorry, Jonathan, but I'm putting you on administrative leave until the cases are solved and we can go back to some sense of normalcy around here."

"Debbie, why did you hire me? I've been doing this job long enough to know how things are done. I've never been contacted about a position that hasn't been floated, let alone a fully funded chair. Why did you reach out to me?"

"It was Rhys's idea. After poor Larry died and we needed to fill the Geddes chair, Rhys said that he wanted to recruit you for Eventide. We take pride in having the best scholars here. He showed me your research into nineteenth-century American literature, particularly your work on Poe. As you know, positions are usually decided by the hiring committee, but Rhys funds the position, so we tend to defer to his opinion in such matters. Rhys and Larry Presspitch were great friends, you know, and he took Larry's death very hard. When we needed to think about filling the chair for the new academic year, Rhys convinced me that you were the best person for the job. Then Rhys and I convinced the hiring committee that you'd be perfect. And you would have been, except for all of this nonsense."

I pushed my glasses back up my nose. "I understand."

"The term is nearly over, and I'm certain everything will be settled soon. You'll be able to come back for the spring term. You'll be paid during your leave, of course. Rhys was adamant about that. I'm sure you'll be cleared soon. You'll be able to begin again as if none of this happened." She opened the door and saw Maeve waiting. "Just stay out of any other trouble so we can get this mess straightened out." Debbie cast a knowing smile at Maeve as she left.

I powered down my computer and closed the blinds. I ran my hands over my books and recalled why I never brought many belongings to new jobs. I glanced around my square of an office. Should I start packing? I could look at it as a paid holiday until I remembered that the police wanted to see me. More than likely, I'd be spending that holiday behind bars if Strongwater believed Simon. As I shoved a few books into my backpack, I realized that I was most disappointed in Leonard. I know all too well how easily people, even the friendliest people, can turn on you if they think it will benefit them in some way. Perhaps Leonard was the murderer, and he was conspiring with Simon to make me look guilty. At that point, I would have believed anything.

Maeve watched me fill my backpack. "Are you leaving?"

"Permanently. Or at least until the murderer is found. I've been put on administrative leave."

"That's not fair. You didn't do it."

"Simon seems to have convinced Detective Strongwater that I did. Apparently, the police are looking for me."

"Then why aren't they here arresting you?"

"That's an excellent question. I suppose I'll have the answer soon enough."

Maeve followed me downstairs. The campus, though always quiet at that time of night, was deserted, as if Maeve and I were the only two people left in the world. We walked in silence toward Cavendish Hall. I expected my sense of dissociation, that breaking away from myself, to return after this unexpected series of events, but oddly, I felt fine, as though everything was happening to someone else while I watched from the wings.

We stopped outside the dorm, the Queen Anne mansion gray in the gloom. No one else was about. We stood there awkwardly, and I felt her question before she spoke it.

"Are you going to the police now?"

"I should." I half-expected to see uniformed officers jump out of the shadows and try to handcuff me. Good luck with that, I thought. But no one was there except Maeve and me.

"But you're not."

Maeve clutched her oversized wool sweater closer to her chin. I kept returning to the same question. Was it Maeve? Could she have done it? To both of them? Good God, I thought. I'm so paranoid that I'm even considering Maeve as the murderer. Often it's the least likely person, the one with the fewest clues attached to them, who commits the crime—or at least that's what Mrs. Griggs's mystery novels say. I had no choice but to trust Maeve. She had divined my secret, and she had not, to my knowledge, betrayed my trust. But we don't ever truly know another person, and Maeve Lang would remain a mystery to me. Perhaps she had seen something between Thomas and Amandine and was compelled to act. As soon as the thought popped into my mind, I shoved it aside, ashamed of the direction my thoughts had taken.

"Maeve." I wasn't sure how to continue. She waited silently, leaning toward me, but the words would not straighten out in my mind.

"It's all right, Professor." She glanced around, saw nothing but a shadow-like sky and skeleton-like trees. "I've discovered some things you should know about. I'm not going to allow you to be caught up in a crime you didn't commit. I think I'm finally onto something."

I too checked our surroundings. Though everyone in that quaint seaside village seemed to be sleeping, and I didn't hear anything besides the howling wind and our whispering voices, I couldn't take any chances.

Maeve gestured toward campus. "We should go somewhere to talk. The trees have ears, and the sky can see."

We walked to the grassy knoll behind the Chisholm Library and made our way to the back door. Maeve let us in using the key Thomas had given her, then quickly punched the security numbers into the pad on the wall. We took the same route as before, down the stairs to the dark, abandoned offices, through the door, and down into the tunnel.

"It's here, Professor." She flipped on the electric lights and led me to the underground library. The space felt alive, as though the books bid us welcome. Maeve glanced over her shoulder, perhaps checking for any peculiar librarians who happened to be about. "After Simon was arrested, I felt something tugging at me, as if someone was trying to speak to me from the other side."

"Who was it?"

"I'm still not sure. The specter was wearing a mask." Maeve shook her head at my confusion. "I don't mean a literal mask. I mean, it looked like they had a face over their face. A face over a face usually means they're lying or hiding something."

"Do I have a face over my face?"

"Yes. That's how I knew there was something different about you." She reached for a book that seemed to lean toward her. "I'm not sure why, but I felt I was being led here, as if there's some answer I needed to find."

Without warning, a heavy book fell from a high shelf. The thud reverberated through the room, rattling the bookcases along with my nerves. I grabbed the book from the floor and studied the spine. *Llewellyn's Witches' Spell-a-Day Alamanack*. Maeve handed me another—*Liber Tenebris: De Corvo Noctis*.

"The Night Raven."

Some thought began gnawing at my brain stem. I handed the *De Corvo Noctis* to Maeve.

"This looks fairly new."

"Some of these books are quite recent, Professor. Someone is still adding to the collection. I've come back a few times, and I've read through a lot of these volumes."

"That was dangerous, Maeve. Anyone could be down here, including that Mr. Venn."

"I haven't seen the librarian since you and I were here together. I mean, someone has to figure out what's happening. The police don't seem to be doing a very good job of it."

"They have to cover all of their options, I suppose. Do you think that evil spirit you were talking about is down here?"

"I think it's been here, yes. In fact, I think it lives here. I have a theory, Professor, and I think you can help me."

My brave Maeve. I realized in that moment that she was beautiful. Dark-haired, amber-eyed, with the courage of a thousand men. I pressed the knowledge away as quickly as it came. I'm not sure how I felt beyond anger at myself for my momentary lapse. I have always had a superstition that if I forget her, even for one flicker of a moment, then I will lose her forever, and I could not bear that. I pressed my confusion about Maeve aside since I did not have time to dwell on it then.

Suddenly, a mass fluttering, like birds flying low overhead, sounded nearby. Only we were underground and there were no birds. Maeve stepped aside as if to move out of their way.

"What was that?"

"It sounded like a flock of birds." I read the spine of the book she held toward me. "What have you found?"

"Every book here is about magic and spells. Some of them are general manuals you can find at psychic bookstores." She led me toward the shelves on the farthest wall. "The books in this section cover elemental magic. The books here," she gestured to the lowest shelf, "cover psychic magic and using someone's mind to affect the world around them."

"Telekinesis?"

"That's right. Moving objects with the power of concentration. The books here are about energy manipulation, and these are about using clairvoyance to gain knowledge about the past, present, or future. The books here," she pointed at a higher shelf, "focus on herbalism and using the magical properties of plants."

"Which you would know about since you're a hedge witch."

"My grandmother taught me how to use Nature to cast spells."

There.

Finally, a connection. I was so happy I could have hugged Maeve. The books in the underground library were similar to the books described in Mrs. Griggs's journal. I wondered if I should mention the journal to Maeve. Perhaps she would know what to make of it.

She walked to a lone wooden bookcase, chipped gray with age. "These interest me the most. Whoever collected all this was most interested in occult magic. The books here are about malefica, or hexing, which is magic intended to inflict harm on someone or something."

"Black magic."

She nodded. "Here are books about mesmerism, glamours, mist generation, and animal transformation."

Thinking of the journal, I asked, "Is there anything here about immortal life?"

"How did you know?" She gestured to the bookcase across the room. "These are, well, I mean, these are..."

"Yes, Maeve. I can see."

There were books about the undead. About using blood, their own or someone else's, as a conduit for healing wounds or empowering curses. There were books about shadowmancy, manipulating darkness and shadows. There were books about the creation of the undead and how the undead pass their curse onto others to create more of their kind.

Maeve searched my face, for what, I couldn't guess. Did she seek traces of shadowmancy? Did she expect to watch me transform into a freakish demon before her eyes? Did she want to see an example of blood magic?

I knew she knew. I had known since she came to my office that first time that she knew. But that didn't stop the concern that came from wondering what she thought of me. What anyone who knew would think of me. Our silence became taut with unasked questions. She was curious about me, perhaps, but she had every right to be. I pressed my palms to my temples, attempting to push the intrusive thoughts away. The harder I tried, the more unsettled I felt. My memories rushed at me from all angles, though none were clear enough to see.

Maeve turned away, her eyes on the ground, allowing me some privacy while I pulled myself together. Finally, she said, "Simon tried to make me believe that you had done it. At first, I said no, it couldn't have been you, but he was so convincing. Then I thought it had to be Simon because why else would he be so concerned about trying to blame you? I was going to try to prove that it was Simon. That was my original plan."

"It's not your job to prove anything. Please, Maeve. Let the police do their job."

"But the answer is in here. I can feel it. Look." She led me to a desk with time-worn tomes, a quill, and ink. A glance revealed that the ink was wet and must have been used not long before. A spiderweb ran from the wall to the side of the desk. "Look at these, Professor."

I glanced through some old newspapers from the 1840s, mainly from New York and Baltimore, some from Boston, some from Maine. I lifted one of the leather-bound volumes, then another, and I realized—they were the works of Edgar Poe. The newspaper was dated 1845, and there, printed for the first time:

Once upon a midnight dreary, while I pondered, weak and weary,

Over many a quaint and curious volume of forgotten lore—

While I nodded, nearly napping, suddenly there came a tapping,

As of some one gently rapping, rapping at my chamber door.

"'Tis some visitor," I muttered, "tapping at my chamber door—

Only this and nothing more.

Maeve picked up one of the leather-bound volumes.

"These are about Poe. His works. Biographies. Literary criticism. All of it."

There.

A memory roared to life, and I recalled the night when my humanity emerged again. I remembered it so clearly I couldn't believe I had ever forgotten it. I had left the forest at the break of dawn, the night's chill still slipping through. I knew with sudden clarity that the life I had been living was not meant for me. I didn't choose it, and I didn't want it. If I tried, perhaps, I might find a way to bring total oblivion upon myself. It seemed the only way I might finally find peace.

Near the town, the streets smelled of freshly baked bread. Smoke from cooking fires filled the air while children laughed as they raced over the cobblestones wet with recent rain. A dog barked in the distance. I staggered, needing to get home, though I was loath to leave. The scene felt—I am still not certain—comforting, perhaps. As quick as a flash, I felt a different kind of hunger. I was weary of empty nights devoid of purpose. I had interests once. I had goals and dreams like any other man. Could I continue to pursue them? Could I be a better man by contributing what I can? I stood with my arms wide, letting the sun warm my skin, though my eyes became painful, and I left. I passed the tavern, inhaled the scent of fresh coffee, and recalled the joy the drink had brought me in better times. My determination took hold of me. I was tired of being invisible. Even if I had to live in the shadows, I wanted to live, however imperfectly, in this world. I have stayed true to that resolution to this very night.

Maeve watched me, an understanding smile on her lips. Could she read my thoughts? She had told me she wasn't a mind reader, but her compassionate expression told me that she had some sense of my inner struggles.

"I think, Professor, with the books about Poe, the books

about paranormal magic, and the Poe-style murders, I think they set it up to make it look like you're the murderer."

"Why me?"

"Because you're the obvious choice."

"The obvious choice for what?"

"For the evil force at Eventide College."

"Are you saying I'm the evil at Eventide College?"

"No, Professor. I know you're not. But someone is, someone close. Someone who wants to make it look like you're the murderer. And we have to discover who before it's too late."

I thought of Poe—slight, black-haired, sad-looking, a study in contrasts with his logical, almost mathematical mind, his serious manner, and his extreme emotions, with his ability to be both affectionate and vulnerable at the same time. I wondered why his works had been at the heart of this mystery, but then I realized—who else could it have been?

Maeve and I returned down the hallway, up the stairs, through the basement, and out the door to the grassy knoll. Standing outside the Chisholm Library, everything was phantasmagoric. Uncanny.

Twenty

Some late visitor entreating entrance at my chamber door; —
This it is, and nothing more.

I walked Maeve to Cavendish Hall, then wandered home on a roundabout route. I felt quite sane then, though by the time I arrived at the corner of Whitley Way, my thoughts became disconnected once more. I asked myself what I knew for certain. I was still a professor at Eventide College, if temporarily paused. I knew that since I arrived in Maine, I had a bizarre sense of being followed. I knew that there were moments when I felt myself losing my grip on my sanity. I knew that two of my students were murdered in the style of Poe's characters while I was teaching the Poe seminar. Detective Strongwater had told me that he suspected Larry Presspitch had been murdered with nitre, the substance from The Cask of Amontillado. I knew I hadn't killed my students. No. I didn't murder them. I was certain it wasn't me, even if my thoughts had been muddled.

I shuffled toward the cottage like a man in a trance, considering everything Maeve and I had seen in the crypt-like library—the grimoires and books about immortality. The old desk, piled high with Poe.

A snap of branches and footsteps. No one. A flutter of wings above me. Nothing. I paused at the corner of Southshore Road and Whitley Way. If I continued down Southshore, I would head toward the police. If I turned left, I would head toward home. I went home. If I were going to avoid potentially dangerous questions, I had to find the murderer first. I had to prove that it wasn't me. I was determined to keep my secret safe.

I turned down the cul-de-sac and paused outside my door, listening for police sirens. Based on what Debbie said, they were likely looking for me, and there weren't many places to hide in coastal Maine. Well, I thought. Let them come. Perhaps it's better to get it over with. I let myself inside, leaving the house in darkness. The darker the better, as far as I was concerned. When I sat at the desk in the sitting room, the bound journal was there. With nothing else to do but wait, I opened the ivory-tinted pages and read.

Tuesday, 9 June 1846
Southshore, Maine

Since learning about the Kalona Ayeliski, I am convinced that the answer I seek lies with the Raven Mocker. My monomania has grown so severe that I have taken to knocking my head against the wall, yelling aloud in a disquieting voice, "Raven! What Raven?" hoping that Helen would finally respond to my pleas. She is the one who infected me with this overwhelming desire. In moments of despair, I think I will never hear her voice again. Other times, I am certain that she will come once I have the supernatural knowledge I need.

My library continues to outgrow itself. I have been adding to it, tome by tome, one ghastly revelation after the next, all of it obscure, forbidden knowledge. What I have done to get my hands on some of these volumes shall not be shared by me. As I struggled to organize this repository of knowledge, I recalled that behind a false panel in my library, there was a secret—an unmarked door leading down to the basement. Eager to examine the space, I pushed past the creaking door and followed the winding corridor underground. The cadaverous rooms are perfect for my new collection. Now I have two libraries—a proper one in the house for polite company, and a secret sepulchral library that no one but I shall ever see.

Saturday, 13 June 1846
Southshore, Maine

I have felt faint and chill since I began working down here. Sitting at my desk, studying books of necromancy, I have seen the ladders shift, repositioning themselves near books I have not reached for. A low fire burns in the hearth, and a faint warmth pulses as if it is some living thing. I look at the books I have pulled to study, and I wonder about the inexorable knowledge they contain. Through the sound of crackling flames, I hear the beating of powerful wings. More Ravens have returned to the area, and now six of them roost in the clock tower. Are they here for me? Has Helen sent them?

Where the Raven cries, she said.

Where the Raven cries, he said.

Have they read Poe's poem? Poe understands the occultish nature of these scavenger birds. He understands their innate connection to the spiritual world and to death. How did they know to come here?

I climbed the stairs to my proper library and pulled aside the velvet curtains to see two Ravens, not in the clock tower, but in the old tree in the front yard. They perched upon the gnarled branches, tenebrous sentinels that they are, living fragments of midnight. I pressed my nose to the glass, studying the creatures of shadow and silence. Their plumage is not merely black, but a sable sheen, richly layered, as though they drink in dimness. Each feather gleamed with a preternatural luster, like woven twilight. The birds turned their heads toward me, sharp, deliberate, precise. Their eyes glistened. I recognized that gaze; it was the cool appraisal of creatures that possess a singular intelligence. They are altogether fascinating creatures.

"What secrets do you have for me?" I asked.

They croaked and flew toward the clock tower.

When I returned to the basement, I heard whisperings. The books spoke to me, all of them—the grimoires, the books of shadows, the books of witchcraft, the occult codices, the stories of the power of the dead as they crossed the veil between worlds. Should anyone find these books here, I should be put into the madhouse, locked away in cursed darkness for eternity, shut away from all that is good and light. But it is not the light I seek. I am content to be consumed by this dark knowledge.

Saturday, 20 June 1846
Southshore, Maine

For one whole week, I have hardly had my head above ground. I spend hours—all day and all night—reading and annotating and rereading and speaking aloud to myself or to the Ravens I see in my mind's eye, those perched outside my window, ah, just like the poem, Poe knows what I am going through, the ominous obsession and the dreadful never-ending madness that follows.

The stone steps leading into the tomb-like library seem to be alive. They are slick, as though they breathe with moisture. The space smells of earth and something more ancient, older than memory. By the time I reach the last step, the world above ceases to exist. I sit hour after hour, still seeking everlasting life. Every page I read is alive, the words moving in time with the flickering candlelight. Sometimes I remember to stand and stretch my legs. Sometimes I remember to eat and drink. Down here, the air is viscous, pressing against my lungs, but I stubbornly remain, determined on my quest. The new shelves, which I constructed myself, rise impossibly high, the spines of my hard-won books blackened and etched with sigils and languages unknown except perhaps to a few. Candles flicker in iron sconces, the feeble flames at war with the shadows, and often they lose.

When I open the books, the words curl before my eyes like smoke, the pages trembling like wings. Here in this grimoire are spells for healing. In this journal are notes about death, resurrection, and eternal life, though I have yet to find a way to create eternal life for myself. The floor is littered with Raven feathers I have gathered from outside. Black and glimmering, I press the feathers into the parquet like offerings, and I use them for quills. Here in this book, the Liber Tenebris: De Corvo Noctis, are notes concerning the Raven of Night.

"Attend the Raven, for it speaks in silence. Its wings bear the weight of forgotten truths, and its shadow falls where destiny stirs."

This half-life of constant study is my destiny. These books waited centuries for me to find them. Their ink seeps into my blood, inscribing their messages onto my bones. I do not read them, but they read me. Whenever I make my way upstairs, I stop to watch the Ravens. They watch me with equal purpose, their eyes glinting. I have asked them directly, "Can you lead me to immortality?" They croak in return.

When I fall asleep at my desk, the room lengthens, the alcoves deepen, and the books multiply like leather-bound blossoms. I will continue until the last secret is discovered. Those who enter here will not find comfortable knowledge. They will find the dangerous hunt for immortal life.

Those were the last words in the journal since the rest of the pages were torn out. I closed the book, and a key rattled in the front door. I froze, certain some specter, or Officer Yellin, had found me. Instead, it was Mrs. Griggs. She dropped her keys on the side table and flipped on the light.

"At home, hmm? No book learnin' tonight?"

I removed my glasses from my pocket and pressed them onto my nose.

"There isn't much happening since it's Thanksgiving this week. Nearly everyone has gone home for the holiday."

"You better not mind that I'm here to do some cleanin' since this is the only time I have before my children and my grandchildren come for dinner on Thursday." She placed a heavy canvas bag with cleaning supplies and rags on the side table. "Not that there's much to do. You were right. You are house-trained. For a man."

She pulled some window cleaner from the bag and spritzed the sitting room windows. She hummed to herself while she worked, some tune I didn't recognize. Since I had the leather-bound journal in my hand and she was there, that would be the time to ask.

"Excuse me, Mrs. Griggs, but I was wondering about this old journal you've been leaving around the house." I pushed the book across the desk in her direction. "It's dated from the nineteenth century, and it seems as if it might be authentic to the era. I thought it might be valuable to you, so I wanted to return it."

Somehow, I knew what she was going to say before she said it. I knew what I had been reading. I knew I had been in that very library on that very night. I knew, though I didn't want to.

Mrs. Griggs continued wiping down the windows, her gnarled fingers moving in a mechanical rhythm. Perhaps it was odd that she was cleaning the windows since she had been so adamant about that not being part of her job description, but there was something about the intensity with which she worked that made me stay silent. Then she stopped. She squinted at the book, her eyes two chips of flint behind her glasses.

"A book, you say?"

"Yes, well, it's a journal, actually. From a man trying to find immortality."

"Well, now. I've seen a lot of things today since the sun came up. Seen a lighthouse frozen in sea spray. Seen a harbor seal with a taste for stolen mackerel. Seen the wind rip the shingles clear off the old bait shack in the harbor. But I haven't seen that book before. It doesn't belong to me, that's for sure."

"This doesn't belong to you?" I waved the journal in the air. "You haven't been moving it around the house when you've come to clean?"

"I don't go lookin' for things that don't belong to me, young sir, and I don't go hidin' books like they were rotten fish on a line. I like books. You know that. I've found you readin' some of mine from time to time. But that book, no. I haven't seen that one before. Someone must have left it for you. That's a book that wanted to be found."

She returned to spritzing the windows and wiping them down as though our conversation hadn't happened. I turned away, the journal hot between my hands. I didn't want her to see how her words had shattered me. I had wanted to believe that the journal belonged to her. I had convinced myself that nothing about the journal was out of the ordinary. Now there was no denying it. Everything was out of the ordinary.

A ghastly panic overtook me, and every instinct I had recoiled in terror. Someone else, someone who was not Mrs. Griggs, had been leaving the journal around the cottage for me to find. The passage about the Raven Mocker was not a coincidence. The mention of the crypt-like library was not a coincidence. Someone wanted me to know.

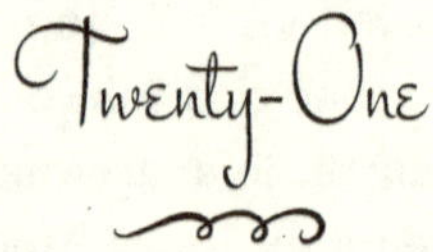

In the deepest slumber—no! In delirium—no! In a swoon—no! In death—no! even in the grave all is not lost.

I left the journal on the desk, removed my glasses, and closed my eyes, unsure what to think. My life was now a Poe story where I was the nameless narrator who slowly descends into a frenzied delirium that would lead to derangement or violence. The scholar in me wanted to examine recent events for theme, foreshadowing, imagery, and symbolism. I still didn't want to accept the journal entries as literal. I still had some hope that the scenes were fragments from an unfinished novel. They certainly had the lost love, haunted memories, and Gothic elements that readers love.

Did Detective Strongwater think I was the murderer? Besides the fact that I was new to Eventide College and the professor of the Poe seminar, and despite Simon's accusations, they had nothing to connect me to the crimes. Or perhaps I didn't know what they had. I couldn't prove my innocence, but then you're supposed to be considered innocent until proven guilty. At least in theory. That's the purpose of an alibi, isn't it? To show that you weren't there when the incident occurred? Yet that was precisely my problem: I didn't have an alibi, at least not a good one. Perhaps I was making more trouble where there wasn't any. Perhaps I should go to the police and answer their questions (keeping the lie as close to the truth as possible). Hopefully, they had some new leads that didn't include me. Hopefully, they would soon solve the puzzle of the Poe-style murders.

An ineffable melancholy overwhelmed me, and I had to fight the urge to run away and leave the madness behind. Solving these crimes was no simple matter. Someone, or more than one someone, was responsible for two and possibly three deaths. The physical strength required for the murders of Thomas and Amandine was extraordinary. I possess that strength. Hopefully, the police did not know that. Thomas's throat was slit to the point of decapitation. Was his throat slit first, and then his corpse was thrown through the window? I had seen his mangled body, grotesque on the ground. According to Maeve, the police were not going with the suicide theory because of the angle of the slice across Thomas's throat. Amandine was an athletic young woman preparing for a brown belt in Taekwondo. Whoever strangled her had the strength to shove her corpse up the chimney. Elias Venn came into my thoughts then, his cadaverous complexion, the way he hungrily eyed Maeve. I knew what he was from the first moment I saw him. What if the murderer was someone beyond the realm of comprehension? Someone not human?

Someone like me.

That had to be the answer. After all, there were no escaped orangutans—that I was aware of.

Mrs. Griggs was pretending not to notice me as she cleaned the kitchen, scrubbing a countertop I never used. But I saw her curious expression, how she watched every movement I made. How much did she know? She was a shrewd woman, certainly. I wouldn't be surprised if she knew everything. Without a word, I left for Cavendish Hall to find Maeve. I needed to know what else she had discovered during her visits to the underground library. There was no question in my mind that it was the same library I had read about in the journal. Was the writer of the journal alive? Did he find his immortality after all?

I had sensed that Maeve was holding back some knowledge. She had taken a chance researching in those archives alone, especially with the spectral form of Elias Venn lurking somewhere nearby, but she was brave, Maeve, more than I was then. I thought of her determined eyes, lit like amber from within. Then Debbie's comment about young students and youngish professors rattled me. No, I decided. I would not involve Maeve any longer. For her to continue on this quest would endanger her, and she had done enough for me. But she had been right all along. There was a malevolent entity haunting Eventide College, and now I had to find it.

That late November night came with a full moon casting a high path across the sky, leaving a bright, cold light. The frozen ground and the sea smoke rising off the water coated the coastline in phosphorescence. Everything was distant and spectral, as though the world turned behind frosted glass. I lingered outside the cottage, considering my options. I might return to Simon's house to examine it again. Perhaps it was Simon after all, and Amandine was his accomplice. That must be the answer. Amandine had helped Simon, and then he had to get rid of his one witness. Yet no matter how many times I went around and around that answer, it didn't sit right. I simply didn't believe that Simon had murdered either Thomas or Amandine. Thomas's murderer must have been an outside assailant, though I wasn't sure how that outside assailant could make their way to an upper floor in Simon's house without being seen. I am many things, but I am not invisible. If the murderer were like me, he would not be invisible either. On second thought, I decided to give Simon's house a wide berth. Simon seemed determined to frame me, and the last thing I needed was for him to see me lurking on his property.

I had to do something, so I returned to the underground library. I sensed that whatever answers I needed could be found there. I flashed across campus, then took my time, surveying the area outside the Chisholm Library, searching for clues. I wasn't certain what I was looking for, but I looked anyway. I was desperate for anything that might help me understand, but there was nothing. The Chisholm Library was just a library, the path across campus an ordinary walkway surrounded by deflated grass and naked trees. I stopped. I listened. No one. Instead of a key, I picked my way in, an old talent I had not used in some time. I had peeked when Maeve punched the security code into the pad, so I knew what it was. Inside the library, I flashed down the stairs and peered into the depths of the tunnel. Black. Grave-like. Morbid. My vision wavered, and I saw a spreading pool of murky water. I blinked, and it was gone. I steeled myself and concentrated on what I was doing. The tunnel felt like a charnel house, too dark for mortals to see. I could not allow my mind to falter. I forced myself to walk into the underworld, one step at a time. Though I was alone, I felt as if the entire world were watching. Poe kept me company.

From ev'ry depth of good and ill
The mystery which binds me still—
From the torrent, or the fountain—
From the red cliff of the mountain—
From the sun that 'round me roll'd
In its autumn tint of gold—
From the lightning in the sky
As it pass'd me flying by—

From the thunder, and the storm—
And the cloud that took the form
(When the rest of Heaven was blue)
Of a demon in my view—

"Ha!" My words echoed in the long corridor. "You knew, didn't you?"

As if in answer, I heard a whisper, soft as breath, repeating phrases from long ago, phrases I thought I had buried.

The Gentleman of Shadows.

The Raven Mocker.

I turned sharply. No one. Why would someone repeat those words after so many years? I must have looked half-mad as I searched everywhere for the speaker. I felt demented enough for ten men.

"Oh, Edgar," I said. "If you could see me now."

To keep control of my sanity, I focused on my actions. I felt the swing of my feet as I crept down the hall. I heard my footsteps on the concrete as I neared the crypt-like library. I searched for clues, ideas, anything that might help me discover the killer and help my remaining students. More selfishly, I was doing it for myself. To keep my secret safe.

A rhythmic sound, soft but steady. I stopped, straining my ears, but I couldn't make sense of it. I pushed the door open and searched the shadows. When no imps jumped out at me, I moved toward the shelves. Near the desk, the cobwebs had been cleared away, the books of Poe stacked neatly. Someone had been there since my last visit. Perhaps it was Maeve. Perhaps it was the author of the journal. Perhaps it was the murderer. Was my guess correct? Was the murderer not natural? I looked for Elias Venn, librarian, embarrassed by my own reluctance to admit the truth to myself. I can detect someone preternatural easily enough. Unless he is as good at hiding as I am.

I scanned the spines, wondering what clues I had missed,

and I found myself standing near the books about immortality. Eternal life is the ultimate dream for so many. Live forever. Just as his wife had bid him. If only I could have explained. Immortality is not what you think it is. So often, we create images in our heads and think that when we achieve this glorious desired end, then we will be happy. If I only had the person I love, I would be happy. If I only lived forever, I would be happy. If only, if only. Then, when we get it, we realize that reality has nothing to do with the perfect pictures we created. All humans think they want to live forever. But forever takes far too long. I have had to explain many times, no, you do not really want forever. You only think you do. But no one ever seems to hear me because their pretty pictures are far too perfect.

While I found such thoughts intriguing, I knew that I wasn't any closer to discovering the murderer. Everywhere I turned was another stack with another hundred books to search. Perhaps I could have used Maeve's help after all.

I returned to the desk and sat in the chair. I put the books and magazines to one side and studied the grimoires. The *Liber Tenebris*, the one about ravens, was no longer there, replaced by *Liber Tenebris: On the Passage Beyond Life*. I opened to the first page and read aloud.

"He who desires the embrace of eternity must first surrender the breath of the mortal coil. Let none presume, for the path is narrow, and the cost exceeds the grasp of flesh."

According to the tome, should one wish to embrace immortality, one needed:

1) A vessel of obsidian, polished to a mirror finish.

2) A chalice of silver, filled with the blood of the seeker.

3) Nightshade, wolfsbane, and the feather of a vulture.

4) A candle rendered from creatures who have never known the sun.

5) A sigil of the Immortal Eye.

Nonsense, all of it, but then some people will believe anything. I flipped through another volume, *On the Gift of the Crimson Shadow*. Again, I read aloud.

"There is a passage between life and the endless night. Few are chosen to walk it, fewer still to return. Those who seek the Second Birth must find the Eternal Ones who are colder than moonlight and whose eyes bear the memory of antiquity. To be emptied is to be filled anew. To lose the warmth of the sun is to gain the wisdom of the moon. What passes between the living and the dead is a covenant. The exchange is not equal. One gives eternity. The other gives everything else. Drink of the shadow, and the shadow will drink of you." I closed the book and shuddered. So he had found it after all. His immortality.

The rhythmic sound grew louder, a faint drum at first, and then a thrumming meter, like clockwork, tick-tock, reverberating beneath my feet. The deeper I moved into the vault, the more the ground shook. Tick-tock. Tick-tock.

I spun around. No one. Whispered voices rolled high and away in a simple cadence, teasing me. I slapped my hands over my ears in a feeble attempt to keep the noise out, insisting that my mind was playing tricks on me yet again. A trembling unease overwhelmed me when something unseen crept toward me like a shadow throbbing in the dark. The further into the vault I crept, the louder the sound became—tick-tock tick-tock—until the tomes exhaled, the candles flickered out, and I stood in darkness. For anyone else, it would have been too dark to see.

Finally, I recognized the sound. It was a metronome, knocking beneath the floorboards in a hideous rhythm like a human heart. Tick-tock tick-tock tick-tock.

No. I didn't want to know. No. No. No. Instead of telling myself where I was and what I was doing, I wanted the opposite. I wanted to be somewhere else, anywhere else, in any other place or time. This wasn't real. This wasn't happening. An exquisite melancholy overwhelmed me as I felt my mind split in time with the metronome, tick-tock, tick-tock, mocking me. Tick-tock. "To die laughing must be the most glorious of all glorious deaths!" Poe said. Only I wasn't laughing.

One of the long floor panels poked up from the ground. I pulled on it until it came away, and the ones next to it. Tick-tock. Tick-tock. The ticking grew louder, louder, and I was the nameless narrator in The Tell-Tale Heart. Except I hadn't murdered anyone. I have never felt more unspeakably doomed than I did in that moment when I pulled up the final floorboard and saw—

Maeve.

My intelligent, brave Maeve, strangled, the vicious gash in her chest empty where her heart should have been, the metronome on her chest, beating the rhythm of her missing heart. A melancholy grace haunted her delicate features. She still smelled of jasmine. In a fit of frenzy, I smashed the metronome against the wall. I pulled her from the ground, splattering myself with her blood. A shroud-like darkness covered me, and everything went blank. Maeve, murdered in the style of a Poe story. I dropped my head onto her shoulder and rocked her, back and forth, until I set her gently down, brushing her hair from her beautiful face. Then the rage began, a fury unlike any I had known for many years. I tore the library apart, one bookcase at a time, yanking the shelves from their fastenings and slamming them to the ground, hundreds of tomes fallen in my furore. With the library demolished and not a shelf left standing, I wondered what to do for poor Maeve. If I went to the police, they would think it was me. That I had killed her. I was covered in her blood, after all. I panicked and searched for an escape. I noticed a second ladder in the corner. Before I climbed it, I knelt beside Maeve, holding her hand.

"I'm sorry, Maeve, but I have to leave you here for now. I promise you, I will discover who did this to you. And I will make them pay."

When I reached the top of the ladder, I pushed the cover open and climbed through. I was not on campus near the Chisholm Library, but somewhere that looked like a garden. The ice had softened, and sleet fell like darts from the sky. The most desolate thoughts crowded my mind. Thomas. Amandine. Maeve. And quite possibly Lawrence Presspitch. Who was this madman? I gasped aloud when I recognized the midnight garden from the night we searched for Amandine.

"What is this?" I said aloud.

The gloomy black bricks and Gothic windows of Eventide Manor bowed toward me in reply.

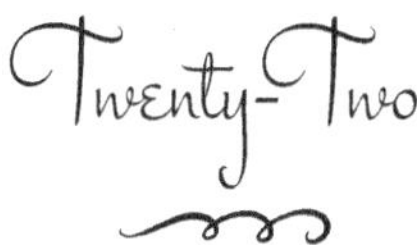

There are chords in the heart of the most reckless which cannot be touched without emotion.

The thought of Maeve, alone, with no one to watch over her or see to her proper burial, was nearly enough to cripple me. But I had to stay focused. These things will be seen to, I told myself. Her family will be notified. I knew that this, whatever this was, would all be over soon. I needed a plan. I needed to think, and the cottage was the one place where I could hide, until, as I neared Whitley Way, I remembered the police. Only they were not there. All right then, I thought. They will have to play according to my rules. I am going back to the cottage. The police may well show up, but if they want to arrest me they will have to catch me first. Showing up at the police station was no longer an option. If this murderer was going to be found, I had to find him. There was no other way.

Sleet became ice, which became fast-falling snow, the moon blanketed by compressed clouds. I smelled the sweet, earthy scent as soon as I turned down the cul-de-sac. A butcher's knife protruded from my front door, pinning ivory-colored pages to the wood. A phantasmal murmur crept toward me through the gloom. Everywhere was midnight and silent. My raven friends were not there. When I pulled the bloody knife from the door, I caught the pages as they fell.

Inside the cottage, I sat in darkness since I dared not turn on a light. With appalling dread, I steadied myself.

There.

The face I had been struggling to remember was still just out of reach, though I felt that he was closer. Where was he hiding in my mind? I couldn't run from the truth any longer, though I wanted to. I have run so many times. After I stay somewhere for too long. After someone looks too closely. After someone notices something that strikes them as odd. Uncanny. It always happens sooner or later. That night, the minutes became hours, which collapsed into seconds, until years sailed past. Faces flipped behind my eyes, features and expressions shifting in and out of focus. My sanity was strained to its limit, and for one mournful moment, I was certain that they were not my memories but someone else's. Half-formed thoughts became glass that shattered into slivers, and when I reached for them, they sliced me.

Stillborn memories continued shifting in my mind. I ran my hand across the floorboards, convinced that Maeve was buried there, that she was haunting me, trying to communicate with me as the man's wife tried to communicate with him. Every one of the dark wood boards had its own sinister intention—I was so certain of it that I could taste it, metallic like the blood on the knife I left carelessly on the dining room table. Dread rose up my throat and down my legs. The ghastly whispers of the newly deceased echoed in the thin chambers of my mind. They were there, and they wanted me. Joy, fear, rage, bewilderment, and melancholy surged unbidden, twisting into grotesque visions. Was I laughing or screaming, crying or smiling? The waking nightmare would not end. A ghostly hand brushed my shoulder, and I flinched. No one. A whisper touched my ear. No one.

I was disintegrating into sepulchral bones and decrepit dust, splitting in two—one self standing, observing, still logical, while the other lurked in the corner, crouching away from the light, gargoyle-like, suspicious and frantic. I reached for my real self, but it slipped from my grasp, disappearing into a shadowy woe that grew darker, darker, and I wondered at what point you are so consumed by madness that you are past the point of no return. Through it all, the sweet, metallic scent from the knife rattled my very instincts. I closed my eyes and turned away. It took forever for the raging thoughts to burn themselves out.

Outside, snow cloaked the roads, the houses, the trees. Visibility narrowed to a few feet. Everything was blurred by gusting flakes and whirling winds. Once again, through the silence, there were footsteps and whispering. The police? Even in my shattered state, I knew that I could not allow them to take me, so I fled toward Eventide College. As I left my cottage behind forever, my two raven friends, black and bold, braved the storm to guide me to campus through the blizzard. Everything in the world was a white haze. Windows glowed dimly through the whiteout, the only signs of warmth. Pines bowed low under their burden, the sea relentless beneath the storm, its sound a heartbeat against the shriek of the gale. Every sound I heard was a heartbeat. I could not shake the rhythmical terror from my mind.

On campus, I wound around Richfield Chapel, the Main Quad, and the Beckham School of the Arts, all of it dreary in the blizzard, to the Eliot School. Thankfully, my passkey had not been revoked. I opened the building without setting off the alarm, though I didn't turn on any lights, keen to avoid suspicion for as long as possible. I crept up the stairs, and shadows shaped like ravens flitted across the walls. I was besieged by nightmarish visions of open graves. Cadaverous hands reached for me as if to pull me down. You belong here, the ghouls screamed. You are like us. Thomas, Amandine, Maeve, and Larry Presspitch pointed at me, calling to me, accusing me as though I had orchestrated this tragedy. A vision of my wife lingering among the murdered assaulted my senses. Though she did not rebuke me as the others did, her dark eyes were sad, so sad, and she turned from me in shame. If I had a heart, that would have destroyed it. I was felled by the remorse that I should have had any part in this catastrophe, and I covered my eyes so I would not have to see them. When the hideous visions faded away, I let myself into my office. I grabbed my scholarly texts—*The Collected Works of Edgar Allan Poe* edited by Thomas Ollive Mabbott, *Collected Writings of Edgar Allan Poe* edited by Burton R. Pollin, and *The Norton Critical Edition* edited by G. R. Thompson. I pored over them compulsively, searching for patterns, clues, hidden warnings, anything that might make sense of these senseless acts. A dreadful knowledge hovered at the edges of my thoughts. The memory I wanted was so close.

There.

No matter how much I wrestled with the murky vision, I could not grasp it. Finally, I left it alone, hoping it would find me when it was ready. To settle my thoughts, I wrote down everything I knew.

1. Larry Presspitch. According to Detective Strongwater, killed by nitre (The Cask of Amontillado)

2. Thomas Lambert and Amandine Wesson. Lambert—sliced throat and shattered bones; Wesson—strangled and stuffed up a chimney (The Murders in the Rue Morgue)

3. Maeve Lang. Strangled, her body left under the floorboards with a metronome to mimic the sound of a beating heart (The Tell-Tale Heart)

Maeve.

Writing her name like that was too hard. Her wise eyes, her easy smile. Her ethereal grace carved as if by moonlight. I nodded at the memory, as though she stood before me. I wanted to reach out to her, tell her it's all right, everything will be all right. But I could only wallow in my horror. The best way I could honor her memory was to find whoever did this to her, so I pressed on.

I read Poe's stories over again, but I was at a loss. There was a connection there, I was certain of it, but it remained in the fog. I closed my eyes, struggling to see. I was so close to discerning its shape, but it slipped away again.

There.

I felt its texture, its weight, its scent, its color, but not its form. Finally, I thought I had it. A vision of Poe. Poe where?

There.

At the farm in Fordham, New York. Then it was gone again. The misty remembrance peered at me from behind the fog, biding its time.

There.

A flash of a face, but nothing about it stood out to me. It was ordinary. Like any face. Then he smiled as though he knew I was onto him. If only I could remember who he was and why he was haunting me. Was this face connected to the murders? Was he the killer? If the killer was trying to make a point, then I still had three living students. Which story might be used to murder the next victim? The Masque of the Red Death? I wasn't sure how someone might engineer a communicable disease. Hanging from a tree or striking the head with an axe, as in The Black Cat? It was a possibility. This murderer wasn't afraid of gruesome violence. The Premature Burial? That story has a happier ending than most Poe tales, which made it an unlikely choice. The narrator, who suffers from cataleptic trances, becomes obsessed with the fear of being buried alive.

After suffering a near-death experience, believing he has indeed been buried alive, he realizes he was merely in a ship's dark berth, not a coffin. Then there was The Fall of the House of Usher, which was also a tale of cataleptic trances and being buried alive, only without a happy ending. Nearly every Poe story shows some horrible way to die. Most of the tales would do.

I returned the books to the shelves and sat on the floor, pondering my next move. The frantic snowstorm pounded the window, and I leaned my head against the wall and listened. Whispers echoed down the hall, first muffled, then clamorous.

The Gentleman of Shadows.

The Raven Mocker.

I have been known by many names.

The whispers grew louder, and the walls vibrated. I opened my door and scanned the hallway. No one. I closed my eyes and listened again. Someone had to be nearby. I was not imagining it. I crept toward the elevator, straining my hearing as far as it would go, but the only sound was the raging storm outside. A snap, a branch perhaps, or something else.

Again, I smelled it before I saw it: that unmistakable scent of earth and iron. The bloody knife I had removed from the cottage door was now pushed through my office door, and the journal pages I had left forgotten were pinned again for me to find. I stopped, listened. Someone was there. Someone was taunting me.

With grim determination, I pulled the knife from my door and gathered the ivory papers. Whoever was following me, whoever was determined for me to have this knife and these pages, was setting me up. I expected the police to arrive at any moment and find me in possession of the bloody knife. I knew I should leave, now, just flash away, but I didn't. I was stubborn, and I wouldn't leave until I knew what secret these pages held for me. The room quivered with the grand reveal. The answers I had been seeking were in my hands, spectacularly presented to me—twice. I sat at my desk while I read.

Thursday, 19 November 1846
Southshore, Maine

I am losing my mind with grief that this long, maddening journey has been for naught.

Robert Beckham is ready to finalize our plans for the campus. He is an artist as well as a scholar of the highest order. Together, we have been planning our college as we prepare to mold our students into young gentlemen with disciplined minds. We mean to provide a Classical Curriculum with heavy emphasis on Greek and Latin, parsing the grammar of Cicero, Homer, and Livy. We will focus on Rhetoric, Oratory, and Moral Philosophy, as well as the Natural Philosophies of Astronomy and Mathematics. Beckham insists that we provide instruction in the arts as well as in the Practical Sciences, such as Chemistry and Civil Engineering.

Our schedule, as it stands, is such:

6:00 a.m.—Morning Prayers at the Richfield Chapel
8:00 a.m.—Greek Recitation
11:00 a.m.—Logic/Rhetoric
2:00 p.m.—Natural Philosophy and Practical Sciences
4:00 p.m.—Art Studies (Painting, Sculpture, et cetera)
5:00 p.m.—Literary Society

Since I have become obsessed with necromancy, I have left everything concerning the campus and the scheduling in Beckham's capable hands. In fact, I have spoken to Beckham about my study of the Dark Arts. I have been honest with him since I had to be honest with someone. Keeping this secret alone was no longer possible. I even told him of my quest for immortality. He did not laugh. He did not smirk or call me a fool or any other number of things he might have said. In fact, he became rather curious about the subject himself.

During dinner last night, we were discussing Typee: A Peep at Polynesian Life by Herman Melville, as well as Mosses from an Old Manse by Nathaniel Hawthorne, highly popular amongst my Transcendentalist friends. We discussed The Redskins by James Fenimore Cooper. I find Cooper's work fascinating, having visited Indian Territory and seen for myself how brutally we have treated our neighbors.

"Have you read Poe in Godey's Lady's Book?" Beckham asked as he passed the bottle of port to me. "The Cask of Amontillado is one of the finest stories I've read about the desire for revenge."

"Yes," I answered. "I've read it. For Montresor, revenge is calculated. He will not be punished for his misdeeds. He intends to commit the perfect crime of revenge and get away with it. And so he does."

Beckham sipped his port, nodding sagely. "Committing that perfect crime because of a thousand injuries Montresor says he has suffered. I've wondered if the thousand injuries actually happened. Were they made up in Montresor's head? Perhaps Montresor was descending into madness already, and Fortunato got caught up in it by becoming Montresor's obsession."

"Ah." I poured more wine into my glass. "And Montresor blames the nitre and the dampness for Fortunato's cough. As they walk through the underground vaults, Montresor repeatedly draws Fortunato's attention to the white crystalline substance on the damp walls."

Beckham stared into his goblet, stroked his moustache, and repeated from memory.

"It is farther on, said I; but observe the white web-work which gleams from these cavern walls...It is the nitre." Beckham

sipped his wine before he continued. "But Fortunato is arrogant and drunk and wants to see this bottle of sherry, so he continues to follow Montresor through the vaults. He chooses to ignore the warning signs, and as a result, he suffers the consequences."

"Death is the ultimate consequence," I said. "Fortunato willingly enters Montresor's catacombs, and the nitre acts as a shroud for a soon-to-be-dead Fortunato."

Beckham grinned as though he had devised the dastardly scheme himself, and he continued stroking his moustache like a theatrical villain. For a moment, I worried for my safety. I checked, and I was not drunk. I had but two glasses of port. Still, I would not allow Beckham to lead me anywhere that night.

"It is the perfect revenge," Beckham said. "Montresor uses Fortunato's weaknesses against him. When Montresor chains Fortunato to the wall and builds the enclosure around him, he gets the revenge he desperately desires. Montresor does indeed walk away with impunity. How wonderful, to get revenge against your enemies, to have them know it was you, and to suffer no consequences."

"Do you have many enemies?" I asked.

"Fortunately, I do not." Beckham laughed as he poured himself another glass. I did not join him. "But we might be onto something with Poe."

"I beg your pardon?"

"With Poe. You have been obsessed with Ravens, the mystical, and immortality. Poe writes about such things better than anyone else. Perhaps he knows something."

"About fictional Ravens, perhaps."

"Perhaps. But it never hurts to ask. I was going to Fordham to see him. His wife is quite ill and has but weeks at best. I've known him for several years now, and I want to help if I can. The end will be hard for him. He is...fragile."

The cunning look that had startled me was gone, and Beckham was once again my wise and kind-hearted friend.

. . .

Monday, 30 November 1846
Fordham, New York

We arrived in New York City via two steamboats and a train, then onto Fordham via stagecoach. Though we dealt with the November snow, it was soft, not ice, and no severe storms impeded our way.

Poe's cottage is a quaint structure, a plain wooden farmhouse, small but sufficient for himself, his mother-in-law, and his young wife, who is not long for this world. Fordham itself is quiet and pretty. On our journey here, Beckham said that Poe hoped the country air would help with his wife's consumption. Sadly, it does not seem to have helped.

Why a man would choose authorship to earn his bread, I could not say. Poe, one of our premier men of letters, is very poor. His wife has a cat, a hearty calico one to be sure, but still only a cat for her warmth. She lies in a simple rope bed, cheerful, but the air is heavy with the knowledge of her fatal illness. I don't wish to make a nuisance of myself to a man already grieving the wife he will soon lose, and I regret having come. This is not the time to bother him about Ravens and the paranormal world. If I knew how to defeat mortality, I would save this young woman.

I will not stay for long, only a few more days, perhaps, and then I will make the journey back to Maine, hopefully before the weather turns too ugly. I know Beckham meant well by bringing me, but I am intruding on Poe's private grief, and I should go.

Thursday, 3 December 1846
Fordham, New York

. . .

One hears such odd things about Poe in literary circles, though in Maine, we are far enough away from the conversaziones. We pride ourselves on granting merit for its own sake. I am not American by birth, though I have been in Maine long enough that I proudly consider myself a Son of Maine. We Mainers are individualists and don't care to have our tastes dictated by the New York literati. My point being, the Poe I have heard gossip of, and the Poe I have come to know, are not the same man.

Of course, he wears his grief in every movement, every expression, every sigh, as I'm certain I did when Helen died of the same wasteful disease. I see nothing of the caustic critic in this sad-eyed, melancholy man. I see no evidence of the Tomahawk Man, who hacks literary mediocrity to bits. But then, his current circumstances do not allow for such displays. There are more important matters to consume his mind than improper grammar. While we have been here, Poe has been a gracious, charismatic host, even though I am, for all intents, a stranger to him. The man is polished in his manners, and he speaks softly but with conviction. He gives the impression of a man who listens more than he speaks. At times, he becomes wary and withdraws, though I believe his wife's illness allows for such actions. In truth, I like the man. I pray he can overcome his impending loss with resilience.

Later, as we walked through Fordham, Beckham was in front, Poe and I behind. With Beckham's encouragement, I decided to explain my quest. I felt he would understand, the author of The Raven, the man with the dying wife, the man who writes so believably about the madness found within the human heart. I told him all. I revealed my innermost soul to this man, who was as much a stranger to me as I was to him.

He said nothing for the longest time. I thought he hadn't heard anything I said. Then I realized he was simply thinking before he spoke.

"I assure you, I am not troubled by your words," he said.

"Only by the echoes they've stirred. Forgive me. My thoughts wander down darker corridors than I intend. It's only that I question your hypothesis. Who would want to live forever? One human lifetime is all too hard." His voice was low and deliberate, and he shaped each word with care. "There is someone here in Fordham you should perhaps meet. He is a professor, formerly of Cambridge."

My ears perked. I was seeking professors for my own college.

"Cambridge? Is he an Anglican priest?"

"No, but his mathematical skills equal his Greek and Latin. He can calculate the orbit of a planet, then write an ode in Ancient Greek. If you want to discuss Aeschylus, Sophocles, or Horace, he's your man."

"What is he doing here?"

"He says he has left his position to take some time away from the rigors of academic life. He wishes to study, think, and write on his own, perhaps for a year or two."

"You suggested that he might be able to help me with my quest?"

"Perhaps. Mind, I am not certain that he will help you, or even wish to help you, since he seems to deny his very nature. But I am afraid he is the only help I can offer."

"Who is he?" I asked.

"He has not told me his name. I call him the Gentleman of Shadows." Poe smiled pleasantly. "Not to his face, of course. But I suspect he knows."

That night, after checking that his wife was as comfortable as possible and leaving her in the hands of her mother, Poe, Beckham, and I walked some distance to an isolated farmhouse, smaller than the one Poe inhabited. Gaslight glowed in the windows. Poe knocked. The curtains fluttered, and the door opened. I was surprised at the handsome young man in the doorway. He nodded at Poe but stared warily at Beckham and me.

"These are my friends," Poe said. "May I introduce you?"

The night passed pleasantly enough. From our conversation, I realized that the young man was a brilliant scholar. He had a keen mind and seemed interested in many subjects, particularly our American literature. That was why he had settled in New York. He wished to consider our books more deeply. He knew Melville and Irving and most of our important literary men and women. The young man and Poe debated about the power of the Transcendentalists, the young man firmly on Emerson's side, Poe defiantly not.

"I believe you're missing the point," the young man said. "Emerson argues that humanity needs to develop an original relationship with Nature since he sees it as a source of spiritual and moral revelation. Through Nature we can find Divine Truth."

"I beg you," Poe said, "spare me the comfort of false optimism. Perhaps they could state their beliefs less arrogantly. How could they possibly know what humanity needs?"

"He's speaking metaphorically."

"Is he indeed. If he could be so kind as to refrain from such conjecture, we might yet rescue reason from ruin. But I must say, your enthusiasm is admirable even if it is sadly misguided."

Their conversation was amiable, and they seemed to enjoy their banter. Finally, Poe made his excuses that he had to return to his wife. Beckham accompanied him, leaving the professor and me alone.

The young man waited, his attention fixed on me. He was taller than most, with gold hair that fell into his dark, no, black eyes, his pale complexion transparent in the gaslight. After reading books of spells, of black magick, of the preternatural, I gasped aloud when I recognized him for what he was. He could not hide his true nature from me. I guessed Poe knew as well. The young man seemed to sense that I knew more than he wished me to. He drew away, in fear, I thought.

"I need your help," I said.

Before he could reply, I told him my tale. As I had with Poe, I told him everything. About Helen. About Helen's desire for me to live forever. About my monomania, my quest, my growing library, and my need to discover one small piece of immortality for myself.

"You can help me," I said. "From the look in your eyes, I know you understand."

He walked to the hearth, staring into the flames as though conjuring something. He turned to me and sighed.

"I cannot help you," he said. "I cannot inflict this," he gestured toward himself, "on anyone else. You do not understand the reality of this life. I too lost my wife..."

"Is she like you?" I asked.

"No," he answered. "And your wife has been gone for some time. Do you really want to live forever without her? Because if I had my choice, I would have died along with my wife."

"But Helen told me she'd be with me always. Not in body. I know that. But here," I tapped my heart, "and here," I tapped my head. He grabbed my hand forcefully, jerking me toward him, and put it to his chest. When I felt nothing, no breathing, no heartbeat, I nearly bolted for the door. He stepped close to me, his face before mine.

"Is this what you want?"

"I want to do as my wife bid me. I want to live forever."

"Does she know you're here?"

"She hasn't visited me in a while."

"How long is a while?"

"Some months. Perhaps a year."

The young-looking professor laughed, a bitter, hollow sound. "When you are like me, some months mean forever." He became thoughtful as he studied me. "But that doesn't bother you, does it? You have become obsessed with the idea of immortality. I'm not sure your wife is even a matter of consequence for you anymore."

His words could not have stung more if he had slapped me. I have felt the inkling of this, that immortality itself has become the goal for its own sake, though I was loath to admit it even to myself. When this young-looking man said it, this being whom I now realized was far older than I could have guessed, I still could not bring myself to acknowledge the truth.

"You lie!" I shouted. I meant to strike him, but his reflexes were too fast. He grabbed my hand before it left my side.

"You want to live forever no matter the cost. I cannot stop you from your quest, but I will not help you. I refuse to be the cause of anyone else's suffering."

"I am already suffering. Please." If he were the kind of immortal that I suspected he was, I knew that he could turn me if he chose. I pulled back my coat and shirt sleeve and offered my wrist. "Do what you must."

The professor looked at my blue veins, and for a moment, I thought he was tempted. He shook his head.

"No," he said. "Never again."

"You've done it before." He turned away. "You can do it again, only one more time. To help me, a fellow sufferer who misses his beloved wife."

"I have walked in places where shadows remember more than the living ever could. I will not help you to that fate."

"Here, look," I said. "This is my wife. Her name is Eleanor. I call her Helen." I took the miniature of her precious face out from under my hat and showed him her dark, curling hair, her wise gray eyes. "Think of all the wonderful things I will do with my time. I am a scholar, like you. I am working to create a college with Mr. Beckham, a wonderful school for men who take learning and research as seriously as we do."

"You can do those things now."

"I want to do them forever."

"Obsession never ends well." He closed his eyes and shook his

head. "I cannot help you. I'm sorry. One day you will thank me."

"I will never thank you for denying me the one thing I have wanted for so long."

Nothing I said, no pleading, no threats of exposure, no bribes, would change his mind. When he had had enough of me, he opened his door, waiting silently, refusing to look at me. Finally, I left. After he shut the door behind me, I banged my fist on his window, shouting so loudly that the dead in the nearby graveyard could hear.

"You will wish you were truly dead, you pallid fiend! One day, I will make you pay for denying me!"

When I returned a few hours later with some hope of yet convincing him, he was gone, the little farmhouse abandoned. There was not one item left behind to show that it had ever been occupied. I am leaving tomorrow for home.

How dare he! How dare he deny me the gift he had been given! Did he not find me worthy? Did I not come up to his exacting standards? Who is he to deny me that which I desire most in the world? I have been searching for this, for him, for years. I found the Raven Mocker at last, and this is how he treats me?

I am nursing my fury in fits and starts. Poe has loaned me his copy of Godey's Lady's Book, the issue with the story Beckham and I discussed. "The thousand injuries of Fortunato I had borne as I best could, but when he ventured upon insult I vowed revenge..."

Ah. Perhaps I have not suffered a thousand injuries from the young-looking professor, but his one injury is enough. Unlike Montresor, I have given utterance to threats, but then the fiend vanished into the night. He has gone to who knows where. But one day I will find him, and I will make him pay. I too must punish with impunity. I will win in the end. I will have my immortality. And my revenge.

All in vain; because death, in approaching him, had stalked with his black shadow before him, and enveloped the victim.

When memory returns, sudden and complete, it is like the sunlight that breaks through the dark of a storm. The recollection had always been there, waiting for me to catch up. My mind, stubborn for so long, now opened wide. How did I miss the signs? He had been hiding in plain sight. That elusive recollection, the one I had been grasping at, finally cooperated, and I realized what I should have seen all along. Am I so detached from my own memories that a clean-shaven face was all I needed to throw me off the scent? He had been the predator all along, right under my nose, and I never suspected. I put the journal pages down and said the passage aloud.

"You, who so well know the nature of my soul, will not suppose, however, that I gave utterance to a threat. At length I would be avenged; this was a point definitely settled—but the very definitiveness with which it was resolved precluded the idea of risk. I must not only punish but punish with impunity."

He had already used The Cask of Amontillado to murder Lawrence Presspitch. What Montresor did to Fortunato, and what the murderer was doing to me, was the same—using our weaknesses against us. What are my weaknesses? In truth, I have so few. I am not physically weak. I need little to survive. I live a solitary life. I have no one I love left in my life. But I remain a professor. What I teach has changed over the years, but my academic life is the one thing that continues to give my time meaning. It is all I have left that provides me with purpose. I care about my students. I care about who they are growing into and how they are growing. I care about igniting a metaphorical fire under them, teaching them how to use words to make sense of the world. At Eventide College, my students were being murdered one by one in a way that cast suspicion on me. Death by Poe. If I weren't at the heart of the horror, if my students weren't the victims, I might have found the plan ingenious. All over one perceived slight that I never meant as a slight at all. I meant to do the right thing. Humans think they know what it means to live forever, but they never do.

That must have been his plan all along. Of course he would return to Eventide College as often as he could. It was his college. He would want to be there. He used his fortune to become a generous benefactor of the department he loved most, and after Professor Presspitch died, he used his clout to lure me to Maine. Since I was taking over for Presspitch, I'd be teaching the Poe seminar. He knew Poe well, but so did I. Poe wrote about murder. He wanted to murder. It was so simple, so perfect. At least, it was nearly perfect.

He had been in my cottage several times, moving the journal around, making certain I would keep finding it. He left me enough to read that would keep my interest, though he kept back the pages that would finally trigger my memory of our time in New York.

Very likely, it was a deliberate attempt to drive me mad. Every doubt I had since arriving in Maine, every step toward hysteria—all of it had been painstakingly engineered. Did my crime match his punishment? The extremes he went to did not make sense, but then those who are mad never do make sense. Centuries of blurred memories weighed me down in the dregs of the river. And then it all came flooding back with the bold-faced realization that he had been at the heart of it all along.

Perhaps I should have been more astonished than I was. Perhaps I should have been overcome with fear and trembling at the lengths he went to for his revenge. He had been the puppeteer, pulling my strings since my arrival in Southshore, jerking me here and tugging me there so I would feel the full impact of his macabre games. Oh, he had been so charming, chatting amiably along the way, prompting me to speak of Poe, pointing me over here, while I wondered which of my students was the murderer. Meanwhile, he was over there, allowing me to wallow in this uncanny world of singular woe.

I had to act quickly. I had to unmask him before it was too late. I could not allow anyone else to die because of his contempt for me. He was staging a narrative as he forced me into the role of a mad Poe narrator, as well as, I guessed, the next victim. That would be his ultimate retribution. Montresor killed Fortunato after all.

As the night grew later, winter swept down from the Atlantic like a living thing—vast and bone-chilling. Along the coast, the wind moaned through the pines, rising to a howl that rattled windowpanes while the storm-battered trees bent over like ailing old men. Salt air and ice rushed sideways, the sea gunmetal gray, the white-capped waves glowing in the dimness. The horizon vanished, sky and snow became one, and the houses crouched low against the gale, their pastel colors obscured by the blizzard, their chimneys trailing smoke that twisted like fleeing ghosts. I could not escape the sound of a heartbeat, a rhythm as old as the sea.

My winged friends, their black feathers iridescent against the snow, once again braved the storm to lead me forward—I knew where. There was a strange, solemn beauty in the way the snow softened every edge. As I ran through the blizzard, the roads folded before my eyes, whispering my names. For a moment, I thought I was being pursued, and again I feared that my grasp on reality was so tenuous that nothing made sense. This time, the strangeness vanished quickly. If I was going to make it out alive, I had to stay alert. I had to be ready to fight.

"You see," I shouted at the birds. "It wasn't me." Though I did not murder my students, I still felt responsible.

"You should have seen it coming."

Yes, I should have.

The ravens perched in the tall oak tree outside the black brick mansion, huddled together against the raging storm. As I stopped outside the wrought-iron fence, every bit and fragment straightened itself out in my mind. The journals, the underground library, the cryptic conversations—all of it.

Immortality seems to be the answer to a million questions. I don't want to die; therefore, I want to live forever. There are many reasons, noble and tragic, why someone might desire forever. The simplest reason is an instinctive terror of the void, of ceasing to exist. Perhaps someone refuses to watch their own body or mind deteriorate, to lose youth and vitality, to lose independence. By remaining deathless, they can postpone the Divine Reckoning, or if they are religious, they might forget the moral consequences of their actions. Humans have an intense yearning to witness the future. Those who study literature, history, philosophy, or science long to taste the sublime, wishing to understand the mysteries that most mortals never grasp. To transcend the limits of flesh and reach toward something beyond comprehension—such a prospect is enchanting to many. This is why he gathered his grimoires and his tomes into his sepulcher-like library. He wanted the mysteries for himself.

I knew his story long before Debbie told me. Born an Englishman, he had become respected and wealthy in New England. His wife, Eleanor Geddes, was from a family that had been in Maine for generations. Eleanor, known as Helen, had a reputation as a fine spiritualist. I knew he had named the chair after her. I had known about the college since that night in the farmhouse in Fordham, and I had been curious about it. However, because of his anger toward me, I dared not approach it. Until that fateful night, sitting in my office at Yale, I listened to Debbie's voicemail. In the back of my mind, when she offered me that prime position at a respected school, I thought it sounded too good to be true. And it was. But I convinced myself otherwise. It will be fine, I thought. It had been so long since Fordham and I hadn't heard anything of Cornelius Everett Eventide since. As far as I knew, he had never achieved immortality. As far as I knew, he had died. The opportunity seemed too good to pass up.

I do not doubt that I made the right choice in denying his request. I could not be the one to grant that man his greatest desire. Something about him did not ring true. There was malfeasance in his eyes. Obsessive determination. He did not appear to me to be a lovelorn man begging to keep some communication, feeble though it might be, with his wife. Perhaps his original desire had been to seek immortality to fulfill a vow to her, to witness her existence through the ages, but by the end, it was about his obsession with the secret knowledge he hoarded.

Some see immortality as a basis for penance, or for righting a wrong that can never be undone. Some believe that with enough time one might earn redemption. Eternal life isn't only about learning from our mistakes. It also allows endless opportunities to repeat them. Some crave endless life to keep a promise, to guard those they love, or to atone for mistakes. I have known them. I have been them. To live forever is not to conquer death but to dwell inside it, to wear it like a second skin, to live always in the black pall of a shallow grave, with one foot in the land of the living and the other firmly underground. To be immortal means to linger long enough to understand that eternity is not life without end but life without release. Perhaps we long for immortality not because we wish to live forever, but because we do not know how to die.

The old house was shrouded in snow, each window seeping as if with ancient tears, while ravens croaked from the trees and the broken clock tower. I examined the desolate black bricks and the curtains pressed together like closed eyelids. The house seemed to rise from the earth like a wound that had never healed, glistening with wet, catching what little light the storm allowed. The gargoyles appeared to crouch more than usual, as though they would pounce on me. The skeleton trees, the shriveled ivy, the dead clock, all of it hung heavy. An inexplicable stillness overtook me, and I was ready for whatever awaited me through that door. I understood, without joy, that I had been right all along. The mansion had been calling to me, anticipating this moment. I would be a fool to cross its threshold. Yet I went forward, as if to my destiny.

The wrought-iron gate groaned when I pushed it, the sound low and human. Every step toward the door felt as if I were descending, the ground itself tilting downward, and I stumbled. The windows watched me, the panes glinting with malice. I stood with my hand on the knob, listening. Nothing.

The air was fine and sharp, not only the chill of a blizzard, but something bolder, a perpetual winter. I turned the knob and heard whispers from within.

The Gentleman of Shadows.

The Raven Mocker.

I needed to go inside, yet I felt a terror more like delirium. Which Poe story was waiting for me? A tremor passed through the hinges, and the door yielded with a deliberate sigh as it swung open, only to snap shut behind me with the smack of inevitability.

The room was dim, the sconces and fires unlit. Dust floated through the corridors like ash. Shadows spilled across the floor like living ink. This was the same hall that dazzled, light and airy, during the ball only one month before. The snap of footsteps inched upstairs, the winding staircase and vaulted ceilings barely visible in the darkness.

"Show yourself. I know what you've done."

Silence. But the house was not empty. He was there. Watching.

In the Hall of Ancestors, which he had steered me away from during the ball, I found the picture he had shown me in miniature, her ivory face catching the weak beams of moonlight filtering in through the gaps in the curtains. The likeness was undeniable. The same wide gray eyes, the same dark hair in ringlets by her ears. I pressed my thumb against the glass, tracing the face. A howling wind blasted down the chimney, and the house exhaled with a passing sigh. And then I saw it: the portrait of him, looking as I remembered, with his lush whiskers, his determined smile, his smirking eyes. He was much the same now, except for the fact that he was clean-shaven. To look at him, he seemed so ordinary. And I never realized. I did not see him because I was not looking for him. The knowledge of how I had disappointed him had been pushed down into a deep river memory, and I had forgotten.

Perhaps it is more accurate to say that I ignored what I knew. It is easier to push away painful memories, even when the proof of them is standing before you.

I entered the library. In the center of the desk lay a letter, its blood-red seal broken, its contents in the same elegant hand as the journal.

My dearest Helen—

If ever you should hear the name Rhys Grimshaw, know that it is only me. In fact, over the years, I will be known by many names to escape the notice of prying eyes. Shall I tell you how it happened, finally, after so long?

After my trip to Poe in Fordham, I was lost. I resumed my travels, wandering the world like a half-living man, fueled by my hatred for the Gentleman of Shadows who denied my simple request. I was determined to show him that I would succeed without him. I crossed continents, chasing rumors of undead men who could grant me immortality. I visited alchemists in Prague who swore they could distill eternity into gold. I saw desert mystics who drank moonlit draughts and claimed to hear the secrets of spirits. I called on scholars in Rome, hunched over forbidden manuscripts that smelled of dust and miracles. Every path led to disappointment, and every promise turned hollow. I did not want scholarly lessons in metaphysics. I wanted eternal life. I wanted my flesh to remain unrotted and my blood to remain warm. I wanted Time to bow to me.

I returned home, still mortal and a failure. I was ready to give up on my quest when, one autumn night, a nearly invisible white-haired man appeared outside my door. Moonlight spilled through the doorway in thin, cold ribbons, and my spine tingled as the flicker of a shadow peeled itself from my wall. His translucent skin, the color of death, glowed in a flash of lightning. He showed me a tome where my name had been scribbled in marginalia by Other Beings who had heard whispers of the man who sought eternity.

"You are Mr. Eventide, correct?"

"Who are you?"

"I am known as Elias Venn."

He passed into the house and flashed to the top of the stairs. "You have been searching, yes?" His voice flickered like falling ash. "Others would have given up and failed. But you continue. I am impressed."

I laughed bitterly. "Most men do not promise their dead wives that they will live forever."

He studied me for a long moment, his eyes glimmering with ancient curiosity. "You understand what must be given? What must be taken?"

"I have nothing left to lose," I answered.

He stepped close to me. "Then you are ready."

The bite itself was like a torturous spike through my body. As he drank of me, I clutched at his shoulders in an attempt to remain upright, and my knees buckled. I collapsed onto the floor while my blood ran warm down my neck.

"Now." He opened his wrist with a deliberate bite. "Here is eternity. Do you have courage enough to take it?"

I took his proffered wrist with eerie serenity. The taste of his blood was electric, like metal and moonlight. I cried out until the world went black. When I awoke, dusk smoldered on the horizon. I rose slowly, feeling my bones being sharpened and remade. The aches of middle age had vanished. I was reborn.

Here I am, my dearest. I have done as you wished. I will live forever. Only I must stay as hidden as I can. Others, if they knew my true nature, would shun me as the very Devil. But you know me truly, and I know that you can see that, despite my eccentric hours and peculiar drinking habits, I am unchanged.

However, this must be said. I have discovered the names of the Gentleman of Shadows. He cannot hide from me forever. If he crosses my path again, if he dares to show his face to me, I will have my revenge.

I knew he was watching me, but he was well hidden. There was a flash of thundersnow, and the air carried the scent of damp earth. Another flash, the click of a latch, and the snap of a closing door. At the top of the winding staircase, a pale curve stretched his mouth upward.

"I'm afraid you've been rather disappointing in the amount of time it took for you to puzzle it out. I was starting to think I would need to be like Hansel in the fairy tale, leaving bread crumbs to lead you to me."

"You wanted me to know it was you, the way Montresor wanted Fortunato to know."

"I'm so pleased you finally figured it out. I have waited a long time, Jonathan. Should I continue to call you Jonathan?"

"Jonathan is fine. Would you prefer Rhys or Cornelius?"

"Between us, I was never fond of the name Cornelius, but it was a family name, and you know how old families are about such things. I haven't been called Cornelius in more than a century. I thought I'd buried that name, for myself at least, though I'm happy for the college to remember it. But then we do tend to go through names, don't we? That's the practical side of immortality. We change our names out of necessity, but our faces stay the same." He patted his clean-shaven face and smiled. "Sometimes simply a shave is enough to throw people off the scent."

He flashed across the room and stood behind me. He touched the edge of the letter with his fingertip, the gesture both tender and haunted. "You remember my wife, of course. Helen. She is my everything."

"Does she speak to you now?"

"Yes. Not often, but it is enough. Our conversations are

like the tender melancholy of a fading night." An apparition flickered on the periphery of my vision. "You see, she visits me too."

I couldn't make out her features, but I noticed an iridescent halo of fragile radiance, wan and exquisite.

He plucked the letter from the desk and held it close. "I was so young then, though I suppose we were all young once. When you're like us, you're young forever."

"We are both exactly as old as we are. What we look like means nothing. We don't age on the outside, but the wear and tear that comes from seeing decades pass still affects us. I feel every one of my years."

"Are you going to quote something from *The Picture of Dorian Gray* now, Professor?"

"I will quote whatever I must to make this stop."

I was speaking nonsense, I knew I was, but I needed time to think. He wanted revenge for something I had denied him, and I had mere moments to stop him. I had no doubt he intended to murder me the way he had murdered Larry Presspitch and my students. I had to keep him talking while I struggled to think of some way out of this trap, meager though my scheme was likely to be.

"Why didn't you tell me who you were after we met at the department meeting or the ball? Why make it all so complicated? And why murder my students? They hadn't done anything to you. Although I have to say that you added a little something extra by murdering in the style of Poe's stories."

Rhys's gaze met mine, his black eyes hard and unflinching. "That's what made this all so fun. Of course, our dear Edgar's stories are especially made for such things, aren't they? I got to play my little cat and mouse game, and now that I have you in my trap, I'm going to torture you until you die."

"I can break free of you. I'm older and stronger than you. What reason do I have to stay?"

"Ah." That cackling laughter. "I'm afraid you are rather predictable. I knew you would say those very words. This is why you should stay." He opened the door to the broom closet. There, bound together and gagged, were Simon, Oliver, and Cordelia, their eyes wide as they struggled to scream through the gags in their mouths.

"They have no part in this. Let them go!"

"But now you will do what I say. You still believe in mercy, and I wanted to remember what that looks like. Since Debbie lured you to Eventide College, I have never had the slightest doubt about you. Your students will go free when you give yourself to me, and I will have my revenge. Patience has its rewards, you see."

I laughed bitterly. "And I suppose you'll give me your word that they'll remain unharmed if I let you kill me?"

"I promise to let them go, but I suppose you'll have to take my word for it because you won't be here to see it happen."

I turned toward my students, struggling against their restraints, their shouts muffled by their gags, their eyes imploring me. I growled in exasperation.

"What do you think Poe would have thought of your violent scheme, Rhys?"

More gibberish, but I had to keep stalling. I felt unmoored, drifting between the past and the present, as if time were folding in on itself. One moment I was here, in horror-filled Eventide Manor, my students bound and gagged. The next moment I was there, in Fordham, New York, saying no to the pleading man.

"You denied me the gift that had been given to you. You took it upon yourself to remain better than me, to look down on me, to belittle me."

"I never belittled you. I was helping you."

"By sending me to my death?"

"You were nowhere near death."

"But I would have been long gone by now. Is that what you wanted? For everything I am, everything I have learned, to be obliterated? For Helen's memory to vanish from the earth as if she never existed?"

"Eventide College is your legacy."

"But I wouldn't have seen it prosper!"

"It happens to everyone. The passage of time doesn't mean you weren't important. It means that it's someone else's turn." I gestured at the walls of the old house. "Are you glad now that you have achieved your immortality? Is it everything you thought it would be?"

"That's not the point."

"That is exactly the point! Immortality is not a gift. It is a slow unraveling. What is the purpose of going on when those we love are gone forever?"

He slid his hands into his pockets, his head bowed. Then he stared into my eyes. "But Helen isn't gone forever, not the way your wife is. She speaks to me. She visits me. I know she's there."

"You contacted her through Maeve."

"As a matter of fact, I did. I liked Maeve, but she became too meddlesome for her own good. You see, she was putting the pieces together before you. I was starting to give you up as a lost cause. You had the journal from the first night you arrived in Southshore. What took you so long?"

"I was hired to be a professor at Eventide College. I had work to do. Besides, you didn't give me the final pages of the journal until tonight."

"I thought you'd figure it out long before then. I have to say, I am disappointed. Really, Jonathan, I thought you were smarter than that. It will be found, in fact, that the ingenious are always fanciful and the truly imaginative never otherwise than analytic."

"You're quoting Poe?"

"It seems as good a time as any."

"Are you saying I'm fanciful or analytic?"

"I'm saying you missed me. You were so caught up in trying to blame your students that you missed me when I was right in front of you, minus one beard."

"You've certainly caught everyone's attention. I appreciate the touch of you leaving me your journal. You thought it would help me remember you. Only it didn't work. I didn't remember you."

"Until you finished reading the journal and finally put the pieces together."

"Why Thomas? Why Amandine?"

"Thomas was an annoying snot from the first day he arrived at the Eliot School. He was argumentative and too nosy for his own good. One night, he spotted me out, and he came to me with some unfortunate questions. He began arguing with Debbie and me, insisting I was some kind of paranormal scary man."

"You are a paranormal scary man."

"Yes, but he wasn't to know that."

"Does Debbie know?"

"I suspect she knows something, but she's not overly curious. I pushed for her to become the next department chair because the only question she asks is when the next check is coming in. I believe she wishes to marry me, isn't that sweet? I'm afraid I can't reciprocate since I still love my dearest Helen. Still, I had to do something about Thomas. I went to his dorm one night and showed him what I was capable of. It was enough to frighten him away for the rest of the year."

"But he came back."

"Yes, he came back. But then he turned his attention to you. He happened to spot you one night, so he started challenging you."

"You know about that conversation?"

"Of course. I know everything you've done since the moment you arrived in Southshore. I have been so close to you, whispering your names."

"The Gentleman of Shadows and the Raven Mocker."

"I know you sensed me there, haunting you, if you will, but you didn't see me. Really, Jonathan, with our instincts, I expected more of you."

"You were at Simon's that night."

"Hiding in the shadows, yes. Thomas was such a scrawny boy, it wasn't hard to knock him out and carry him upstairs, where I slit his throat and tossed him through the window. It wasn't hard to sneak away in the darkness. There was no moon that night, you know."

"Yes, I know."

"And we see well in the darkness."

"Yes, thank you. I know that too. But why Amandine?"

"I needed another death to complete the pair from the story. That one was easier to orchestrate. I've lived in Eventide Manor on and off for nearly 200 years. No one knows this house better than I do. She was standing near the staircase after everyone else had drifted away. It wasn't hard to lure her upstairs when no one was looking."

"And Lawrence Presspitch?"

"He was the first, yes. He had his suspicions about me. We were rather friendly, actually. I was a bit careless one night, and he saw more than he should have. He became a danger that needed to go away. I knew you were at Yale, and I knew that you had been publishing about Poe. That's when I realized that murdering in the style of Poe's stories would be perfect. You would come here as the new Geddes chair, and I would make sure that Larry and your students would die in some ghastly way invented by our friend. Larry was the easiest. Nitre is easily passed over as a heart attack, and he did like his coffee."

"Detective Strongwater is onto you."

"He knows about the nitre, but no, he's not onto me. In fact, they were rather apologetic when they had to search the house after Amandine's death. They genuinely had no clue that I was involved. In fact, I think they felt rather sorry for me. Police work is rather inept these days, isn't it? Too bad they didn't have C. Auguste Dupin to assist them. With Larry gone, I knew you would be interested in joining us here. You took the position easily enough. It was as if fate wanted to hand you to me."

"But Simon Hayes was trying to convince the police that I was the murderer. It would have spoiled your plans if I had been arrested."

"I was fairly certain that you would not allow yourself to be taken, although you're right, it would have slowed things down. Simon was becoming a nuisance, and I was wondering if I would have to take him down as well. It would have been a shame, though. The Hayes family has been here nearly as long as I have. I knew Simon's great-great-great-great-grandfather, Raymond. But the boy was interfering with my plans, and if he had continued being bothersome, he would have had to go too."

"Which Poe death did you have in mind for him?"

"I hadn't yet decided."

He spoke so calmly about the murders, as though he were speaking of something fictional instead of something real. As I listened to his smooth voice, my fragile defenses crumbled, and everything I had tried so hard to forget returned with ghastly vividness. He was still talking.

"... at least until this generation dies out and I can return. There's always some new name, some new biographical detail, some new place I can begin again. I have to leave for some years, and then I can return. You know how it goes. You do the same, or you did, until now." He moved toward the staircase. "Come, Professor. There's something I want to show you."

It's funny how time can stretch onward forever or end in a split second. When I thought I was out of time, all I could think was that I didn't want to go just yet.

"Let the students leave first. I'm not going anywhere until you let them go."

Cordelia, Oliver, and Simon, visibly exhausted from struggling against their bonds, looked terrified.

"Come with me, and then I'll release them."

Police sirens sounded in the distance. The way Rhys tilted his head, I thought he heard it too. Were they on their way to my cottage? I thought of my house, small and unprotected in the dark cul-de-sac. I thought of the hours I had enjoyed there, reading in the recliner before the fire, making my way through Mrs. Griggs's mysteries, never guessing in those first nights that I'd become immersed in a suspense story of my own. I tried to will the police to the black brick mansion.

"Come with me, Jonathan."

"Why should I?"

"Because if you don't, I'll kill them." He looked up the winding staircase. "Mr. Venn? If you would."

The white-haired man with the death-like pallor appeared on the top step. He was well-dressed in his black nineteenth-century suit and his royal blue cravat.

"Mr. Grimshaw?" Venn said.

"Will you help me escort the Professor of Eventide to the downstairs library?"

Rhys grabbed one of my arms and Venn the other. I might have been able to break away from them, but I was concerned about my students, so I played along for as long as I could.

"I see that you retained Mr. Venn's services after he granted your greatest wish."

"Indeed. You see, I'm nothing if not loyal. He gave me what I wanted, and I gave him what he wanted in return—a place to belong. You rather like being the keeper of our secret knowledge, don't you, Mr. Venn?"

Mr. Venn bowed even as he gripped my arm. "You have all the knowledge of the world on your bookshelves, Mr. Grimshaw. It is a privilege to be in charge of maintaining such a library, sir. Even if it is going to take some time to get everything back in order." Mr. Venn glared at me for daring to disturb their collection of ancient tomes.

Rhys bent forward as he spoke, as if the darkness itself leaned closer to listen. "And what did you think of my little collection, Professor? Before you tried to destroy it, I mean."

"I think perhaps it's not so little. Why do you hoard those books? Others would like to study them."

"Perhaps one day I will share them. Perhaps not. It's my knowledge, and it's hard won, as you well know. When someone won't give you the knowledge you want, you have to grab it and keep it for yourself. Since I will never die, I will have it forever. I like to think I'm rather like Poe. He made the macabre beautiful, not in a glamorous way, but in a haunting way, in a mournfully poetic way. That is what I intend to do. I want to make the macabre beautiful."

"Why the tunnel from your underground library to the Chisholm?"

"Ah. Well. One always needs an escape route. Just in case."

"What is my escape route?"

"Alas, my friend, there isn't one."

All I could think was, here I am, willingly following Rhys and Venn to my death. Fortunato did not realize until too late what he was in for. I had complete knowledge of Rhys's plan —or at least I knew that he meant to kill me.

Rhys opened the crypt door. Instead of the library, he brought me into a side room. At first, I saw, heard, and smelled nothing, and an eerie silence overwhelmed the pitch-black room. Rhys and Venn seemed to have vanished, which is not, to my knowledge, one of our talents. With my arms free, I groped my way along damp stone walls. Then the atmosphere became close and heavy, and the room reeked of hot death as a gust of air wafted upward from what I guessed was a gaping hole in the floor. When I discovered that the chamber was roughly square and smaller than I expected, I froze, terrified as the slick walls seemed to lean toward me.

His voice boomed from somewhere above. "This was the construction I had to keep everyone away from during the ball."

"Didn't the police look here after Amandine died?"

"They saw there was construction, and they glanced at it, but they didn't notice anything particular about it, so they didn't look too closely. I certainly didn't point out the interesting odds and ends the room contains. Do you understand now how I will get my revenge?"

"The Pit and the Pendulum. Not one of my favorites, as it happens."

"Nor mine, but it is a rather proper ending, don't you think?"

"I don't know how proper it is. Either I fall into the pit or I'm sliced in half by the pendulum."

"Correct."

I struggled to see into the pit, but it was too dark even for me.

"Any clues about what I'll find at the bottom of the pit?"

He laughed. "Very funny, Professor. No, I'm afraid there will be no clues from me except to say that it's lethal to our kind of people. As is being sliced in half."

"I guessed as much. You may not recall that the narrator of The Pit and the Pendulum doesn't die. The pendulum stops just before he's cut to pieces."

"Alas, I dislike changing anything about one of dear

Edgar's stories, but I'm afraid your tale doesn't have a happy ending. Goodbye, Jonathan Ferrars."

He flashed away, and I let go of the wall, blind in the blackness, careful to keep my balance on the slippery floor. I reached out a tentative foot, wary of the deep pit in the center of the room. One wrong step and I would fall into that death trap. I had to stay calm and think rationally, though my mind went to every conceivable horror that might be waiting for me.

Suddenly, a blinding light, a mysterious, hellish glow, flooded the chamber, and I knew what to expect—walls of smooth, black, painted metal. A slashing sound crossed above my head as a massive pendulum appeared, the blade crescent-shaped and sweeping back and forth, glinting in the hideous light as it descended. I wasn't bound, which gave me an advantage over Poe's narrator, but only a slight one.

Rhys appeared in the corner of the room, far enough to be out of harm's way. He looked as he always did, that smirking smile, his absolute ordinariness. Even now, there was nothing remarkable about him—except that he had me cornered. He looked the same as he did when I saw him at the faculty meeting, at the colloquium, and at the ball. You would never guess that his greatest wish, for this revenge, was about to be granted.

"Here for a closer view?"

The swinging pendulum, its sharp blade slicing the air, descended at an oddly slow pace. For longer mental anguish, perhaps.

"I want to watch you die, Professor. And I want you to watch me watching you die."

The open pit gaped like a mouth from a nightmare—wide, endless, and looming. I edged forward as much as I dared, struggling to see what was down there, though all I could make out was darkness. The pendulum continued swinging, the gleaming blade slicing the air in a slow, rhythmic arc. With every pass, it whispered, a sound half metal and half sigh, as if the room itself mourned what it was about to witness. The blade continued its downward arc with inevitability, like the pendulum of a clock marking the end of time. Tick-tock. Tick-tock. Marking the end of my time, certainly. I stood at the pit's edge, every muscle taut, my arms flapping against the draft that rose from the depths. Undecided whether I should take my chances and jump into the pit or stay, I remained at the edge of the precipice. Rhys watched from across the chamber, his figure caught between shadow and flame, his eyes bright with triumph and madness in equal measure. Tick-tock tick-tock tick-tock.

"So this is how it ends." My voice echoed strangely, swallowed by the depth of the pit. "You, the scholar who would be eternal. And I, proof that eternity is a curse. All your careful years, your lies, your murders. It comes down to this. You have murdered innocent people because of some petty slight. Only it wasn't a slight at all. I was trying to save you from this curse."

His bare teeth looked sharp in the flickering light. "You are the curse. You are the failure. How could you not see what a great gift we have been given?" The pendulum's swing edged closer, and the air recoiled with a hiss. "You have squandered what you were given. Immortality is not an ending but a continuation. We are a story that will never end. Now you will die, but I will go on. Now that I have found my revenge, I am free to pursue my next goal."

"Which is?"

"To restore Helen."

"She's been gone too long to revive her. You know that."

The whooshing of the pendulum grew closer. It was halfway down. I didn't have much time to decide how I wanted to die.

"I have gleaned some promising ideas. Some spells that

have never been tried. Mr. Venn has helped me discover them. I will bring Helen back to me. I will resurrect her as Ligeia was resurrected. What say you now, Professor Ferrars? Can a mind plagued by love, grief, or obsession force reality to obey it?"

"You seem to have forgotten that the narrators of those stories couldn't tell the difference between presence and memory. You have the same problem. You've lost track of what is real and what is not. The women in those stories *may* have been resurrected. Or they may not."

"I will succeed. I would say that you will see," he glanced at the dropping blade, "only you won't."

My hands trembled, not from fear, but from the force of unwanted knowledge dragging me down.

"You are mad! All this..." I gestured at the pendulum, swinging closer, closer, "Lawrence Presspitch, Thomas, Amandine, *Maeve*!" I shouted her name.

"I knew her death would hurt the most." He tilted his head, the blade's silver reflection tracing light across his cheek. "Tell me—how many sins have you renamed as retribution?"

His words struck me like a blow. My thoughts blurred as they flipped through faces and an endless procession of nights. For a heartbeat, I saw myself as he saw me, an immortal wretch, clinging to the ruins of his mournful remembrances.

The pendulum swung, closer, closer, the rush of its movement deepening to the hum of a human heartbeat. I flashed to the side as much as I dared, and my left foot nearly caught at the edge of the pit. I steadied myself and clawed my way over the chasm. With one last show of bravado, I leapt far enough across to collide with Rhys. We grappled, our bodies twisting against each other.

"If you had turned me when I asked, we could have remade the world. You could have stood beside me."

"I don't think we would have worked well together. I've seen what happens when we mistake survival for impunity."

"Then you've learned nothing."

The air slapped my face as the pendulum passed just above my head, close enough to stir my hair. His laughter broke into a snarl as I knocked him back, our feet slipping on the damp floor. The pendulum swung closer, closer, its hiss violent now, screaming in my ears. He lunged at me, grabbing my shoulders and pushing me toward the pendulum, or the pit, I couldn't tell which. I felt his threatening strength, certain that this was the end. And then he faltered. As the pendulum breathed its final descent, I twisted free of him, yanking him toward me with all my strength. He stumbled, and the blade passed between us, whispering finality in its swing. I struck, not with fury but with resignation, a final attempt to save myself. When he tripped, his eyes grew wide. Elias Venn flew out of the darkness, his feet slipping on the wet stones, his arms flailing. He tried to save Rhys and himself and failed. They fell backwards, and the pit took them in silence. As if on cue, the pendulum stopped. It was over. Rhys Grimshaw, or Cornelius Eventide, or any other name he had used, was gone. Elias Venn was gone. And I remained.

I stood trembling, the hell-like lights flickering across my face. Though the pendulum had stilled, I continued to hear it in my mind, unhurried, terrible, eternal, even though it was no longer a menace to me.

In pace requiescat.

Twenty-Four

Never to suffer would never to have been blessed.

I released my students from their bonds and saw them safely away. I sent an anonymous message to the police, letting them know where to find Maeve. I didn't include anything else in my message. I didn't bother to explain. It would sound all too fantastical to believe. Let them make sense of what Cordelia, Simon, and Oliver told them. Let them make sense of what they discovered at Eventide Manor as they would.

With my message sent, I went to the bay. The storm had passed, but its presence lingered in the restless sea while ragged clouds covered the sky in black ribbons. Lobster buoys bobbed on the water, their colors, including Mrs. Griggs's aesthetic orange, dulled to ghostly smudges, their bells ringing a thin chime. In the distance, the islands crouched low and dark against the slick rocks glistening with melted sleet, glowing under the vanilla moon, brilliant in her fullness. The lighthouse's eye flashed—open, closed—in a knowing wink. I thought again of Poe's quote about beauty exciting the sensitive soul to tears. As I stared into the night, I felt the same. I looked out over the Maine shore one last time while the wind dropped to a steady whisper. I nodded and said goodbye.

I made one final stop at Eventide College. It was after midnight and deserted. I walked the snow-laden pathway, beginning at the Eliot School and past the Beckham College of the Arts. The four spires of the bell tower of Richfield Chapel stood tall. The plentiful trees were spindly and naked, bowing low beneath the strength of the storm that had just passed. I paused at the statue of Cornelius Everett Eventide. I stood there for a long time, wondering at him as he posed for eternity. He had found that eternity, but it was not enough. And yet, despite his wicked deeds, his college would go on. Students would continue their studies, they would graduate, and they would move on with their lives. Professors would apply for positions, and if hired, they would research, publish, and teach. And no one would know. No one had to know, as far as I was concerned. He was gone, his dangerous games vanquished with him into the pit constructed by his own madness. I glanced at the Chisholm Library but didn't stop. There had been enough sadness under that ground to last all my lifetimes. The chapel clock chimed two a.m., hollow against the pensive silence. I stood at the threshold of campus, casting a last glance at the red colonial bricks, the neoclassical façades, and the winding walkways. Eventide College would indeed go on. But without me. As I left, the road unfurled before me like a pale thread through the fog. The frigid night air was sharp enough to sting, and I welcomed it. I traveled without haste. I was leaving the horrible weight of this term—and everything that had ever bound me—behind.

In literature, hero stories are about change. These stories resonate with us because they reassure us that life is about growth. We leave our homes behind to face challenges. If we are lucky, we come through the other side with the wisdom to live more fully. But Poe's stories are rarely heroes' stories. Instead of a journey toward wisdom, his characters descend into dissolution. Poe's characters are not trying to save anyone. They wish to satisfy their own dark obsessions. No mentors are showing them the way. All they have is their own deteriorating sanity with its melancholy lies. Instead of returning triumphant, Poe's characters are entrapped, or they end up insane, or entombed, or they die. If they survive, like the narrator in The Pit and the Pendulum, like me, they return with trauma, not triumph. There was no triumph here, not for me.

I tilted my face toward the winter moon, bright and sharp. The two ravens, I might say my only friends in Maine, circled above and flew away. I waved farewell and retreated into the shadows. The shadows always recognize me. As I left Southshore, I felt the weight of every name I have worn.

Suddenly, I heard her laughter.

"You should have seen it coming."

I blinked, hoping for a glimpse of her face, but there was only light and fog. So I moved on. Behind me, the campus faded into shadow. Its corridors, its knowledge, its ghosts, all receded into silence. I thought that discovering the murderer would save me, but nothing is ever that simple. In the end, I felt empty and scraped clean of any illusions about what any of it meant. He was dead, the mystery solved, yet the rot remained.

I traveled until the mist gave way to rain and towns appeared behind drizzle, then vanished. Nights folded into one long, ethereal dream. Sometimes I would pass a window, curious about what my reflection looked like. Am I still Jonathan, I wondered? I shook my head with the sad realization that, no, I cannot be Jonathan anymore. When Rhys

Grimshaw fell to the bottom of the pit, Jonathan Ferrars vanished with him. The police will always be searching, and I cannot take that risk.

I still think of them. Cordelia's earnest wonder. Simon's willfulness. Oliver's determination. And Thomas, who never had a chance to understand the talent he already held within him. And Amandine, who had so much to offer. And Maeve. Dear Maeve. Whenever I pass through a forest, I think of her, the hedge witch, performing some spell or other. I wish I could tell her I'm sorry. I meant to protect her, and I failed. That knowledge will haunt me forever. Poe said, "The eye, like a shattered mirror, multiplies the images of sorrow." That is all I can think of when I recall Eventide College—the tremulous grace of the young lives that were lost for no reason at all. There are times when, in the deepest night, when the lamps burn low and the fog curls along the road, I am mesmerized by the echo of my own footsteps, and I wonder if I ever really left Eventide after all. It is hard to accept that the whole horror show was about time. The time he felt I owed him. The time he demanded. But eternal time is not a gift. This is what he refused to understand. Endless time is the absence of meaning. When I reappeared in his life, he chose to give his time a dreadful meaning. He chose murder. He nursed one imaginary slight until his fury became fathomless. And still, after all the terror, in time Eventide College will be relegated to just another memory that I easily recall, or not. Even the most dreadful ordeals can lose their edge. Nights blur into decades, and I drift through it all, a ghost trapped between tides. There are evenings when I awaken, certain that I have lived this night already. And perhaps I have.

As for the flashes of madness? They have not returned. Perhaps they were brought on by my study of Poe. Perhaps they were brought on by the phantasm of memory overwhelming me, prompted by Rhys's desire for revenge. Perhaps they were brought on by knowing, somewhere so deep I couldn't quite touch it, that something evil wanted its way with me. Perhaps somehow I recognized him, but I pressed the knowledge aside because I feared what the truth would reveal. Perhaps the madness will return. Perhaps not. Only time will tell.

There was a time when I might have called this freedom—the open road, the quiet night, the peace of no one in the world knowing where I am. The more I have to flee like a thief in the night, the more I have to begin again, the more my existence feels like exile. But I am here, so I must continue to make something of the time I have, or else what is the point? When I left Southshore, I decided to stay hidden in some out-of-the-way place. Later, when I am ready, I will reinvent myself yet again. My road does not end. It simply dissolves into other roads.

Once again, I am a nameless traveler. The night stretches before me, the luminous, guiding moon high in the sky, endless yet merciful in her companionship. Somewhere out there, the living go on dreaming while I remain a shadow, labyrinthine and half-remembered, a whisper in the dark. I am a book without an ending, though perhaps endurance provides its own kind of conclusion. I used to believe that we could contribute to positive change, that we could improve the world through acts of creativity, deep thought, and lovingkindness. Mainly through lovingkindness. I am not as certain anymore. But I will continue to try. I will continue to follow the wind under the everlasting night and the sound of my far-echoing footsteps. I will continue to search for yet another new beginning, with Poe's words for company.

Is it therefore the less gone? All that we see or seem is but a dream within a dream.

Author's Notes

First, as always, I thank my readers from around the world, some of whom have been following me since 2011. You are more appreciated than you will ever know.

I was inspired to write *The Professor of Eventide* after reading Donna Tartt's *The Secret History*. I loved the story of Richard and his fellow Classics students so much that I wanted to write something similar. Since I love a good paranormal story, paranormal elements gradually found their way in, and over time *The Professor of Eventide* became its own entity. Other important influences on this story were Leigh Bardugo's *Ninth House* and Susanna Clarke's *Jonathan Strange and Mr. Norrell*. I'm not sure what to say except that one day, as I was working on *The Professor of Eventide*, I began writing about Mr. Norrell's library. I like to take my inspiration where I can find it, so I went with it.

Longtime readers of mine will not be surprised to learn that I originally intended for Charles Dickens to be the author studied by Professor Jonathan Ferrars and his students that fateful term at Eventide College. Whenever I write about my books to myself, I always use the acronym, which for *The*

Professor of Eventide is TPOE. There it was, right in front of me—Poe. And fate was correct. Poe was the perfect author for this story. Although I'm still not sure what the T stands for... If you were not a fan of Edgar Allan Poe before you began this book, I hope you are by the end.

I love hearing from readers. You can find me on my website at www.meredithallard.com. Join me for my weekly blog posts and my monthly newsletter.

About the Author

Meredith Allard is an award-winning author whose work explores the intersection of history, memory, and the human psyche. She is best known for the bestselling *Loving Husband Trilogy* and the Victorian novel *When It Rained at Hembry Castle*, which was named a Best Historical Novel by *Indie-Reader*. Her prequel, *Down Salem Way*, earned the B.R.A.G. Medallion and was a semi-finalist for the Chaucer Award in Early Historical Fiction.

A recognized authority on the craft, Meredith is the author of *Painting the Past: A Guide for Writing Historical Fiction*, a #1 Amazon New Release in Authorship and Creativity Self-Help. For over twenty years, she has mentored writers of all ages, helping them find their voices while honing her own signature blend of meticulous research and haunting prose.

When she isn't unearthing the secrets of the past, she can be found in the hills of Southern Nevada with her cats and a cup of coffee.

Books By Meredith Allard

And Shadows Will Fall

Christmas at Hembry Castle

Down Salem Way

The Duchess of Idaho

Her Dear & Loving Husband

Her Loving Husband's Curse

Her Loving Husband's Return

Painting the Past: A Guide for Writing Historical Fiction

The Professor of Eventide

The Swirl and Swing of Words: Embracing the Writing Life

Victory Garden

When It Rained at Hembry Castle

Woman of Stones

www.ingramcontent.com/pod-product-compliance
Lightning Source LLC
La Vergne TN
LVHW090550110826
845146LV00001B/88

* 9 7 9 8 2 1 8 5 7 1 2 7 6 *